The Alchemy of Bridges

Charlene Williams

Also by Charlene Williams

Unexpected Places – A Collection of Short Stories

For Ericka

Every morning you have two choices –
Continue to sleep with your dreams
or wake up and chase them.
Liz Adams

Part One 7

Part Two 75

Part Three 195

Epilogue 347

Part One

New York City
December 1968

Ronan

Trudging up West 51st Street, shoulders sagging under his winter coat, arms wrapped tightly around himself, and head hung low against the winter wind, Ronan couldn't imagine things getting much worse and he wasn't sure he'd care if they did. Ever since Carrieann's death he didn't seem to care about much, even the loss of his job last year barely caused a ripple.

He always thought his job would be secure. He never thought he'd be unemployed, especially before he was thirty. After all, longshoremen would always be needed. He never thought otherwise. That is, until containerized shipping began gaining popularity. The piers on the West Side were starting to feel the sting. While many were still on the job, Ronan and quite a few of his co-workers found themselves unemployed. With few other skills, the search for new work had been difficult and, so far, fruitless.

That wasn't the only change. Ronan often contemplated the changes in his neighborhood since he was a kid. He was too young to remember the construction of the Lincoln Tunnel but had memories of his father complaining about the access roads destroying the place. After retiring, his parents picked up and moved to the mountains in Pennsylvania. This was his home, though, even if it did have a bad reputation. Hell's Kitchen had certainly earned it; it was always a gritty and rough neighborhood ruled mostly by gangs. Since the thirties and especially after the war, it started changing. The Port Authority terminal and high-profile businesses moving in were giving it a different look.

Now the piers were changing, too. The livelihood he had counted on was gone. He had figured something would turn up sooner or later, but so far there'd been nothing. He had made a comment to his sister about becoming a member of the Westies since he was Irish and, having grown up here, knew the city like the back of his hand. She didn't find joining organized crime funny. Walking down the street now, Ronan once again wondered if it wasn't a bad idea. They would take care of him, at least. He'd have to break laws and maybe even rough some people up but at least could afford food. His unemployment benefits had run out. He had no money coming in at all. He knew he'd never be able to hurt people, though. It wasn't in him. He felt as if nothing was in him anymore. Nothing mattered.

Carrieann had mattered, though. With her, his life had meaning. The day he married her he was in awe. He could not comprehend how a girl so lively and kindhearted had said yes to him. Carrieann had made everything, even their tiny apartment, a beautiful and loving place. She was the kind of person that saw the good in everyone. She didn't need a fancy apartment on the Upper West Side to be happy. She often said all she needed was her man and an occasional trip to Coney Island to ride the Wonder Wheel. Carrieann had always loved the view from the top.

Ronan made sure he was there. He didn't hang out at the bars with the guys after work. He didn't gamble away his paychecks. He made sure Carrieann had everything she wanted to turn their apartment into a home. He took her to movies and dances and, on one special occasion, took her to see *Fiddler on the Roof* at the Imperial Theater. But it was always the top of the Ferris wheel that made her happiest so he took her as often as he could. He was never sure why it made her so joyful, and he didn't ask. He knew now that he should have. It was one of the things that he didn't know about her and it bothered him.

The day he came home to find her lying on the kitchen floor, already dead, was the day his life ended. He would find out later it was due to a brain aneurysm, but it didn't matter. He wasn't there. He had promised he would always be there for her, and he wasn't there when she needed him the most. It didn't matter what his family or friends told him, that he couldn't have saved her, he blamed himself and he always would. He believed if he had been there, he might have gotten her to the hospital in time for them to do something. No one could tell him otherwise.

It was also the day he stopped caring. He shut himself off, told his family he was fine and his friends that he was doing well. He limited contact with his parents, declined invitations from ex-coworkers or friends, and only spoke to his sister on occasion. Once he lost his job, he stopped answering his phone and would only answer the door if it was the rare visit from his parents - during which he would put on a show of being okay, life moved on, he would find something and he would prevail. Although, most days would find him alone in his living room staring into space, his thoughts full of the life he once had - the life he thought he would share forever with Carrieann.

Ronan knew his problems were more than grieving. His whole life he had seen people move on after losing a loved one. He watched as one of the guys he worked with had also lost his wife, had grieved, and felt lost for a while but then, somehow, was able to go on. He didn't understand why he wasn't able to. When Carrieann was alive, he had felt a sense of purpose. Now, he felt nothing. He could barely find a reason to get out of bed each morning. He couldn't talk to his parents. His father would tell him to toughen up, pull himself up and get on with it. He doubted his father had ever experienced the sense of loss, the depression, that Ronan was now feeling.

Seeing a doctor was out of the question. He no longer had insurance and couldn't pay for it himself. Besides, he knew his father would belittle him and his mother wouldn't understand. His mother would say she could help him. He could save his money and talk to her instead of seeing a quack - as his parents called all doctors involved in mental issues. He had no one. He wasn't even sure a doctor could help him. They couldn't bring Carrieann back nor did he feel there were any words that could be said that would give him any reason to believe this life was worth living anymore.

On this cold December evening he didn't care if the elements took him. He thought hypothermia would be a good thing since all he'd been feeling lately was numb. Arriving at the stoop to his building, he took a seat on the bottom step. Logic would dictate he should go inside but he didn't want to. As he often did over the last two years, he looked toward the sky and wondered if Carrieann was looking down on him. He knew she would be disappointed in him but then he also felt she would understand that going on without her was impossible.

He searched the sky, looking at the few stars that were visible, once again hoping to see some kind of sign. He had no idea what he was looking for but thought maybe he would know when he saw it. Anything that might tell him what to do, how to go on or, more than anything, that Carrieann was somewhere near him.

After several minutes, Ronan sighed, placed his hands on his knees, paused for a moment and then got up and made his way up the steps into his building. At least he could sit among her things in the apartment. Making his way up the steps and down the hall he saw something taped to his apartment door. As he got closer he saw it looked like a legal document. When he reached the door and took it down, he wasn't at all surprised to see what it was.

He was being evicted.

Emily

Ronan was hurting and Emily knew it. She'd known for weeks. As she followed him up 51st Street she felt the sadness jump off him. She'd felt it for a while but tonight was different. Tonight there was also resignation. He was sinking deeper, and Emily could physically see it. His shoulders slumped lower, his eyes were almost vacant now and he rarely lifted his head anymore. Except when he sat on the stoop. She wondered why that was the only time he would look up.

She also wondered why no one was helping him. She knew he had family. She had seen them visit him, although those visits were now fewer and farther between. While she couldn't draw from her own family experiences, Emily knew that families were supposed to take care of each other. She had witnessed it with her own friends or, more accurately, the small circle of people she pretended were friends. She saw the way families would circle around a member that was hurt or had stumbled in life and the way they would help them. It was confusing to her that neither his parents nor his sister were there to assist him at a time it was so obviously clear he needed help.

It was also clear that, unlike herself, Ronan hadn't done anything to hurt or disrupt his family. It appeared they loved and cared about him. The only conclusion she could come to was that he hadn't asked them for help. She knew men had a difficult time with that. Men had to be the strong ones, the bread winners, the rock. Men were not allowed to be emotional or weak. Asking for help would be a sign of weakness and most men would rather die than be seen as weak. But even if he hadn't asked, it was clear he was coming unraveled. How his family could not see that was beyond her.

Watching Ronan now, once again sitting on the stoop and staring at the sky, Emily knew something was going to happen and it wouldn't be good. She knew he was reaching the end of his rope and it wouldn't be long before he decided to do something drastic. She sighed and resolved herself to help him. If his family wouldn't step in then someone had to. She had seen enough to know that Ronan was a decent enough man. She saw no reason why someone like that should flounder and do something he might regret.

Emily followed as Ronan made his way up the stairs. It was clear to her that he had lost too much weight in recent weeks, and she wondered how much food he had left or if he even had money to get any groceries. She was bewildered as to how someone could let themselves get to a point where there wasn't enough money for food. She had never come across anyone who didn't have enough money for a healthy breakfast and a good dinner every day. If she were honest, she'd admit that up until recently she had never come across anyone who didn't have enough money for *anything*.

There were many things that stunned Emily lately. She began noticing things she had never taken the time to look at before. As she took her walks through Manhattan, she noticed the people only a few years younger than herself, the ones everyone were calling 'flower children'. Many of them slept in the park and, to her amazement, were happy about it. There was a time she would have snubbed her nose at people that slept on park benches and under bushes. The idea that those who were obviously without money could be happy was strange to her. When she first encountered them, she thought maybe they were people she could help but she quickly realized they weren't. They were fine. They *wanted* that life. She thought it was disgusting but they were happy and that fascinated her.

Then she encountered people who were shouting about the war. She had been aware there was a conflict going on in Vietnam but had been too absorbed to pay attention. She knew there was growing resentment about the United States becoming involved in it. She'd heard a few stories of injured soldiers returning and not seeming quite right, but she had never concerned herself with things that didn't directly involve her. Now, she was curious about it. It was one of the things she realized had been happening in what seemed like a different world to her.

On her walks she became aware there was an entire city involved in things that she had never known, never cared about or, in many cases, had turned a blind eye to. Not only the flower children and the war but children in hand-me-down, out-of-date clothes; women who wanted independence but were faced with institutions who still wouldn't let them do anything without a man's consent; people in their twenties or thirties strung out on some kind of drug; black people organizing and marching for equal rights. Some days it was almost too much for her to absorb but she kept on walking.

It was on one of her walks when she noticed Ronan. He wasn't doing anything that should have drawn attention. Like her, he was just walking. It was the grief radiating from him that caught her attention. Emily could feel the anguish and it made her watch him. She followed him daily and learned of his losses. Like Ronan himself, she was bewildered that he could not seem to pull himself out of his darkness.

Watching him today, Emily knew something had to be done. He was getting worse and now, she was sure, he wasn't eating. He was still alert, she noticed. He wasn't stumbling or passing out, so he had to be getting some nourishment. At least his clothes were clean, she thought, as she watched him labor up the steps. She mused that he could use a shave and maybe a haircut. She had noticed a while ago he wasn't a bad looking man under the sadness and unkempt look. Concluding he must have been somewhat modish for his means before his life fell apart, she also concluded that he could have been more ambitious. After all, she had never known anyone who willingly lived in this part of the city.

Reaching his floor, she stood at the top of the stairwell and watched as he rambled down the hallway toward his apartment. She looked on as he took down the paper tacked to his door. She heard him mumble some words she couldn't make out before crumbling the paper and throwing it on the hallway floor before taking out his keys and entering his apartment.

Silently, she walked down the hall and picked up the ball of white paper. Straightening it out, she took in its meaning. While Emily didn't consider it much of a place, it was the only home he had. She gathered he would be too proud or, more likely, embarrassed to ask his parents or his sister for a place to stay. Images of the various shelters available in the city went through her mind. No, she thought. She wouldn't wish those on her worst enemy. . .and she did have a few enemies.

Previously, Ronan wasn't someone she would associate with, nor would she be caught dead in this section of the city. There was something, though, that stopped her when she saw him that day on the street. Whatever it was, it had been strong. She strengthened her resolve to help him. She wasn't sure how or what she would do first, but she'd figure it out.

Giving one last look at his apartment door, she straightened her back, nodded and headed back down the hallway.

Ronan

He hated confrontation. He didn't like arguing with people to begin with and right now he was too tired to put up much of a fight. The building manager, a burly man with thick hair growing well below his shoulders, stood in front of him. Ronan wanted to ask him what was so appealing about long hair and peace signs lately but refrained from doing so.

"Look, man, rules are rules. You signed the lease; you know what it says. The owners ain't gonna let me give any kind of extension to anyone. No one. They want their money. You got until Friday, pal. After that, locks are changed. Orders from the owner."

"Come on," Ronan tried again. "I've always had it in on time. We. . .I. . .have lived here going on five years and I was never late. You can't give me just another week? You know what's happening down at the docks. You know how many of us lost our jobs. You gotta give me a break."

"Wish I could, brother, but it ain't happening. I got orders, man. Owners want their money when it's due. Anyone late, they got three days to come up with it then it's adios, amigo. Sorry. Friday. That's it."

Ronan ran his hand through his hair and took a deep breath. He had no idea what he was going to do now. Unless he found a job fast, he'd be out on the street.

"Look, brother, I'm sorry. Really, I am. I can't do nothin'," the manager muttered.

"You know," Ronan raised his voice, "ain't isn't a word, it's 'I can't do *anything*,' you stupid hippie, and I'm not your brother."

The manager only raised an eyebrow and closed the door on him. Ronan wasn't sure what was coming over him. He had never been rude to anyone before. There were a lot of things he wasn't before. There were also things he *was* before; things he did and things he accomplished. He used to be the one who found solutions, the one who fixed things, and built things for the apartment. He used to be the one who got things done. Now, it seemed, he couldn't fix a single thing.

Back in his apartment, sitting in the worn vinyl recliner and staring at the wall, Ronan went over his options. He found he had very few of them. He had to find a job, no matter what it was or what it paid, he had to find one. Sighing, he grabbed the paper off the side table and opened it once again to the Help Wanted section.

Several days later he was back in the same chair, in the same position. He had gone to more places than he could count but no one was interested in hiring him. He even talked to a local grocer who had advertised for a delivery boy. That didn't even pan out. Nor did the job at the sanitation department or the one at the construction site. He had applied to countless jobs, attended interviews, spoke to owners, foremen and managers but none of that had led to a job offer.

As he sat in that familiar chair, he couldn't help but feel defeat wash over him. He didn't know if he had done something wrong or if he lacked the necessary qualifications. But what qualifications did he need that he didn't already have to deliver groceries or pick up garbage? Reflecting on his journey, he realized that finding a job also required a bit of luck. It appeared as though luck was just not on his side. It hadn't been for quite some time.

The rumble in his stomach reminded him it had been quite a while since he'd had something to eat. He tried to remember the last time he had something. He was pretty sure it had been close to two days. Wandering into the kitchen, he opened the refrigerator door to find a bottle of ketchup, a jar of pickles and an almost empty bottle of milk. He hung his head and closed his eyes. He never thought he'd find himself in this position. He was only twenty-seven. How could this have happened? He thought about calling his sister but immediately felt ashamed. His parents were out of the question.

Ronan felt useless, hopeless and empty. He was disconnected from his friends and he kept his family at arm's length. He felt trapped by his circumstances and couldn't see a way out. He realized this must be what people mean when they say they've hit rock bottom.

Deciding he couldn't sink any lower, he grabbed his coat and headed out. The desperation gnawed at his stomach, urging him to find something by any means necessary. As he walked down the dimly lit streets, a glimmer of hope sparked within him. He remembered hearing stories of how restaurants often discarded perfectly good, barely touched food. It was a gamble, but he was willing to seize the opportunity. Hunger drove him forward, eradicating any remnants of pride or concern about where his meal would come from. All that mattered now was finding something to ease the rumbling ache in his belly.

Turning into an alley, the aromas coming from the kitchens of the few eateries on 9th Avenue made his mouth water and his stomach growl louder. Each whiff of cooking meat and freshly baked bread fueled his determination. The dimly lit dumpsters lined the back walls, almost beckoning to him. With a mix of caution and just a bit of disgust, he approached the first one, carefully lifting the lid. His heart sank as he found nothing but empty containers and scraps of wilted lettuce. He moved on to the next, and then the next. Minutes turned into an hour as he searched through the refuse and then, with a combination of disbelief and gratitude, he uncovered a still-wrapped sandwich.

In that moment, he also realized just how wretched his life had become. He stared at the sandwich. Tears sprang to his eyes as he thought about Carrieann. She would be disappointed, even horrified, at seeing him like this. He knew it would break her heart if she could see him. Contrary to every other time she entered his mind, this time he hoped against hope that she was not looking down on him. He could not bear the thought that she could possibly see him in this sorrowful position.

Unwrapping the sandwich, the thoughts of Carrieann faded away. He wasn't willing them away; they were being replaced with something else. There was something vague at the edge of his mind. Something was trying to work its way in. He stopped unwrapping and stood still. An image of the grocer near 48th and 10th Avenue floated through his mind. He remembered it was permanently closing. In fact, yesterday would have been the last day it was open. It would still have food. It wouldn't be cleared out yet, would it?

Taking a bite of the sandwich, Ronan turned south. His thoughts were only on still-stocked shelves of food in a closed store. With any luck, if he had any bit of it left, the owners would be waiting until the weekend to start removing everything. He could stock up on canned goods and boxes of cereal. It wouldn't help him pay the rent but at least he wouldn't be hungry, he thought. Maybe once he ate more than the sandwich he'd be able to think more clearly and figure out a way to either scrape up the money for the rent or talk the landlord into an extension.

His pace picked up as he thought that maybe, just maybe, he'd catch a break.

Emily

Emily smiled as she watched Ronan nearly break into a run. She'd been willing him to remember that Pop Murphy's store was closed. She wasn't sure if she would be able to do it, but she tried and, to her amazement, she succeeded. She'd read about the powers of the mind and had been fascinated by it. She was never truly convinced that any of the techniques described in her reading would work. Until now, that is. She had been so disappointed this week that it felt good to finally have a small win.

Putting multiple job opportunities in front of Ronan hadn't worked. She had watched as he went from place to place. It was clear to her early on that no one was going to hire him. He was sullen, mumbled when he spoke and looked as if he couldn't be less interested in finding work. No one in their right mind would have hired someone like that.

As if Emily wasn't already confused by Ronan, this confused her more. He needed to work, he needed the money, but he was acting as if he didn't care whether or not anyone hired him. She didn't understand it. She thought he would be eager, excited and make a good impression on those he spoke to. He hadn't and it was a puzzle she couldn't work out.

Whenever something she was after was within her grasp, she never had any qualms about doing whatever it took to get it. Sometimes that meant hurting people. Sometimes it meant she would have to bend the law or use questionable tactics. She hadn't cared. Emily had kept her eye on what she wanted and she didn't stop until she had it.

Although that seemed like a long time ago, it wasn't. So, when she witnessed Ronan lacking the enthusiasm or the determination to get not only what he wanted but what he *needed* it was something she was unable to understand. She was frustrated at the dejected manner in which he had conducted himself. It was disconcerting to her that she had put these opportunities in his path, and he had squandered them. Still, she knew he needed help, and she knew that somehow, she would be able to provide it.

She wasn't quite sure how she was going to handle the job situation but, for the moment, she was happy that at least one of the techniques she read about worked and Ronan was on his way to getting food. Once his stomach was full and he had enough food for at least a week or so he would be in better shape. She'd be better able to guide him toward something once he was stronger.

Following him down 10th Avenue, Emily tried to put together the puzzle that Ronan had become to her. He seemed to be an intelligent man, but he had not extended himself to go beyond what he was comfortable with. He was comfortable in the neighborhood he'd grown up in, comfortable doing the work on the docks that so many in that area had done and he had been comfortable in his marriage. She knew all of that was good but he had never thought beyond that. He had never imagined what could be. He had only gone with what he knew.

Then there was his family, whose visits had been seldom and lately, not at all. His friends that he once had who didn't call him anymore. All of this, she realized, was by his own doing. He had intentionally pushed everyone in his life away. Any intelligent person knows you need people. Emily knew that. Even if you did not like them, you needed them for something.

She had surrounded herself with people, some of which she despised, but she needed them because they served a purpose. She was sure most of them didn't like her, either, but without her many of them wouldn't get the things they wanted, either. Previously, she had viewed people as transactional. She viewed them in terms of what they could do for her and, if needed to complete the transaction, what she would be able to provide them.

It was yet another bewildering point about Ronan. He did not reach out to someone, anyone, and make a deal with them to get what he needed to survive and offer them something in return. She, again, knew men had a difficult time admitting defeat or asking for help but she didn't think making some type of arrangement with someone would be seen as weak. Clearly, he was not able to get himself together on his own, yet he wasted each job opportunity and had reached out to no one. He did not make sense to her.

Her thoughts were interrupted when she realized Ronan had reached Pop Murphy's. She watched as he surveyed the front of the store. He stood silently for a bit before he walked around to the back of the building. She knew there was an unlocked window behind the pile of boxes. He'd find his way in without much trouble.

He got this, she thought. He'll get what he needs and while he was getting some of his strength back, she would figure out what to do next.

Ronan

It didn't bother him that what he was about to do was a crime. Breaking and entering wasn't something he aspired to do but the thought of going hungry outweighed the risk of getting caught. Ronan really didn't care if he got caught. In fact, maybe he should get caught. He would get three square meals a day in jail and wouldn't have to think about what he was going to do anymore.

He thought about breaking the window on the back door but then realized that would be too loud. He looked toward a pile of boxes a few feet to the left of the door. If he was remembering clearly, there was a window behind them. He walked over and took a few of the top boxes off the pile until the top of the window frame revealed itself.

Minutes later he found himself in the storeroom. He wished he would have had the foresight to bring a flashlight with him. The dim light from the alley would have to do. He began looking through the shelves. Many of them were already empty but there was still enough left to tide him over for a while. He began setting aside cans, cereal, and bags of rice.

As he was reaching for a bag of noodles, the sound of a police siren stopped him. He froze, his hand still extended toward the shelf. He listened as the siren got louder. He realized it was heading in his direction. He held his breath and listened. The siren grew louder until it passed in front of the store and then began to fade. Ronan exhaled and brought his arm down.

He stood back, leaned against the wall, and took a deep breath. He closed his eyes and stood there silently for a few minutes. Then he rubbed his face, shook his head, and sighed. He couldn't do this. He thought he could. He had been determined to. The siren seemed to have brought him back to himself. He couldn't steal what was left of a family business that had been bought out by one of those big companies moving in down here.

Ronan looked around the storeroom, pushed himself off the wall and crawled back out through the open window. He shut the window and placed the boxes back onto a pile. He looked up at the back of the building and pondered what had brought him here. How could he believe he could steal anything? Had he changed this much?

Maybe he had. Maybe he had changed along with everything else that was changing around him; his life, his neighborhood, the world. It was all changing. The country was involved in a conflict that was causing a lot of division and unrest, racial tension was at an all-time high, businesses were moving into his neighborhood, the city was trying to clean it up and get rid of its bad reputation once and for all. His life, well, he would never again get back the life he once had. He didn't think he could keep up with it anymore. He didn't think he *wanted* to keep up with it anymore.

For a brief moment, he thought about signing himself up to go to Vietnam but then realized he wouldn't pass the physical fitness test in his current condition. He let out a soft hiss. He couldn't even serve his country. He wasn't good enough to deliver groceries or pick up garbage and he'd fail if he tried to join the service. He'd become completely useless.

He wandered back onto 10th Avenue and began walking toward 51st Street before he stopped. He wasn't sure why he was walking back to the apartment. All he would do was sit in the recliner, sleepless, and wait for the building manager to throw him out in the morning. He supposed he should box up Carrieann's things but he didn't know what he would do with them. He had no place to go with them.

Lowering himself onto the curb, he put his face in his hands. It didn't take long before the tears came. Ronan realized he was tired - not just physically tired - he was also mentally and emotionally tired. The sobs increased and he let them come. He couldn't go on like this anymore. There was nothing left, he thought, nothing left for him in this city or in this life. He raised his head toward the sky, the tears wet on his cheeks. He said a prayer to Carrieann to forgive him. He wanted to be the man she had known but that man had slipped away and he couldn't find a way to bring him back.

Wiping the tears away with the back of his hand, Ronan stood up. There was one thing he wanted to do. He wanted to go to Coney Island. He wanted to see the Wonder Wheel. He wanted to know why Carrieann was enthralled with the view from the top. It would take him a little over an hour to walk to the Brooklyn Bridge. Then he figured another 2 ½ to 3 hours to get from there to Coney Island. He could do it. He had nothing else to do and nowhere else to go.

He turned south toward 47th and began walking when he realized there was something else he wanted to do. He dug around in his pockets and pulled out a nickel. He'd need another nickel to make a phone call. He began looking on the sidewalk and the gutters as he walked. People were always dropping spare change without realizing it. He had a long walk ahead of him, surely someone had dropped a nickel somewhere. He thought his best bet was to walk to Times Square and look around there. Then he'd just go south on 5th Avenue.

It had always amazed Ronan how many people were in Times Square no matter what the weather or the hour. On this night, however, he didn't look at them or care about what they were doing. He only cared if they had dropped any change. They had. By the time he reached 5th Avenue and 30th he had picked up 70 cents and had stopped at an open deli for a soda, another sandwich and to get warm for a few minutes. He had more than enough money left for a phone call. He realized he should have thought about looking for street change earlier in the week. He still wouldn't have made the rent but at least he wouldn't have been so hungry.

He found a phone booth a couple blocks north of Washington

Square Park. He stepped inside, closed the door and was glad the light would provide a tiny bit of warmth. He pulled out his change and dialed the number. When the familiar voice answered, he greeted it in what he thought was the same manner he always had.

"Hey, sis. What are you up to?"

Emily

Emily was astounded when Ronan emerged from Pop Murphy's without anything in hand. She couldn't understand why he had blown yet another opportunity she had placed before him. Ready to give up on him, Emily was about to turn away when Ronan suddenly slumped onto the curb and burst into tears. In that vulnerable moment, a wave of compassion washed over her. She felt a softening in her heart, realizing that she couldn't simply abandon him in his time of need. Something inside her seemed to melt. She couldn't walk away.

Watching him weep stirred feelings inside her she hadn't felt for a long time. He was in need of more than a job and some food. He was broken. Helping people who were struggling on the inside was something Emily had no experience with. She had shut out any feeling of compassion long ago as she had concluded that emotions only clouded solid judgment.

Ronan had been sad. She had felt that but had not bothered to address it. She thought she would help him by addressing his external needs. She had believed if she could assist with the job and food situation that would be where her part ended. He would be better off and would continue on with his life. She would continue her walks through Manhattan and that would be that.

It wasn't that simple and she wasn't sure what to do. This was something that had become almost foreign to her. It had been years since she had felt anything akin to compassion and sympathy toward someone. When she was a young girl, she had been the most compassionate in her family. Often taking food to stray cats in the park or helping other kids in school who were falling behind, her brother once called her the Mother Theresa of the Upper West Side.

Those days were gone, though. Emily had been sixteen when, after a traumatic experience, she shut off her emotions. From that point on she let logic and determination run her life, void of feeling. She had been called cold and calculating more than once but, as she would point out, she had become wildly successful by the age of twenty-six. She was not anticipating empathy would return to her and she was not completely comfortable with it.

When Ronan got up and began walking again, she decided she wasn't going to try anything new. No putting anything in front of him, no mind tricks to guide him anywhere. She was going to let him be and see what happened. Maybe she could get a glimpse of something that would help put this perplexing puzzle together and give her something to work with. This was territory she was completely unsure of.

Emily shook her head as she watched Ronan pick up pennies, nickels, and a few dimes out of the gutters or off the street. It was such a simple way for him to get some food and neither one of them had thought of it. She wondered if he had begun to think a little more clearly since he'd eaten that sandwich earlier. She was pleased when he stopped in the deli to warm up and get another one.

Maybe, she thought, some nourishment had been exactly what he needed after all. He seemed to have a purpose as he walked. What it was, she didn't know but his shoulders weren't as slouched as they had been, and his steps were just a bit faster. Emily knew he definitely had something in mind as he continued down 5th Avenue. She didn't recall Ronan ever walking this far before.

When he stopped at the phone booth, Emily paused. She needed to know who he was calling. She wanted to hear the conversation, but she didn't want to risk him seeing her. How would she explain eavesdropping? She thought, again, of the book on methods of the mind. She wondered if she could get close enough to try another technique. She walked as close as she could without thinking she was being obvious. She closed her eyes and concentrated.

After a few moments, her eyes snapped open. Emily had tapped into something, but it wasn't the conversation. It was a feeling of hopelessness, of nothingness. Her hope that Ronan had begun thinking clearly vanished. It was now clear to her that he had lost all hope. The feeling that had swept over her was one of deep despair and a resignation that there was nothing left worth living for. It made her dizzy and she had to take deep breaths to keep herself on her feet. She was frightened. She had never felt something so dark and agonizing before, not even the night she had turned off her own emotions.

She reached up and wiped away the tears she hadn't realized had fallen. There had been something else Emily had felt. She sensed the goodness in Ronan, the kindness. Under the loss and despair there was a soul that was gentle, loving, and honorable. There was a man who was capable of great things and great love who had fallen into a pit of depression, loss and heartbreak and could see no way out. This was a man who did not need material things to get back on his feet. He needed to see why his life was still worth living.

Emily took a deep breath and exhaled slowly. Her mind was spinning. She was completely out of her element but knew she had to do something quickly. Regardless of whether or not Ronan caught sight of her, she moved closer to the phone booth until she could hear his end of the conversation. She realized he was speaking with his sister. She closed her eyes again and concentrated as hard as she could.

One way or another, Ronan would get the help he needed tonight.

32

Ronan

Michelle's voice came as a comfort to him. "Ro! I'm glad you called. How are you?"

"Fine," he replied. "I'm doing alright." He hated to lie to Michelle but he felt he needed to. "Hey, look, I know I haven't been around and I'm sorry about that."

"Ro, don't. It's okay. I understand."

"I know you do but I had to say it. I've been thinking about you, though. I've been thinking about a lot of things lately. It's funny how things you haven't thought of in years find their way back into your head. You know, like the time we were in the Catskills and I left you on that raft in the middle of the lake."

Michelle let out a laugh. "Oh, how could I forget that? I was 10 and you just left me there. You swam back to shore because some girl was sunbathing and you didn't want your kid sister weighing you down." She paused. "What made you think about that?"

"Like I said, I've been thinking about a lot of things. We had some good times, didn't we?"

"Yes, we did. A lot of good times."

"And I'm sorry I haven't been around much lately and—"

"Ronan - "

"I just want to tell you I'm sorry, okay? I know I kinda froze you out and you didn't deserve that. You've always been good to me, even if I did leave you out on the lake, and I want you to know I appreciate it."

"Ro– "

"Let me say this. You were one person I could always count on. I never told you enough how much you mean to me and I'm sorry for that. You meant a lot to Carrieann, too. And maybe we took you for granted at times. If we did, I'm sorry."

"Stop, Ronan," Michelle began to feel worried. "I never felt taken for granted. I know you and Carrieann appreciated me. What's going on?"

"Nothing. Really. Can't a brother get a little sentimental with his kid sister?"

"Yes, he can, and a sister can be worried about her big brother."

"Don't worry about me, okay? I'm gonna be fine. It'll all be fine. No one will need to worry about me. You just take care of Jack and June. You tell that little girl that her uncle. . ." Ronan's words caught in his throat, he took a breath before continuing, "her Uncle Ro loves her very much."

"Ronan, what's happening? You're not alright, are you? Talk to me. Tell me what's going on."

"There's nothing to tell. Nothing is going on."

There was silence on the line for a few seconds. It was broken when Michelle said the words Ronan needed to hear. "I love you, Ro."

Fresh tears sprang into Ronan's eyes. He took a beat before responding. "I love you, too, Misha." He hung up the phone and, hand still on the receiver, leaned his head against it.

He hoped Michelle hadn't realized what he was really saying. He didn't want to hurt her. She was the one person besides Carrieann that was always there for him. Through the good times and the bad times, she had never wavered in her support. He had thought about leaning on her after Carrieann's death, but she was pregnant with June and had too much on her plate to burden her. A part of him also felt it didn't matter what she might have done, nothing would have changed the fact that his wife was gone.

Stepping out of the phone booth, Ronan shoved his hands in his pockets and looked toward the sky. The only thing he didn't like about living in the city was the sky was never clear enough to see all the stars. Only the brightest ones could be seen on a clear night. He imagined

Carrieann being one of them. He wouldn't doubt if she was the one that shone the brightest. A tiny smile appeared on his face as he imagined her up there spreading her glow and making everyone happy. He wanted to be up there with her.

The smile faded as turned back to his plan. He figured he'd be at the bridge in about a half hour. He continued on his walk; his steps not as quick as they had been. His mind alternated between thoughts of Carrieann and thoughts of Michelle. Carrieann at their wedding; Michelle playing in the fire hydrant stream as a child; Carrieann dancing in their apartment; Michelle chasing him through their parents' apartment. Back and forth the scenes went in his mind. In all of them there was laughter. Once there had been so much laughter and joy in his life. Carrieann and Michelle had been responsible for almost all of it. Those days were now just memories. His mind went to images of the empty apartment, the docks, and Carrieann's grave.

Yet again he wiped tears from his eyes. He could barely see the sidewalk in front of him. He had never felt like this. Ronan had never experienced feelings so dark. He tried to change his thoughts and think back on the things he had accomplished and was able to do over the years but none of that mattered as his mind told him he had become useless. The voice in the back of his head reminded him there was nothing left for him here.

He reached the bridge and stopped. Staring up at the massive stone archways he was no longer sure if he wanted to continue on to Coney Island. He was tired. He was aching. He was hurting. He walked onto the bridge and through the archway. He walked past the third lamp and stopped. Placing his hands on the railing, he looked down at the cars passing underneath. He was done.

Michelle

"I have to go."

"What? What do you mean you have to go? Where?"

"To Ronan," Michelle answered her husband. "Something is wrong. I feel it. Something is telling me I have to get to him." She grabbed her coat and hat from the hall closet and found the car keys on the hall table.

Jack rose from the sofa and walked toward her. "Was that him on the phone just now? What's going on?"

Michelle stopped. Looking at her husband, she shook her head. "I don't know. He said he was fine, but I know he's not."

"Do you think you're overreacting? Maybe he's just having an off night."

"No!" The word came out stronger than Michelle intended. She took a breath. "No, I'm not overreacting, Jack. He called me Misha. He hasn't called me that in years." Her hand went to her forehead and she closed her eyes. "I can't even remember the last time he called me that."

"Okay, did he say anything else that makes you think he's in trouble?"

Opening her eyes, she looked at her husband with a resolve that he had never seen before. "I just know. Everything in me is screaming that he needs me, that something is horribly wrong. I have to go."

Jack nodded. "Okay, go. June is down for the night. I'll watch over her."

Michelle spoke slowly, thoughtfully. "I don't think he's at his apartment. It sounded like a pay phone." She looked up at Jack. "How am I going to find him?"

She dropped her hands to her side, worry filling her soul. Jack was about to speak when an image flashed through Michelle's mind. It took her by surprise and filled her with a dread she had never known before. In that moment, she knew where he was and why he had called her by her childhood nickname. It terrified her.

"I know where he is." Without another word, Michelle ran from the house, jumped in the car, and sped away from the curb.

It would take close to 40 minutes to get to the Brooklyn Bridge from her home in Jackson Heights. Going on 11:00 pm, Michelle was praying there wouldn't be too many people on the road as she sped down 34th. If there was hardly any traffic she could make it in 30, she thought as she accelerated. Once over the bridge, it wouldn't take long to get to Washington Square.

Her eyes slowly filled as she thought about her brother. She was upset with both Ronan and herself. She didn't understand why Ronan had not talked to her. Whatever it was, he could have told her. She would have listened. He used to tell her everything. She was angry he had not called her, had not come to see her. She would have been there for him as she always had. How could he not know that?

Michelle became angry at herself, too. Why didn't she check up on him more often? She knew his grief over losing Carrieann had overcome him. She knew he was not coming out of it the way most people do. She had been there constantly in the beginning but then had given birth to June. No one would blame her for shifting her focus to her newborn baby, but Michelle didn't feel that way at the moment. She blamed herself for not calling more. She should have gone to his apartment more often. She could have taken June with her. Instead, she chose to believe him when he said he was fine. *Stupid*, she thought, *you were stupid. You could have found time.*

Ronan had always been self-sufficient. He had taken the right paths all through high school and after. He had always been her rock, the one who gave advice, the one who helped her through every family crisis, every boyfriend drama and he was the one she turned to when her first love, Dean, had lost his life in the early days of Vietnam. It wasn't often he needed help, but when he did, she was always there. She had been there for all his triumphs, all his worries, all his ups and downs. Through it all, he always had his head on straight. He was always thoughtful and logical.

Michelle had no idea what it was that could have gone so wrong that he felt he could not tell her. She knew grief was a powerful thing but she also knew, though she couldn't explain how, that this was more than grief. This was more than the loss of a wife and a job. The realization struck her that she didn't even know if he had found another job yet. The anger at herself grew

"Hang on, Ro," she said out loud to the dark night in front of her. "I'm coming. You'll be okay."

Emily

Standing under the archway of the bridge, Emily was unsure of what to do. She had hoped with all her might that his sister had picked up on the thoughts and images Emily had tried to project to her. Failing that, she hoped that the tone of Ronan's voice and undercurrent of his words hadn't been lost on Michelle. She closed her eyes again and tried to project an image of the bridge. Emily had never been the praying type but at that moment she said a silent prayer that his sister received the message, one way or the other.

She could feel the bond Ronan had with his sister. It made her sorry that she had distanced herself from her own siblings. Distanced wasn't the right word, she knew. She had deliberately alienated them. She wished that things were different and that she had the closeness with them that Ronan and Michelle seemed to share. She wondered if they would ever speak to her again. Probably not, she surmised, not after what she had done. She had been methodical about what she had done and she had known they would be angry, hurt and would resent her, maybe even hate her.

Emily shook her head and brought herself back to Ronan. He was who she had to focus on at the moment. He was just standing there, holding onto the railing. The despair was palpable but he wasn't moving. He appeared to be interested in the cars going by underneath, but Emily knew what his mind was encouraging him to do. He didn't deserve this, she thought to herself. He was a good person who didn't deserve to lose so much. She contemplated what a complex place the mind was. It could take an otherwise rational person and send them into a deep well of darkness. Without some kind of help that pit could swallow a person whole.

She wished she had spent more time on the chapters of the book that explained depression and other mental disorders. She had been too interested in the methods to bend people to your will than in the many ways the mind could play tricks on you. Emily had read through them but had not taken in enough to remember anything useful. The only thing she knew as fact was that Ronan's mind was playing tricks on him and he'd fallen into a pit.

At that moment, more than anything, she wanted to rescue Ronan from that pit. Emily weighed her options. She could wait to see if his sister showed up or she could do this herself. A part of her was hoping Michelle would show up and take over. The other part of her wanted to reach out to Ronan and talk to him.

Her decision was made for her as she saw Ronan lift his leg to climb on top of the railing. Her heart dropped and panic set in. She began to run toward him.

"Ronan! Stop!"

Ronan

As the cars passed by underneath him, Ronan began to wonder about the people inside them. Where were they going? Where were they coming from? Did they have a family or were they single and heading home from a bar? Were they happy? He hoped they were happy. He hoped their lives were full of love. He hoped they had everything he once had and he hoped they would never lose it.

He sighed heavily. For a moment he wondered if he should really do this then he thought of what he had to go back to. Nothing. In the back of his mind, he kept hearing that voice that told him he was of no use to anyone. He had failed and his life no longer had any meaning. So what if he hadn't gotten another job? What difference would it have made? Sure, he would have been able to keep the apartment but so what? That was the question that kept going through his mind. *So what?* It wouldn't have mattered. He still wouldn't have his life back. No one had hired him anyway but *so what?* He probably would have hated another job.

His parents would be upset after this but *so what?* It would save them the embarrassment of having a failure as a son. This way they could tell people it was an accident instead of explaining why their son was unemployed and homeless. Michelle would be hurt, he knew that. But, again, *so what?* It was better that she be hurt for a while, grieve and move on instead of having him as a burden in her life. She didn't need his problems on top of taking care of a toddler. It was better this way, all the way around, for everyone.

There'd be one less person in the world. *So what?* The world was better off. He had nothing to contribute to it and it had nothing left in it for him. Ronan shrugged his shoulders and let out another sigh. He was going to do this and *so what?*

He lifted his right leg up to straddle the railing. He began to feel something close to relief. Relief that it would be over soon. Everyone could go on with their lives and never have to worry about him. More than that, relief that he would no longer feel the pain he had been carrying around with him. He would no longer feel anything. *Finally*, he thought, *I found a way out of this hell.*

"Ronan! Stop!"

The voice screaming his name startled him. He brought his leg down and turned to see a woman running toward him, past the few other people on the bridge that he hadn't noticed before. As she got closer he could see she was scared. She hadn't taken her eyes off him. It confused and unnerved him.

"Ronan," she started, "don't do this. You can't do this. Stop. Just take a moment. Please."

Ronan was stunned into silence. He stared at the woman for a few moments, her breath visible in the cold air as she tried to catch it. "Do I. . . do I know you?"

The woman shook her head.

"Then who are you? Why are you here?" He was suddenly angry. He was moments away from finding peace only to be stopped by this woman who had no business here. "Go away. Just let me be." He turned back to the railing.

"Ronan, please listen."

He snapped his head toward her. "How do you know my name? Why should I listen to you?"

"You're hurt."

He said the phrase that had been going through his mind the last several minutes. "So what?"

"So what?" the woman repeated. "So what?! This isn't the answer. This will only cause more pain for more people. And you. . . you. . ."

The woman fell silent. The anger Ronan had felt began to

dissipate slightly. He noticed her eyes. They seemed to hold something. He wasn't sure what that was but there was something in them that struck a chord. He felt a pull that told him he should listen to her, but he didn't want to. He only wanted a release from the agony he'd been feeling for so long. He tried to shake off the feeling but, instead, he turned toward her.

"How do you know my name?"

She hesitated before speaking. "I'm Emily. I've seen you around but that doesn't matter. What matters is you." She brought her gloved hands up to her face, covering her nose and mouth, and breathed in. She seemed to be figuring out what to say next.

Ronan didn't care what she had to say. "Well, Emily, I don't matter. So, please leave."

Emily's hands immediately fell as she screamed, "NO!"

The word was said with such force that Ronan froze and could only stare at her.

"No," Emily continued, "I will not leave." Her hands went to the top of her head. "I'm not good at this. I have no idea what I'm doing but what I do know is that your life is worth living. You are a good man, a kind man. You have so much to offer, so much you are capable of. You can't do this. You are too good."

Ronan's brows furrowed and he squinted at her as she dropped her hands to her sides and leaned against the railing. Multiple things went through his mind in a split second. He didn't think he had ever seen this woman before, yet she seemed to know him. Before he could utter a word, Emily continued.

"You won't understand. It would sound crazy if I tried to explain it and there's no way you'd understand but that's okay. You don't need to understand. Please just listen."

It appeared to Ronan that she was looking for agreement from him before continuing, so he nodded.

"Okay," Emily started again, "Okay. So, I know you are hurting. I know what you've lost."

Ronan shifted his weight at the last sentence. He was not going to get into a conversation about Carrieann with a stranger. Especially one that sounded like she'd been stalking him. What else would explain this? He started to speak when she held up her hand.

"Like I said, you won't understand. I know a lot about you, Ronan. I know that you're kind, that you have a big heart. I know that you love your sister and would never want to hurt her. I know that things have been extremely rough for you for quite a while." She paused. When she continued her voice was softer. "I know that you loved your wife very much."

Ronan inhaled sharply. While his mind railed against any conversation with this woman, something inexplicable was taking over inside him. He lowered his head but didn't speak. He knew Carrieann would have been weeping silently wherever she was if he had not been interrupted by this woman. The familiar grief and guilt began to well up inside him once again.

Emily turned toward him. "It was not your fault. You are many things, Ronan, but you are not God. There are many things that happen that we will never understand and that will haunt us, but this is not one of those things. Carrieann had an aneurysm. You did not cause it, nor could you have done anything about it. Even if you had been home with her, she would not have made it to the hospital. You are not God. You could not have changed what happened. What you need to know is that she loved you as much as you loved her."

Ronan brought his head up and looked at Emily, if he spoke he knew he would break down again. He bit his lower lip and looked out over the water. He shook his head and closed his eyes.

"It was not your fault," Emily repeated.

Though he had heard those words many times before, it was the first time he thought he might be able to believe them. Somewhere inside he had known all along but his mind couldn't seem to handle it. His entire life he had found solutions to things and fixed them. His mind seemed to block all reason when it came to this; the one thing that he would not have been able to fix. He had needed something or someone to blame. Someone had to be at fault. He had to blame himself. It was easier to blame himself, to feel the anger over not being there to fix it, than it would be to deal with the sorrow alone. The anger gave him a break from the grief.

Still unable to speak, Ronan only nodded before opening his eyes and looking back at Emily. He was exhausted, emotionally drained and didn't feel as if he could stay on his feet much longer. He sat down on the bridge and leaned against the railing. He let his head rest against it and exhaled deeply. Emily carefully sat down beside him.

"Carrieann saw the best in you. She saw the good man that you are. She saw the man that worked hard so she could make a home for you, the man who loved deeply and cared so much about her and his family. The man who cared about everyone. The man who would give up a night with his friends just to take a walk with her and see her smile. The man who could figure out anything. She saw how smart you are and how there wasn't anything you couldn't fix or build. That man is something special. That man still has more than just a little bit left. That man has a lot left to say and do. That man is still in there, Ronan."

"Is he? I'm not so sure."

"Of course, he is. You need to find him again instead of giving up. You just need some help, that's all. I don't profess to know much about this stuff, but I do know that this is more than mourning and loss. You need to reach out to someone and let them help you. What you were about to do wasn't going to give you peace. It would have given you nothing. Nothing is worse than sorrow, it's worse than pain."

Ronan snorted. Who was this woman who thought she knew so

much? What did she know about what he was feeling and what he's been struggling with? By the looks of her it didn't appear she'd ever struggled a day in her life. It looked like her biggest tragedy would have been her father taking away his credit card.

"What would you know about any of that?"

"Because I know about feeling nothing and let me tell you, feeling anything is better than feeling nothing at all."

"Yeah, okay," he replied somewhat snidely. "You look like someone who's idea of a bad day is Daddy not buying you a brand-new Mustang." Ronan caught himself. He had never judged people by the way they looked before. Why was he starting now? He realized he was trying to pick a fight with this woman. He was trying to be angry with her because it was easier to fight than acknowledge any truth in what she was saying.

"I'm sorry," he said. "I shouldn't have said that. I don't know why I did. It wasn't fair."

"No, it wasn't," Emily replied, "but, to be completely honest, I could see why you would think that. To be even more honest, there was a time that wouldn't have been too far off the mark, unfortunately. However, we're not here to talk about me. But, you know, if taking shots at me helps you, go ahead and take your best one."

It was never in him to demean anyone and he was sorry he had done it now. He knew that this woman, whatever her reasons might be, was here to help him. There was even some truth to what she was saying before he was rude. He did need help. Ronan shook his head. "No. No shots."

"Okay, then. Talk to me, Ronan. Get everything out. I won't interrupt you. Just, finally, start talking."

And he did. Ronan didn't know why he started but once he did, he couldn't stop. He let his anger, his sadness, his despair spill out. He told her the story of how he met Carrieann, he talked about their wedding, their life together and he told her everything about the day he came home to find her on the floor. Emily had listened quietly; he was thankful for that. When the sobbing began, he let her put her arms around him. He leaned on her shoulder and let it out. The sobs wracked his body as the emotions he tried to push down with anger and resentment found their way out.

It was several minutes before the sobs became low moans and, eventually, quiet sniffles. When he gathered himself, he spoke about losing his job. He talked about not being able to talk to his parents, how he didn't want to put any more weight on Michelle. He lamented how everything was changing and it was too much for him. Again, Emily had listened quietly.

Lastly, he told her how he felt about himself. Ronan believed he wasn't useful to anyone anymore and there didn't seem to be a job he was qualified to do. He couldn't hold himself together anymore. He was a complete failure with nothing left and he just wanted it to be over.

He was shocked when Emily was no longer silent. "Well, that is the biggest load of bullshit I've ever heard."

Ronan didn't know how to respond. He thought she would be sympathetic. He was expecting her to agree. He thought she would commiserate. He wasn't expecting her to say those words.

"What?"

"Not able to do anything? That's bullshit. Not qualified? That's bullshit. Did you listen to your own story? Did you hear yourself? Your problem isn't that you have no skills or can't do anything. Your problem is you are too far down this hole to recognize all the skills you *do* have and all the things you *can* do."

Not knowing what to say, Ronan let Emily continue, her voice much softer. "I can honestly say I can't imagine what you went through or what it must feel like, but I do know that you are a strong enough man to come out of this. You can pull yourself out of this. You just need to take the first step."

"What's the first step?"

"Reaching out to someone and admitting you need help."

Ronan's first instinct was to resist. However, he knew she was right. He'd known for a long time he needed help. Maybe having someone be so blunt with him was what he needed. He looked at Emily and nodded.

Once again, he was struck by her eyes. He wasn't sure why. They weren't a special color; they were the dominant brown most people had but he saw something in them. Looking into them filled him with a warmth he had forgotten existed. He was drawn to them. It was almost as if he could see himself in them, as if he had already been a part of her life and knew her. Except that he didn't.

He realized he knew nothing about this woman who had stopped him from making a devastating mistake. Looking her straight in the eyes, he asked, "Okay, so what's your story?"

Michelle

Of course there has to be traffic, there always is. Michelle checked her watch. She was a few blocks from the bridge and at a standstill. If only these cars would get out of her way.

"Move!" she screamed. "Come on! Get out of the way!" Not that anyone could hear her, but it made her feel better to scream at the cars in front of her than to panic over the possibility of being too late to find Ronan.

She tapped the steering wheel impatiently. The image of the bridge had floated through her mind a while ago and she knew he had moved from the square and was on the bridge. She was so close, but she was not able to move. The thought of abandoning her car and going the rest of the way on foot crossed her mind. If she had put her winter boots on, she probably would have done it. As it was, she was stuck in the car.

Having already prayed to God twice to get her there in time, she gave it another try. "Are you listening? Do you answer prayers anymore? Please. Please, let me get to my brother. Please let him be alright. Please, God, he needs help. Let me get to him."

Slowly, the line in front of her began to move. Michelle looked up, "Thank you. I will never doubt you again."

Inching along, she saw what the holdup had been. She saw the flashing of police lights ahead and what she thought was an ambulance. As she got closer, she saw the wreckage of a vehicle moved to the side and an officer directing traffic slowly through one lane past it. She hoped everyone involved was alright and prayed those would be the only emergency lights she saw tonight.

Without warning, the feelings of worry and panic waned. Ronan was okay. He still needed her but he was safe. Michelle had no idea how these thoughts, images and feelings were coming to her but she didn't care, she'd think about that later. Right now, she was glad her brother was safe, she would find him and, together, they would figure everything out.

Emily

Relief had washed over her when Ronan nodded in agreement to needing help. She had relaxed and knew he was going to be okay. Eventually. She was thinking about the process he'd take to get better. She was not prepared for his question. Startled, her eyes widened, her mouth dropped, and her brain froze.

"I asked," Ronan continued, "what's *your* story?"

"I . . . I heard you," Emily replied, "but I'm not important here. You are."

"I need to know what brought you here tonight. I need to know how you know so much about me. I don't think we have ever met before but here you are." He paused. "You literally saved me. I need to know how."

Emily sighed. She knew she could never explain this to him. She wasn't even sure she understood it herself. The walks she took, the people she thought she could help. It was hard to understand herself why she did it, all she knew was that she felt she had to. What was driving her, she couldn't say, so how could she explain it to someone else?

"I told you," she answered quietly without looking at him, "you won't understand. Honestly, I don't even understand it. Let's just be glad I was here and leave it at that."

There was silence and Emily hoped Ronan would drop the subject. She also hoped that Michelle would get here soon. Even though she wanted to sit and talk to him longer, she did not want him to know anything about her. She knew someone as honest as Ronan would take an instant dislike to her.

She closed her eyes tightly when Ronan began speaking again.

"Okay, but at least tell me *something*. I told you everything. All I know about you is your name."

Emily couldn't argue with that. It was true but she didn't really want to tell him anymore than that.

"Do you have family?"

Okay, this she could answer. "Yes. My parents are gone but I have an older brother and a younger sister."

"Are you close?"

"No."

"Oh."

Damn it, she thought, *I should have said yes. Now he's going to want to know why.* She was wrong.

"So, let me ask you this. Earlier, you said you knew about feeling nothing. Tell me about that. I'm all tapped out over here. It would help me if you talked. It's your turn."

She turned that over in her mind. He might be right. Maybe it would help him if she shared that part of herself. She doubted she would see him again after tonight so what would it hurt? Ronan would see that he wasn't the only one who had emotional problems, he wasn't alone in that. That she could handle, that she could share. The rest she would keep to herself. She did not want him leaving here thinking she was evil.

"Well," she began, "my parents weren't exactly warm people. In fact, they didn't raise us. Our nannies did. We had two of them."

"Excuse me? What?"

Emily chuckled. "Yes. Okay. Alright." She held up her hands. "My parents were very rich. I'm an Upper West Side brat, okay?"

Ronan let out a low whistle. "Okay but just remember you said 'brat', I didn't."

Emily looked over at him. "Noted."

"Go on."

"When I was in elementary school . . . a private one, of course."

"Of course."

"I noticed other girls whose parents would drop them off or pick them up. I would watch as they hugged each other. When I went to birthday parties I would watch as their moms and dads did things with them, played with them and sang to them. My parents never hugged us. They never did anything with us except come in at night to say goodnight. I wanted so much to have parents like some of the other kids, you know? So I started trying."

She paused and cleared her throat. When she didn't start speaking again, Ronan took the moment to reflect on his own parents. "You know, my parents aren't the easiest. They can be rough and they can be strict but at least they played with us. My mom would sit with me and help me build things with my logs and she'd play dolls with Michelle. My dad taught me baseball basics and he'd take Michelle up to Bryant Park to play."

"You're lucky."

"I didn't always think so. I didn't think so today, as a matter of fact. I guess all parents can be rough and do things that screw up kids but, yeah, my parents paid attention at least – and they hugged us."

"Mine didn't. They didn't hug or pay attention. Like I said, I started trying. I would ask my mom to bake something with me and she'd tell me to go ask Terry. She was one of the nannies. I'd ask my dad to do something, a walk, a movie, anything, and he'd brush me away. I desperately wanted their attention. My brother seemed to be okay with it all - as far as I could see, anyway, and my sister was younger; I didn't pay attention to her because I was too busy trying to get my parents attention.

"The only person who paid any attention to me was my grandmother. She moved to Paris when I was ten. I cried for days. When she came back to visit once she brought me this beautiful replica of the Eiffel Tower made of crystal. It sparkled. Oh, how it sparkled. I loved it. It was my most prized possession. So, anyway, after years of trying to get my parents to do anything with me, I got angry. I figured if they didn't notice me when I was good maybe they would notice me when I was bad. I started to do things."

"Like what?"

"Pick fights at school. Break things. Sneak out at night. Stuff like that. All that happened was they had the nannies keep a closer eye on me and took away my phone privileges. When I was sixteen, I started smoking and drinking. I'd take bottles out of their liquor cabinet and sit in the living room. I'd light a cigarette and drink from the bottle. All they did was put a lock on the liquor cabinet and had the nannies go through my room three times a day to look for lighters and cigarettes."

"They never talked to you?"

Emily shook her head. "Not really. They sat me down once and told me they were disappointed and if I kept it up, they would cut down on my allowance." She noticed the look on Ronan's face. "Stellar parenting, I know. My grandmother had passed away by then, so there was no one to keep me even a little in line. So, one night I managed to sneak out and one of my friends had smuggled a couple bottles of wine out of her place, along with some weed. We drank in Central Park and smoked as we tried to stumble back home."

She stopped. Suddenly, she wasn't sure she wanted to go on. The feelings that came with that night had been shut off for so long. Before tonight, she had been able to reference things from the experience without emotion, as if it had happened to someone else, but now she was beginning to choke up. The feeling of panic and helplessness she had felt that night came back to her. Ronan must have noticed. He told her she didn't have to continue.

"No, no. I think I do." Emily wasn't sure why she'd gotten this deep into the story. She hadn't intended to, but now that she was here, she felt she had to tell it all. The next part came out in a rush. "We were drunk and didn't notice the guys following us. We were assaulted. The one guy had me pinned down. . .he. . .it happened so fast. . .I tried to fight back. He was going to rape me and very nearly succeeded but someone, I don't know who, pushed him off and started punching him. I got up and ran as fast as I could. I didn't stop until I got home."

She paused and let out a slow breath before continuing. "I ran inside the apartment and into the living room. My parents were still up having their nightcap." She said the last word with disdain and rolled her eyes. "When they saw me with my torn clothes and bloody lip, you know what they said?"

"I'm afraid to ask."

"They didn't ask me what happened. They didn't ask if I was okay. My father said, 'For heaven's sake, what have you done now?' Yup. That was it. I started crying and screaming, trying to tell them what happened. They weren't concerned about me. They were angry with me. My mother started babbling on about what it would have looked like if I actually had been raped. People would say it was my fault and they'd be right. I was trouble and they should have sent me off to boarding school. I ran to my room and they followed me. I was screaming at them for not caring. I asked them why they didn't love me. My father, whose attention I had once craved so much, this man who I had looked up to as a little girl, looked at me with such disgust and asked me what there was about me to love. He said just because you had children didn't mean you had to love them. Love is a wasted emotion and gets in the way of what is important in life. Then he walked across the room, looked me dead in the eyes and told me I should take a good look at myself. I was asking to be raped and would have deserved it. No one would ever love a slut like me. No one. Ever. I screamed that I hated him. He laughed and said 'No, you don't'. Then he went over and picked up my Eiffel Tower and threw it against the wall, smashing it to pieces. As he walked out of my room, he turned and said 'Now, you do'. And that was it. At that moment I shut down. I turned off all my emotions. I began to feel nothing. Nothing and no one was ever going to hurt me the way I had been hurt that night.

"That's how I lived after that night. No emotion. Everything was a calculated, logical, and methodical decision. I went through the rest of high school and college with straight A's. My parents couldn't have been more thrilled, but I no longer cared about what they thought or what they said or what they did. I no longer cared about them at all. I went to work in my father's business because it no longer mattered to me that he didn't love me. He was nothing more to me than a means to an end. I wanted to work my way up, I wanted money, and he had the business I could do it in. It was a transaction. I was efficient and extremely good at my job, and, in return, he paid me well and promoted me. When they died in that car accident, I felt nothing. All I thought about during the funeral was taking over my father's business and what I would have to do to make that happen."

Emily paused for a moment, tugging at her gloves. "I really thought shutting down was good. I thought feeling nothing had worked well for me. I really believed that. But now. . . ." She caught herself before she let out the rest of the sentence.

Looking slowly up at Ronan, she saw he was staring at her with an expression she could not discern. She began to think she had made a mistake telling him. She was afraid he thought she was a tramp or, like her father, she might have asked for the assault. Emily didn't know if she could handle Ronan thinking so poorly of her.

Her fear was put to rest when Ronan took her hand and said, "Emily, I'm so sorry that happened to you. You deserved so much better than that." In a mirror image of earlier, she let Ronan put his arm around her and she buried her head in his shoulder as she let out ten years of pent-up emotion.

When she started to pull herself together and sit up straight, she heard Ronan softly say, "Well, aren't we just two rays of sunshine in the middle of winter."

They started to laugh at the same time. Emily reveled in it. It had been so long since she had felt this - the power of laughter through tears. She didn't know what it was about Ronan or why she had decided to follow him that day on the street, but he had managed to do something no one else in her life had managed. He made her feel again.

When the laughter subsided, she was caught off guard once again when Ronan asked her to finish her sentence. He had noticed she had cut herself off without completing the thought. It was a sentence that was better left unsaid, she thought. She shook her head and told him she didn't remember what she was going to say.

"Yeah, I heard Upper West Side brats are forgetful."

Emily's mouth dropped and then, "And I heard Hell's Kitchen men are insufferable."

"And needy and sometimes suicidal." Ronan added

"Well, Upper West Side brats steal booze and sometimes weed." Emily continued.

"In Hell's Kitchen we'd have the booze and weed back before you even walked a block."

"On the Upper West Side your neediness would smell like fresh meat; lions would circle."

"So here we are," Ronan lifted his hands palms up.

"Just two rays of sunshine in the middle of winter," they said in unison followed by more laughter.

After a moment, Ronan became serious. "Thank you, Emily. I mean, really, thank you."

Emily smiled. "You're welcome, Ronan. I think we helped each other tonight."

She was about to say more when she heard someone calling Ronan's name. Michelle was coming down the bridge from the

Brooklyn side. It was time for her to go. A large part of her didn't want to leave Ronan but she knew she had to. He was going to be okay. His sister would help him get further out of the pit and he would go on.

Pointing down the bridge, she gave Ronan one last smile and said, "I believe your ride is here, sunshine."

Ronan

Following Emily's finger, he saw Michelle running down the bridge. His heart leaped at the sight of his sister. For all his determination not to put anything more in her lap, he couldn't hide the fact that he was both thankful and relieved that she was here. She was calling his name and looking at the faces of people as she passed them. He cupped his hands around his mouth and called out to her. He watched as she stopped and scanned the bridge. When her eyes fell on him, he knew he'd be okay. Help had come.

Ronan was trying to get up when Michelle reached him. She helped pull him to his feet and drew him into a hug. He held her as tight as he could and held it for a while, letting the warmth of it overtake him before whispering in her ear, "I'm sorry, Michelle. I'm so sorry."

"It's okay, Ro. I'm here. You're going to be okay," she replied.

Pulling away from her slowly, he momentarily went back to his old habit. "I'm okay. . ." he started but stopped. He shook his head and looked at his sister. "No, I'm not. I need help."

"I know."

Ronan gave a soft chuckle. As he turned to look down at where he had just been sitting, he said "I took the first step." The space was empty. No one was sitting along the railing. He looked down the bridge but wasn't sure what he was looking for. It was as if a fog came over him. He stared toward the archways and tried to remember, tried to recall why he had just said that.

"Ronan? Who are you talking to?" Michelle's voice took on a worried tone.

Turning back to Michelle, confusion set in. "I don't know. I thought. . .it seemed like. . .I don't know."

"Was there someone here?"

Looking around again, Ronan answered, "I don't think so, but. .

.maybe." Looking back to Michelle he said, "I feel like something happened but I can't remember what it was."

Michelle nodded. It was clear to Ronan that she didn't know what to make of that. Neither did he. He felt different than he had when he first walked onto the bridge, but it was going blank. He didn't know why. He remembered watching the cars below and then nothing. Nothing until he heard Michelle calling for him.

A moment came back to him in a flash; he staggered a bit. He was thankful Michelle was there to catch him. He leaned back against the railing and put his hands to his face. He was going to have to tell Michelle. If he was going to get the help he needed, he was going to have to be honest about everything.

"Ronan, what is it? What's wrong?"

Bringing his hands down, he took Michelle's and, without looking at her, quietly told her, "I was going to jump. I came close. I even had my leg up on the rail. I wanted everything to be over. I remember thinking that I would finally be at peace."

"Oh, my God," Michelle whispered.

He looked her in the eyes. "Something stopped me. I don't know what. I can't remember." Releasing her hands, he turned around and put his on the railing. "I was here; I put my leg up and then. . . nothing." He looked back at Michelle. "The next thing I remember is sitting here and hearing you call my name."

He felt Michelle put her hand on his shoulder. "Whatever it was, I thank God it stopped you. Maybe it's best if you don't remember for now. Maybe what you need to do now is focus on what to do from here." He let her turn him toward her. "Let's get you home and we'll figure things out."

Another admission he needed to make. "I don't have a home anymore. Well, I do for the next few hours, but I couldn't make the rent. As soon as the sun comes up, I won't be able to get back in."

"Why didn't you tell me?" Ronan could hear the anger and disappointment in her voice. "Let's go. I'll call Jack when we get to your apartment. He'll bring over a check in the morning."

"Mich–"

"He'll bring over a check. You won't lose your apartment. You will pay us back when you get on your feet. No argument. It's done."

Ronan knew that voice and he knew it was useless to argue with her. His sister could be as stubborn as a mule. He reached out and hugged her again.

"Okay, Michelle, take me home."

Michelle leaned back and said, "We have to walk over to Brooklyn first to get my car." She smiled at him.

"I gotta go to *Brooklyn*?" Ronan asked in mock disgust.

"Watch it or I'll make you walk all the way to Queens."

Keeping their arms around each other they started to walk down the bridge. Ronan figured he'd make another confession. "Before I decided to stop here, I was actually going to walk to Coney Island."

"Are you insane? I don't know how you managed not to freeze here on this bridge. What made you think you could walk all the way there? And for what?"

Ronan shrugged. "I had nothing else to do and there's something I wanted to see."

He knew Michelle was aware of Carrieann's fascination with the Wonder Wheel. He knew he could say it and she would know what he meant without explaining it.

"I want to know what is so special about the view from the top."

He saw Michelle turn toward him out of the corner of his eyes. He felt her squeeze him a bit tighter and then, "Well then, we'll have to make sure you get up there."

"Okay."

"Okay."

Emily

Emily got off the bridge as fast as she could. The tears had started as soon as she had gotten to her feet. She found the first bench at the bottom of the ramp and sat down. Now she was weeping uncontrollably. She could barely catch her breath. Leaning over, her head nearly touching her knees, she tried to regain control of herself.

After several minutes, she sat up, taking deep breaths. Removing her gloves, she dug into her pockets looking for a tissue. She was startled when one appeared in front of her. She looked over to see a middle-aged gentleman extending it toward her. Taking it gingerly, she nodded a thank you and turned to blow her nose. When she was finished, she used her hand to wipe her eyes and cheeks. Noticing the gentleman was still sitting next to her, she decided she'd better get herself together and start back toward uptown. She began putting her gloves back on.

"It's alright, Emily," the gentleman spoke. "You are fine. In fact, you did better than we expected."

"We?" Emily stared at him. "Who are you? What are you talking about?"

"Oh," the gentleman seemed to remember something and gave a quick wave of his hand.

Emily seemed to start a bit and then sighed. "You again."

"Yes, me again."

"Why are you here, Marcus? What did I do wrong now?"

"Absolutely nothing. Can you tell me why you are crying like this?"

"How could you not know? What just happened was. . .I can't explain it. I'm so tired. Ronan was going to jump and it terrified me."

"But he didn't."

"No, but he's a good person, Marcus. I saw it. I felt it. He deserves happiness and love not trapped inside a mind that tells him he's nothing. He's. . ."

"He's on his way to getting help. We will talk about him, but first – like I said, dear, you did better than we expected. Honestly, you lost me a bet. I didn't think it would happen for at least another two months."

Emily was lost, "You didn't think what would happen?"

Marcus answered with a question. "Emily, what is the last thing you remember about your life before you started taking your walks?"

"My life? But, Ronan–" Marcus shook his head and Emily relented. "Okay. I remember a lot of things. I took over my father's business, I work long hours. Rob and Maggie have no real part in it. I live in my parent's apartment since they died and I took it over. I also took control of my grandmother's apartment in Paris. In fact," she searched her memory, "I was in France recently for a little break."

"Yes," Marcus replied, "all that's true but it's not what I was getting at. Let me start over. When was the last time you went to your office?"

Emily looked down and went into deep thought. She couldn't remember. Her recent memories were of her walks; of noticing the things and the people she hadn't bothered to look at before; of trying to help people where she could. She had to have been in the office at some point. There was no way she'd stay away for any period of time. Even when she was in Paris she had made dozens of calls to stay on top of everything.

She looked at Marcus, "I don't remember. Why don't I remember?"

Again, he answered with another question. "When was the last time you slept in your apartment?"

"What? That's —", she was about to say it was silly when she realized she couldn't remember that, either.

"You don't remember, do you? It's okay. Now that we're sitting here, don't you wonder why you don't go to the office? Why you haven't been to your apartment? Why you only remember your walks?"

Emily realized it was true. She remembered her walks clearly. The ones before Ronan and all the ones she took when she began to follow him, but she didn't remember going to sleep anywhere. She hadn't thought about why she wasn't going into the office. Whatever had been possessing her, she only knew she had to keep walking and seeing if she could help people. After she thought she had successfully helped someone, Marcus would show up and tell her she hadn't succeeded. He'd tell her what she did wrong or that what she had done hadn't helped anyone at all. So, she'd start all over again.

"Marcus, what's going on?" For the first time since she began her walks, she felt scared. "Why can't I remember going home or going to work? Why did I decide to take walks?"

"You didn't decide that, Emily. We did."

"What are you talking about? Please, start making sense. What's happened to me?"

Marcus gave another short wave of his hand and a flood of memories hit Emily like a tidal wave. Most of them she already knew. She hadn't bought out her brother and sister, she had taken both her parents' and her grandmother's apartments out from under them. She had maneuvered it so that her siblings had small stakes in their father's business but not enough to have any say in the operation. She had made deals that were technically criminal except the paper trail would be too complex for any lawyer to unravel. She fired long-time employees loyal to her father and replaced them with people she knew would get whatever she needed done. They were also people she had enough dirt on that she could control them. These were all things she already knew about her life. It was the last memory to come back that hit her hard.

She had just gotten back from Paris. It was early spring. Central

Park was coming back to life. She was waiting to cross the street in front of the Dakota building, wanting to take a long walk through the park to clear her mind. It wasn't the push she felt first, it was the placing of hands on her back. At first she thought she was being mugged and, as was the case since that dark night ten years ago, she went into defense mode. The feeling of panic set in and she turned to confront whoever had set their hands on her. That was when the shove came. She went into the street sideways, stumbling and losing her balance, she saw the flash of a car and heard the screech of tires.

The next thing she remembered was taking walks through Midtown. She remembered taking in some of the sights as if she was a tourist and not a resident of the city. Then she was sitting on a bench in the park observing the flower children and wondering if they were people she could help.

"I was hit by a car. . . and then the walks started." She turned to Marcus. "Did the accident do something to me? Did it damage my brain and my memory? Do I walk because I can't work?"

Marcus chuckled. "No, honey. You're in a coma."

Emily was shocked, "I'm *what*?"

"I said you're in a coma, dear."

"Yes, I heard you. How is that possible? How can I be in a coma and be here at the same time? That makes no sense, Marcus."

Marcus sighed and leaned back. "The details are boring, Emily. Let me just give you the short version. Over the years, we've had decisions to make about you. I have always felt your soul was worth saving. It was easy at first but this last time it was much more difficult to make a case for you. I managed to do it, though. However, it came with strings. You had to prove you were worth saving, so I sent you out to see if you could find yourself again. Once upon a time, you had a good, kind soul but you buried it. We had to see if you could uncover it and let it out before we could decide what to do."

Emily was getting agitated. None of this made any sense to her. Marcus' explanation sounded more like a fairytale than it did anything close to reality. She shook her head. "You can't possibly expect me to believe that."

Once again, Marcus sighed. He turned his head to her and gave her a look that conveyed his annoyance at her disbelief. It only increased Emily's agitation. "Okay," he said, straightening himself, "how did that horse manage to take an abrupt turn when you were eight? Did you ever find out who pushed the guy off you in the park?"

"How. . ." Emily blinked several times. She had forgotten about the near-miss during horseback riding lessons. Her brother was having trouble getting his mount to stop and nearly ran over her if not for the horse suddenly taking a right turn without guidance from Rob. Then there was the park. She never did find out who had saved her. She sat silently for a few minutes trying to understand and process what he was saying.

When she spoke, she was quiet. "So, what are you? Are you my guardian angel?"

"Guardian angel?" Marcus shook his head. "Not exactly. It's not as if we guide people to take the right paths. There is something called 'free will' and we don't interfere with that. Like I said, the details are boring. In short, some souls are worth saving and some aren't. Sometimes we have to decide."

"Decide whether to let them live or whether to let them die?"

"That's the gist of it."

Emily nodded. "You thought my soul was worth saving so that's why I'm in this limbo? I'm in a coma but I'm here talking to you. Is all of this in my head? Was none of what's happened real?" Suddenly the thought of Ronan being a figment of her imagination felt devastating to her. She didn't want to imagine that Ronan did not exist.

"It was all real, Emily. Everyone you interacted with are real people. All of them had problems you tried to help with. Some of them, as we discussed at different times, still have those problems."

Breathing a sigh of relief, Emily almost smiled with the knowledge that Ronan was a real person but her thoughts went quickly back to the others she had tried to help. She realized that giving them a blanket, offering them money, or helping them find some good clothes didn't really help them. Those things gave them temporary comfort but did nothing to solve their troubles. She had failed them.

"I didn't really help them," she lowered her head.

"You did, a bit, but not in the way they needed it. What made Ronan different?"

Emily didn't look up. She considered the question and turned it over in her mind. There were several things she could say; there were a few reasons she stuck with him. After a few moments, she said "Because he has a good soul. He's a good person, a kind person."

When Marcus didn't respond, Emily looked up and saw him nodding. She wasn't sure if she should go on or not. She figured he already knew everything that happened but then something compelled her to keep talking. "He doesn't deserve to be hurting the way he is. There's so much life for him to live yet. He was different, I guess, because his main problem is his mind. He did need things yet he rejected the things I put in his path."

"He did. You didn't give up, though. Why?"

"I don't know. I just didn't." Emily didn't want to talk about this further. She could already feel the tears returning to her eyes.

This didn't seem to deter Marcus as she felt him shift on the bench and speak again. "You know why. You need to answer, Emily."

She turned and looked at him fully. "Because I could feel it. I could feel how low he was but I could feel the soul underneath and. . ." Emily paused for a moment. "I could see and feel the pain and I just wanted to lift it from him. I wanted to help him get better. I wanted to bring that kind, compassionate, intelligent, and loving person back to the surface. I want to see him go on and live a life he deserves."

Emily waited for Marcus to speak. It was true. She did want to see him go on and find happiness again. She hoped Michelle would help him get back on his feet and that Ronan would discover the things he was so capable of achieving. Emily felt he deserved it. He only needed to control the demons in his mind that were holding him back. She was sure he was strong enough to do it.

"And in return?" Emily noticed the slight sarcasm in Marcus' tone.

"Nothing," she seemed incredulous. "I don't want anything. I only want him to be well."

She watched as Marcus broke into a full, beaming grin. "That is why I knew your soul was worth saving. I knew that girl was still inside there somewhere."

Emily did not return the smile. She thought of all the people she had used over the last ten years. The ones she held things over; the ones she made deals with; the ones she discarded when they were no longer useful. So many people she needed to make amends with. She thought of her brother and sister and felt a guilt so profound it almost took her breath away. That was a bridge she wasn't sure she could rebuild.

"I have a lot of forgiveness to ask for and a lot to atone for. There are quite a few people that quite literally hate me." She let out a long breath. "This isn't going to be easy."

She saw Marcus shrug before answering. "It never is but it's in you. You can do it, of that there is no doubt. You have shown great brilliance, albeit, not exactly in a good way but your intelligence is nothing to be questioned. A female running a vast business by the age of twenty-six was no easy feat. In fact, it's unheard of." Emily began to speak but Marcus held up his hand. "Yes, I know you used . . . well, let's just say *questionable* . . . tactics but you made it happen. The big question is – what are you going to do now?"

Emily's reply was immediate. "I'm not going back to that. I'll assign others to run the business; changes will have to be made; no more corrupt deals or blackmail to get things done. I'm done with all of that."

"And what will you do instead?"

"I don't know. There's so much that needs to be done." She waved a hand to encompass the city. "There are women that need help, soldiers that need help. I mean how many more people out there are like Ronan? There are a lot of people that need help with mental issues but don't get it. That needs to be fixed. Racism is out of control. Violence is out of control. The country lost two good men this year who could have made a difference in this world.

"But first, I need to repair my relationship with Rob and Maggie. If they'll speak to me, that is. I need to make this a real family." She stopped. For the first time in a decade she knew what she had been missing more than anything. A family. She wanted to make things right and, with luck and a lot of redemption, maybe it was possible for them to be one again. She wasn't sure where to start but she knew it was up to her to repair it. A thought lurched into her mind and she asked, "Will the mental powers I had here still be there when I go back?"

Marcus' laughter gave her the answer. "Oh, Emily, you never had powers. We helped you along with those. We planted the images and feelings in both Ronan and Michelle. We knew what you were trying to do so we helped you but, no, you didn't have those powers here and you won't have them when you go back, either."

"Well, that's unfortunate. I thought I was doing it all myself. I didn't realize angels were doing it for me."

"Angels? Well, if that's what you want to think, I guess that's fine."

Emily looked questioningly at Marcus. "You're not angels?"

"We're many things, Emily. If viewing us as angels works for you, that's all that matters."

Emily sighed, she knew it would be useless to get a straight answer out of him. Her thoughts returned to Ronan. She had to know he would be okay. "Marcus, can I. . ."

"No," he interrupted her, "you cannot see Ronan before you go. I can tell you that his sister is taking him back to his apartment. She will be of great help to him. You won't be able to see him when you go back, either."

That shook Emily. "But why not?"

"Because you won't remember him. His memory of you has already faded. When you wake up you will be what you were before - complete strangers living in different circles in different parts of the city."

"Why? Why do we have to forget? Please. I don't want him to forget me. I don't want to forget him. Marcus, don't do that." She was almost pleading.

"Those are the rules, Emily."

"I don't accept them."

She heard Marcus snort. "This isn't something you can negotiate. You don't have a choice. Look, Emily, you proved to us that your soul was worth saving. You have good things ahead of you if you use both the time given to you and your free will wisely. I was right to gamble on you. You and Ronan learned things from each other, and you helped each other. If, in the future, you are meant to cross paths again, it will happen, but it will be like meeting for the first time."

A feeling of resolve came over Emily. "I will remember him. Somehow, I will."

Another smile crossed Marcus' face. "It's wonderful to see you caring about people again, dear. Try not to lose that this time." He bent his head and looked into her eyes. "You can make a difference in this world if you don't lose that."

Straightening his head again and clearing his throat, he continued, "I have one last question for you, Emily. This will tell us if you took the time to understand the person you were helping. Ronan's wife loved the view from the top of the Wonder Wheel. Have you figured out what she saw there that he did not?"

"She saw an endless sky; she saw beyond the horizon, and she saw infinite possibilities. He saw what was already there. He never looked beyond the horizon. He only saw what *was,* not what *could* be."

"Very good. How did you come to that conclusion?"

"Ronan is a creature of habit and the familiar. He felt safe in his comfort zone. Change is hard for him to handle. Partly, because of how his brain works. His mind limits his ability to see all that is possible."

"You are very insightful when you take the time to understand someone. Let's see how you use that power from here on out. It turns out you *will* leave here with a type of power. We've given you a new horizon, Emily. You need to look beyond it and see the possibilities. You need to use this power and be wise about it."

"Marcus, can I please see Ronan one more time? I don't have to talk to him. I just want to see him."

"I'm sorry, dear. It's not possible."

"Why?"

"It's time for you to wake up."

At that moment, three things happened simultaneously. Marcus waved his hand, Emily disappeared from the bench and at Lenox Hill Hospital in the Upper East Side a coma patient opened her eyes.

Part Two

September 1975

Ronan

Thriving and settled into his loft in Tribeca, Ronan knew the move he made three years ago was a smart one. His building in Hell's Kitchen had been sold and he considered himself lucky to find this space. Since industry had moved out of this area, he, along with quite a few artists, found that renting space in a building that was once a factory was both inexpensive and versatile as it lent itself to being both a work and a living space. Ronan's move to Tribeca marked a significant transition for him.

The charm of Tribeca's emerging, vibrant atmosphere, combined with the history and character of the building, appealed to what he now referred to as his second chance at life. Having discovered his talent for fixing and building things could be transformed into a home improvement business, he had started building a client list and began working on apartments and homes before he made the move to his loft. Over the last three years, with more space, he found he could expand. He used his loft for his home, his office, and a work area for another endeavor, building unique wooden furniture he could incorporate into his business.

Ronan found Michelle's support invaluable in his journey to this point. After helping him through his breakdown, she joined his business as his office assistant. It allowed her to earn her own money and, with Ronan being flexible, it also allowed her to take paperwork home during the summer while June was off from school. Ronan, however, loved the days Michelle would bring June with her to the loft. He adored teaching his niece about woodworking. He would give June little pieces of wood to whittle and form. The decision to work together not only strengthened Ronan and Michelle's bond as siblings but also created a nurturing environment for June.

Ronan attributed much of his change to their trip to the Wonder

Wheel years ago. It was during that visit when Ronan unraveled a deep realization - what Carrieann had been seeing from the top. She saw the open space and the endless possibilities of life. With the help of therapy and a nudge from Michelle, Ronan had finally seen what Carrieann had been seeing all along. He learned how to look for new opportunities and embark on new endeavors. It wasn't easy to break old habits, to go beyond what was comfortable, but once he took that first step, he realized he could move forward and create a new life for himself.

He knew from his therapy that his brain didn't always work the same way others did. Therapy and the Librium he was prescribed were helping, though he still had days where bleak thoughts would creep back in and threaten to take control again. Ronan knew those thoughts were, more or less, tricks his mind was playing on him. His therapist had gone over what his brain was missing and had given him methods to curb those thoughts and move beyond them. He was given a prescription for valium for the days that became too overwhelming, though he preferred not to rely on it.

When he wanted moments of introspection and clarity, Ronan found himself walking to the Brooklyn Bridge. He had begun this ritual when he first started his therapy. It had become his sanctuary, a place where he could witness the ebb and flow of the water while contemplating the second chance that had been granted him. He still could not recall what happened that night seven years ago, but he now views the bridge as a catalyst to his new life and of what possibilities lay ahead. It serves as a source of comfort and inspiration.

Ronan's determination to come out of the dark place he had been in, his self-discovery, his move to Tribeca, the establishment of his home improvement business, the support of his sister, and his contemplative moments at the bridge shaped him into the person he was becoming. He found purpose, passion, and gratitude for the opportunities that have come his way. For the first time since

Carrieann's death, he was in a place where he was beginning to enjoy his life but, more importantly, he was beginning to like himself again. He resigned himself to the fact that he would always be a work in progress, he would still have the off days, but he could control them.

On this oddly chilly September morning, Ronan found himself deep in thought as he was working on an oak bench a client was sure would look fabulous on the porch of their Long Island home. He was contemplating how word of mouth had driven quite a few people to his business looking for their own one-of-a-kind pieces. Always deeply appreciative when someone was pleased with his work, it still amazed him when they would recommend him to their friends and family. He advertised here and there but it was his clients recommending him that brought in most of the requests for furniture. He wasn't getting rich, but he was comfortable and, also for the first time in seven years, felt somewhat secure. Byrne Improvements was slowly gaining a solid reputation.

He was thinking about Michelle's suggestion of more targeted advertising when the buzzer startled him. As he got up to answer it, he once again made a mental note to replace the obnoxious buzzer with a regular doorbell. Strolling across the work area and through the office space, he swung open the huge metal door to find one of the other tenants on the other side.

"Hey, George, what can I do for you?"

George looked disheveled and a bit out of sorts. "Hey, man, have you heard the news?"

"What news?" Ronan became a little concerned. "Why don't you come in?"

Stepping through the door, George took the first seat he found. "I was talking to that guy on the second floor, you know, the one who had a thing for the owner's daughter?"

"What owner?"

"The owner of the building! That guy, Marty, had a thing for his daughter, remember?" When Ronan shook his head, George continued, "Anyway, you know that J-51 thing? It has to do with tax relief or something."

"Yeah, I know what it is but what about it?"

George sighed. "We're going to get evicted, man."

"What are you talking about? J-51 doesn't have anything to do with us. Why would we get evicted? It's not like they can do much else with a building like this."

"Oh, yes, they can. According to Marty, there's a thing floating around that has a real good chance of getting passed next year. It would expand J-51. Apparently, it would include a big tax break for anyone who renovates industrial buildings into multi-family residential buildings. He says the owner is going to take advantage of it and anyone on the second floor and up is going to get the boot unless they agree to the renovations and make their lofts residential-only."

Ronan fell silent and tried to sort through the implications of what he just heard. Rubbing the back of his neck, he took a seat and looked over at George. "Okay, but we don't know if it's really going to pass, right?"

"No, we don't know for sure, but Marty said it more than likely will. We're in a recession here, unemployment is at what? 9%? The city almost went freakin' bankrupt! President Ford had to bail us out. They're trying to make it more attractive to people to move in. Renovating a place like this, with its architecture and all, could get more people here. There's no more industry here so there's a lot of buildings they could turn into apartments. They could easily cut all of these lofts in half and make two apartments. If they make everything but the first-floor apartments, they'll charge the same rent we pay now or more and then everyone like you and me will have to go out and rent another place for our work. The landlords and the city get more money."

"Why not the first floor?"

"Businesses only. This is bullshit, man. A lot of us can't afford paying two rents. Can you? If we do stay here, I know we'll end up paying the same rent for half the space. Then what am I going to do with all my glass and machines? It's bullshit!"

"Okay, calm down. We'll figure this out. Let's get all the tenants together and talk this through. There's gotta be something that can be done." He stood up and led George toward the door.

"Yeah, we can do that. Strength in numbers and all that. Mayor Beame has got his head up his ass if he thinks we're all going to stand for this."

"We'll get everyone together. Until then, relax. There's a lot we don't know yet." Ronan opened the door and paused. "George, do you know who owns the building? I mean I know who we write our rent checks to but are they part of a bigger company?"

"Not that I know of. Why?"

"Just checking. Corbyn owned my last building and almost evicted me. They would have, too, if not for Michelle. I was just thinking if it's Corbyn, we don't have a chance against those bastards."

"It's not. Besides, I heard that Corbyn changed. They just donated money for a new wing on the Babies Hospital up there by Columbia-Presbyterian."

"Money for hospitals is good but it doesn't mean the people giving that money are good. Those people aren't good. I don't care if they changed their image, they kicked a lot of people out on the street back then and didn't give a damn. I doubt they really give a damn now. They have mob ties, you know."

George shrugged, "That was the rumor, sure, but all I know now is this building isn't owned by them so don't worry about it."

Ronan nodded, "We'll get everyone together and have a meeting. No one is going to lose their lofts here if we can do something about it."

"Okay. Thanks, Ronan," George said on his way out.

Ronan closed the door and sat down at the desk usually occupied by Michelle. He tapped his fingers for a few minutes while thinking things over. He was not going to get an eviction notice for the second time in his life. He got himself to a place where he could enjoy both his work and his life again. He wasn't going to have the rug pulled out. He picked up the phone.

Emily

Approaching the door to Safe Haven Clinic, Emily checked the time. With a sigh of relief, she realized she had half an hour until her first patient. Swinging the door open, she greeted the receptionist with a warm smile.

"Good morning, Jean!"

"Someone's been well caffeinated." Returning the smile, Jean handed Emily her messages.

Setting down her briefcase, Emily looked through the slips of pink paper. "I got a great night's sleep. So, how does Michael like school this year?"

Letting out a laugh, Jean replied, "He hates it! He doesn't like that there's no recess this year. He says the girls all have cooties and the teacher looks like Oscar the Grouch."

Emily leaned her arm on the desk, "Well, tell him girls get rid of their cooties in seventh grade, he's too big for recess and as long as his teacher doesn't *smell* like Oscar the Grouch, he's good for the year."

"Got it," Jean replied as the phone began to ring, "I'll tell him his Auntie Em said stop being a baby."

"Don't you dare. You know I love that boy." Though not actually related to Jean and her son, the sentiment was true. Emily loved Michael like he truly was her nephew.

"He loves you, too, but you know I will," Jean said as she answered the phone.

Picking up her things and heading down the hallway, Emily heard Jean yell. "Margaret is on line one."

"Thanks," she said over her shoulder as she opened the door to her office.

Emily's sister usually didn't call her at the clinic, so it was a bit disconcerting to her. Settled at her desk, she picked up the phone and cradled it against her shoulder as she pulled files out of her briefcase. "Hey, Maggie."

"Hi, Emily. Listen, have you seen or talked to Lyle Kettering lately?"

Emily paused. Lyle was one of the people she had fired from her father's company shortly after she had taken over. He had threatened her when she gave him his walking papers but she hadn't taken him seriously. Nothing had happened during the time she ran the company nor in the years since. She had tried to reach out to him in the months after coming out of her coma, but he had refused to see her. Instead of the in-person apology and restitution she had planned, she had written him a letter. No response had been received. She knew that one can apologize, and one can try to make up for horrible behavior but what can't be controlled is how the person on the receiving end will respond to it.

There were many people she had spoken to during those months. She apologized to people in-person; other apologies were done over the phone as there were some people that were willing to speak to her but not see her. Those months had been hard on Emily, but she reached out to everyone she had hurt and did what she could to atone for any hardship she may have caused. She did not expect, nor did she ask for their forgiveness, but she knew they all deserved, at the very least, an apology and to know that she recognized and took ownership of her behavior and was truly sorry for it. She was no longer the person they once knew.

After emerging from her coma, to everyone's shock Emily made the decision to hand over the reins of the company to her brother and sister. She retained a small share of the business, but her priorities had shifted, and she no longer wanted any active role in it. No one knew what to make of this sudden change and bets were placed on whether Emily was going to really follow through. Many were skeptical but when the terms were agreed upon and the papers were signed, Emily turned her back on it, knowing her siblings would run it efficiently and, unlike she had been, would be honest, fair, and above board. After that, she dropped from sight. Page Six speculated Emily had gone insane, and her siblings had her put away somewhere in Europe.

The reality was Emily began to change everything about herself. She changed her wardrobe, hairstyle and began her attempts to atone for her past misdeeds. Starting with Rob and Maggie, the three of them reached an agreement to sell their parents' apartment, yet Emily chose not to pocket her portion of the proceeds. Instead, she divided the money equally between Rob and Maggie, the first step in repairing the damage she had done. She had also officially bought out their shares of their grandmother's Paris apartment. It was the one thing from her previous life she wanted to hold on to.

Emily knew it was going to take a lot more than money and giving them their rightful place at the company to fix the fractured relationship, but she was determined to be a family again. She understood that actions speak louder than words, so she began a gradual process of rebuilding. She made a conscious effort to be present in their lives, attending their family events and showing genuine interest in their well-being. Despite the hard resistance she initially encountered, Emily persisted with a sincerity neither one of her siblings had seen since she was teenager.

Time had proven to be both an ally and a test of Emily's commitment. Month after month and year after year, she continued to put in the effort. Through her consistent actions and determination, Emily demonstrated that she had indeed changed. Slowly but surely, Rob and Maggie began to acknowledge the transformation.

It took nearly three long years for them to fully soften their hearts towards Emily. As they observed her resilience, remorse, and her generosity toward others, they gradually allowed forgiveness and healing to take over from the anger and resentment. Finally, they reached a point of reconciliation, where they could let go of their past grievances and embrace each other as a loving and supportive family.

In the midst of putting the pieces of her family together, Emily had decided she did not want to have the family name any longer. Maggie understood the need to change, though Rob was not happy. He felt if Emily was being truthful about wanting a family again then she should keep the family name. Emily listened but explained to her brother that she needed to start over completely. She wanted to get rid of everything associated with the person she once was and, to her, that included her name. In the end, she changed her name to Emily Walton.

As Emily Walton, she delved into a personal endeavor that surprised even herself. A newfound fascination with mental health care had bloomed within her. She had awakened from her coma with a desire to help those with mental disorders. She feverishly worked to establish a clinic dedicated to addressing this crucial aspect of human well-being. In her pursuit of this mission, Emily decided to hire recent college graduates to give them a good start to their careers in a time when unemployment was on the rise. She picked several whose compassion and drive matched hers and together they formed the Safe Haven Clinic.

Fueled by her passion to contribute more in this field, Emily embarked on her own education. She went back to college and studied vigorously, taking on double course loads, and obtained a PhD in Psychology. Armed with her qualifications and a compassionate heart, she strove to make her clinic accessible to all. By deliberately keeping her rates low and introducing special rates for veterans, Emily ensured that her services were within reach for those who needed them most.

Emily made other significant changes in her life. She decided to relocate from the Upper West Side to the Lower East Side. She would be closer to the clinic, which she opened in the Williamsburg part of Brooklyn, and she would be much closer to the bridge. For reasons she couldn't explain, she found herself often taking a cab from Uptown down to the bridge, walking out a little past the third light and then stopping to lean against the railing and look out at the water. Even though it was bustling with more and more people over the years, she found inspiration and peace there. It made sense to her to move closer to the bridge and to Brooklyn.

In addition to her clinic and education, she had also become part of the women's movement. Attending numerous marches, writing letters, and speaking one-on-one to women across the city, she worked tirelessly to advocate for women to be heard, respected, and treated fairly. Celebrating the victories of Title IX of the Education Amendments in '72 and the landmark Supreme Court ruling on Roe v Wade in '73, Emily knew there was still much more work to be done until women were seen as equals. Her commitment to making a real, positive change in the world only grew stronger with each passing day.

Looking to expand, Emily set her sights on opening another clinic in an old industrial building in Tribeca. By strategically locating it in that neighborhood, she aimed to reach a wider demographic and extend her reach to those who could benefit from mental health services. With each step, Emily remained steadfast in her pursuit of providing compassionate and effective mental health care, driven by a deep-rooted desire to help those in need and make life better for each patient who came through the door.

Emily found herself in a place where she felt she was finally making a difference and truly helping people. Once, when her brother commented that she could be making more money if she came back to the company, she told him the progress of her patients was more valuable to her than any amount of money. The company, she said, was part of her past; a past she had closed the door on and would never open again.

"Emily? Did you hear me?"

Emily was startled out of her thought. She almost forgot she was on the phone. "I'm sorry, Maggie. Yes, yes, I heard you. You caught me off guard. No, I haven't talked to or seen Lyle Kettering in years. Why?"

"You might want to sit down for this. Rob got a call from Tim Jackson this morning."

Tim Jackson was the lead lawyer for the company. Immediately Emily's mind went to an impending lawsuit. "Is Lyle suing?"

"No. However, you know Tim's firm also does work for Knopf Doubleday, right?"

"Yesss," Emily dragged the word out, confused as to where this was heading.

"Lyle is publishing a book."

"Okay, well, that's good for him. He's found a new career."

"Emily, the book is about you."

"*Me?*" Emily was incredulous.

"Yes. It's about you, the company, how you ran it, things you did when you were in charge. Apparently, he got some people to talk and is going to expose some of the deals you made . . . and other things."

"Why? Why would anyone want to publish something like that? I guess it's a story but it's no Watergate or Manson Trial, for God's sake. Even the breakup of the Beatles is more interesting and that was five years ago. I was only in charge for a couple years and left seven years ago. Who cares about it anymore?"

"Emily," Maggie sounded exasperated, "you were a woman - *a very young woman* - who took over a company and was absolutely ruthless about it. You fired men who had been in executive positions for years. You changed the rules on how everything ran, from the existing projects to the development deals, and you–"

"Don't say it. I know. I was there, remember?"

"Men don't want women in business. They didn't want it in 1968 and they sure as hell don't want it now. The women's movement made waves and men are resisting it. Hating it is the more accurate term. This book is going to paint you as a spoiled, rich bitch who cared about no one but herself, had no business being in the corporate world, and nearly destroyed a company."

"Well, some of that is true, if we're being honest, but I didn't nearly destroy it. It made a lot of money."

"That's not how it's going to be portrayed. You are going to be the poster child for why women should be controlled, barefoot, pregnant, and back in the kitchen. You are going to be the cautionary tale of scatter-brained women who think they can do it all but are inept and have no place in the business world."

"Scatter-brained? Lyle can accuse me of many things but one look at the growth that took place will tell anyone that I was far from a scatter-brained little girl."

"I know that, you know that. The average reader won't. They will drag you through the dirt and while they may not be able to prove a lot, they will imply you were more than a little dishonest. Your name will be synonymous with Virginia Hill or. . .or. . .Lizzie Borden."

"Okay, Hill I get but *Lizzie Borden?* I didn't kill anyone with an ax, Maggie."

"No, but they'll say you got away with murder. Now you know why Lyle wouldn't respond to you. He wants revenge. You're a woman who took his career away. He's going to try to make you look like Satan. Once the book comes out, people will look for you and you'll be easy to find. Changing your name and dying your hair isn't going to hide you. This could ruin your clinic, not to mention what it will do to Rob and me."

"I know. We'll have to find a way to stop this book from coming out. Can you arrange a meeting with Tim?"

"Rob's getting that set up already," Maggie paused and then, "Are you okay?"

Emily read between the lines. She knew her sister feared this news might cause the old Emily to resurface and use her old tricks in order to stop the book.

"Yes. We'll listen to Tim."

"Good."

"Maggie, trust me."

"I do. You've come so far. I just–"

"Maggie, I'm Emily Walton. Emily Corbyn vanished in 1968 and she's not coming back."

Ronan

The noise in the loft was giving Ronan a headache. When he suggested getting the rest of the tenants together, he didn't realize the rumor of a possible eviction had made them so irate. He was expecting some confusion, maybe a little fear, and, yes, some anger, but he hadn't expected them to be at the torches-and-pitchforks level of mob mentality so quickly. It had been a struggle to calm them down so a rational conversation could take place.

In the end, Ronan was pleased with how it went. The first step was to find out if the rumor was true and the J-51 Tax Abatement would be expanded to include the remodeling of industrial buildings. If it was, the next step would be a meeting with the landlord. As luck would have it, they wouldn't need to hire a legal team. They had Jack.

Michelle's husband was a junior partner in an uptown firm. Ronan hadn't needed to ask Michelle to speak with Jack. As soon as he called after George's visit, she wasted no time in asking Jack to look into whether or not J-51 was being expanded and what the tenants could do if they faced eviction. Jack had promised Michelle he'd find out and, if needed, he'd get something together if the landlord confirmed eviction. Ronan used that to ease some of the tension in the beginning, and during, the meeting.

Even though the meeting itself was over, half the tenants were still in his loft, talking to each other, talking to Michelle about Jack, or trying to get Ronan's attention. The noise and the scattered pieces of conversation were ringing in Ronan's ears.

"Everyone!" Ronan's voice boomed over the fray. "Everyone!"

The chatter began to dissipate as the attention turned once again toward Ronan. He continued in a lower, calmer voice. "There's not much we can do until we know the facts. It's been a long day. Why don't you all head home, write down all of your questions and concerns, and we'll discuss them all when we know what's what? The rumors could be true, or it may turn out to be nothing. In the meantime, let's all relax a little and we'll pick it up again when we know more."

It took nearly another half hour before the last tenant left, leaving Ronan alone with Michelle. He sighed heavily as he closed the door and leaned against it, closing his eyes. His head was throbbing, and he was tired.

"How're you doing?"

Ronan opened his eyes and looked over at Michelle. "I'm fine. Let's have a drink." He pushed himself off the door and headed to the kitchen area. He opened the refrigerator, retrieved two bottles of beer, and handed one to Michelle. As he was searching for, and found, the bottle opener, he grumbled, "I'll tell you, though, I will not get another eviction notice."

"You won't," Michelle replied as Ronan took her bottle back and opened it for her. "If it comes down to it, Jack will find a way to keep you all here."

Settling on the sofa, Ronan leaned back. "I hope it turns out to be nothing. I know it's probably *something*, though. The city has to do something in this recession. The president already bailed it out of trouble, it's got to stay on its feet somehow."

"Strange times we're living in. Changes are going to keep coming."

"Change is the only thing that is constant in life."

"Your therapist say that?"

Ronan laughed. "No, some Greek philosopher, I think, but it's true. I mean, just look at this decade so far. It started out with the Beatles breaking up and it's been all downhill from there."

"Are you blaming the Beatles for everything?" Michelle laughed.

"Yes, I am. Damn mop-tops should have stayed together."

"Of course, they should have," Michelle picked up the thread. "If they would have stayed together, we wouldn't be in a recession, Watergate wouldn't have happened, and unemployment wouldn't be so high. What else is their fault?"

"Apollo 13."

"Okay, anything else?"

"The gas shortage."

"Yes, because Paul McCartney caused the Arab oil embargo."

"Actually, it was John Lennon," Ronan quipped, "and you know he lives on the Upper West side by Central Park. I think we should go have a little chat with him."

"You're on your own there, Ro. As far as I'm concerned, Yoko broke them up and I'm still very angry about it. I'm not going near her."

"My therapist may have some openings if you'd like to make an appointment and talk to him about your Beatles obsession and your immense dislike of Yoko Ono."

"Speaking of therapy," Michelle took the opening to ignore the comment and turn the conversation. "I heard that Safe Haven Clinic is looking to rent some space on the first floor. If the landlord will make the first floor all businesses, then they really wouldn't have to do anything to the rest of the floors."

"In theory, but it wouldn't get them a tax break and that's what they're looking for. Also, the city wants people to move in. They need more multi-family housing. They need more affordable apartments to attract people." Ronan paused. "Where did you hear that Safe Haven was looking at space?"

"The guys that are cleaning out the offices the travel agency vacated. I guess a couple of the doctors are coming to look it over. Why? Thinking about changing therapists?"

"Nope. I was just curious. I heard they're good, but Dr. Parks has gotten me this far, I'm sticking with him."

"You've come a long way, Ro." Ronan nodded. Michelle continued, "Look at what you've built here. You have a successful business, a family that loves you. There's only one thing missing."

"That's right!" Ronan made a mock gesture of slapping his forehead. "Something *is* missing. I forgot to take my valium before the meeting."

"Stop," Michelle chided. "But I have been meaning to ask. Didn't you say your doctor was going to try something new with you? Instead of the valium and Librium?"

"Yeah, something experimental. He called it an SSRI. I forget what those letters stand for. It's some kind of inhibitor."

"You're going to take something experimental?"

"I haven't made up my mind. I've been doing fairly well but, you know, I have some off days. Nothing like before but it would be nice if there was something that would keep the dark stuff at bay every day."

"Dr. Parks think this inhibitor will do that?"

"He does. He says a lot of research is being done and if I take that along with staying in therapy, he thinks my brain may function as close to normal as everyone else's. Apparently, it's not producing some kind of chemical."

"What kind of chemical?"

Ronan shrugged. "I don't know. Science, medicine, all that, not my scene. It all sounds like a foreign language when he starts talking about it."

"Maybe you should start writing that stuff down so you understand it." Michelle suggested.

"Look, I'm just glad they didn't stick me in a state hospital like they used to do years ago. Or give me heavy drugs that turn people into zombies. They've come a long way with mental problems."

"Yeah, I can't see Bob Newhart giving his patients a

lobotomy."

"He should give Archie Bunker one. That's one show I don't like. The guy's a racist fool."

"That's the point, Ro, and he's always wrong."

Ronan turned sideways to face Michelle. "I'm serious. I've been waiting for this country to find some peace but for every problem that is solved there's a new one right around the corner. It never ends. Just look at the last ten years. Vietnam protests everywhere - even against our own troops - the Manson Family, Watergate, gas lines, racism, the Equal Rights movement, inflation, recession, unemployment-"

"You don't have to list it all, Ro," Michelle interrupted. "I've lived through it, too, you know."

"Yeah, well, TV shows don't help. *All in Family* uses black people as punch lines, real families aren't like *The Partridge Family* and war isn't as funny as *MASH* makes it."

"True but that's why it's called entertainment, Ronan. People have enough reality just going through their daily lives. At night they want to be entertained. We all know those shows aren't real life, but they make us feel good for a half hour. By the way, *The Partridge Family* isn't on the air anymore."

Ronan sat back and let out an exaggerated breath. "Well, there's the bright spot I've been looking for. David Cassidy is off the air. He's too good-looking; the rest of us don't have a chance. I swear every girl east of the Mississippi has a thing for him."

"West of the Mississippi, too, in case you were wondering."

"I wasn't."

"But that, dear Ronan, is what I meant when I said something is missing."

Ronan gave Michelle a surprised look. "David Cassidy on my TV?"

"That would be a whole different conversation," Michelle replied. "I mean, have you gone on any dates lately?"

"Too busy."

Michelle shook her head but did not reply.

"I guess it's just not a priority. Besides, I took Carol to the movies once over the summer and all she did was scream and vow never to swim in the ocean again. First and last date. You know that."

Michelle's mouth dropped open. "You are such a typical man! You don't take a girl to see a horror movie on your first date! What is wrong with you?"

"What?" Ronan looked confused. "Everyone was raving about *Jaws*. It was the number one movie all summer. Why was it wrong?"

"Okay," Michelle stood up, "I don't have time to re-teach everything you need to re-learn about dating. I have to get home. Jack is probably climbing the walls dealing with June by himself."

Ronan stood up and followed Michelle to the door. "Tell Jack we're all grateful."

"I will. He's really not doing much yet; just checking to see if it's really going to be expanded or not."

"Yeah, but I appreciate it."

Michelle opened the door and was about to leave before she turned around. "Oh, and Ronan? Yes, I have a Beatles obsession, I know exactly where John Lennon lives, this country has never known peace and probably never will, television is not reality - it's entertainment - it's a distraction, David Cassidy has nothing on you and you should have taken Carol to see Monty Python."

"Goodnight, Michelle." Ronan shook his head as he nudged her out the door.

"Goodnight, Ro, love you!"

"Love you, too."

Ronan shut the door and began straightening up the loft, all the while pondering a few of Michelle's comments. He realized she was right when she said the country had never known peace. Each decade brought its own struggles. He knew television was entertaining but also felt a lot of it was a waste of time. He figured she was also right about writing down the things that Dr. Parks told him about the experimental drug. He was doing okay without it and was pleased with where he was but wondered if it would help with those days when the thoughts crept back in.

As he was heading for bed, he thought about all the times he ignored Michelle's comments about his lack of a relationship. There was a time he couldn't imagine himself with anyone other than Carrieann, but that time was gone. He knew it was possible to love again. He also knew that there was someone out there for him. He never said anything to Michelle, but he carried this feeling around with him that the right person was out there, he didn't know who she was or what she looked like, but he was positive he would meet her. That feeling was getting stronger the last few months.

Ronan shut off the light, settled in bed, and drifted off, peaceful in the knowledge that somehow, some way, things were going to work out; he wouldn't lose the loft and, soon, he would meet that person.

Emily

"This is a great place, but it needs some work," Emily stated as she walked through the office space in Tribeca. She looked over at Theresa, one of the first psychologists she hired right out of college when she opened the clinic, and pointed to the ceiling where several cracks were visible.

"I know. It's also in need of paint. Can we do paint instead of this awful paneling? Who decided wood paneling was a good idea? I've always hated it." Theresa replied.

Emily laughed, "I completely agree. We can take it down and paint."

"We?" Theresa's eyes widened. "You do not want me to use a paint brush, trust me."

Emily chuckled. "No, we'll hire someone to do some renovations."

Emily was excited about the new office space. The clinic in Brooklyn was doing well. She felt one in Manhattan would do well, too. They could reach more people in need of their services, particularly the Vietnam veterans who were having a hard time readjusting to civilian life. She had personally counseled several vets and was horrified by the stories they told. Her heart broke with each session. She had managed to help several of them, but recognized others were in need of more than she could provide and referred them to psychiatrists who would be able to diagnose them with what was commonly referred to as 'battle fatigue' and prescribe something to help them sleep through the night.

More research needed to be done concerning victims of trauma and Emily was already knee-deep in her own work in the area. Having read through many dissertations and research papers already, she connected the patterns between combat veterans, Holocaust survivors, victims of sexual trauma and other victims of disaster. The current diagnosis of 'adjustment reaction to adult life' was not sufficient enough to cover this area.

The research had forced her to finally face and work through her own assault. She was able to openly discuss her own experience and recovery with her female patients who had been through the same or, in too many cases, worse. It helped them to understand they were not alone and, above all else, it was not their fault. This also aided her in her activism for women. It was a very rare exception when a woman won a rape case in court. The defense would put the blame on the victim every time. The Women's Movement was trying to raise awareness and change the public perception by pointing out that what a woman was wearing, how many drinks she may have had or where she was walking alone was no excuse for the violent behavior of men. It was an uphill battle that they were currently losing but she continued the fight.

"How many new hires for this place?" Theresa asked, interrupting Emily's thoughts.

"I don't know," Emily replied. "What do you think? Two plus a receptionist and a secretary? I might split my time between here and Brooklyn. That's something you, Patrick and Ian might want to do as well."

Theresa mulled it over. "That will work. When will you place the ads for the two new hires?"

Emily smiled. "You forget. I don't place ads for counselors."

Nodding, Theresa recalled how she was recruited by Emily fresh out of Columbia. "You'll go for the graduates again?"

"Yes. I already have a list of recent NYU and Columbia graduates. I just need to screen them before bringing them in for interviews."

"Master's Program or PhDs?"

"PhDs this time around. If they're going to work with veterans, they need the experience that comes with the doctorate program. That's essential."

Theresa furrowed her eyebrows. "How many people with a PhD do you think you'll get to work here? I'm not trying to discourage you by any means but that's a lot of money to put out on an education. Don't get me wrong, the pay here is more than expected given how you keep the rates low, but they won't get the money here that they could at other places."

"Ah, you forget again, Theresa. That's what separates the ones we want working here from the ones we don't. We are looking for people with a drive to help people. People who understand that help with mental disorders should be affordable and accessible. If they are graduating with dreams of immediate six-figure incomes and a fancy car, they're not for us. That's why our clinic works. You, me, Patrick, and Ian; we get that. We're here for those people who desperately need us but can't afford the cost of those uppity Park Avenue doctors."

Theresa snorted. "Uppity. That's a good word for some of them. They spend three days a week listening to the problems of socialites or celebrities and then look down on clinics like ours. They wouldn't know what to do with half our patients."

Emily shook her head. "Don't minimize the problems of others, Theresa. Socialites and celebrities are just people. They have problems like everyone else. Money can't fix what goes on in the mind. With that said, I won't argue that their doctors charge exorbitant amounts and do, in fact, look down on us. It doesn't matter, though. We're here for the rest of the city."

"Yes, we are. Making the city a better place one patient at a time."

"We should make that our slogan," Emily said as she walked toward the large windows facing Leonard Street.

"Only psychologists? No psychiatrists?"

"Correct," Emily answered as she looked out over the street.

"You know I don't believe in medication as the first line of treatment. It's necessary for some but I've seen too many psychiatrists put their patients on medication that only numbs them but doesn't solve their problems. There are so many people out there who need our help."

"You don't think medication is beneficial?"

Turning from the window, Emily replied, "Yes, in some cases, it is. Very much so. However, I think it's too easy to write a prescription instead of giving someone the tools they need to overcome whatever their problem might be." Emily paused and eyed Theresa. "You know I published a paper on this topic, right?"

Theresa nodded as Emily continued, "Take the soldiers, for instance. We've helped quite a few of them but there are some that have been through hell and back. It's more than battle fatigue and it's more than re-adjusting to society. It's the reaction and mental condition that comes immediately following a crisis, a disaster, or other cataclysmic event. That's why I refer them to someone else. Some of them only sleep one or two hours a day because the effects of what they have gone through are too strong, their minds can't escape it, nor does it let them deal with it. Those poor men are stuck in a limbo they can't get out of unless they are medicated. You know this, though. Are you advocating for a psychiatrist?"

"Maybe," Theresa admitted. "I don't know. The breakthroughs being made with SSRIs might be very advantageous and I think if we don't have someone here that could prescribe something like that once it becomes available, people might look elsewhere."

"That's a different subject and there is a way around that should the inhibitors work as suggested. We send them to their family doctor for the prescription."

"Brilliant."

"I'm very interested in SSRIs," Emily went on. "If they increase serotonin activity, as it seems they do, that could help a tremendous amount of people. I wonder how many people have been misdiagnosed over the years when all it could be is the chemicals in their brain aren't producing as they should. It's fascinating. I'm not against all forms of medication, Theresa. I only want to make sure prescriptions aren't the only thing relied upon. Taking a pill doesn't make one's problems magically vanish."

A sudden knock on the doorframe interrupted their conversation. Emily turned to see a young man with paint-stained jeans and tousled hair standing in the doorway.

"Hi, ladies," the young man smiled, "moving in?"

The exaggerated up and down glance at both women was not lost on Emily and she found it repulsive. She stiffened.

"Possibly. Is there something we can help you with?" Emily's tone was icy, her face a mask of stone.

"Just stopping in to be neighborly," came the reply, he smiled a little broader. "I live up on the sixth floor."

"Good for you," Emily didn't mask her annoyed tone.

"Okay, lady, I just wanted to say hello and tell you if you're moving in here there's something you might want to know first."

"Oh? What's that?" Emily crossed her arms.

Theresa jumped in, "Is there something wrong with these offices or the building?"

"Nothing wrong with the office," the young man turned his attention to Theresa, "except it needs some work. No, it's about the city expanding a tax thing for building owners." He gave them a shortened version of what he'd heard at the tenant meeting.

Emily paused for a moment as several thoughts flashed through her mind. She heard Theresa ask a question, but she didn't wait for the young man to reply.

"I know about that and, yes, it's certain to go through next year. It wouldn't have an effect on us as most owners are interested in bringing in businesses for the first floor of buildings like this. Renovating serves two needs of the city - attract businesses to help the economy and bring people into the city willing to work at and/or frequent said businesses. Has the owner issued any kind of statement regarding this?"

The young man was caught off guard and took a moment to respond. "No, we heard it from a guy that used to date his daughter. We had a meeting the other night and there's a lawyer that's going to find out if it's true."

"It's true," Emily replied. "I can already tell you that. Technically, the owner can't outright evict you without probable cause until your leases are up, however, there may be some loopholes that can be used to enable him to do it. Now, I'm just guessing at the rent tenants pay when I say this but with the first floor as business-only and tenants in the rest, it's still a lucrative building. The difference is the tax break for renovating and the ability to split up the lofts to bring in twice the money. By the looks of you, I'm guessing you use your loft to live in as well as create your art, am I right?"

"Yes," replied the young man, somewhat surprised.

"I'm sure a lot of other tenants do the same thing. The rent is reasonable, and you don't have to pay to rent for separate work areas," she mused. "Splitting the lofts and restricting work areas on the rest of the floors could theoretically put some of the tenants out of business. Banded together in a union-style way the tenants could launch a suit against the owner should it come to that and have a decent chance of winning under the current law."

"Damn, lady, there's a brain behind that pretty face. You should have been at the meeting the other night."

Emily's eyes narrowed as she gave the young man a level stare. "My name is Dr. Walton, thank you. Yes, there is a brain in here as is the case with all women. If I had known about the meeting I would have attended. Do me a favor . . . what's your name?"

"Jim."

"Jim. Do me a favor, please. Let the rest of the tenants know they don't have to worry about it. They won't be evicted."

"How do you know that? Do you know the owners?" Jim asked.

"I've dealt with them, obviously," Emily waved her hand around the office space.

"Okay," Jim hesitated. "I'll spread the word. You sure about this?"

"Yes. I'm very sure."

Jim started to leave but turned back and pointed to the cracks in the ceiling. "There's a guy on the fifth floor that runs a home improvement business. The name is Ronan Byrne. He could probably fix that for you and anything else you want done around here. I'll tell him to stop in."

"Thank you, Jim. That would be nice."

"You're welcome, Dr. Walton. See you around."

Once Jim had retreated from sight, Theresa, who had been silent throughout the exchange, let out a long breath and stared at Emily. "How did you know all that and how on earth can you assure him they won't be evicted?"

"I know people in the business world. Real estate development, to be exact, among other things. They talk, I listen." Emily wasn't lying. She had, indeed, listened to Rob go on at length about what the expansion of J-51 would mean for real estate. He already had Corbyn buy a few buildings that would qualify.

"But how do you know they won't be evicted?"

"Same people," was all Emily said as she began to gather her coat and purse.

Theresa did the same and as they walked toward the door, she decided to approach Emily about something she had noticed. "Emily, can I give you a little advice?"

"Always."

"Keep doing the exercises that have helped you deal with your past traumas."

Emily stopped and turned toward Theresa. "I did it again, didn't I?"

Theresa nodded. "I'm not saying Jim didn't deserve it with that drooling stare he gave us but, yes, you almost turned to ice right in front of me."

Emily rubbed her eyes and sighed, "I didn't realize it. It's a reflex anytime I see a man look at a woman like they're a steak. Oh, and that comment about a brain behind the face, I wanted to slap him." She smiled at Theresa, "So, give me some credit for not doing that, at least."

"I do," Theresa replied. "You need to keep going with those exercises, though. Men aren't going to change anytime soon. Unfortunately, you'll have to find a way to deal with those comments without shutting down and turning into an ice queen."

"I despise the notion they still think it's a man's world," Emily shook her head.

"Well, it is. It's horrible but we have to play the game until we're in a position to make our own rules. We're not there yet."

"Speak for yourself," Emily began walking again.

Theresa followed and, once out on the sidewalk, asked "What do you mean by that?"

"I never played their game, Theresa. I play by my own rules. I always have. It's not our job to keep placating male egos by acting like second-class citizens. It's our job to start motivating more women to take a stand and demand to be seen as equals."

"Gloria Steinem must be very proud of you."

"She is," Emily laughed, "but I hear what you're saying, Theresa. I do shut down at the first sign of conduct like that toward women. I know it's still a residual effect from what happened to me. I really did not feel it this time, though, which does bother me a bit. I promise I will continue working on it."

"That's all I'm asking. Are you heading back to the office?"

"I don't think so," Emily looked around. "I need to find a phone booth. There's someone I want to talk to, and I don't want to wait. I'll catch up with you tomorrow."

After saying their goodbyes, Emily found a phone booth, stepped inside, and dialed Rob's office number.

"Rob, I need you to do me a favor," she said after being put through.

"That depends on what it is, Em," came her brother's reply.

"I need you to buy the building on Leonard Street, the one where I'm opening the clinic."

"Are you serious?"

"Yes, I'm serious. I want Corbyn to buy it, but I don't want it to become part of the renovation boom that's going to take place."

"Then what's the point in buying it?" Emily should have known that would be Rob's reply. He needed to see what the return on the investment would be before even considering buying a property. This building wouldn't bring in the return of a renovated building. She would have had the same reaction a few years ago.

"The point would be that it's still a lucrative building without the tax break and renovations. The point is that Corbyn could use it as part of its new image by not forcing the current tenants to agree to renovations or be evicted. Corbyn realizes that would put unnecessary hardship on these people, effectively putting some of them out of business or possibly out of a home."

The silence on the phone told Emily that Rob was considering it. She continued, "Rob, it's already a great building. It could use some updates, certainly, but it's a good investment as it is. The first floor would be for businesses and the rest of the floors could stay as is. The rent from the businesses alone, including mine, would pay the company back and turn a profit. Let's not make life harder for these tenants. It's hard enough for them as it is right now with the recession. Let Corbyn be the good guy."

"First, it's not for sale so we'll have to convince the owners to sell. You realize we'll end up buying it for more than what it's technically worth."

"I know. Is there a second?"

Rob sighed, "Second, I'll put one of the guys on it and get back to you."

"Thank you, Rob," Emily said, "you're the best brother!"

"About time you realized that. While I have you on the phone, I set up a meeting with Tim about Kettering's book."

"I've been caught up in expanding the clinic, I almost forgot about that. Does Tim have an idea how we can stop it?"

"He does. He said he already had it delayed and it will probably be buried entirely. He still wants to meet, though, in case it finds its way back out. He wants you to be prepared."

"Okay. But right now, it's delayed. That's good news. Now, all you have to do is buy me a building."

"You mean buy Corbyn a building and you better hang up before I change my mind."

Stepping out of the phone booth, Emily smiled. Feeling optimistic, she decided to walk home instead of catching a cab. Reflecting on the day, she made mental notes of a few things that needed attention at the office as well as the work that needed to be done on the new space.

"Ronan Byrne," she said out loud to no one. "I like that name."

Michelle

"So, it's going to happen," Michelle sat back in her chair and folded her arms.

"Yes, but it doesn't mean Ronan will lose his loft."

Michelle looked over at her husband and shook her head. "People are greedy, Jack. You know that. If someone could make twice the amount they are and get a tax break to boot, why wouldn't they?"

"There are legal avenues Ronan and the others could take if they're facing eviction. I know the law, Michelle. There are ways people can get around it but there are some laws people, including building owners, forget exist. If it comes to it, I'll represent them. Don't you worry. He'll be fine."

Softening, Michelle replied, "I know. It's just that, you know, he's come so far. I'm so proud of what he's done these last few years. I don't want to see him have a setback."

"This won't set him back, Michelle. Stop worrying about him so much. He's not a child. He's a grown man, for God's sake."

Michelle did not reply. Talking about Ronan's problems with Jack had always been futile. Jack did not understand psychological problems and never tried to. He was not a proponent of therapy and was of the mindset that all Ronan had to do was "toughen up". She'd heard more than enough comments over the last few years regarding Ronan's "whining", "weakness", and how he should "be a man". She often wanted to remind him that they were no longer living in the dark ages.

The Women's Movement was also a sore subject with Jack. Michelle learned carly on not to push the issue. The only reason Jack agreed to her working was because it was with Ronan. She was able to accommodate June's schedule and be home in time to get dinner on the table. Michelle often felt torn between the things she was hearing out of the movement and the things she had learned growing up. She was trained to believe men were the head of the household but like many other women these days, she wondered why it couldn't be an equal partnership.

There was no question she loved her husband. Her only wish was that he would learn to adapt to the changing times. She wanted to progress out of the same mindset their parents had where Jack seemed dead set on keeping it. He was never outwardly disrespectful but last year when his firm hired its first female lawyer, she was aghast when he said he was concerned how the new lawyer would perform her job during 'that time of the month' and what would happen if she got herself pregnant. They ended up in one of their rare arguments when Michelle challenged him by asking how a woman goes about getting herself pregnant since it usually takes two people. In the end, Jack admitted it was a poor choice of words but would not relent that women were more emotional than men and he didn't feel that was a good fit for a lawyer. Michelle resigned herself to the fact that Jack would always hold these old-fashioned beliefs. Her hope was that as time went on, he would see for himself that women were just as capable - if not more so in certain areas - than men.

As far as Ronan was concerned, Jack had been more than willing to help in the days and weeks after his breakdown seven years ago. But as time went on, he had a hard time being sympathetic. He felt Ronan was given plenty of time to get himself together and shouldn't need as much of Michelle's attention. He didn't want to hear about therapy or how Ronan would continue to struggle with his mental health for years to come. Jack began to view Ronan as weak. Though being pleasantly surprised by Ronan's success with his business and his move to Tribeca, he still had the impression that Ronan was soft and needed to develop a thicker skin. Michelle gave up trying to explain things to him.

The phone saved Michelle from further discussion. Jack picked it up and she immediately gathered it was another lawyer at the firm.

Whatever the topic was, Jack did not seem happy about it. She was sure she would hear about it as soon as the conversation ended. There was always one crisis or another going on. Hopefully, this one didn't involve the woman lawyer, or she might be up all night listening to him.

Hanging up the phone, Jack burst out, "How does Corbyn do it?"

"Do what?"

"You know Tim Jackson used to work for us, right?"

"Yes, but then he moved to another firm. I forgot their name."

"Tyler and Smith."

"That's it."

"Corbyn is one of their clients. Anyway, he had dinner with Don tonight. Apparently, after a few shots of whiskey, Jackson let it slip that the book about Corbyn is being delayed and possibly shelved for good."

"What book?"

Jack sighed, "I told you about this. One of Corbyn's ex-employees wrote a book about the few years that witch had control of the company. It supposedly had some interesting dirt in it. The book was supposed to come out in December, but Jackson got it delayed, if not killed."

Michelle didn't know which issue to address first, so she decided to go with the easy one. "Can I ask why that would even be news anymore? That was a long time ago. I doubt anyone even remembers her name. I mean, yeah, in the city people knew her but why would the rest of the country even care?"

"Revenge, Michelle. I don't think the point was to make millions from it. I think the point was to ruin her in the circles that she moves in. I would say, as well, it would serve as a reminder to people why women aren't cut out to run a company and that, honey, is what would appeal to the rest of the country."

Michelle rolled her eyes. "If you say so, dear, but it's old news. I don't think anyone is going to care. Besides, didn't I hear she had a breakdown of her own and her brother shipped her overseas somewhere?"

"That was the speculation, but I don't buy it. She was in that coma, came out of it and then dropped out of sight. She may be overseas, but I don't think she went crazy. That woman was vicious. Wherever Emily Corbyn is, I hope she's burning."

The way Jack was speaking surprised Michelle. "Why did you call her a witch? Why do you hate her so much? Your firm never did business with them so why are you so angry?"

Jack didn't answer right away. Michelle thought he looked caught off-guard by the question. When he spoke, his voice was calmer.

"Because she had no business taking over her father's company. She fired some good men. Decent, hard-working men, who had been there for years. She stepped on too many toes and dealt with the wrong people. Let's leave it at that."

"Jack, there's more, isn't there?" Michelle couldn't just sense there was more, she knew it.

"No. That's it in a nutshell."

"No, it isn't. Is it because she was not only a woman in control but a *young* woman? I know your views on women in positions of power. Is that why?"

Jack leaned forward slightly, "It's because she was a woman who used blackmail to get what she wanted. You don't want to know who she employed to assist her in the execution of those deals. All justified by the fact that Corbyn was making money."

Michelle nodded. She wasn't naive to the ways of business, having listened to Jack talk about his clients all these years. "I'm curious, honey. If she had been a man, would you have the same reaction? Or would you be saying he did what he needed to do to get the job done? Would there be a book about it if she'd been a man?"

"I'm not answering that."

"Of course, you're not. Doesn't Fred Trump and his son have mob ties? You're the one that told me it's an open secret. Where's the book on that?"

"Are you trying to defend Emily Corbyn?"

"No. I'm pointing out your hypocrisy. They both have ties to the mob, but you hope Emily burns while Fred Trump gets the deal done by any means necessary. I find that interesting."

Jack leaned back and grabbed the newspaper, "It's not interesting at all. I'm done with this conversation."

"I'm not. I hope Emily is thriving in Europe."

Jack shot Michelle a surprised look.

"Why shouldn't she? She didn't do anything men don't do. Why should she burn for it while the men keep doing it?"

"You think what she did was okay?"

This time Michelle leaned forward. "No, I don't. I don't think blackmail and dealing with the mob is okay. But you burn them all or none at all. I'm sick to death of men getting away with things but as soon as a woman does the same thing, she must be stoned in the street. It wasn't okay for any of them so if you burn Emily at the stake then you burn the men, too." Michelle got up and began walking out of the room.

"You spend too much time with Ronan," Jack said to her retreating back.

Over her shoulder, Michelle replied, "And you don't spend enough."

Ronan

Grabbing his toolbox and heading out, Ronan went over in his mind the work he had scheduled for that day. He'd be spending the morning doing a kitchen remodel at a house in the Bronx. It was almost complete, and he could finish up the woodwork this morning; the rest was on hold until the new appliances arrived. An appointment at an apartment building on the Upper East side was scheduled for the afternoon. The woman wanted shoe racks installed in her closet and he needed to see the space before giving her an estimate. He'd end his workday back at the loft re-working Adirondack chairs for a couple that lived in Brooklyn.

He was pleased his day was filled. Keeping busy was a tremendous help. Whenever he thought business would slow down, he was proven wrong by more calls for estimates and work. Michelle was after him to hire more than Mike, the temporary employee he used a couple days a week. He was considering it. If he hired Mike full time and hired someone else in the temporary capacity, he could take on more jobs. He was already looking for a work van. He'd outgrown the small pickup truck he'd bought a couple years ago. It had been great for the small jobs but now that bigger ones were coming in, he needed something he could haul drywall in.

As he stepped off the elevator on the bottom floor, he saw Jim coming toward him. He liked some of the art Jim created and even recommended his pieces to a few of his clients. Ronan considered Jim a pretty good guy even though his manners could use some work. Seeing him now reminded him he wanted to follow up on the rumor he heard around the building.

"Hey," he greeted Jim when he got closer, "how's it going?"

"Pretty good, man," Jim replied. "Can't complain. Looks like some of my paintings might end up in that exhibit in the park."

"That's fantastic! I hope they sell." Ronan was glad for him.

"We'll see. People don't seem to be in the mood to spend money these days. I can't blame them, really. This recession is hitting everyone, even the theater district is feeling it. Not a good sign when you can get really cheap discount tickets to *Pippin*. Although, without Ben Vereen, I'm not sure it's worth seeing anymore."

Ronan shrugged. "I'm not into going to the theater much. I'd rather see movies, I guess. But, hey, I've been meaning to talk to you about something. I got word that someone with the clinic told you we didn't have to worry about eviction or renovations or anything. That true?"

"Sure is. I was meaning to swing by your place to tell you myself, as a matter of fact. Her name's Dr. Walton. She said we had nothing to worry about and I should let everyone know. Don't ask me why she's so sure but she is. Smart lady and built like a brick house but a bitch, man. Anyway, the offices they're moving into need some work. I told her about you. I told her I'd tell you to stop in and take a look."

"Did she say anything else about J-51?" Ronan asked, ignoring the brick house comment.

"Oh, she knew a lot about it. Even said if we band together we'd beat the landlord in court if he evicted us."

"She would have been useful at the meeting the other night."

"Yeah, that's what I said but I gotta tell ya, man, she's a stiff. I mean, I told her she was pretty and had a brain and she got mad." Jim shook his head, "I just don't get women these days."

Ronan laughed, "I know you don't." He'd been around Jim enough to know that he wasn't always tactful when it came to women. "But I am curious why she's so sure we'll be fine."

"Don't know. Maybe she's got some kind of deal going with the landlord. Who knows? As long as we can stay and everything remains rent-controlled, that's all I care about."

"That's what we all care about and, hey, thanks for recommending me to her. I'll stop by there either this afternoon or in the morning and see what needs working on."

"Cool," Jim replied and then switched subjects. "Man, not to be a downer or anything but are you watching this Operation Baby Lift thing going on? I mean, we brought all those kids over from Vietnam a couple months ago and now they're being adopted here. Why? Why do we want more people here, especially Asians?"

Ronan paused and inhaled before answering. He'd come across a lot of xenophobic people lately. It always amazed him that they all thought everyone felt the same way they did. "Jim, where'd your parents come from?"

"Jersey."

"Okay, how about your grandparents?"

"Germany."

"Okay, well, then it's a good thing when they came over there weren't people standing around questioning why we'd let krauts into the country, isn't it?"

"That's different," Jim replied.

"How so?"

Jim didn't reply. Ronan saw him searching his mind for an answer.

"Look, man, I'm not trying to start a fight or anything," Ronan continued. "I just want you to think about it. Look around the city; everyone is from somewhere else. We're a nation full of immigrants. My grandparents came over from Ireland. Growing up in Hell's Kitchen I kept hearing all the stories of fights between the Irish and the Italians and it was stupid. All our parents or grandparents came over here for a better life. Why are people so against others doing the same thing? That's all I'm saying."

"You feel the same way about the Mexicans and the Puerto

Ricans?"

"Why wouldn't I? We all bleed red, Jim. We're all people."

Jim shook his head. "Next you're going to say you're an honorary Black Panther. Think what you want, Ronan, but some people should just stay in their own country."

"I'm not fighting with you, Jim. I think, though, you might want to figure out why you don't like people that don't look or speak like you. You also might want to take a look at which politicians are using them as scapegoats. I gotta run. See ya around."

Ronan was glad to be on his way. He had thought of Jim as a good guy who just needed work on his rough manners. Now, he wasn't sure he even liked him anymore. He was tired of people degrading others based on their race or religion. He was tired of the bad jokes on television and of the politicians that point to them as the reason for the ills in the country. He wondered if he was the only one who understood that it was a trick. Politicians get people angry at immigrants so they don't notice it's really them and their policies that are screwing up people's lives. It wasn't people coming here from Puerto Rico that caused the recession. Bringing children in from Vietnam didn't make the city need a bailout.

He was trying to pull himself back into a good mood when he passed by the office spaces for Safe Haven. Their front windows looked out onto Leonard Street which, in his opinion, was a prime spot. Stopping at the doors to what he assumed would be the front office, he peeked through the glass. He noticed a few cracks in the ceiling but couldn't see much else. He decided to leave a note and, hopefully, someone would be there the next morning.

Before putting the paper back in his bag, he made a note to ask Dr. Parks about Safe Haven at their appointment but, more specifically, Dr. Walton. He was intrigued. He'd heard about Safe Haven keeping their rates low so that the average person could afford treatment. The fight to get psychological care covered properly by insurance wasn't getting anywhere and many people couldn't afford on-going care. He thought the model Safe Haven was using was admirable. He was also intrigued by Jim's description of her. Clearly, she was intelligent and if she worked for Safe Haven, she would also be someone who was compassionate. Ronan ignored the negative comments from Jim. He knew Jim immediately labeled anyone who rejected his advances a bitch. He thought Dr. Walton was obviously insightful if she rebuffed Jim on first sight.

As Ronan left the building and headed toward the garage to get his truck and begin his workday, his mind remained on Dr. Walton. He decided she was a woman he definitely wanted to meet.

Emily

"Thank you, Dr. Walton. I'll see you next week."

"Yes, you will, Phil. Have a wonderful rest of your day." Emily closed her office door as her last patient of the day left. Settling back in her chair, she reviewed her schedule and was pleased she had time to stop by the Tribeca office before meeting Maggie for dinner.

She needed a relaxing dinner. She'd been up into the early morning hours finishing her latest paper on the use of hypnosis in treating patients. Emily was a strong advocate of finding the root cause of the problem. She'd read and observed too many psychologists and psychiatrists who felt the root cause was irrelevant and focused more on adjusting the current behavior. Emily was different. She felt finding the cause and addressing it at the source was the most effective way to help her patients move forward.

Having rejected many of the "old school" methods of immediately addressing a patient's childhood, she began searching for a more constructive way to reach the answer. While many scoffed at the idea of being able to control one's mind through hypnosis - thinking only of the stereotypical exaggeration of hypnosis - Emily found it appealing. Using a variation of the idea, she began using it in many of her sessions. The results were better than she expected. When people were lulled into that meditative level of consciousness it was amazing what the subconscious often revealed. If she was able to get her paper peer-reviewed and published, she thought it would be a wonderful step forward.

Her briefcase packed, coat on, she headed out. As her cab crossed the bridge, she could feel her muscles begin to relax as she looked through the window at the water. Her mind drifted back to the one thing she was never fully able to explain; how she woke up from her coma with an intense desire to help other people through psychology. She had thought about it, off and on over the last seven years, during those rare occasions when she found herself with some down time but could not figure it out. She had tried to meditate on it and went so far as to have Theresa use hypnosis on her but to no avail. It was as if she couldn't reach that part of her mind that would give her the answer.

By the time the cab dropped her off on Leonard Street, she was no closer to finding a way to reach it. Emily was pleased with where her life had taken her after the coma. She began to think that she should just be grateful for it happening and let go of trying to figure out why it had. Emily *was* grateful. She was more than grateful. She hadn't realized how empty and dark her life had been before her coma nor how horrible a person she had been. She only wished she knew what she could attribute the change to.

Fishing her key out of her purse, she noticed a note taped to the office door. Grabbing the note, she began opening the door and saw the area completely cleaned out, no remnants of the previous occupants in sight. Putting her keys and the note in her purse, she looked over the front office area.

"This is good," Emily said out loud. "This is going to be really good." She knew there were so many more people she could reach in Manhattan. She'd always known it but wanted the first clinic to be in Brooklyn to gauge the viability of a practice that would cater to the average, working-class person.

After going through the offices and taking more notes on what was to be done, she left for the restaurant and found Maggie waiting patiently at a corner table.

"It's about time," Maggie said upon Emily taking a seat. "I was beginning to think you forgot."

"Of course not," Emily replied. "I just wanted to stop by the new offices and finalize a list of the work that needs to be done. Has

Rob made progress on buying the building yet?"

"He'll make it happen. I just don't understand why you care. It won't affect you or your patients. Companies don't stay in business and make a profit by giving up revenue, Emily." Maggie picked up a menu and began scanning it. "You, of all people, know that."

Emily fell silent. A mixed bag of emotions surfaced with Maggie's comment. She didn't pick up the menu nor take her gaze away from Maggie. She had often instructed her patients to process their emotions before responding to anything in order to avoid an emotionally charged response. She was taking her own advice. The sudden rise of emotion surprised her. It was a mix of confusion, anger, and sadness. Her eyes began to water, and she took a deep breath.

"I think I'm going to have the grilled salmon," Maggie concluded as she closed her menu. She was about to pick up her glass of water when she looked over at Emily and stopped suddenly. "Oh, Em! I didn't mean that the way it sounded." She reached over and took Emily's hand.

Emily only nodded before Maggie continued. "I'm sorry. I only meant that you know the business world, that's all."

Emily shook her head, cleared her throat, and held up her hand. "No, no, it's okay, Maggie. I know you didn't mean anything by it. I don't know why I got so emotional over it. Maybe I'm just tired. I was up until almost three this morning finishing my paper and then trying to get this new office together on top of it, along with keeping up with my patients. I'm burned out is all."

"We've tried to tell you to slow down. It's wonderful that you're doing all these things, not to mention your activism, but you have to give yourself a break. You've been in high gear for too long. When was the last time you took a vacation?"

"When we all went to the apartment in Paris."

"Emily, that was how long ago! You can't keep going on like

this without taking a break now and then."

"I know. I do take breaks. I meditate and I make sure to give myself some quiet time. I take my walks to the bridge. I'm fine."

"No, you're not." Maggie was about to say more when the waiter interrupted. After giving their orders and having their drinks arrive, Maggie picked up again. "Talk to me, Emily. I understand being burned out and tired, but I saw your eyes. Something else is going on in there."

Emily paused. Her first instinct was to deflect the conversation away from herself, but she suddenly felt the need to talk. She wasn't sure what would come out, but it felt as if something needed to. She took a sip of her drink and then decided to drain the glass before setting it back on the table.

"I don't know. I really don't. I guess I'll start with what you said. I care about Rob buying the building because it will help the people who already live there. I don't see why it's necessary to renovate a building that is already turning a profit. Sure, it would bring in more money and there's the tax break, but it would hurt some of those tenants. It might possibly put some of them out of business if they can't work and live in the same place. Maybe I care because when I ran the company, I knew that I kicked quite a few people out on the street. Well, not me, personally, but for the apartment buildings we owned, I'm the one that made the policy that tenants were given only three days after the rent was due or they'd be locked out. That was me. I knew some people had nowhere else to go and I didn't care. I guess some things just remind me of that horrible person. Some days I forget she ever existed and then when I remember I feel ashamed. You might think that I do what I do as penance or to make up for the past but that's not the whole truth. I woke up from that coma with this desire to get out there and help. It's so rooted in me. I had no desire to change before the coma but as soon as I woke up that was all I wanted to do.

"That brings up another thing. I can't seem to figure out what caused it. Obviously, I understand how certain events can change people but there is usually a reason, a realization, an epiphany of sorts caused by the event. In my case, there was the event but there's been no epiphany. There's nothing I can point to that I can say 'that's why I changed, that's why I decided to open a clinic and go back to school.' I can't seem to unlock the part of my mind that contains the answer."

She paused for a moment and took a breath. She signaled to the waiter for another drink before continuing. "I still have residual trauma from the assault as well. Theresa picked up on it the other day. I hadn't even noticed the change in me. Usually, I can feel it happening but that time I didn't. I don't know if it was because I was focused on something else or if the guy triggered the response. It was just a look. I had gotten to a point where I could handle something like that without a problem. This was different, though. I don't know why."

"Of course, you'll have residual trauma," Maggie replied. "I can't imagine that you wouldn't. Do you think maybe working yourself into the ground might have had something to do with that?"

Emily chuckled. "It's not that bad, Mags. I like working. I like having busy days and I love what I do. It's been a lot lately and, yes, I'm tired and I could use a break, but I don't think that was it." She shrugged her shoulders. "I know I have to work on it, though."

Maggie reached over and took her hands again. "Emily, you are the strongest, most intelligent, most caring person I know. It's true you weren't always. It's true I thought I'd never speak to you again, but I thank God every day that you emerged from that coma as the Emily you once were. The one I knew when I was younger. I'm so very thankful that you found yourself again. I'm so damned proud of how far you've come and everything that you have built. If you ever have a moment where you doubt yourself or the residual trauma hits or you just need a shoulder, you have me. You have Rob. You have Theresa. You have

Jean. You have people who love you. You don't always have to be strong. We are here for you. I've heard doctors are the worst at asking for help. Don't be one of them. Ask."

"Thank you. I will, I promise." To lighten the mood, Emily added, "I do ask for help, you know. You don't think I'm going to tear down that hideous paneling in the new offices and paint it myself, do you?"

Maggie shook her head and sat back. "You're such a smart ass."

"Oh! That reminds me," Emily bent down and rummaged through her purse for the note. "This was left on the door at the new place." She unfolded the paper and read it. A small smile appeared on her lips.

Leaning over, trying to make out the writing, Maggie asked, "Who's Ronan?"

"He lives in the building and does renovations. He's stopping by tomorrow morning to look over the offices. See? Help is on the way."

Maggie narrowed her eyes. "What made you give that smile, though? Is he good looking?"

"Oh, don't start. I haven't met him and it's only business. I don't even know if I'm going to hire him yet."

"So, what was with the smile?"

"I don't know. I like his name. Ronan Byrne. Don't you think it has a nice ring?"

Twelve hours later, Emily opened the door to the new office, set her things on the floor, walked over to the wall of windows facing the street and took a sip of the coffee she'd brought with her. She had her notes ready for Ronan and was more than ready to begin the transformation of the area into a welcoming, comforting place.

Thinking of the list of recent graduates she was scheduled to call after lunch, she hoped there were as many good candidates as there had been the year she opened the Brooklyn clinic. Emily had been very particular when she had interviewed for those positions, and she would be even more so now. It wasn't enough to have the grades, the intelligence, or the drive. She had to know where their heart and their passion lie.

Her head snapped up as soon as she heard the knock. She took in the tall, well-built man with dark hair and piercing blue eyes. Her breath left her lungs and a sensation she hadn't felt before went through her body. She knew him. She was sure of it. She didn't know how or from where, but she could feel it was true. She could feel this man was important to her, though she did not know why.

The man at the door looked as caught off-guard as she was feeling. "Are you Dr. Walton?"

"I'm...I'm sorry," Emily stammered without thinking. "Do I know you?"

Ronan

As soon as the woman looked up Ronan had the feeling he already knew her. More than that, he felt a click in his brain, something that switched on and told him this was the woman he'd known was out there somewhere. It was a feeling he wasn't prepared for and it nearly knocked him off his feet. He logically knew he hadn't met this woman before yet everything in him was telling him he'd known her forever. He had gathered himself but was once again stunned when she responded to his question. He momentarily froze with the realization that she, too, felt as if they had met before.

"I'm sorry. Excuse my manners. Yes, I'm Dr. Walton." She began to walk toward him. "But, please, call me Emily."

Composed once again, Ronan smiled. "Ronan Byrne." He extended his hand and as they shook Ronan noticed they held each other's eyes a moment longer than was normal. He was sure his expression matched the quizzical look in her eyes.

As they dropped hands, Emily took a step back. "I know this may sound a bit odd, but have we met before? I feel as if I have seen you somewhere."

"It doesn't sound odd because I was about to ask you the same thing. I don't think so, though. I'm fairly sure I would remember meeting you." He said the words but as he looked into her eyes he knew he had seen them before. Something was scratching at the back of his mind. He was sure he had once gotten lost in those eyes.

Ronan noticed Emily had not responded. She was staring at him as if she were trying to place him. It was a moment before she spoke again. "I don't know. I have a very strong feeling that I've spoken to you." She paused and then chuckled. "If we have met before, I'm sure it will come to us at some point. Why don't we get started?"

The next three-quarters of an hour was spent going over the

offices. Ronan took notes, reviewed the notes Emily had taken and offered advice on how to best utilize the space. He was relieved to focus on the potential job, it took his mind away from the feeling that he had finally met the only person besides Carrieann who he could spend his life with.

He knew he would have to talk to Dr. Parks about this. He was aware of how it sounded but he had carried this feeling with him for the past seven years. He knew she was out there. He knew it was only a matter of time until he came across her. The time had come. Here she was and he was completely unprepared for it. He also knew it was illogical and if he put a voice to it, he would sound off his rocker, but the feeling was strong.

"Well, Emily, I think I have all I need. I'll have a quote written up and have my sister bring it down tomorrow. If no one is here I'll tell her to slide it under the door."

"Your sister?"

Ronan smiled, "Yes. My sister works for me as an office manager, secretary, receptionist, billing, payroll. Who am I kidding? She runs the business, I just do the work."

Emily laughed, "Well, I look forward to meeting her."

Lingering a moment longer, many thoughts ran through Ronan's mind. There was so much he wanted to say but felt none of it was appropriate for their first meeting. He was relieved when Emily went first.

"You haven't thought of it yet, have you?"

"What?"

"Where we may have met."

Ronan shook his head, "No."

"Me, neither," Emily said. "It's a strange feeling, though. I'm sure I've talked to you before."

"I don't think it's a strange feeling. It feels more like…" Ronan couldn't find the right words.

"Like finding someone you lost a long time ago."

They stood frozen for a moment. Ronan could see Emily hadn't meant for the words to come out. She looked almost embarrassed at having said them. He was glad she had, though, as it was exactly how he was feeling. Seeing the look on her face, he wanted to relieve her of any unease she might be feeling.

"Something like that, yes."

Emily straightened up and smiled, "Well, like I said earlier, if we've met before I'm sure it will come to one of us sooner or later. In the meantime," she waved her hand around the area, "we've got some work to do."

"That we do. I'll be in touch."

After leaving Emily, Ronan called Michelle to give her the details of the job for Safe Haven and then headed to the Upper East Side to finish work on an apartment. It did not go smoothly as this particular client was hard to please. In addition, she looked down on what she referred to as the "hired help". It didn't help that Ronan's thoughts had been completely occupied by Emily. He completed the job, handed the client his bill and was out the door before she could complain about a minute dust particle or how his jeans were dirty.

Fighting his way through the Mid-Town traffic on the way to his appointment with Dr. Parks, his mind went in several directions. He loved his work, but he didn't always like some of his clients. The one he had just left was a good example. There had been a few times he had wanted to tell them that having money didn't make them better people. In fact, there were times it made them horrible people. It didn't matter, though, and he knew it. He could say it, but it certainly wouldn't change their attitude. He could not understand how some people who had the means to make a difference in their community, in their world, were the ones who ultimately only thought about themselves. He realized not all of them were alike. He knew some of them were very charitable. However, it seemed to him that lately the ones who weren't charitable were becoming the majority. Most of the time he didn't let it bother him but there were days like today where it got under his skin.

From there his mind floated back to Emily. He was certain she was the one he'd been waiting for. He had been happy about it on the drive up to the Upper East Side but now, on the drive home, it began to bother him. What if he wasn't ready for it? What if it was only a coincidence that she had the same feeling, and it really wasn't something that was 'meant to be'? He began second guessing himself. By the time he got to his appointment, he had all but convinced himself that he might be wrong.

As he walked through the door, he felt the downward spiral. He hadn't had a bad day for a couple weeks but the knowledge that bad days would eventually come was always there. He once explained it to Michelle as not being able to fully enjoy a sunny day because the storm is around the corner. He could appreciate it; he could get out in the sunshine but knowing the storm was never far away was always on his mind. He had felt the storm clouds gathering on the drive here.

He decided to ask about the experimental drug and this time he would write everything down so he could relay it to Michelle. If Dr. Parks could assure him this drug didn't have any horrible side-effects, he'd agree to it. Rationally, he knew today was a good day but emotionally he'd fallen into the hole of thinking he'd been wrong about his feelings, he was wrong about a woman being out there and his client had every right to criticize his appearance.

Emerging from his session, he felt a bit better and had agreed to begin the experimental drugs. He was given additional exercises to navigate through the rough days. What had made him a little more optimistic, though, was when Dr. Parks began exploring his feelings, instructing him to trust his gut instincts. His feelings regarding Emily were not discounted by Dr. Parks. In fact, they were reinforced, though Ronan didn't quite listen to everything the doctor relayed to him about the chemical reaction his brain had. He was never interested in the science part of things. He was only interested in the knowledge that the reaction had happened because of a connection and that when your instincts are telling you something, you should listen.

Though he felt a bit better, the nagging thoughts persisted in the back of his mind as they always did on days like this. These were the days he needed to train his mind to listen to the logic and banish the negative. It was always easier said than done and Ronan was praying this new drug would help him keep the negative away.

Getting off the elevator and heading toward his loft, he noticed George heading toward him down the hallway. He was about to greet him when George cut him off.

"Did you hear?" George asked, somewhat frantically.

"Hear what?"

"The building is being sold. The deal hasn't gone through yet but there's no doubt it will. I came looking for you because I knew you'd want to know. I remembered what you said the first time I came to see you about all the J-51 stuff."

Ronan was a little bewildered. "George, slow down. I haven't heard about this. Who's buying it? Why? How do you know?"

George took a deep breath. "Okay, so, yeah, Marty's been talking to the owner's daughter again, you know, seeing if they could start things up. Anyway, she agreed to hook up with him and they've been talking, and she said they're going to sell. I came straight up to tell you because of what you said."

"What did I say?"

"About Corbyn. That you didn't like them. Get this. *They* called. *They* initiated it. Our guy wasn't looking to sell but they called him and made an offer."

Ronan leaned his head back and sighed. "That's not good news."

"It is, though!" George seemed excited. "Apparently, they're not going to do anything. The news is they're going to keep everything as it is. They're still going to bring in businesses for the first floor but we're all safe."

"I wouldn't be too sure about that." Ronan fished his keys out of his pocket and headed toward his door with George right behind him.

"Come on, man, don't be a downer. This is good. We don't have to worry about anything."

Putting his key in the door, Ronan paused and turned toward George. "Corbyn doesn't buy buildings to do nothing with them. It wouldn't make sense for them to buy this building and not take advantage of the expansion once it goes through. I don't trust them."

"I know you don't. That's why I came to tell you. I wanted you to know that even though they're the ones buying it, nothing's going to happen. I told you they cleaned up their act."

"I'm not convinced but thanks for the information, George. I really appreciate it." With that, Ronan let himself into his loft, dropped his things and leaned against the closed door.

His mind went back to being a jumble of thoughts. There was too much noise going on in his head. He slid his tool bag against the wall, turned around and went back out. He needed to clear his thoughts. He decided to take a walk to the bridge.

Emily

"Look at you, all glowing!" Jean couldn't help but poke a little fun at Emily. She had never seen Emily talk about a man the way she was talking about the contractor she'd met earlier.

"Stop!" Emily chided. "It's not like that. I'm going to hire him to do a job. That's it. Well, I'll hire him if his bid comes in at a reasonable price."

Jean nodded and smirked, "Okay. So, how many other bids did you get?"

"None." Emily lowered her eyes.

"See! You like this guy!" Jean couldn't contain her glee.

"Okay, okay," Emily conceded, "there's something about him." She took a seat on the corner of Jean's desk before continuing. "I feel like I know him already. He said the same thing. It's as if we've met somewhere before but neither of us can remember when. It's odd, I know, but I can't shake the feeling that I've talked to him before. I felt it the moment I looked at him."

"Love at first sight! That's so romantic!" Jean gushed.

"No, it's not love at first sight. I don't believe in that. It's like…" Emily paused as she remembered the words she said to Ronan. She felt the same flush of embarrassment that came over her the moment those words had escaped her mouth.

"You're blushing," Jean was incredulous. "I don't think I've ever seen that before. It's like what, Emily? Tell me."

"It was like finding someone you lost a long time ago. It really was the strangest feeling but what makes it even stranger is he felt the same thing."

"Oh, Emily, can I tell you that it's so good to see you interested in someone?"

Emily smiled. "He *is* kind of cute."

Jean laughed and patted Emily's knee. "This is wonderful. I may have to go up to the new office and check him out. Oh, and I did put word out that you'll be needing a receptionist, and that the new clinic is in the triangle below Canal Street."

"They call it Tribeca, Jean, and thank you for doing that. If anyone gets back to you, have them send me their resume."

Jean huffed and shook her head, "Tribeca. Did they really need to give it a name? Yeah, yeah, it's short for triangle below Canal but it's just lazy to shorten it."

"No different than Hell's Kitchen or Soho. What do you think Soho stands for?"

Jean shrugged and Emily laughed, "It stands for south of Houston Street."

The phone rang as Jean was about to say something. Instead of replying she simply picked up the phone as Emily removed herself from the desk.

"One moment, please," Jean pressed the hold button and looked up, "It's a Mr. Jackson for you. I'm going to take off now unless you need anything."

"No, I'm good. Thanks, Jean, and give that sweet little boy of yours a kiss for me when you get home."

"Will do!" Jean replied as Emily headed to her office.

A sense of dread came over Emily as she closed her office door. She was hoping the book was permanently buried but if Tim was calling it could mean that isn't the case. She dropped into her chair and took a deep breath before picking up the phone. "Hey, Tim, what can I do for you?"

"Emily, I'm glad I caught you. Listen, we've been successful in delaying Kettering's book but I'm not sure we can kill it completely. I got an advanced copy and I have someone going over it with Rob and, so far, it all seems to be accurate. If we can't find anything false or otherwise misleading, we won't have grounds to kill it."

"What if I try to reach out to Lyle again? Do you think he might listen? It's been a few years. Maybe there's a chance he'll meet with me now."

She heard the sigh and knew the answer before he spoke. "Not advisable, Emily. This is a revenge book. He's bitter. Apparently, it's only grown over the years. There's a good chance he'll come out of the meeting saying you threatened him or tried to pay him off."

"I know. You're probably right. In fact, I know you're right." She tapped her fingers on the desk. "Tim, I want to read it. Does Rob have the copy?"

"Yes, he does. I was going to ask you to read it. Rob didn't think it was a good idea. He doesn't want you reliving what you've put behind you."

"Well, I can't say I'm looking forward to it but if there is anyone who can tell you if anything is false, it's me. I'll get in touch with Rob and get it from him."

"In the meantime, there are still a few legal technicalities and bullshit maneuvers I can use to keep pushing the release back but, eventually, we'll run out of options."

"I understand. Thanks, Tim. I'll be in touch."

Emily set down the phone and sat back in her chair. There had to be a way to stop the book from reaching the public. She knew Tim was right. She had to stay away from Lyle Kettering. He could twist any contact into something incendiary. Tim was also right that if everything was accurate there was no legal way to stop it.

She sat up straight in her chair. Her mind raced. There may be no legal way but, as she was well aware, there were definitely other ways.

"No," she admonished herself. She brought her hands up and rubbed her face. "No. Stop it. Don't even think about it. The ends never justify the means. You are not that person anymore."

In addition to the trepidation of the book, she was now feeling both anger and disappointment in herself. The thought of using other means had flickered in her mind for only a moment, but it was enough to make her feel ashamed. She hadn't had thoughts like that since she woke from the coma and untangled herself from Corbyn. It unnerved her that her mind had regressed to thinking that way when she was intent on getting something done. Yes, she wanted the book stopped but not enough to go back to any of her old ways. She was so sure she had grown past the old unscrupulous business habits.

All the confidence and optimism she had been feeling all day vanished as she put her elbows on her desk and sank her head into her hands. *Okay,* she thought, *what would you do if this was one of your patients?* Emily knew the answer. She would tell them not to be so hard on themselves; that they had caught themselves before acting on it; that they knew they were no longer that person and never wanted to be that person again. She would have congratulated them on having the intelligence and strength to immediately shut down the train of thought. She would have called it growth. However, like almost every other psychologist she'd met since embarking on this path, she was not good at taking her own advice or instruction.

Sighing heavily, she got up and grabbed her coat and purse. Locking up the office, she decided she needed some time to clear her head, get her thoughts back on track and regain the optimism she'd been feeling earlier. She hailed a cab and climbed in the back seat.

"Brooklyn Bridge, please," she told the cab driver.

Michelle

Finishing up the estimate for the Safe Haven Clinic, Michelle pulled the last sheet from her typewriter, separated the carbon, and placed the pages in the folder. She was pleased that Ronan's business was doing well. It kept him busy, and she loved to see the light in his eyes when he told her of a project he thought he'd done a top-notch job on. There were times she watched him as he created one of his furniture pieces. He would get lost in the process. There were times it would take him over a month to finish a side table or chair, but he didn't care about speed, he cared about quality, and it showed in each piece he finished. She thought he underestimated the value of those pieces, but he was too stubborn to raise his prices.

If Michelle had her way, his business would be twice the size it currently was but that was another area they tended to butt heads on. She tried to resign herself to the fact that Ronan wanted to remain a small business and not expand to a point where the jobs became impersonal to him. She understood that to an extent, though it frustrated her when she thought of the opportunities he was missing.

Overall, she could not be prouder of her brother and the progress he had made over the last years. The only thing she felt was missing was a good partner and not one of the business variety but of the personal kind. He had a rough time coming to terms and accepting Carrieann's death. She hadn't understood how hard it was until that night on the bridge. She had tried over the years to forgive herself for not being there when he had needed her the most, but the guilt remained. Both Jack and Ronan repeatedly told her that June had rightfully been her first priority but seeing him that night, knowing he had been ready to jump and knowing that if she had only made some time to visit him, maybe he would not have gotten to that point. She didn't know if she could ever forgive herself for that.

Michelle often thought back to that night. To this day she had no idea what had guided her to him. She often thought it was the bond they shared. She had read of how people with strong familial bonds or married people often felt the other's pain even though they were separated by miles or knew something had happened to them before they were ever told. Some days she thought it was God that guided her. Other days she thought it might have been Carrieann. She may not be able to identify who or what guided her, but she was sure of one thing; that it had been some kind of higher power and for that she was forever grateful.

When she thought of that night, she wondered who Ronan had thought he was talking to. He had said something and turned as if to say it to someone else, but no one had been there. She remembered him looking around and being confused. She had even asked him if someone had been there, and he thought maybe someone had but he couldn't remember. It was the one thing Ronan couldn't explain, even now. He told Michelle that his therapist had tried on quite a few occasions to break through the block and get him to remember. Nothing seemed to work. There was still that blank space between getting ready to jump and then hearing her call for him.

Maybe it was for the best, she often thought. She was no expert, but she did know that the mind sometimes blocks out memories that are too horrible for the person to recall. Maybe it was like that and, if it was, then it was best that he couldn't remember. She only knew that he had come out the other side of that night ready to get the help he needed and ready to move forward. He may never know what happened during that time, but it no longer seemed to bother him. He had once told her he didn't need to know, whatever happened got him to where he is now and for that he was thankful.

She was still worried about him. That would never go away. Only it was a different kind of worry these days. Some days she worried he might have a setback but most times she worried that he was lonely. The times Michelle tried to talk to him about his personal life it was met with jokes, sarcasm, or distractions. She knew several women who were nearly chomping at the bit to have Ronan ask them out. He showed no interest, though, and there was usually nothing she could do to persuade him. The last time she talked to him about it, it was clear he had intentionally sabotaged his last date and had shut down any conversation about future dates.

The phone interrupted her thoughts. She picked it up to hear Jack telling her he'd be a little later and not to hold dinner for him. Michelle was almost relieved by the news. Ever since their conversation about Corbyn there was a slight chill between them. It wasn't enough to be overly concerned about, but it was just enough to make life a bit uneasy at times.

Michelle still could not understand Jack's reaction to Corbyn since his firm didn't do any work directly for them. She was more confused by his hatred of Emily Corbyn. His reaction was a bit intense, and she had intended to ask him if Corbyn or, more specifically, Emily, had done something that had impacted people in his firm or friends he had in other firms. It was the only thing that made sense to her. That, and the fact that he thought women had no business being in any position of authority or power. She hadn't asked him, though, as the chill had not subsided since that night.

Looking at the clock, she realized it was time to make dinner for June and then, hopefully, she could take a long, uninterrupted bubble bath before sitting with June and reading with her before bedtime.

Taking the folder off the table, she placed it in her tote to take to Ronan's in the morning. As she did so, she realized Dr. Walton shared the same first name as the woman her husband despised. Michelle wondered how Jack would respond to Dr. Emily Walton if they were to ever meet. She was a woman who was not only clearly smart but ran her own clinic in a field Jack thought was hogwash.

She chuckled as she realized that whether Jack liked it or not, times were changing. Women weren't going to be quiet any longer. The number of women in the House of Representatives was up to 16, women were coming out of college with degrees in fields dominated by men and were determined to break through, the Equal Rights Amendment passed Congress three years ago and only needs to be ratified. Women were coming out of the kitchen and Jack was going to have to deal with it.

Michelle was still smiling as she started up the steps to get June washed up for dinner. She wanted to tell Jack that while one Emily may have disappeared there was another one out there making her own way in this "man's world" and being quite successful at it.

Ronan

Walking out to his usual spot, Ronan took in the breeze coming off the water and began to feel more at ease. It didn't matter how many people were on the bridge, he just loved to walk out, lean against the railing, and take in the water. He could look to one side and see Manhattan, his home with all the noise and flurry of activity that made it come so much alive and to the other side, Brooklyn, the borough that always got the bad rap, but the one Michelle loved the most. His attention when he walked out here, though, was always the water. Looking out over the horizon now, Ronan felt the muscles in his neck begin to relax.

As he usually did when coming here, he began to go through the good things he had going for him. It was one of the exercises given to him; to count at least five good things for every one negative. He looked at it as a sort of mental balance sheet. In his mind he could visualize it and see the positives as a much longer list than the negatives. From there, he would focus on one of the positives. In this case, it was the side table he was currently working on. His customer was very specific in how he wanted it to look and so far, Ronan was not only meeting the original vision, but he was pretty sure he was exceeding it.

His mind then wandered to Safe Haven. He hadn't been given the job, yet, but he was pretty sure he would be. His estimates were always reasonable, and he was certain Dr. Emily Walton would give him the green light. He wondered, again, why the feeling was so strong that he had met her prior to this morning. As he had talked through it with Dr. Parks, the logical answer was that the instant chemical reaction to the connection only made it *feel* as if they'd known each other before. It was logical but the only way it made sense was if Emily had the same chemical reaction since she, too, thought they'd met. However, Dr.

Parks was also of the mindset that reactions such as those, combined with instinct, happen for a reason.

"Ronan?"

Ronan knew the voice instantly and turned to find Emily standing only a few feet away. He was a bit stunned as it seemed his thoughts had almost conjured her there. He thought she looked beautiful with the lowering sun shining on her and the breeze sweeping her bright auburn hair away from her face. His heart seemed to skip a beat as he looked at her and smiled.

"Dr. Walton. What brings you here?"

Emily walked over and stood next to him at the railing. "Please. There's no need to be so formal. I'm Emily. Mind if I share the rail with you?"

"I don't mind at all," Ronan was more than happy to have her interrupt his time of reflection. In fact, he couldn't think of anything he'd like more at that moment. "So, what *does* bring you here?"

Emily shrugged and looked out over the water. "I do this sometimes. When I need to decompress or when I just need some time, I come here, stare at the water, clear my head, and regroup." She looked over at Ronan and was startled by the look on his face. "What?"

"That's interesting because that's exactly what I do." Ronan was amazed to hear Emily had the same habit. "I've been doing it for years now."

"Are you serious?"

Ronan nodded. "It's funny because you'd think there are quieter places to go if you want to clear your head or get some peace but, I don't know, I was drawn here after..." he hesitated and restarted, "I was drawn here one night. and it just seemed to be the right place for me."

"I know what you mean. It really isn't a place one would think of to find peace," she motioned to the people around them, "but it works for me, too." She paused for a moment before continuing. "You were drawn here after what?"

Ronan had been hoping she hadn't caught that. He shook his head. "Nothing."

"Okay," Emily replied, "you don't want to talk about it. That's perfectly fine. So, what brought you here today?"

Ronan smiled, "No small talk? You just get straight to the point, don't you?"

"Occupational hazard, I guess. You said you come here to get some peace. I'm assuming something happened to facilitate your visit here. But look," Emily held up her hands, "if I'm overstepping, I'm sorry."

"No need to apologize," Ronan looked out over the water again. "I have a lot on my mind recently, that's all."

"Anything you want to share?" Emily followed his gaze out onto the water.

Ronan paused for a moment before responding. When he did, he was still looking out over the water toward Governor's Island. He opted for his more general concerns over the personal ones. "We live in some crazy times right now, don't we? This country is so divided even though we got out of Vietnam, the recession is hitting a lot of people…although, luckily, my business is still doing alright. I keep waiting for this country to find some peace but there's always something."

"Countries don't find peace, Ronan. They never will."

Ronan turned his head toward Emily, though he didn't respond. Emily looked back at him and gave a small shrug. "It's true," she continued. "As long as there are politicians working in a broken governmental system there will never be peace. These politicians seek to divide us. They use us as pawns for their own agendas. I don't believe any of them truly work for the average citizen. There will always be conflict within the country. There will always be war because war is money."

Ronan knew what she was saying was correct, though he wanted to remain optimistic about the country coming together and the government working together to find real solutions to what was happening across the country. He was about to say something when Emily continued.

"Countries don't find peace, Ronan, people do. People find peace."

Nodding, Ronan turned back to the water but did not respond. He mulled Emily's statement over in his mind for a minute and then said, "Not everyone seems to want peace."

"Well, that's true," came her response. "There are always those people that thrive on conflict and separation. We can't control those people, though. We can only control ourselves and what we do." She paused. "So, is that why you came out here today? The state of the country? Because that's too big a problem for one person to solve."

Ronan chuckled, "No, it's not. I do think about it a lot, though."

"A thinker," Emily remarked.

"I guess I am. I had a conversation with my sister not long ago. We talked about everything from the state of the country to the shows on television."

"What conclusions did you come to?"

"That David Cassidy has women wrapped around his finger, the Beatles breaking up is the reason the country has gone to hell, and that I think too much."

Emily laughed out loud. "That must have been one hell of a conversation."

"Well, let's face it. The decade started off with the Beatles breaking up and look what's happened since."

"Well, then, you should take it up with John Lennon. Want his address?"

"That's what I suggested we do!" Ronan continued the joke, "But Michelle won't go. She hates Yoko."

"Ah, yes, the scapegoat for the Fab Four disbanding. On the bright side, we have Wings and The Plastic Ono Band, and both have put out some good music. So, look, there's a silver lining to everything."

"Is there?" Ronan turned serious. He turned his body toward Emily and continued. "Can I ask you a professional question?"

"Sure."

"What do you know about SSRI's?"

Emily was quiet for a moment which made Ronan think he shouldn't have changed the subject so abruptly and asked the question. She was a psychologist, he realized, not a psychiatrist. Maybe she didn't know too much about them. He also realized by asking the question he may have just admitted to her that he was struggling with mental health issues. He didn't want her to think he was looking for free counseling.

"I'm sorry. This is your off time. I shouldn't have asked."

"No, it's okay. I can answer your question. If the research I've read is accurate I think they could be very beneficial to many people."

"How do they work, though? In simple terms, please," Ronan decided to be honest with her. "My doctor explained it but I'm not much into science."

Emily paused for a moment and then said, "Think of it as a broken bridge. There's a broken bridge in your brain and the chemical that is needed to balance out emotions can't cross that bridge. It falls into the water. The SSRI's fix the bridge which inhibits the water from absorbing the chemical, therefore, allowing the chemical to cross it."

"Thank you. That's a better way of understanding it for me." Ronan paused and then said, "So, now you know I'm in therapy. I see Dr. Parks. He spoke highly of you and Safe Haven, by the way."

Emily let out a half-laugh, "You checked up on me?"

Ronan blushed slightly, "If you want to say that. I hope you don't mind. I had an appointment this afternoon and after meeting you this morning, I was a little curious about you and the clinic."

Emily nodded. "Well, then, I'm glad Parks spoke highly of us. He's a good guy. I've referred patients to him a few times. Is that why you came out here? Are you contemplating taking the experimental SSRI?"

Ronan noticed she side-stepped his obvious hint at interest in her. Maybe he had told her too much too soon. On the other hand, he thought, maybe it was best to tell her all this upfront instead of hiding it and having to tell her later on. Looking at her, he began to think that maybe she was out of his league but then the feeling that she was the one that he'd been looking for crept over him again. He decided to go on being as honest as he could.

"I've already told Parks I'll take it. I have to go pick them up next week. That's not the only reason I'm out here, though. It's been a strange kind of day and I found out our building is being sold." A realization struck him. "You should know this, too, actually. I found out Corbyn is buying the building. The rumor is they're not going to take advantage of the J-51 expansion. I don't buy it, though."

Emily looked a bit concerned before she responded. "Why don't you buy it?

"You've heard of Corbyn, right? I mean they're the big real estate developers, among other things. Everybody in the city knows who they are. I almost got evicted a couple years ago because of them. Thankfully, my sister and her husband helped me out. Some of my friends found themselves out on the street, though. I don't trust them at all. I know people say they've changed and are more community-minded and all that, but I don't think I believe it."

Ronan noticed Emily's eyes lower and a look he couldn't read crossed her face. She seemed to harden slightly as she looked back toward the water and did not respond. He didn't think he had said anything to upset her, but she appeared to be bothered by something.

"Emily? Are you okay?"

Emily

Emily was not prepared for Ronan's reaction to Corbyn, nor had she been aware that his friends were tenants she had evicted from their home and that he had almost been one of them. It was one more thing from her past that came up today, only this one was harder for her to handle than the book.

She had been surprised and thrilled to find Ronan standing on the bridge. He hadn't been far from her thoughts all day. The feeling that they had connected somewhere before was stronger than it had been earlier. The ease she felt in talking and joking with him was something she hadn't experienced with a man before. She took the fact that he had been honest with her about going to therapy on only their second meeting as a sign that he felt the same.

Then his honesty about Corbyn shook her. As she looked at the water, she had to remind herself that she was no longer that person. That person was buried years ago and was no longer around to cause any harm to innocent people. She spent the first years after her coma trying to make amends but here she was, faced with a man she felt a strong connection to who came very close to being one of her victims.

"Emily?"

Emily turned and looked at Ronan, she could see concern in his eyes. She wasn't sure how she was going to handle this. He had been honest with her but, at the moment, she didn't think being honest with him was a good idea. She didn't want him to walk away from her. She wanted him to get to know Emily Walton.

"Are you okay?" Ronan repeated.

"I'm sorry. Yes, I'm fine. I do have a question for you, though." Emily hesitated a beat. "Do you think it's possible for people to change?"

"Sure, people can change. I did. I'm a much different person than the wreck I was years ago. It took a lot of work, but it happened. I think it depends on the person, though. I'm not sure everyone can change. Some people don't seem to have it in them. I see it with my clients at times. I don't think there's anything that would get them to change who or what they are."

"I changed," Emily replied. She looked directly into Ronan's eyes. "Years ago, I wasn't such a good person. In fact, I was pretty much a horrible person. I was estranged from my sister and my brother. I kept everyone at arm's length and there wasn't a whole lot that I cared about."

"I find that hard to believe," Ronan replied.

"Well, it's true," Emily continued. "I did a lot of things I'm not proud of. I have a lot of regrets from that time. When I realized I no longer wanted to be that person, I worked hard. I tried to make amends the best I could, but I know there are some I still need to make." She paused and looked back at the water. "Lately, things have popped up that remind me there is still music left to face. I'll face it. I don't know what the outcome will be, but I'll face it."

"And your brother and sister?"

Emily turned back to Ronan. "That is a broken bridge that I fixed, I'm happy to say. It took years to regain their trust, but we are a family again. There are still other ones that are broken, though."

"So, we both have broken bridges."

"Yes, we do. The point is that people can change. I see it with my patients every day. Yes, it takes work, but it happens. There are many factors that can make a person become awful and cruel, but they don't have to stay that way. Once they come to terms with things and once they realize they want to be better, to do better, they can change."

"I'm not saying that isn't true. All I'm saying is that I don't believe everyone is capable of it. I think there are some people that aren't. Look at Charles Manson. That guy is never going to change."

Emily brought her hands up to her face and took a breath. She needed Ronan to understand what she was trying to say. She'd been honest so far about what she'd said about herself even if it wasn't the whole truth. She wanted to keep being honest, but she felt blurting out she was actually Emily Corbyn was out of the question.

Bringing her hands back down, she continued, "Okay, I agree that there are people who don't want to change and never will. There are also people who will revert back to their old habits no matter how much therapy they go through. I get that. What I want you to see is that there are people, like me, who put in the work and overcome things from their past in order to be better people."

"I do agree. Emily, I'm not going to ask you what you've done in your past, if that's what you're worried about. If you want to tell me, I'm here to listen but that is up to you. I know this is only the second time we've talked but I know you feel this, too. I know you feel like we've already been through this, that we already know each other. I can't explain it, you can't explain it, but the feeling is there. It makes me want to tell you that none of that matters. What matters is who you are now and what happens from this point forward."

"I do feel that, Ronan. That's why I want you to know that I've accepted and taken responsibility for things I did but I also want you to know that I'm nothing like that person anymore. I need you to believe that."

"I do believe it. I believe you have done things you regret, and I believe you have changed. I believe you will do whatever is right to fix whatever broken bridge is left. I believe that you are a good person. I'm beginning to think you are an exceptional person."

Emily felt Ronan reach for her hand. She gripped it and smiled up at him. "Thank you for that. You're not the only one who thinks the person in front of them is exceptional."

Ronan smiled, "So, we were both different people at one time.

That's the past. We're here now, as better people."

"True, but with still more work to do."

"Then we work. Look, Emily, this has never happened to me before. For a long time, I had the feeling that someone was out there. I didn't know where and I didn't know when I'd meet her, but I knew. This morning, when I saw you, I knew that person was you. Logically, I know it's been less than 24 hours, but it feels like…"

Ronan paused but Emily had the words he was looking for, "It feels like we've picked up right where we left off somewhere. It's like I said this morning, it feels like we found someone we lost a long time ago. I understand, Ronan. I didn't have the feeling that someone was out there but when I saw you this morning, I felt something I'd never felt before. I could have sworn in a court of law that we already knew each other."

"You're the psychologist. Are we insane?"

"You want my professional opinion? If a patient came to me and told me this story, I would caution them against doing anything too quickly. I would recommend they take it slow. I would probably give them a short synopsis on how the chemicals in the brain react when there is an attraction. I would agree they should follow their instincts and trust their intuition, but with caution."

"Your personal opinion?"

"I think, for the first time in my life, I'm not going to over think this. The fact that we both felt the same way this morning and then we both end up here on the bridge tonight…some would say that's a coincidence, but I believe it's something more. I think the universe is telling us something and maybe we should listen."

Emily took in Ronan's boyish smile in reply and began to feel at ease again. The worry seemed to fade away and the feeling that she'd found the piece of her life that had been missing grew stronger. She squeezed his hand.

"Look at us," Ronan said, "aren't we just two rays of sunshine—"

"In the middle of winter," Emily finished and looked at Ronan with a confused expression.

"Oh my God, Emily," Ronan said, "that's exactly what I was going to say except I realized it isn't winter. How did you know?"

"I didn't. It just came out." If Emily hadn't been sure before that they were connected, this would have cemented it for her.

She saw Ronan tilt his head as he was searching her eyes. "Maybe we knew each other in a past life," he said. "Maybe that's why I'm so sure I've looked into these eyes before."

"That's one explanation," Emily replied as she watched, seemingly in slow motion, Ronan lean down and kiss her lightly. She responded by dropping his hand and wrapping her arms around his neck. She felt his arms encircle her waist as they melted into a deeper kiss. Emily could feel her heart expanding. It was a joy she had never felt before.

As Ronan lifted his head, he smiled and brushed away the hair on the side of her face. "What do you say to a proper date? Say dinner on Friday?"

"Dinner on Friday." Emily smiled as Ronan shook his head and chuckled. "Yes, Ronan. Dinner on Friday would be lovely."

"I'll even make it. How's my loft at seven?"

"I will be there." Emily tried to calm her emotions. Inside she felt like a high school girl who just got invited to the prom by the most popular boy in school. She hoped she looked more mature on the outside.

After Ronan said his goodbye with one last kiss, Emily watched him walk down the bridge before turning back toward the water. Her smile broadened as she thought about the impending dinner. She had never met someone who could melt away all the exterior things about her and bring out the joyful, joking girl inside of her. For a moment she had almost forgotten she was a Doctor of Psychology with published papers who owned one clinic and was opening another one.

She had also almost forgotten she had once been Emily Corbyn, even after being reminded. Her smile faded. This was a broken bridge. She was going to have to fix it. She wasn't sure if she could. She had seen his reaction to the name Corbyn. Finding out it was her that almost had him evicted might end this before it even had a chance to start. However, she realized he had told her she didn't have to tell him about her past if she didn't want to. Emily decided it might be possible to cross the bridge without having to tell him who she once was.

Ronan

"What?"

"You heard me," Ronan looked at his sister. "Corbyn is buying the building. Rumor is they're going to keep everything as it is, though."

He took another sip of his coffee and waited for Michelle to put her things down on her desk. Since he woke up, his thoughts had alternated between Corbyn taking over the building, and his time with Emily. He had already decided on the menu for their dinner, all he had to do was pick up the groceries before tomorrow night. Not since Carrieann had he been looking forward to seeing a woman this much. He wondered if it wasn't a past life that made Emily and him feel the way they did but Carrieann up there pushing him toward someone. Maybe she had orchestrated the entire thing. By the time he poured his second cup of coffee he decided not to worry about how it happened and decided that he, like Emily, wasn't going to over think it and just enjoy it. As for the building, he wanted Michelle's opinion.

"What is with Corbyn, lately?" Michelle asked as she hung her jacket on the back of her chair. "I didn't hear their name in quite a while and then Jack goes off about them the other night and now they're buying the building." She walked toward the kitchen area to grab her own cup of coffee. "Are you sure they are?"

"Pretty sure. George got the information. He said it comes straight from the owner's daughter so I'm going to say it's accurate. Do you think they'll really keep it all as it is?"

"Hard to say," Michelle leaned back against the counter. "They've definitely changed their public image. They've been donating to charities and various community projects but...I don't know. Why would they buy a building and not take advantage of an opportunity to turn much more of a profit?"

"That was my question. It doesn't make sense. I don't trust it." Ronan put his cup down and headed toward Michelle's desk and scanned the calendar. "In any case, we've got work to do. I got two calls this morning for estimates. I'm going to swing by both places and then I'll give you a call to type up the formal quotes."

"Got it."

Ronan looked up and saw Michelle looking lost in thought as she tapped her coffee mug. "What's on your mind?"

Michelle looked up and shook her head. "Nothing, really. It's just that Jack got a phone call the other day. Apparently, there's going to be a book coming out about the woman that ran Corbyn years ago. I guess Corbyn got the book delayed and Jack was upset about it. I mean he was really upset. Now I'm wondering if Corbyn just might keep this building as it is in order to look good when the book hits. You know, kind of a 'yeah, that all happened but look at us now' type thing."

Ronan nodded, "Could be. It's certainly a possibility. Why would Jack be upset about a book, though? Why is there even a book? I don't think anyone outside of the city would care about that."

"That's what I said but Jack said it's not about sales and money, it's about revenge against her. Oh, and, in Jack's words, a cautionary story about how women shouldn't be running businesses and should still be at home taking care of the house and kids. I'll tell you, though, he really despises that woman."

"Did he know her?" Ronan asked, ignoring the comment about women as he was already well aware of Jack's stance on women in the workforce.

"I don't think so. His firm never did any business with them, to the best of my knowledge. I'm just guessing it's because she was young and successful, even though she did do some nasty stuff."

"Like evicting people?" Ronan asked.

"Yes, among other things. It doesn't matter anymore, really. No one has seen or heard from Emily Corbyn in a while." Michelle took another sip of her coffee and then, "Oh, speaking of Emilys, I have the quote typed up for Safe Haven. If you're going to be tied up, I'll run it down to their office."

"Thanks, that would be great." He hoped Michelle hadn't picked up his change of tone.

She had. "What's with that little smile?"

"Nothing. I'm just glad the business is doing well, and we've got enough work in front of us to survive this recession. Can't a guy be happy about that?"

Ronan saw Michelle nod but knew she wasn't convinced. He wasn't ready to talk about Emily Walton with his sister. He wanted to keep it to himself for a little while and enjoy it without the pressure of family surrounding it. If he talked to Michelle, she would never let up on him. She'd been waiting for him to meet someone, and he knew she would be all over him with questions. It would only be a matter of time before she called his mother. No, he was not ready for that.

As Michelle walked to her desk, Ronan saw that thoughtful look again. This time he didn't ask what was on her mind as he wasn't sure he wanted to know. She reached into her tote and pulled out the papers she had prepared the night before. Ronan turned and was about to head toward his workspace when Michelle stopped him.

"Ro?"

Giving a small sigh, he turned back around, "Yes?"

"Didn't you tell me that Emily Walton was the one who told Jim no one needed to be worried about eviction?"

"That's right, why?"

"Hear me out. How would she know that? She tells Jim and then Corbyn offers to buy the building. Now, I'm no genius but it would seem like Dr. Walton might have some ties to Corbyn. Her first name is a little ironic, too, wouldn't you say?"

"It's a common name, Michelle, but I did think about the other thing earlier." He shrugged. "Maybe Corbyn had already reached out to the owner and when she signed the papers for the clinic and he told her about it. Who knows? I would like to think she doesn't have any ties, even if she does think people like that can change."

"What? You've talked to her about Corbyn? How did that happen?"

Ronan sighed. "Okay, I ran into her when I took my walk to the bridge last night. We didn't talk about Corbyn that much. I mentioned them and then she started talking about how people can change. It ended up not being about Corbyn at all. She seems to think there's more hope for people than I do. I mean, yes, people can change. I'm living proof of that and so is she, apparently, but I don't think everyone has it in them."

Michelle stifled a laugh, "You talked to a therapist about the capacity for people to change? I don't know, Ro, I think you were out of your depth there. I think she might have just a tiny bit more experience in that area. At least now I know why you gave that little smile earlier."

He saw the grin on Michelle's face and knew he would have to give her something or she would continue to question him. "She's an interesting woman, okay? I enjoyed talking to her, that's all."

"I know you, Ronan Byrne. You like her. Are you going to see her again? I mean outside of the realm of work?"

Ronan relented, "Michelle, please don't start with a barrage of questions, okay? But, yes, I asked her to dinner tomorrow night. Now, drop it. I don't want to talk about it and I mean that. No questions, please. Just let me do this without you giving me all the sisterly advice you're so good at."

Michelle raised her eyebrows. "Okay, big brother. I got it." Ronan turned again and was on his way back to his work area when he heard Michelle call after him. "I *am* good at the sisterly advice, though!"

Emily

Emily loved her Friday schedule. She saw patients during the morning hours but intentionally left the afternoon hours open. During a normal week, she would have spent the afternoon in her office doing billing or researching another paper. But not on this Friday. She left the office shortly after lunch, picked up a new outfit to wear for dinner and was now at home, sitting in front of her vanity, starting her process of getting ready.

She had promised herself she would not analyze this thing with Ronan, and she had been successful. It seemed every time she tried to think of it from a logical, methodical viewpoint, her mind shut it down and she was left with her feelings of happiness. She tried to remember when she had ever felt this way and could not. Before the attack, she had only been 16 and had very little experience with boys. After the attack, she hadn't let anyone get close enough to her. Her relationships, if they could be called that, had been short. In truth, they had been nothing more than a series of 'friends with benefits' or more accurately, 'acquaintances with benefits'. It was a textbook case of trauma victims keeping their wall intact and controlling their environment.

Ronan, she knew, would get through that wall. This was not only the opposite of those 'relationships' but he was the opposite of all the men she had engaged in those benefits with. She could not explain how but he had managed to melt the ice around her heart the moment she had laid eyes on him. In the past, she would size a man up and determine whether or not he was someone she could spend some time with without getting into any type of serious relationship. There were never any personal conversations, no holidays spent together, and no birthday or Christmas presents exchanged. She had told Ronan more about herself in their two encounters than she ever divulged to any other man. He was the one, she was absolutely sure of it.

Picking up her foundation, she was about to begin applying it when she looked in the mirror and caught sight of a man sitting on the chair in the corner of her bedroom. She let out a horrified scream as she dropped the foundation bottle, and the man gave a short wave of his hand.

"Damn it, Marcus," Emily let out her breath. "Don't scare me like that. At least give me some warning." She turned around to face him. "It's been a long time. Have I done something wrong?"

Marcus smiled, "No, dear, not yet, anyway. In fact, we are all quite proud of you. *I* am proud of you. You have done wonderful things over these last seven years."

Emily smiled. "Thank you, Marcus, I appreciate that. It's been so rewarding, and I can't begin to tell you how happy it makes me when I see one of my patients having a breakthrough. I know with this new clinic we'll reach many more people who really need our help."

"That is true, Emily. Unfortunately, that's not why I am here."

The smile faded from Emily's face. "Then there is something wrong." She tried to scan her mind to figure out what would bring Marcus back to her. She couldn't think of anything. She was running the clinic well; she hadn't gone back to any of her old habits and the only other thing was Ronan. She hadn't hurt Ronan in any way, though, so her confusion only increased.

"Emily, you can't build a relationship on a faulty foundation."

It *was* Ronan, Emily realized. She didn't respond. Instead, she bent down and picked up her makeup bottle, set it back on her vanity and turned once again to face Marcus. She knew what he was implying and she couldn't say that he was wrong. She said the only thing she had at her disposal for a defense.

"Ronan himself said I did not have to disclose my past if I didn't want to. I choose not to. Not now, anyway. I want him to get to know the person I am right now. I don't want it to be tainted by the knowledge of who I used to be."

"Do you believe, as a psychologist, that lying to Ronan from the start is the best way to begin any type of relationship with him?"

Emily shook her head, "I haven't lied to him."

"Technicality, Emily. You know that. It's a lie by omission. I ask again, as a trained professional, is it the best way?"

She was cornered. She knew it and Marcus knew it. Emily drew in a deep breath and exhaled. She turned back to her mirror and picked up her brush. It was not the best way. She'd known it the other night on the bridge. She'd only been trying to convince herself of it ever since. She ran the brush through her hair a few times before quietly setting it back on the vanity. Without looking up, she quietly asked, "So, what do I do?"

"You tell him," replied Marcus, "and you remember."

Emily looked up. Without turning around, she looked at Marcus through the mirror. "Remember what?"

She saw Marcus give another short wave of his hand and a tidal wave of memories flooded through Emily's mind. She had to grab the sides of the vanity to steady herself. At first, there were little flashes; central park, homeless people, offering people money or a blanket. Then the flashes turned into longer, complete memories. She saw Ronan, his depression, his tears, the closed grocery store, the phone booth, the walk to the bridge.

A gasp escaped her throat as the memory of that long ago night on the bridge came back to her. Her mind played back the scene of Ronan ready to jump, her scream to stop, the conversation that ensued, the comfort they gave each other as they confided in each other the darkness they had experienced. She also remembered the laughter and then his sister coming. The last memory to come back was Marcus telling her they would not remember each other.

Shaking slightly, with her eyes glistening, she turned around to face Marcus. "But we did remember each other."

Marcus nodded, "Somewhat, yes, you did. Remarkable, actually. A first, to be honest. You did tell me you would not forget him. In fact, you were quite determined. Somehow, you both embedded the encounter into your subconscious. We're usually quite thorough in wiping the memories. I'm not quite sure how that happened but you're the psychologist, maybe you can figure that part out."

Emily had no desire to try to figure it out. She sat there with the knowledge that she had followed and helped Ronan at his lowest point, that she had spoken to him about things she had never discussed with anyone at that time, that they had found some comfort and even some laughter in each other's company, it was too much for her to process.

A thought struck her as she was trying to organize her thoughts. Her eyes widened and she asked, "Does Ronan remember?"

"No, he does not. There is only one way he will remember that night."

Emily was afraid to ask but she plowed ahead, "What way is that?"

Marcus cleared his throat and leaned forward. He stared directly into Emily's eyes for a moment before answering. "You must be honest with him. You must tell him who you once were."

Emily fell silent. She knew that would be the answer. Her mind was buzzing with the memories. She brought her hands up to her ears to quiet it. She heard Marcus continue.

"I cannot tell you what to do. I can only give you the information. It is up to you as to what you do with that information. Now, there are a few minor loose ends."

Bringing her hands back down, Emily looked questioningly at Marcus, "Loose ends?"

"Yes...or as you put it, 'broken bridges' that need to be fixed."

"It's really rather frightening that you know everything that I've said and done throughout my lifetime, Marcus. Is there some big screen somewhere that you watch me on?"

Marcus laughed, though Emily did not share in it. "No, dear, there's not. We don't sit in lounge chairs with popcorn watching you. We see little snippets of time and the information comes to us. We don't see everything you're doing but we know what you've done."

"Well, at least now I know you're not watching me shower, so that's one good thing." Emily sighed and then straightened herself up. "So, what are the loose ends?"

"You already know one of them. Lyle Kettering. I'm not sure if his book can be stopped. You will need to prepare yourself in the event it comes out. Some people will try to find you for comments and media fodder, not to mention the people you angered during that time. Your sister was right, Emily. You didn't do a very good job of hiding yourself. Changing your hair and last name was not enough. It won't take a journalist worth his salt very long to find you."

"I know but it's worked so far." She turned back to the vanity mirror and picked up her brush again. "I didn't want to leave the city. I love this city. Maybe I should have. Maybe I should have changed my first name as well but it was my grandmother's middle name and I didn't want to give it up. If the book comes out and someone finds me, I'll face it. I'll own it. Is that all?"

Marcus leaned back in his chair. "You're a strong person, Emily. There's no doubt you will own whatever revelations come from the book. You're also very perceptive. That's not all. You left one thing go that has bewildered us all. Why, Emily, did you never pursue finding and prosecuting the person who pushed you into the street and caused the subsequent coma?"

Once again, Emily looked at Marcus through the mirror, though she didn't hesitate in responding, "Because, on some level, I thought I had deserved it."

Nodding, Marcus stood up. Emily turned and rose to her feet as well. He walked over to her and gave her a brief hug. When he stood back, he gave her a small smile.

"I would rethink that, if I were you." With that, he turned and began to walk from the room. "Now, go and enjoy your dinner but don't forget what we've talked about here."

"You're not going to wipe my memory?"

Stopping at the door, Marcus turned around, "No, not this time. You will keep your memories of that night and you will keep your memories of me. You have free will, Emily. I cannot force you to do one thing or the other. Whatever you do with what you've learned here this evening is completely up to you and you alone."

Emily watched as Marcus left. She sank back down into her chair and sat silently for a few minutes trying to organize and make sense of her thoughts. She knew she would have to tell Ronan the truth, but it wouldn't be tonight. She had to process and think through everything first. Tonight, she decided, she was going to put this on hold and, as Marcus instructed, enjoy the evening ahead of her. She hoped.

Her hand was still shaking as she once again picked up her foundation bottle and began to apply her makeup.

Ronan

"So, she turns around and points to the other side of the room and asks why we can't just remove the whole closet in one piece and move it over there."

The sound of Emily's laugh brightened Ronan's evening. They were just finishing dinner, during which he had regaled her with stories of some of his more extravagant clients.

"Did you tell her you were sorry, but you left your magic wand in your other toolbox along with your rabbit and top hat?"

This time Ronan chuckled, "No. No, I did not. I was a bit more technical than that."

Dinner had gone smoothly, Ronan thought. The conversation came easily, it felt as if they'd done this a thousand times before. He had to remind himself at times that this was their first official date. They had covered a range of topics from movies to current events to the stories of his clients. There was no awkward lull as one topic seemed to flow seamlessly into the next. Emily seemed to be relaxed and Ronan found, much to his delight, she seemed to share the same odd sense of humor he had.

As he poured more wine into both their glasses, he said, "We covered movies, television, books, and I've told you enough about my clients. Tell me about you, now."

"Oh," Emily laughed again, "I would love to tell you about a few of my clients. Trust me, some of their stories would make you laugh until you cried but you know that I can't. On the flip side, there are some clients whose stories would make your heart break."

"I don't doubt that. What made you get into psychology?"

Ronan noticed Emily hesitate a bit before answering. "I'm not really sure," she started and then stopped, seemed to regroup, and then continue. "I think it was the fact that years ago I ran into someone who I thought had relatively easy problems to solve but, as it turned out, it was much more than that. The mind had fascinated me before that, but it was then that I realized how it could play tricks on a person, how it can malfunction, for lack of a better term, and throw people into a pit of depression they can't see a way out of. I realized that if this person was like that then how many other people were out there with the same issue and that's when the passion to help those people was ignited."

"Did you help this person you ran into?"

Ronan again noticed a bit of hesitation before she answered. "I'd like to think so."

"So, you started a clinic? That's impressive. Actually, that is one of the things I wanted to talk to you about. You keep your rates low and while I think that is extremely admirable, how do you stay in business? How do you keep qualified therapists on staff?"

Emily smiled and took a sip of wine before responding. "I keep the rates low because I believe that everyone should have access to mental healthcare. I think it's vital that mental issues be seen the same way as any other medical issue. Unfortunately, insurance companies are not quite on board with that train of thought, yet. The average person can't afford some of the rates that are being charged out there, but they need the help. I'm not going to lie, it wasn't easy, but I found a way, an investor of sorts, and over the last couple years we've managed to not only keep the doors open in Brooklyn but also expand. We could charge more, yes, but our reputation grew mostly by word of mouth. We are, and will remain, the most qualified clinic with the most reasonable prices. I don't hire anyone who doesn't share that vision. They have to possess a passion for helping people in need and not a passion for a Park Avenue penthouse."

"I wish everyone possessed your passion to help people in need. I think the world would be a much better place. Maybe I should rethink my profession."

Ronan was surprised by Emily's reaction. "Don't you dare!" she exclaimed loudly and then lowered her voice. "You have a passion and you're following that passion. You turned what you love to do and what you're good at into an entire business. Not many people can say that, can they?"

"No, they can't," Ronan replied. "And yes, I do love what I do, especially the furniture. I just meant, in comparison, you're out there helping people and making a difference. I'm just giving them a place to sit or something to put their clothes in."

"Ronan, you do the same thing I do, and you don't even see it. You help people by not over-charging them. You could double the price of your furniture and it would sell, there's no doubt about that. You don't. You could charge more for your renovations. I know because, as you already know, I signed your quote. I know you could charge more but you don't. You *are* helping people, and you don't even realize it. We're not that much different. I work and help with my mind; you work and help with your hands. At the end of the day, people benefit from our services and that's what it's all about."

At a loss for words, Ronan simply looked at Emily and shook his head. He straightened himself in his chair and leaned on the table, never taking his eyes off her. "You are an amazing woman, Emily Walton."

"Not really," came the reply, "just observant."

"No," Ronan argued, "you're more than that." He noticed she lowered her eyes. "You don't believe that, do you?"

Emily looked up and returned his level stare. "Do you believe that *you're* amazing?"

"That's a bit different," Ronan replied. "I'm an average guy. I work with my hands. I'm not rich. I don't have a college degree. I enjoy the simple things in life. I was broken at one time, and I can't say I'm completely fixed but I'm on my way there. I'd rather stay in and watch an old black and white movie than go to the theater. I'd rather read a novel than see an opera. I'd rather have a conversation with someone who stimulates me and makes me think than go to horse races. I'm not sure any of that makes me amazing."

"It all does. I've met a lot of people in my life and I'm here to say that you are, indeed, incredible. Not only did you pull yourself up, have the strength and courage to ask for the help you needed, but you did the work and created your own successful business. You make people comfortable, you listen, you empathize. I can see that beautiful, caring soul underneath the calluses. It's why you fixate on the state of the country. You yearn for a better place for your niece to grow up in."

"Well, that part's true," Ronan replied. "I do worry about this country. Something you said the other night has stuck with me, though. You said countries don't find peace, people do."

Emily nodded and replied, "It's true. We will never find peace if we keep waiting for the country to find it. Not every problem is ours to fix. We have to find our own peace and help others to find theirs. We can engage in activism, we can use our voices and use our votes but at the end of the day, we have to find our own way of making our lives peaceful. No one, especially the government, is going to do it for us. Name a time the country was at peace with itself. In fact, I'll treat you to an elaborate dinner at Rosie O'Grady's if you can name one."

"After World War II," Ronan said confidently and then hesitated. "Wait, no, there was segregation."

Emily nodded. "Don't say the 1950s. That was the Korean War and McCarthyism."

"The early 60s. I can't think of anything there."

Emily shook her head. "The Cuban missile crisis. JFK's assassination. Let's not forget there was still segregation."

Ronan sighed, "Right, how could I forget JFK? Okay, the summer of love?"

"You mean in the middle of Vietnam, the Stonewall Riots, protests, and segregation was replaced by sundown laws."

"There has to be a time. Okay, 1900?"

"When women didn't have the right to vote?"

"Damn. Okay, 1910?"

Emily hesitated. Ronan could see her searching her brain. He thought he had her until she announced, "Ah! The race riots that were started when a black boxer beat a white boxer in a match. Not to mention women still didn't have the right to vote."

Ronan leaned back again. "I concede. No dinner for me. You're right. The country really has never been at peace with itself. I may have lost dinner, but I'm not losing hope. At some point this country has to get its act together."

He heard Emily chuckle, "Well, don't give up on dinner yet." He gave her a smile before she continued. "Like I said, it's up to us to find our own peace with our lives. Once we achieve that, we help others find theirs. We build bridges with our neighbors based on common ground. We connect with people of other races, cultures, religions and we learn from them as they learn from us. Bridges go both ways, we need to stop being stuck on one end."

"The country would definitely be better off with more bridges, the physical kind and the ones between people."

Emily lifted her glass, "Here, here." She finished off her wine and set her glass down. This, Ronan thought, was what he had missed more than anything. Conversations about everything and nothing, about important subjects and silly nonsense. He knew with Emily he could talk about anything; express any feeling and she would listen.

Ronan suggested moving to the living room, where they finished off the rest of the wine and spent nearly two hours in lighter conversation where they made each other laugh, teased each other, and discovered more about each other. It was when Ronan asked about her childhood that he noticed Emily intentionally looked at the clock and announced it was getting late.

"I sort of skipped out on some of my work this afternoon," she said. "I have to go into the office tomorrow and catch up on the billing. Jean will not be happy with me if I don't hand it to her neatly finished so she can type everything up and get it in the mail."

Ronan nodded, "I have work of my own to get done, too. I didn't notice the time." He stood up, gathered the glasses, and walked them to the sink as Emily retrieved her coat and bag.

Standing at the door, Ronan was only sure of two things. The first was that he didn't want her to leave. He wanted to sweep her into his arms and take her to his bed. He wanted to wake up with her in the morning and make her breakfast. The second was that he knew she had to leave. Whatever happened between them, he wanted Emily to be comfortable and on the same page he was every step of the way. He knew from the few times she hesitated, and her evasion talking about her childhood, she wasn't quite there yet.

"Emily, I had a wonderful time tonight. I hope we can do this again."

His heart lightened when he saw the smile cross her face and she replied, "I'm counting on it."

He leaned in and kissed her, a deeper, more passionate kiss than they'd had on the bridge. He felt Emily lean into him and heard the soft murmur escape her throat. Ronan wanted to burn this moment into his memory. This was the woman he was going to spend the rest of his life with. There was no doubt in his mind.

Emily

Sitting at her desk, trying to concentrate on the papers in front of her, Emily couldn't stop thinking about Ronan. The previous evening had been more than she had expected. She couldn't remember being with a man where the conversation didn't end after 15 minutes, and the 'date' didn't end in the middle of the night with her quietly getting dressed and leaving before he woke up. She had always been in control of where, when, and how long her relationships would last. If they could be called relationships.

Leaving Ronan's apartment last night, she realized she was not in control of this. If she were to follow this into a relationship, she knew it would be a partnership. She wouldn't be the one dictating everything. Ronan wasn't like the other men. She was interested in his thoughts, his dreams, his opinions on things.

More than that, for the first time in her adult life, she had spent hours alone with a man and she had felt safe. She wasn't on guard; she wasn't closing herself off. She talked more to him than she had to every other man combined. Emily knew, however, that she was going to have to tell him the truth. She was aware he had noticed the couple of times she hesitated answering questions and it was quite obvious she side-stepped answering him about her childhood by saying it was late.

Picking up the papers, Emily tried to focus on them. Her mind wandered back to telling Ronan her real identity. She put the papers back down in a rush, several of them fluttering to the floor. She bent down to pick them up. As she sat back up, she was momentarily startled to find Marcus sitting in one of the chairs on the other side of her desk.

"I thought I told you to give me a heads up when you decided to visit."

Marcus only smiled back at her.

Emily arranged the papers neatly and set them back down.

Eyeing Marcus, she wasn't sure why he was back so soon. She waited for him to speak but he seemed to be waiting on her. She cleared her throat and looked down at the papers again. She thought about telling him she had work to do so this wasn't a good time.

Finally, she heard Marcus speak, "You have questions."

She looked up but didn't reply right away. There were some questions that had gone through her mind, but she was sure she wouldn't get a straight answer from Marcus. She never did. It still wasn't clear to her who or what he was. She decided to start there.

"Can you finally tell me who you are?"

She saw Marcus give a kind of snort before replying, "Why is that important? I'm here. I already told you, if you want to think of me as a guardian angel that is perfectly fine. Emily, at some point it will all become clear to you, trust me. Let's just focus on the matters at hand."

Emily shook her head. She should have known better. Rolling her eyes, she asked, "Why are you here?"

"Because you have questions."

Hesitating for a moment, she decided to go ahead. "How will he take it if I tell him the truth?"

"That you were once Emily Corbyn? I can't say. I told you; everyone has free will and we don't interfere with that. He will react the way reacts. He will do with that information whatever he chooses to do. I can't tell you what that will be."

Emily sighed. She should have foreseen that answer. Marcus had told her several times before they didn't interfere with free will. It was her hope, though, that he would have some glimpse into the future and give her some hint as to what might happen. A thought struck her.

"You can't tell me because you don't know what will happen or you *won't* tell me because it's against the rules?"

Marcus did not reply. He only folded his hands in front of him and leaned back further into the chair.

"Damn it, Marcus. You said you were here because I had questions. If that's the case, why won't you answer them?"

"I'm sorry I didn't answer your first question to your satisfaction, but I did answer it. The last question is irrelevant."

Emily lowered her head and began to rub her forehead. Without looking back up, she asked, "My connection to Ronan is so strong that I can feel myself spending my life with him. I know the initial feeling was because some part of me remembered that night on the bridge. I understand that, but this feeling…that I'm supposed to be with him…is it fate? What is it?"

"What is it that you tell your patients? You tell them that they should always trust their instincts and their intuition. If your instincts are telling you that, maybe you should listen."

She looked up to see Marcus giving her a knowing look, one eyebrow raised and a slight smirk on his lips. The urge to slap the smirk off his face came over her. Instead, she laughed. He was correct, that is exactly what she tells her patients, with one exception.

"You know if one of my patients told me this story, I would not suggest they dive feet first into it right away. I do tell them to trust their instincts, but this? This is a whole different ball game."

Marcus gave a short laugh. "I don't think you will ever hear a story quite like this from one of your patients, though. Your instincts are telling you something, aren't they?"

Nodding, she picked up a pen, lowered her eyes and began to play with it. There was something else that she was turning over in her mind. "You said Ronan won't remember that night on the bridge unless I tell him the truth."

"Correct."

"What would happen if he found out some other way? What if someone found out and told him? Or…the book comes out?"

"Emily, look at me." Emily noted the serious tone in Marcus' voice. She lifted her eyes and met his. "It has to be you. If he finds out any other way, he will not remember. You are the one that must tell him."

Emily closed her eyes. She knew that would be the answer. It frightened her to think how Ronan might react. The fear of him rejecting her overwhelmed her. The truth had to come out or their relationship would not survive. She knew this as a therapist and as a woman. Emily always thought of herself as someone who could face and deal with anything. This, however, scared her; a feeling she was not used to.

When she opened her eyes again, Marcus was gone.

Michelle

"Spill it, Ronan!" Since she had walked into his loft, she had not let up on him. Michelle wanted details of his date with Emily.

"I told you; it was good. Now, please stop, Michelle. Where's June, by the way?"

Noting the exasperation in his voice, Michelle decided to back off a bit. "Okay, no more questions. June is with Jack's parents. They wanted to take her to the Bronx Zoo today. I could have gone with them, but Jack's father drives me insane, so I decided to come here and find out how things went but it looks like I would have more luck getting answers from the zebras."

"That's probably true," Ronan responded without looking at her.

Frustrated, Michelle asked, "Why won't you tell me? You used to tell me about these things." She saw Ronan put down his sander and run his forearm across his forehead. Michelle knew she was pushing him, but she was too curious to let it go.

"I don't know, Michelle," Ronan replied. "I think, for now, I just want to keep this between Emily and myself. I'm hoping things will continue to go well but, we'll see. That's really all I feel like saying right now."

"Okay," Michelle answered, disappointed. "I get it. But you know," she continued, "I could always walk down to Safe Haven and meet her myself. Maybe she'll give me more details."

"Nice try. She's not down there today. It's Saturday. I'm going down later, though, to start some of the work."

Michelle fell silent as she watched Ronan return to the side table he was working on. Her mind turned over all she knew about Emily Walton, which wasn't much. There had to be something special about her, though, if Ronan wasn't willing to talk about her. She was used to Ronan discussing almost everything with her. For him to not want to discuss it signaled that Emily was different from the others. She went back to the same thought she had the other day.

"I still think it's odd that right after she told Jim not to worry, Corbyn decided to buy the building." She heard the sigh as Ronan turned off the sander. He took his gloves and goggles off and rubbed his temples. Michelle saw his frustration and almost regretted what she'd said.

"You're entitled to think that, Michelle. There could be several valid explanations for it. What we do know is she runs Safe Haven. She doesn't work for Corbyn. Okay?"

Michelle nodded, "I'm sorry. I shouldn't push." She tried to reverse course, "I will say, though, that it's good to see you interested in someone. I mean really interested. You should bring her to our house for dinner."

Ronan held up his hands, "Slow down, Michelle. It's been one date. While you're here, why don't you make your visit useful and type up some of those quotes? We have three more requests. One is for a complete first floor remodel for a house in Brooklyn. There's also some invoicing that needs to be done."

Sitting at her desk, Michelle began reviewing the first quote. She looked over at Ronan and she realized that her comment may have planted a seed. Once again, she regretted saying it. She said a tiny prayer that there was nothing to it.

Ronan

After putting the first coat of stain on the side table, Ronan left Michelle to finish up the quotes and invoices and went down to begin the work on Safe Haven. He was relieved to be out of the loft while she was there. He adored Michelle but what she had said about Emily and Jim tugged at the back of his mind and that annoyed him.

Emily had left the key to the offices when she had left the signed quote in his mailbox. He let himself in, set down his toolbox and crowbar and looked around. He decided to start with pulling off the wood paneling first. Ronan found that this type of physical work was good when it came to clearing his mind.

He was almost done with what he assumed would be the receptionist/waiting room area when he heard the familiar voice behind him.

"Is this what they mean when they say things get worse before they get better?"

He spun around to find Emily standing in the doorway. He was aware of how sweaty and dusty he looked as well as the mess of discarded paneling laying haphazardly in the middle of the room. He was also aware that there were rusty nails and jagged edges among the mess.

"Stay there," Ronan warned, "It's not safe to walk around until I get this cleaned up." He took off his goggles and mask and carefully made his way to the door.

"I wasn't expecting you to be here," Emily said, "I was only stopping by to see if anything had been dropped off. I was expecting some of the office equipment."

"I wasn't planning on it, but I decided to come down and get a head start," Ronan looked back over the room. "Don't worry. I'll have this cleaned up by Monday morning. Although, you might want to hold off on any more deliveries until I get the paneling out of the back offices."

Emily came further in and took a seat on one of the windowsills. She looked around at the shambles the outer office had become. Ronan came up and took a seat beside her. "Don't worry. It will be exactly as you imagined by the time I'm finished."

"I don't doubt that one bit," she replied.

As she continued to survey the mess, Ronan debated on whether the thought that had been nagging at him should be approached with her. He decided it was best to get it out of the way instead of having any doubts lingering.

"Emily, I need to ask you something."

"Sure. Ask me anything."

"Well," he hesitated a moment. "So, you told Jim to let everyone in the building know that we had nothing to worry about as far as getting evicted and all of that."

"That's true," she replied.

"Then we find out that Corbyn reached out and offered to buy the building. Did you know that? Do you know people at Corbyn?"

Ronan noticed that Emily stiffened and drew in her breath. She looked down and seemed to be gathering her thoughts before she answered.

"Our families were close," she finally said. "As you know, real estate development is a huge part of their business. I've known Rob for a long time. I spoke to him about it, yes. He agreed to acquire the building and do some upgrades, but everything will remain as it is. They're not going to take advantage of the expansion next year."

"Is that because of you? I mean, it doesn't make sense for them to do that when using the expansion would benefit them financially."

"Partly because I asked but also because…" she stopped and let out a breath. "They're not the same, Ronan. Trust me. They'll stick to this deal."

Ronan didn't reply at first. He thought back on his conversations with Michelle. Then he looked back at Emily and asked, "Do you know Emily Corbyn?"

"Yes," came the clipped reply.

"Do you know what happened to her?"

"Yes," another short answer.

Ronan noticed that Emily had not relaxed. In fact, if possible, she seemed to harden more, and he wondered if there was more to the relationship than simply being family friends. "Do you know where she is?"

Emily looked Ronan in the eyes and responded, "She's closer than you think she is."

Ronan nodded. "Any truth to the rumor that she had a breakdown?"

A short chuckle escaped from Emily before she said, "No, there was no breakdown."

"Michelle noted the two of you share a name, but you couldn't be more different. That Emily hurt people; people I know. You help people."

Once again, he heard Emily take a sharp intake of breath. She reached for his hand and he gave it to her. He had the strong sense that something important and consequential was coming.

"Ronan," she started, "there's something I need to tell–"

"There you are!" Ronan looked to see Michelle coming in the door. He shot her a look that he hoped conveyed it was not a good time to interrupt. Either Michelle didn't catch it or she ignored it. "I'm on my way out and I wanted to find you first. You must be Emily. I'm Michelle, Ronan's sister."

Ronan looked on as Michelle came toward Emily with her hand extended. Emily took her hand and acknowledged that she was, indeed,

Emily Walton.

"It's so nice to meet you," Michelle went on. "Ronan has had nothing but wonderful things to say about you."

He noticed Emily glance his way before turning back to Michelle. "That's good to know," she smiled, "he speaks very highly of you as well."

Michelle smiled at Ronan but before Ronan could say a word, Michelle turned back to Emily. "My big brother here thinks I'd be out of line by asking this, but I don't care. Why don't the two of you come over to my house tomorrow after church? I'll make a roast. We'll get to know each other."

Ronan closed his eyes and silently cursed Michelle. He opened them and looked at Emily. "It's okay if you don't want to. Michelle gets a bit ahead of herself sometimes."

To his surprise, Emily replied, "No, it's fine. I think that would be wonderful. Thank you, Michelle. What can I bring?"

"Oh, nothing. Nothing," Michelle was delighted. "Let's say one o'clock?"

Ronan and Emily agreed on the time and Michelle went on her way. Ronan apologized to Emily for the interruption and the invitation, but Emily didn't seem disturbed by either one. He already knew, somehow, that Emily would fit seamlessly into his life, but he didn't want her to feel rushed. He especially had not wanted Michelle to rush the family introduction. It amazed him that Emily not only seemed to take it in stride, but she seemed to relax a bit. It made him feel a bit guilty to go back to their earlier conversation.

"So, what were you about to say before my lovely sister interrupted us?"

Emily gave a small laugh. "Actually, she *is* a lovely person. It's clear you love her very much. I also think tomorrow is more than an invitation to a roast dinner. It's an interview. She wants to see if I'm good enough for the position of her brother's girlfriend."

Ronan agreed with that statement but did not let her get away without answering his question. "What did you need to tell me?"

He noticed her smile fade, and she was quiet for a few beats before answering. "It was nothing important. It can wait."

184

Emily

The cab ride on the way to Michelle's house in Jackson Heights was filled with laughter and easy banter even though Emily had a knot of guilt gnawing at her. She knew she should have told Ronan the truth when she'd had the opportunity, but she was taken with Michelle's friendliness. As she was getting ready earlier, she made herself a promise; she would tell Ronan before the day was over. Her thought was to ask him to her apartment after dinner. Hopefully, he would be able to see how far she had distanced herself from the person she'd once been.

"I can't believe you agreed to this," Ronan said.

"Why not?" Emily asked. "Your sister was very nice. I understand she's very curious because, I'm assuming, you haven't dated much. She only wants what's best for you."

As Ronan shrugged and gave a little smile, Emily thought back to her conversation with Marcus. She wanted this to work with Ronan. The feeling they were meant to be together only grew as each minute passed; she felt it in the depths of her soul. She knew she had to tell him before he found out any other way. The sooner the better, before the relationship progressed beyond dinners and meeting sisters.

"No," she heard Ronan say and snapped back to the present, "I haven't dated all that much. I wasn't very interested. I told you. I knew you were out there somewhere. I never told Michelle that, so as far as she could see, I wasn't having much luck with women. She's been a great sister and friend, especially these past several years. I don't know what I would have done without her, but she can be a little overbearing."

Emily corrected him, "You mean over-protective. There's a difference."

"Oh, no," Ronan laughed, "I meant overbearing. I love her but if she wants to know something or has an idea about something, she won't let up. She'll back off for a bit but, sure enough, she'll come back around to it. I need to ask you something, though."

"What's that?"

"Why do you insist on taking cabs everywhere? The subway would have been a much cheaper way to get there. This fare is going to be ridiculous."

Emily bit her lip and hesitated a moment. "I have a fear of being trapped in spaces that have no immediate exit." It was the truth. The only part she omitted was it was a result of the assault she experienced.

"Oh," Ronan replied. "We all have a fear of something. Are you claustrophobic?"

"Something like that. Tell me about June and Jack," Emily was eager to change the subject. Besides, she did want to know as much as she could about Ronan's family before meeting them.

As Ronan filled her in on Jack, with a thinly veiled warning about some of his more misogynistic ways, Emily bristled slightly. She had dealt with men like that over the years, and she was never one to hide or downplay her accomplishments. Yet in the best interest of making a good impression on Ronan's family, she decided to deflect any conversation away from herself and focus on the others.

June was a different subject. Based on the way Ronan was describing her, Emily couldn't wait to meet the little girl described as vivacious, inquisitive, and smart. It warmed Emily's heart the way Ronan talked about his niece. It was clear they had a close relationship, and that Ronan was proud of June. The idea that Ronan might someday want children of his own flitted through her mind. She surprised herself when she realized the thought hadn't scared her.

As they got out of the cab in front of Michelle's house, Emily felt Ronan reach for her hand. She looked up to see his reassuring smile and, yet again, she knew this was exactly where she was supposed to be;

by Ronan's side.

Michelle greeted them at the door, Ronan gave her the bottle of wine they brought with them, and Emily could hear June running down the steps shouting for her uncle before she saw her. She couldn't suppress her smile and quiet laugh as Ronan swept the girl into his arms and swung her around.

Setting June back down, Ronan turned her toward Emily. "June, I'd like you to meet Emily."

"You're pretty, just like my Mommy said you were," June smiled at her.

Emily bent down to get eye-level with the girl. She tapped her on the nose and said, "Thank you, but you are prettier. I hear you like to help your Uncle Ronan make things out of wood."

"I do!" June exclaimed and launched into a commentary of her favorite things to make and how her uncle helps her when it's time to use the sharp tools.

"That's enough, June," Michelle interrupted, "Let Emily and Ronan come in and sit down. Why don't you go get your daddy?" She ushered June out of the room and came back looking more than a bit flustered. "Dinner should be ready in about 15 minutes. I don't know what's keeping Jack."

"Relax, Michelle," Ronan said. "It's just us. There's no need to overdo it or get fancy."

"I know. I wasn't expecting church to be longer than usual this morning. Then Jack's mother almost invited herself over but, thankfully, I managed to get around that. June has been bouncing off the walls all morning. You know how excited she gets when you come over. Then, of course, Mom had to call just as I was starting everything. You need to call her, you know."

"I will," Ronan replied. "Calm down; you're off the phone, I'll take care of June, we're here and we'll help you get everything out.

"Absolutely," Emily chimed in. "What can I help you with?"

Before Michelle could answer they heard the sound of heavy footsteps coming down the stairs, followed by the lighter sound of June's. They heard a man's voice call from the dining room. "Ronan, I'm assuming you'll take a beer. Can I get your lady a glass of wine?"

Ronan looked to Emily, who nodded, and he called back, "Yeah, that'll be fine, Jack. Thanks." He turned to Emily again and shrugged.

"You'll get used to him," Michelle added.

June, carrying several books, ran back into the living room and straight to Ronan. He bent down to inspect and discuss them as Michelle gave Emily a rundown of what was on the menu and insisted that no help was needed. Emily didn't care what was being served. She was wrapped up in the atmosphere of family. She had never experienced this kind of family life. Even when she spent time at Jean's with her son, it was always a birthday or a holiday. This was everyday family life; church, a child, Sunday dinner. It was a new experience she was taking in and, so far, she couldn't imagine being anywhere else.

They were interrupted as Jack entered the room. Ronan stood up to accept his beer and as she turned to meet Michelle's husband, Emily realized she could not have prepared herself for what happened next. She froze and her heart began to race. Jack was standing a few feet from her. His arm extended to offer her the glass of wine but he, too, was frozen. Emily realized he was studying her face, and it would only take a few seconds.

Withdrawing his arm, his eyes widening in recognition, Jack shouted, "What the hell is this?"

Without thinking, Emily turned to stand in front of Ronan, facing him. "Ronan, we need to leave. We need to leave right now! Please. Take me to the bridge and I will explain everything, but we need to leave. Now!"

With that, Emily ran from the house, hoping Ronan was following her.

Ronan

Unsure of what was happening, Ronan set his beer down and ran after Emily. Catching up with her on the sidewalk, he could see she was frightened.

"What's going on? Emily, talk to me. What was that?"

"I will tell you everything but please get a cab. Please!"

"Emily, I'll have to call for one. Calm down, talk to me."

Ronan was stunned when Emily turned and began walking down the street. He caught up and began walking beside her. "This is my fault," she said softly. "I shouldn't have…this was a mistake. I should have…oh, my God…where's a phone booth?"

Taking her arm, Ronan stopped walking and made Emily face him. "Stop. I need you to tell me what's going on."

He watched as Emily took several deep breaths before replying. "Ronan, I need you to trust me right now. I need to get out of here. Please take me somewhere where we can call a cab. I promise I will tell you everything you need to know. Please, take me to the bridge."

Instinctively, Ronan put his arm around Emily, and they walked to the nearest main street, found a phone booth, and called a cab. Emily remained quiet and Ronan had the same feeling he had yesterday; something important and monumental was about to happen. Emily's reaction to Jack had him worried. He could clearly see she had been frightened when she fled the house. While she was calmer now, he could feel how upset she was. He needed to know how Jack could have this effect on her.

The cab dropped them off on the Brooklyn side of the bridge. They walked in silence as Ronan let Emily lead him to the familiar spot closer to the Manhattan side. His mind raced with possible scenarios to explain what happened but none that made sense. How did Jack know Emily? What did he do that would cause that reaction from her?

When Emily reached the spot where they had talked the other night, she turned to face the water. He stood beside her at the rail, arm around her. He would give her as much time as she needed. He knew she would tell him. He would listen. They would work it out.

After several minutes, Emily began to speak. "I need you to remember our conversation from the other night. I need you to remember that people can change."

"I do," Ronan reassured her.

Emily turned to face him. He dropped his arm and watched as she took his hands and looked down at them. He felt her grip them tightly and take another deep breath before looking up. He noticed her eyes had begun to water. He was about to say something, but she shook her head. He waited for her to speak.

"I'm scared, Ronan, but there are things you need to know. Things I need to tell you. I told you about how I changed. I told you I wasn't a very nice person years ago. I worked very hard to become who I am right now, and I did change. When I did, I also changed a few other things. I changed my hair. My natural color isn't red. I'm a brunette."

"Okay, that's…" Ronan started but Emily shook her head again.

"I also changed my last name. The name I was born with was not Emily Walton."

Ronan felt a knot form in his stomach. Though he didn't want it to be said, he knew what she was about to say before the words came out.

"Ronan, I'm Emily Corbyn."

The knot turned in his stomach and he dropped her hands. Taking a few steps back, he ran his hand through his hair and tried to wrap his mind around it. Too many questions were going through his brain, too many thoughts. He took hold of the railing, trying to make sense of it. He felt anger start to rise in his chest and he gripped the railing tighter.

"Ronan, please," he heard Emily say, "I need you to remember."

"Remember what?" he replied in a clipped voice.

He was about to tell her to leave when he felt a rush of something. It was as if a strong wind blew through him. He held tighter to the railing as the memory of that long ago night came back to him. It was vague at first and then it formed into a clear memory. He was getting ready to jump, he heard Emily yell to stop. He remembered it all. Their conversation, their tears, their confessions. He tried to steady himself but just like that night seven years ago, he turned, took a seat and leaned back against the railing.

Clearly seeing her in his memory, sitting next to him, holding him while he wept, letting him get out his dark thoughts, talking him through it, it was all there. The blank space in his memory of that night was filled in. He could hear the words she said to him that night reverberate in his head. What sent his head reeling was the realization that it was her, Emily Walton - Emily Corbyn - who had stopped him from jumping that night.

"It was you," he said without looking up. "You saved me."

He felt Emily sit down beside him, just as she had done that night. "And you saved me."

Ronan didn't reply. He went back over that night in his mind, remembering all that he had told her. He had poured his heart out to her about Carrieann, about losing his job, about feeling useless. It was Emily who had told him the first step was asking for help. It was Emily who had made him see what he was good at, what he could do. It was Emily who stayed with him until Michelle arrived. It was Emily who had been there with him on the lowest, darkest night of his life and had gotten him through it until Michelle could take him home.

Something else struck him. "It was me," he said. "I was the

person you ran into. I'm the one who had the problems you thought were easy but found out weren't. I'm the one that started you thinking there were others out there like me that you could help; the reason you became a psychologist."

"Yes."

Ronan fell silent again. He sat with that knowledge for a few minutes before his mind fell on the things she had confessed to him that night. The conversation about her parents, about her assault and how she had shut herself off from feeling. He understood. He understood why she had become the person she'd been, and he understood that, somehow, he had been the catalyst that helped her to change into the person she was now.

He realized that's why she shifted the conversation the other day from Corbyn to people being able to change. It had been important to her that he knew she had changed. He had been reassuring but, at the time, he hadn't imagined her past being anything he couldn't handle or understand. Being Emily Corbyn was something he wasn't prepared for.

He turned to her slowly, "Why didn't you tell me when we met in your office that day?"

"I didn't know then," Emily replied. "I was like you, remember? It felt like I knew you, but I couldn't remember from where. We both had that feeling. We both knew there was a connection. We both felt that pull that we belonged together. You said it yourself. Now, we both know why."

"When did you remember?"

"Friday. I wanted you to get to know the person I am now before telling you who I was then. Yesterday, when you asked me about the building, I tried to tell you but then Michelle interrupted."

Ronan nodded, "I remember."

"I understand if you don't want to see me anymore but, Ronan," she hesitated and then took his hand. "I want you to know that you saved me that night. More than that, this past week you have opened places inside of me that have been closed for as long as I can remember. I hope that you can find it in your heart to forgive me." Ronan heard the catch in her voice, and he looked up to see the tears beginning to fall. "But I'll understand if you can't."

He reached over and held the side of her head, wiping a few tears away with his thumb. Dropping his hand back in his lap, he held her eyes. "This is a lot to take in."

"I know. I'm sorry."

"Emily, you saved my life that night. You wouldn't let me give up on myself. You forced me to see that I was anything but useless. If you hadn't been there, I wouldn't be here right now. This past week, all I could think about was you. I've been so sure you are the one for me." Ronan stopped. The emotions he was feeling were overwhelming him. He cleared his throat and went on. "We don't have to figure this out today. Maybe we both just need a little time alone to work it out."

Ronan pulled himself to his feet and helped Emily up. He didn't release her hand. He looked into her eyes and the feeling that they were meant to be together crept through him again. She had been honest with him, both that night seven years ago and today. He had too many questions, though, he had things he needed to say, things he wasn't sure he'd be able to work past but, as he said, it didn't have to be today. And then it hit him.

"Emily, was it Jack that assaulted you? He did, didn't he? That's why you ran out, that's why you were so frightened." Ronan could feel anger rising in his chest. In the split second it took to think that, he also envisioned himself confronting the brother-in-law he never really cared for and making him pay.

He saw Emily swallow and brace herself before answering.

"Jack is the person who pushed me into the street, Ronan. He's the reason I was in a coma."

Part Three

November 1982

Emily

Shifting positions under the glaring studio lights, Emily couldn't understand how someone could do this day after day without melting. She looked across the table at Marilyn Dumont, anchor for New York's number one morning news program and noted how calm and cool she remained. Emily mused they must get used to it after a while. She doubted she ever could.

After rejecting on-air interviews over the last several years, she still wasn't sure it had been wise to agree to this one. She preferred print interviews. The printed word remained year after year and could be referenced verbatim. Verbal interviews were often picked apart, clipped to suit a narrative, or twisted based on appearance, silences, or certain words used on the spur of the moment. Still, Emily had agreed. She felt the message needed to be heard and a larger audience reached.

Hearing the person behind the camera do the countdown to return from the commercial break, she straightened her shoulders and folded her hands on the table. She watched as Marilyn shifted and straightened her papers then smiled at the camera. Emily listened as Marilyn gave the viewing audience a recap of their pre-commercial interview before turning toward her once again.

"So, Dr. Byrne, as we had been discussing, your main concern for President Reagan's repeal of the Mental Health Systems Act is that it could result in less effective mental health care."

"It *will* result in less effective mental health care, Marilyn. Without federal funding, many places will be forced to cut back on staff and other needed resources. Additionally, clinics and hospitals will have a difficult time keeping their doors open. Many states will see these institutions closing with many patients having nowhere else to go for the help they need. President Carter gave the field of mental health a much-needed spotlight and the funding was invaluable. Thousands of patients benefited greatly. We, as a country, were making great strides toward making mental health as important as physical health. This repeal has taken us more than just several steps backwards."

"If hospitals closed their doors, wouldn't these patients be able to seek help from other places? A clinic such as yours, perhaps?"

"Unfortunately, not every clinic operates as Safe Haven does nor are there clinics like Safe Haven in every state. There will be far too many people without the tools they need to get by. Not only is mental health not yet covered by health insurance in the same way physical health is, it is still a battle to get things covered at all. Even when they are covered, the coverage is still woefully inadequate. The average American cannot afford to continue seeking the assistance they need."

Emily watched as Marilyn checked her notes, waiting for the next point to defend the appeal. "But, Dr. Byrne, you must know that the Patient's Bill of Rights remains intact. That has not changed regardless of where a patient may live."

Trying to stifle a chuckle as she knew this point would be made, Emily responded, "Yes, Marilyn, it does remain intact. However, a state such as New York may be able to weather the repeal and keep its state hospitals afloat, however, a state such as Mississippi may not be able to shift state funds to its hospitals. We know this. When it comes to health, especially mental health, leaving it to the individual states puts an unnecessary burden on them. Many states simply cannot afford to shift funds away from other necessary areas."

"And you believe the federal government should continue to shift funds away from other necessary areas?"

"Do you feel our health is not a necessary area? Should a government not care about the well-being of its citizenry? It should. In fact, the United States is well behind all other industrialized, first-world countries when it comes to taking care of its citizens both physically and mentally. Marilyn, the writing is on the wall. In the next few years, this country will see a rise in the number of homeless people as a result of state hospitals having to close their doors. Again, thousands upon thousands of people nationwide will have nowhere to go, no family to take care of them. They will end up on the streets. Is that how a government should take care of its people?"

"The vote to repeal was bipartisan, so I would say that members of both parties, not just Republicans, agree the states are more than equipped to take care of their people within their borders. Relying on the federal government for things would be a form of socialism, wouldn't it?"

"Politicians in both parties should be listening to the experts in the field. They should be listening to their constituents. They should not be listening to the CEOs of insurance companies nor should they be using mental health issues as a way to slash the budget when there are many other areas where there is wasteful spending. By the way, social security is a form of socialism but I believe citizens of both parties cash those checks, don't they? Federal highways and fire departments are also a form of socialism. The way to dissuade people from supporting something is to associate it with an "ism", socialism, communism, fascism. It's an old, tiresome trick. This country is heading toward a mentality of every man for himself and that's not a healthy attitude for any country. We should be focusing on the community. When a community takes care of each other, no one needs to worry for they know they will also be taken care of. That's not socialism - or any other kind of ism - that's just common sense and it should be bipartisan.

"As for leaving mental health up to the states, there are far too many states who are not *more than equipped* to take care of mental health issues and, as we know, there are more than just a few states who are governed by people who, sadly, still do not believe that mental health is an issue that requires attention and resources. We know this, too."

"You don't believe people should work to earn things? They should just be taken care of?"

"That's an unnecessary spin. If someone wants a new house, a new car, a television - yes, they should work for it. That's not even a question. I'm not talking about material things here, Marilyn. Of course, people should work to earn things. However, I do not believe both physical and mental healthcare should be solely for people who can afford the best coverage. It should not be a privilege reserved for the well off. Every person should be able to get the care they need regardless of their income."

Once again, Emily watched as Marilyn checked her notes. She anticipated the next point before Marilyn began speaking again.

"You are not a big proponent of Prozac, are you? I would think that with the use of this drug, there would be less need to have people placed in hospitals."

"Prozac is not a cure-all, Marilyn. In fact, I have cautioned against seeing it as a cure for depression over the last year. Prozac is not a cure. What it does, as will the other drugs similar to it that are currently in development, is it restores the chemical balance in the brain. That's in the simplest terms. What it does not do is solve the patient's issues. It helps a patient think more clearly and restores their rational, logical thought but it does not take away their problems. Taking the drug without further treatment does little to help people. Prozac and its successors should not be viewed as a kind of wonder drug that will solve all mental health issues. They simply do not. We have already witnessed this. The research and evidence are already there so, no, Marilyn, it would not reduce the need for state hospitals. Reagan promised when he campaigned he would repeal the Mental Health Systems Act and he managed to get enough Democrats on board. He has taken us backwards in this field and I fear the repercussions will be felt for quite some time if we do not do something to restore the funding for clinics and hospitals nationwide."

Marilyn nodded. "I still have a few more questions, doctor." She turned to the camera. "However, right now we have to take a break but we'll be right back with Dr. Emily Byrne and later we'll be bringing you the latest on the Tylenol murders and how Johnson & Johnson has made their product tamper resistant as it once again becomes available to consumers. We also have Boy George from the new group that's making waves, Culture Club. You don't want to miss it. Stay tuned."

Emily watched as Marilyn took a few beats before exhaling and turning to her. "You certainly are a tough one. You do realize I have to make the counterpoint whether or not I believe it, right?"

"I do," Emily responded. "We are going to end up with more homeless people, Marilyn. Homeless people who are not mentally equipped to take care of themselves. That doesn't speak to a caring country."

"No, it doesn't. I do want to go into your paper on . . ." Marilyn flipped through her notes again.

"Post-traumatic stress," Emily finished.

"Yes. I find that very interesting."

Emily knew that while Marilyn may disagree with the repeal of MHSA, it was clear she did not care very much about its ramifications as they would not directly affect her. She found that to be the case with many people who had the means to get any kind of care they needed with or without insurance coverage. In fact, she found that to be the case with many things. She found more and more that people were uninterested in standing up for anything if it didn't affect them directly. They'd rather ignore it, turn a blind eye to it, rather than do what was needed to help their fellow citizens. She was becoming horrified that the country was entering a very self-centered era where all that mattered to people was themselves and not their community as a whole.

When they returned from the commercial break, Emily was

lobbed easy questions about her work with veterans and post-traumatic stress. It took a few years for the American Psychiatric Association to acknowledge and accept it as a diagnosis but once the research was irrefutable, it was officially entered into the Diagnostic and Statistical Manual in 1980. While it was still a relatively new diagnosis, it provided a much clearer picture and a better treatment plan to patients who had experienced trauma.

Vietnam veterans were no longer being treated for battle fatigue but for the stress and psychological damage that occurred during their tour. It was the same with victims of assault and for patients who had experienced other types of devastating trauma; they were no longer diagnosed as having "adjustment issues". The effects of the trauma did not always materialize immediately following the event. Sometimes it could be weeks or months afterward but the signs of post-traumatic stress were very similar across the spectrum; inability to sleep, feelings of isolation and anxiety, inability to concentrate. These were usually coupled with a fear that the traumatic event is happening again or will happen again. Emily answered these questions with ease and used both her work with veterans and her own experience as core examples.

Citing the suicide rate among Vietnam veterans was a point she wanted to drive home as she was adamant that if mental health was taken as seriously, and put on the same level, as physical health, the vast majority of those veterans would still be alive. She tied in patients with severe depression and thoughts of suicide who often go either misdiagnosed or untreated simply because of the stigma of mental disorders and the reluctance of those in power to see mental illness as an area that needs support, funding, and coverage.

Once the questioning was finished, Emily thought the interview was coming to a close until she was blind-sided with topics she did not know were coming.

"Dr. Byrne, there's a few other things I'd like to talk to you about quickly and then we'll let you go. You made headlines back in '75 for a couple of reasons. One, of course, was Lyle Kettering's book which detailed your time running Corbyn. Your brother, Rob, gave a press conference before the book's release. In fact, I'd like to show a clip of that."

Taken aback, Emily watched as the monitor showed Rob in front of the Corbyn building. She hadn't wanted Rob to do it but on the advice of Tim Jackson, Rob decided to get ahead of the narrative and diminish the book's relevance. She didn't know what part Marilyn was going to show until the tape rolled.

"Emily's journey following her coma reflects the resilience of the human spirit and the transformative power of personal experiences."

Emily thought Rob looked more like a politician than a CEO. He spoke eloquently as a slight breeze went through his hair.

"Understanding what she had previously done, Emily did all she could within her power to atone for her prior actions. That included reaching out to Mr. Kettering, who declined to meet with her. He chose to make a profit off her instead of doing the decent thing and speaking with her. Had he sat down with her he would have immediately seen that the Emily that once ran this company no longer exists. He would have met a woman who is deeply remorseful and eager to make retribution. Instead, he chose money over humanity. You see, through her actions, Emily has exemplified the capacity to change, to transform oneself, to find new passions and most importantly, work tirelessly to improve the lives of others. That is what she has done, is doing now and will continue to do. Since recovering from her coma, Emily has devoted herself to helping those in need of mental health services. In doing so, she has improved the lives of countless people. She has become an inspiration. I know that for many people, she is a source of hope in a world where compassion and understanding have become paramount."

The tape ended and Marilyn turned toward Emily. "You spoke of spinning things earlier, Dr. Byrne. However, it seems your brother did quite a spin there. He succeeded in making you a sympathetic figure and Lyle the villain when, in actuality, Lyle was really the victim. Don't you agree?"

"Well, Marilyn, I don't see how rehashing old news from years ago does anything to help with the topics I was asked to discuss here. I would call this an ambush with material I had no warning was going to be presented. As for my brother, Rob, there was nothing in his speech regarding Lyle that was not true. I did, in fact, try to reach out to him a few times. He declined. He chose to, as my brother said, make money instead. There is no spin there."

"Okay, but was Lyle not a victim of –"

"I've answered every question about the book seven years ago in various interviews. That part of my life is closed now. Do you have any other questions regarding the topics we've discussed earlier?"

Emily noticed Marilyn bristle but quickly regain composure. "There is something else. Your brother was correct in that it seems you *have* become an inspiration, Dr. Byrne. Your concern for the well-being of people, not only here in New York but across the country, is quite apparent. Standing up against the repeal of the MHSA shows that. However, you have a family now. In fact, you have a young son at home. How will you continue to find the time?"

Emily smiled. "Do you ask men that question?" She saw Marilyn flinch slightly before she continued. "It's curious that only women are asked about working while having a family while men aren't. Don't worry, Marilyn, I'll let you off the hook. I have a wonderful husband and we have a marriage that is a 50-50 partnership. That's how I find the time."

"Wonderful!" Marilyn responded. "I don't think very many women have that kind of luxury in a marriage. One last question. Also in the headlines several years ago was the arrest and trials of Jack Beaumont. I won't go into details as we are all familiar with the story. He went to jail for, among many other things that had been uncovered, causing the accident which resulted in your coma. He is coming up for parole very soon. Our sources tell us his chances of getting that parole are fairly good. How do you feel about that?"

Not expecting Jack to be mentioned during the interview, Emily felt her stomach turn.

Ronan

"Hear that, Michelle? I'm a wonderful husband," Ronan lifted his coffee cup toward Michelle and smiled broadly.

"I think Emily was right. It was a little shitty she brought up the book and tried to corner Emily into saying Lyle was a victim. I mean, yeah, he did lose his job, that part is true but he didn't have to write a revenge book." Michelle grabbed her cup and lifted it toward Ronan. "But, yes, Ro. You *are* a wonderful husband."

Turning back to the television, they both fell silent when they heard the last question put to Emily. Ronan looked over at Michelle, whose face had turned to stone. The first few years after Jack's arrest had been difficult on Michelle. Ronan helped Michelle stay in the house in Brooklyn for the first year but after all of the revelations came out, Michelle no longer wanted the house. She no longer wanted any trace of Jack in her life.

During that first year Ronan had also been working things out with Emily, though, it had not taken him very long to overcome the fact that she had once been Emily Corbyn. He understood her. He had understood it all that day on the bridge when he remembered everything. Ronan knew that the trauma she had endured had shaped her into that person. He also knew the person she was now and how much work she had done to face her past, become the person she wanted to be and to reshape her future. Having been through, and still going through, his own journey, he more than admired her for the strength she possessed on hers.

When Michelle no longer wanted to stay in the Brooklyn house, it was Emily who suggested Michelle and June move into the loft. Ronan readily agreed. With Michelle in the loft, they spent more time discussing the business and, reluctantly, Ronan had agreed to expand. After Ronan had proposed to, and married, Emily, Michelle and June moved into Emily's apartment.

Ronan had been more than grateful to Michelle for her perseverance in expanding the business as it grew to the point where they rented a small office space on the bottom floor of the building. With the business taking off, it enabled Michelle to earn enough money to pick up the rent on the apartment.

It was in their office where they were now watching Emily's interview on the small black and white television Ronan had put in his private office. Ronan noticed Michelle's frozen expression, not taking her eyes off the screen. Just as she had been there for him after his breakdown, he had been there for her through the arrest, the discovery, the trials, and the eventual divorce. There had been many late nights of sitting with Michelle, comforting her, while she quietly sobbed, feared for June's future or, at times, screamed her hatred for the man she had once loved. Ronan was proud of Michelle for landing on her feet, raising June and continuing to move forward when many others might have crumbled.

He turned his attention back to the television when he heard Emily begin to speak.

"Well, Marilyn, I don't feel anything. It is up to the justice system to determine if he has paid his debt to society. Thank you for having me on the show. I appreciate the time to discuss the ramifications of the repeal of the MHSA with you."

Ronan turned it off and looked at Michelle. "Are you okay?" He watched as Michelle took a breath, cleared her throat, and shook her head slightly. He walked over and put his arms around her. They had already known Jack's parole hearing was coming up and Ronan knew the stress it was putting on Michelle.

After a few minutes Michelle pulled away. "You know, just when I think I'm okay and can handle everything, it sneaks up again and hits me." She reached for a tissue. "I know we've talked about this so many times already but . . ."

"It's okay, Michelle," Ronan said, "Talk as much as you want."

"I didn't know how unhappy I was back then. I thought everything was fine and that's how life was. It wasn't until we moved in with you and really got to work. Then watching you and Emily together I realized how empty that life was. I really was just going through the motions and being a dutiful wife like we were all brainwashed to be. I never thought to question him. I never thought to look beyond the things he was telling me, even when I knew some things didn't quite add up. I mean, what choice did I have? I thank God every day that June is living in a time when women can finally be who they really are and not what some archaic society wants them to be, reliant on a man to survive."

"Emily will be the first one to tell you not to let the media fool you. The country isn't there yet. There's still that . . . what do they call it? The glass ceiling?"

Michelle snorted, "Yeah, I know, but we're making strides." She paused and took a deep breath. "I worry about June. She hasn't seen Jack since the day he was arrested. I've been successful in the provision that Jack doesn't get to see her while he's in prison but now that he might get out it's going to be a different story. She doesn't want to see him. His lawyers aren't going to stop, though. They already contacted me. He wants joint custody upon his release."

"And we'll fight it."

There was no love lost between Ronan and his former brother-in-law. After Emily revealed what Jack had done to her, the rest of the story came out in pieces. Ronan had not yet known the entire story before he called the police. He wanted Jack as far away from his sister as possible.

Jack had been the lead lawyer in a deal between Corbyn and one of his clients. Jack needed the deal to go through because, as it was discovered, he had been living two separate lives. Not only was he in heavy debt for a gambling addiction but he also had a girlfriend he was supporting and often stayed with when he'd told Michelle he was working and staying at the office.

Emily had backed out of the deal and Jack had threatened her. She used her investigators to dig up the dirt on him and blackmailed him with it. The deal went through but the client ended up selling for much less than what the original deal had stated. Jack did not get the money he had envisioned that would have helped him get out of debt. When he threatened Emily again, she threatened to blow his entire life apart as she had much more than a hunch that he had embezzled money from his firm.

Jack went to jail for embezzlement and attempted murder. His lawyer tried to get the attempted murder charge lessened to simple assault and battery, except Jack lost his temper during a deposition and admitted he'd wanted Emily dead.

Ronan did all he could to make sure Jack was put away. He worked with Emily as she dug through old boxes to find what she had uncovered back in 1968. He had spoken with Jack's law firm as they did an analysis on the cases and clients Jack had worked with. Jack had covered his tracks fairly well, but not well enough to survive a forensic analysis. At the end, they had discovered he had embezzled close to three hundred thousand dollars over the years. Emily referred Michelle to an expert divorce lawyer and paid for all the legal fees.

Ronan had prepared for the parole hearing and was ready to testify in front of the board. As the brother of one victim and the husband of another, he was armed with enough evidence of what they had gone through as a result of his actions. He also knew Jack's former law firm was ready to present evidence to the extent of the damage he caused to their reputation and clientele. Jack would not be getting out if Ronan had anything to say about it.

"I know we'll fight it," Michelle answered and then sighed.

"You don't need this, Ro. You have enough going on with the business. You guys have Jonathan now. Emily will have her own worries. You don't need to worry about me, too."

"Stop. Both Emily and I will do whatever is necessary to protect you and June. You know that." Ronan noticed the change in Michelle's voice when she spoke again.

"I'm terrified. Ro, if he gets out, what's it going to do to June?"

Michelle

"You know that your Aunt Emily gave an interview today, right?"

June didn't look up from her plate. "Yeah, I know they brought up Jack." She lifted her fork and took another bite of the pork chop Michelle had made for dinner.

"How did you hear that?" Michelle took note again of how June never referred to her father as Dad. She insisted on calling him Jack. She once told Michelle she did so because he'd never really been a father and certainly was never going to be one so she wouldn't give him the honor.

Swallowing and taking a sip of her water before responding, June still did not look up. "Amy. She was late to school today and I guess her mom had it on. She was talking about it at chorus rehearsal."

"Do you want to talk about it?" Michelle was concerned how June seemed to compartmentalize her emotions. When it came to Jack, you could have sworn June was talking about any random person instead of her own father.

This time June stopped eating and looked up at Michelle. "No, Mom. I do not want to talk about it. I do not care about him."

Michelle sighed. "I know, honey, but if he does get parole you know that he will try to see you and you need to be prepared for that. I'm afraid you're keeping too much inside."

"You sound like Aunt Emily."

"She's not wrong."

June set down her fork and folded her arms on the table. "Okay, what do you want to know? If I'm okay with him getting out? No, not really but there's nothing I can do about it. Uncle Ro already told me that he and the place Jack worked for are going to try to block it. Let's hope they can do it. Okay?"

There were times Michelle found herself ill-equipped to deal with a teenage daughter. There were times she longed for the days when June was a toddler and wanted nothing more than to talk and play. Those days were gone and now June was a moody teenager who often let Michelle know how out of touch she was. But there were still times, however rare, that June would come to her to ask for advice or to simply talk. Michelle was hoping that tonight would be one of those nights they could talk.

"Stop, June. This whole thing is putting a lot of stress on all of us. Me, your Uncle Ronan, and Aunt Emily, not to mention your grandmother. Please don't sit there as if you are unaffected by the thought of him getting out. I know you're not."

Michelle was met with silence. It looked as if June wasn't prepared for that response. Michelle guessed she thought her attitude would shut down the conversation and Michelle would let it go. She wasn't going to let it go. She met June's stare across the table.

June leaned back and let out a breath. "Okay. Fine. You want to know what I keep thinking about? That day. I still vividly remember that day when Jack recognized Aunt Emily. I remember her running out of the house and Jack screaming at you, asking you why you allowed her to come in the house. I remember you being confused and not knowing what was going on. I remember Jack hollering about who she was and how stupid you were not to know it. I remember him throwing things and breaking things. I remember it all, Mom. I remember that day more than I remember when the cops came for him. You know why, Mom? It's because that was the day I realized that my so-called father was nothing more than an asshole. The way he kept screaming at you and blaming you for something you had no idea about. I remember all the words he used to put you and Uncle Ro down. The way he kept picking things up and throwing them and then telling you to clean them up. I know I was young but I remember thinking he was the one breaking everything so he should clean it up. That's the bottom line, Mom. He's the one who made the mess out of everything in his life and he's the one who has to clean it up. Not you, not me, not Uncle Ro. Him. He never will, though. I know that. He blamed everyone else then and he'll continue to blame everyone else now. That's the kind of person he is and I don't need to be around him."

June stopped and drank more of her water. Michelle sensed more was coming so she remained silent. This was the most June had spoken about Jack in a long time. She wanted June to continue uninterrupted.

"I didn't know then why he was blaming you and Uncle Ro for everything but I do now. Uncle Ro was dating Aunt Emily and you let her in the house. It was only a matter of time before she would have let you guys know everything he'd done. He wasn't going to take responsibility for it. No, he was going to blame all of you. If Uncle Ro hadn't met her then you wouldn't have invited her in and all his secrets would still be safe. So, it's all your fault. And Uncle Ro's. He's not sorry he did any of those things. He never will be. We were a cover, Mom. We were the 'look at the perfect family I have' cover he paraded around like a devout church-going family man when the truth is he was anything but that. But you want to know why I'm okay?"

"Yes, honey, I do."

"Because of you. You took me with you everywhere you were able to. You took me to Uncle Ro's when you had work to do there. He would spend time with me and teach me things with wood. You spent time with me at home, read to me, did my hair, helped me with homework, taught me right from wrong. Then we moved in with Uncle Ro and, really, the only thing that changed was where we slept. He still did things with me and taught me a lot of other things besides woodworking, you still read to me and did my homework with me. When we moved here, it was okay because Aunt Emily was moving in there and she helped me a lot, too. You see, Mom. I had a dad. It wasn't Jack, though. I still have a dad. And all of us? That's our family. So, you see, I don't need Jack. I don't want Jack and I don't want to see Jack. I'm not angry. I'm not anything when it comes to him. I feel nothing for him. When my friends say anything about me not having a father I tell them that's not true. I have my Uncle Ronan."

Michelle was at a loss for words. She realized her daughter was wiser than she had ever given her credit for. At some point June had grown into an insightful young lady right under her nose. She hadn't realized her eyes had been watering and she blinked back the tears.

"Oh, honey, I love you," Michelle said. "And you're right. This is our family. But you know I worry about you. I always will. If Jack wants to see you, we'll figure it out. I promise I will do all that I can to make sure you don't have to."

"I know you will, Mom, and if there's no way around it and I have to see him, fine. I'll deal with it."

"How?"

"Well, they might make me *see* him but the law doesn't say I have to *talk* to him. I'm sure he won't be expecting a mute daughter."

"Oh my God, June!" Michelle laughed.

June shrugged and laughed as well. "It's true. I don't have to talk."

"Yes, that's true."

"Let's just hope it doesn't come to that. Uncle Ro seems to think that between him and the firm, they'll deny his parole. I'm good with that. Black and white stripes are a good look for Jack."

"I think they wear orange jumpsuits now."

"Even better!"

They laughed for a bit and then Michelle said, "Just so you know, I'm not going to tell your Uncle Ro what you said about him. His head is big enough. We don't need it any bigger."

June chuckled, "I think he already knows."

After dinner, Michelle began to clean up as June went into the living room and turned on the television. Michelle heard the familiar theme of MTV and shook her head. It amazed her what teenagers had these days that she wouldn't have imagined when she was that young. When she was finished she joined her daughter on the sofa.

"Who's that?" Michelle asked, pointing to the blonde woman on the TV.

"Nina Blackwood. I love her hair. She's so pretty. I think she's the coolest of the veejays."

"Of the what?"

"Veejays. You know, like a DJ but it's videos not records. God, Mom, what was the great potato famine like?"

"Funny. I get it. I'm old and out of touch."

"And Irish. By the way, Michael Jackson's Thriller video is going to premiere in a couple weeks. Is it too much to ask if you could learn how to program the VCR before that?"

Michelle sighed. She had no idea how she was going to keep up with all the new gadgets that were coming out. "Sure. I'll try."

As she put her arm around her daughter, she said a silent prayer that Ronan was right and Jack would stay exactly where he was.

Emily

"The way you called Marilyn out on how she twisted things was definitely something to behold," Theresa shook her head and continued. "I especially enjoyed the part where she implied you were an advocate of the government taking care of *everything*."

In the Brooklyn office, Emily, Jean, and Theresa were enjoying the early morning quiet and some coffee before the patients started to arrive. The other two doctors, Patrick and Ian, were already in their offices getting ready for their day.

"I think my favorite part was Prozac will stop people from needing in-patient care," Jean chimed in.

"Marilyn told me during the break that she has to give the counterpoint to everything whether she believes it or not. Personally, I don't think she cares too much about any of it. I'm sure she has great insurance through the station so why should she care if there are people that go without it? I often think about France. The difference in culture is amazing. Over there, it's about community. It's about looking out for one another. Here it's starting to be every man for himself. Too many people are starting to think that way."

Emily took a long sip of her coffee as Jean expanded on the comment and lamented how people were becoming self-centered and weren't as neighborly as they once were.

"The French hate us. Besides, I think some people were always self-centered and mean," Theresa said evenly. "I don't think it's a new thing. I just think more people are bringing it out in the open."

Emily caught the tone in Theresa's voice and was about to say something when Jean continued the thought.

"Do you think people just got tired of all the political stuff? You know, Vietnam, Watergate, Iran taking hostages and all that? Maybe they just started thinking about their own lives." Jean offered.

"Maybe," Emily replied. "But, Theresa, the French don't hate us. They hate when Americans come over and act like they own the country."

"Well, they would be speaking —"

"Don't say it," Emily cut Theresa off. "That's one of the things that leaves a bad taste in their mouth. They are well aware and don't need it thrown in their face by the 'ugly Americans'. Anyway, Jean, you might be right. It could be that people are tired from the never-ending political garbage. It could also be the political parties dividing us and telling people what they should be concerned about."

"Whatever the reason, I agree with you. It's not a good road for the country to go down. We're all in this together yet people are starting to forget that. You haven't. No matter what Marilyn tried to throw at you."

"All that stuff at the end?" Theresa asked.

"Yes," Jean replied, "and Emily, I wanted to tell you. I loved your answer when Marilyn asked you how you find time for your job now that you're married and have Jonathan. You were right. People even ask *me* how I get things done at home and take care of Michael when I work full-time but they never ask Barry that."

"I thought you meant about the book and Jack," Theresa said.

"That stuff, too," Jean answered. "You know, Emily, I said this before but your life could be one hell of an ABC Movie of the Week."

Emily knew it was only a matter of time before the end of the interview came up. After that day at Michelle's house, Emily sat down with Jean, Theresa, Patrick, and Ian. She laid everything out on the table for them from start to finish. She included the personal things she divulged to Ronan that long ago night on the bridge, how she was raised and how her parents had reacted after her assault. She omitted the parts that concerned Marcus but explained she found a new passion after awakening from her coma. In detail, she relayed all she had done to make retribution for her misdeeds.

Emily had expected someone, or maybe even all of them, to resign. Instead, after a long silence, Patrick had thanked her for her honesty. He went on to say that he had seen how tirelessly she worked both at the clinic and the causes she advocated for. Jean seconded that and told her she wasn't leaving. Ian and Theresa echoed them and, together, they continued to grow the Brooklyn clinic and pushed forward with opening the Tribeca clinic.

Jean and Theresa stood by her when everything came out publicly. Theresa had stayed with her for several days to help with the media who insisted on camping out in front of her apartment building. Jean took her home for dinner often. After Rob's televised press conference, it died down a bit.

Naturally, after Jack's arrest, the media picked up again but were more sympathetic and the attention turned toward the trials and focused more on the embezzlement and double life. Emily's attempted murder was almost a footnote. Nothing captivated the country more than a man who appeared to be an upright, squeaky clean member of society having a shady double life.

Through it all, Jean's and Theresa's friendship never wavered. They were in court the day she had testified against Jack. They stayed at the clinic to make sure she got to her car safely, even after things began to quiet down. In return, Emily did whatever she could to help her friends. Babysitting for Jean, taking Theresa out to dinner, staying with Jean after she lost her father to a heart attack, and helping Theresa complete and publish papers. She valued them and was beyond grateful for their continued support and friendship.

"There are far more interesting stories to turn into a movie, Jean," Emily replied. "Everything was put out there in '75, no need to go backward. I want to tell both of you, again, how very grateful I am that you stood by me. I have no idea how I would have gotten through it without the two of you." Emily leaned forward and reached for their hands. "I could not ask for better friends. I love you both."

"And we love you," Jean squeezed Emily's hand.

"We sure do," Theresa added.

"Okay!" Emily released their hands and stood up. "Time to get moving. I've got a patient coming in soon. We've got work to do."

Emily headed toward her office but not before she heard Theresa mutter in a dry tone, "Yup, there's work to do."

Ronan

Ronan turned to Mike and asked, "You mind taking this chair up to the Bronx?" He'd taken on Mike full-time once the business expanded, as well as hiring another full-time employee and two part-time. The last two years hadn't been easy as the country found itself in yet another recession but Ronan was always grateful that the one thing he could count on was people would need home repairs.

"Sure," Mike replied. "Are you gonna bring another one down from the loft to show off down here?"

"You mean display?" Ronan laughed. "Yeah, of course. I've sold quite a few pieces by showing them off down here."

"Just ribbing you," Mike replied. "And, hey, thanks for recommending that place in Queens. They hired my brother. It's been rough for his family."

"No problem. It's been rough for a lot of people. You saw how slow we got last year and the beginning of this year."

"I know. Seems like every time I turn around we're going into another recession. This one was bad, though. Recession, inflation, taxes. That's all you ever hear about anymore. I know a lot of guys still looking for work."

"Yeah but we're coming out of this one. Hopefully, unemployment will go back down."

"Reagan seems to be doing some good things. His plan sounded pretty good and it looks like we're recovering."

Ronan shrugged his shoulders. "I don't know. Maybe short-term but I don't think some of the things he's doing are going to be good long-term."

"What do you mean?"

"All this top-to-bottom stuff. I think Bush was right when he called it voodoo economics. I don't think it's a good thing. I don't think his cuts are going to pay for themselves like he promised. I don't see it happening. It's going to be the middle class that'll carry the tax burden. I think his plan makes it too easy for people to get greedy. It'll be easier for the people at the top to keep the money instead of passing it on to the workers." Ronan shrugged again. "Just my thoughts."

"Okay, so what do you think he should've done?" Mike asked with a touch of sarcasm in his voice.

"Look, I know I'm no politician or economist, that's for sure, but I think it should be from the bottom up. I mean, think about it for a minute. If you take care of the workers, if you take care of those with lower and middle income levels they're going to put their money back in the economy because they'll have more money to spend. The more that gets put back in the economy, the more products and services are needed, the more profits are made, the more companies thrive. If you starve the lower and middle income people and they don't spend, the money doesn't go back in the economy and the only people thriving are the ones at the top. Don't get me wrong, I think there are things that Reagan is doing that are good but not in this area. I think this will just cause a bigger gap between classes. Again, just my thoughts."

"Lucky for you we just got slower and didn't hit too much of a dry spell." Mike laughed. "But you're right. I didn't think about it until now, but for months we were only doing work for people who were . . . what's the polite way of saying it? . . . better off than most people."

"Yup, the jewelry rattlers kept our doors open."

"Jewelry rattlers?"

"You don't remember what Lennon said when The Beatles played The Royal Albert Hall? He told the people in the cheap seats to clap their hands, then he laughed and said, 'the rest of you can rattle your jewelry.' He always did like to ruffle feathers."

Mike fell silent. "Yeah. I can't believe it's coming up on two years since he died. You think Michelle will go up to the Dakota again?"

Ronan nodded. "She went the night he was shot and she went last year, even took June with her."

"Two years and it's still hard to believe," Mike sighed. "Anyway, yeah, back to work. I'll take the chair up to the Bronx. Anything else? If not, I'll just head home after that."

"That's it. I'm closing up down here soon, anyway. I have to relieve the babysitter."

After Mike left, Ronan wrote up a couple of quotes and left them on Michelle's desk for her to type up and mail in the morning. He locked up the office and retrieved the mail from the mailbox in the lobby before heading up to the loft.

As soon as he closed the door he heard the patter of little feet running across the floor and the high-pitched squeal of "Daaaddy!" Ronan never got tired of it. He threw the mail on the table and scooped up Jonathan. This was his favorite part of the day.

"How's my big boy? Were you good for Ellen today?"

He laughed as Jonathan nodded and let out a mischievous giggle. Ellen walked toward them, coat already in hand.

"He was as good as any 3-year old can be," Ellen quipped. She ruffled Jonathan's hair and said, "I'll see you tomorrow, cutie."

With Ellen gone and after chasing Jonathan around the loft for several minutes, Ronan settled down on the floor with his son and began playing with his train set. They were on their 5th time around the track when he heard the door open and Emily come in. Jonathan scrambled to his feet and once again went running across the floor.

"Mommy!"

"There's my little man!" Emily dropped her coat and briefcase where she was standing and bent down to pick up Jonathan.

"Daddy's playing trains," Jonathan informed her.

"Just Daddy? Were you playing with him?"

Ronan watched as Jonathan nodded and they began walking over to him. He winced as he got to his feet and noticed it didn't get by his wife.

"You really need to get that knee looked at," Emily chided.

Ignoring the comment, he smiled, "Where's the kiss for your tall man? Or do you reserve them all for the little man?"

After Emily gave him a kiss and turned back to Jonathan, Ronan noticed the tired look in her eyes. He didn't think she'd been sleeping well lately and figured it was Jack's parole hearing weighing on her. They'd talked about it a few times but there really wasn't anything they could do anymore. They just had to wait, testify and then hope the board didn't grant him parole.

"I know it's your turn for dinner but what'd you say we order in tonight?" Ronan asked. "You look worn out."

"Thank you, darling. You look wonderful, too." The playful tone that usually accompanied comments like that wasn't there.

"Are you okay?"

"Yes," Emily sighed. "It was a long day, that's all. Plus, I think it must be a full moon. Everyone seemed a little off today, especially Theresa. I'm sorry, honey. Yes, ordering in sounds wonderful. Thank you for suggesting it."

Later, after dinner had been ordered, eaten and cleaned up, Ronan gave Jonathan his bath and put him in bed. Then he sat on the sofa as Emily took over. He could hear her in Jonathan's room, reading to him. Curious George had become his favorite. Tonight's tale was about George and an escaped bunny. Ronan closed his eyes and continued to listen. These were the moments he wanted to engrave in his memory. The family moments in their otherwise busy world.

It was also during these moments that Carrieann would go through his mind. It wasn't as often as it used to be but when it happened he would feel a sense of guilt. He felt it was unfair that he was living a life that she had been robbed of. He had several conversations with Emily about it. Emily had felt his pain that long ago night on the bridge when he no longer wanted a life without Carrieann, when he didn't want any life at all. She helped him understand the guilt was a normal emotion and that Carrieann would forever be a part of him.

Ronan loved Emily more than he could have imagined. She understood him in ways that even Michelle didn't. She made him understand that there was enough room in his life for all of them; for her and Jonathan, for Michelle and June, and for the memory of Carrieann. When he added in the fact that she handled his depression in a way that didn't make him feel like he was broken, he sometimes wondered how he got so lucky. He never felt embarrassed nor did he feel he had to hide it from her. Even though he still struggled with it, and always would, he had never felt more complete than he did the last few years.

"What's on your mind?"

Ronan opened his eyes. He didn't realize Emily had come into the living room. He held his arm out and wrapped it around her as she snuggled on the sofa beside him. "How much I love you," he replied.

"I love you, too, honey."

"Jonathan asleep?"

"He was out before the bunny was even found. Did you two run a marathon before I got home? He was really tired."

Ronan laughed, "We did do several laps around the loft before getting the trains going. I'm getting old. It's hard to keep up with him sometimes."

"Tell me about it. That's what we get for having a child this late in life."

Ronan squeezed her, "I wouldn't trade it for anything."

"Me, neither."

"Feeling any better?"

"Eh," came Emily's response. "I can't get rid of this headache."

"Want me to get you anything?"

"Anything but Tylenol," Emily elbowed him.

"Oh, that was bad," Ronan shook his head. "I'll get you some aspirin."

"That's okay," Emily said, sitting up. "I'll get it. You want anything?"

Ronan shook his head and Emily headed to the kitchen. He heard her ask if there was anything new on the Tylenol case. It had been two months since 12 people died in the Chicago area from taking cyanide-laced Tylenol capsules. It was only a few days since they were reintroduced back on the market with new packaging. The tamper-proof boxes put it back in the news and reminded the nation the case had still not been solved.

Even with the new seals, Ronan wasn't about to go back to capsules. The scare had everyone on edge as to what else could be tampered with and people had become suspicious of a lot of things besides over-the-counter capsules.

"Didn't you stay to hear Marilyn talk about it after your interview? There's really nothing since they started looking for this Lewis guy," Ronan called back. "They seem to be focusing on him. There haven't been any other deaths or bad bottles since the recall. They're all talking about how they're all sealed now so people can't mess around with them."

"I'm still trying to understand the motive," Emily said from the kitchen as she took the aspirin. "Was he trying to kill one specific person and putting other bottles out there to cover his intended murder? Or was he going for mass murder? If he wanted mass murder, you'd think there would be more than eight bottles. That's the scary part. No one really knows how many bottles were actually tampered with since everyone threw them out."

"Who knows? If he wanted a mass murder, maybe he should

have tampered with the Kool-Aid."

"Oooh," Emily replied, "that was a bad one, too, Ro. Although, I'm sure Jim Jones is smiling up from Hell."

"I don't think you're allowed to smile in Hell. Are you coming back in here?"

"Yeah, I just want to get the mail."

Ronan once again wrapped his arm around Emily after she retrieved the mail and sat down again.

"By the way, Ro, it was Flavor-Aid not Kool-Aid."

"I know but who drinks Flavor-Aid? Anything important in the mail?"

"Bills," Emily replied as she flipped through the envelopes.

Ronan closed his eyes again and heard Emily open a few of the bills and toss them on the coffee table. It was when she let out a gasp that he opened them again and looked at her. She was holding a sheet of paper in her hand; her other hand had gone over her mouth. Her eyes had widened and she no longer looked tired. She looked frightened.

Without asking, he took the paper from her hand. A chill ran through him as he looked down at the neatly printed block letters. There was no salutation, no name on the bottom. It was one sentence:

Your days are numbered.

Emily

"Doesn't look like the police can do much."

In the days since Emily had received the letter, she'd been on edge but refused to alter her schedule. They took the letter to the police and a report was filed. It was dusted for fingerprints but having gone through the postal service, there were too many sets. Rob offered to hire a private investigator but both Emily and Ronan had declined.

Sitting in her Tribeca office, with Jonathan on her lap, she was once again explaining to Rob why she did not want a private investigator.

"They can't do much because there are too many fingerprints on the envelope and none on the letter except for mine and Ronan's. There is literally nothing to go on. What can a private investigator possibly do in a case like this?"

"They can look into people and see if there is anyone who took an unhealthy interest in you recently. But alright," Rob held up his hands. "I won't hire one. However, I *am* going to hire someone to watch over you."

"What?"

"You heard me. You won't even know he's there. There are far too many crazy people in this world to take chances. I wish you would have taken Ronan's advice and cut back on your patient schedule."

"No. I will not be intimidated."

"Mommy, put me down," Jonathan began to squirm.

Emily set Jonathan down and set him up with Legos before turning back to Rob. "Ronan thinks it was Jack. He thinks he had someone send it for him. In fact, he's going to the prison today to talk to Jack. I tried to stop him but he had his Irish up."

"My initial thought is Jack as well. I don't blame him for going. I don't know if it's the wisest decision but it's what I would do. Let me know how that talk goes." Rob sat on the floor next to Jonathan. "What are you going to build, buddy?"

"A wall."

"A wall? That's boring! How about a big tower instead?"

"No! A wall so the bad man can't get Mommy."

Emily's eyes widened. She and Ronan had not talked about the letter in front of Jonathan but he must have overheard something. There was nothing in her conversation with Rob that a 3-year old would understand as a bad man trying to get her. He couldn't have possibly understood what they just talked about.

Rob spoke before Emily could. "Hey buddy, what makes you think there's a bad man trying to get your mommy?"

"Ellanen said it."

"Ellen? What did she say, honey?" Emily bent down to talk to her son.

Jonathan didn't look up from the blocks. "A man wants to hurt you."

"Did she tell you that?"

"No," Jonathan shook his head. "On the phone."

"Honey, look at me," Emily put her hands on either side of her son's face. She looked directly into his eyes. "No one is going to hurt me. You don't have to build me a wall because no one is going to get me. We are all okay. Do you understand?"

Jonathan nodded and wiggled his head out from her hands. He turned to Rob and said, "Okay! Big tower, Uncle Rob!"

Emily stood up and took a deep breath. She looked over at Rob, who was looking back at her. "Okay."

"Let me talk to your mom for a minute and then I'll be right back to help you with the tower, okay?"

Rob got up and walked with Emily to the other side of the room. In a lower voice he said, "Okay, what? Do you want me to hire someone to watch over you or do you want me to hire a private investigator?"

"Both. I didn't realize he'd heard anything. I don't think he understood anything we were talking about before but he definitely understood whatever Ellen said to whoever she was talking to." Emily looked over at Jonathan and then back at Rob. "Hire both. The sooner we find out who sent it the better."

"Consider it done. I'm placing my bets on Jack and that's where I'll tell him to start."

Emily nodded and walked back to her desk. She sat down and watched her son put his Lego blocks together. She'd have to talk with their babysitter about certain subjects being discussed in front of Jonathan. She knew children were far more receptive than adults were aware of and admonished herself for her lack in judgment talking about it with Rob in front of him.

She looked up when Rob took the seat on the other side of her desk. "So, I forgot to tell you. I saw your interview. Nicely done, sis. I have to say, though, the best part was when they showed my clip. I'm such a handsome devil, don't you think?"

Emily smiled, "A handsome devil with a big ego."

"I have to ask, though. When did you become a liberal?"

"I'm not a liberal." She noted Rob began to smile and quickly added, "I'm not a conservative, either. I think both parties forgot who they work for years ago. It's only going to get worse."

"There's some truth there. On a different note, where *do* you find the time to juggle work and a family?"

Emily shook her head and let out a loud breath, "Stop." Then she stood up and started to walk toward the door. "I have a few things I have to check on. Can you watch Jonathan for just a few minutes?"

"Sure! We'll finish that tower, won't we, big guy?"

Emily walked out as Rob was getting back on the floor with

Jonathan. She leaned back against the closed door and exhaled. For Emily, coming after her was one thing, but if it remotely affected her family, that was a whole different thing. It broke her heart that Jonathan wanted to build a wall to protect her. Walls don't work, though. One only needed to look at East and West Germany. Walls divide people but they don't keep people from doing what they have their mind set on. Emily knew this. She would have to instill in Jonathan that it is far better to build bridges, but the fact that he wanted to keep her safe from the 'bad man' was more than her heart could take at the moment.

Her thoughts moved to Ronan. She had never been happier than she'd been these past few years. With Ronan, she found that piece of her that had been missing. He'd gotten her to slow down, take more time to enjoy the simple things life had to offer. He was creative where she was scientific, he brought out the softer side of her, allowed her to be all the things she was and supported her continuing journey into who she wanted to be. Ronan saw her flaws and accepted them as easily as he accepted her good traits. He wanted nothing more from her than to be his partner and she was. They were partners who completed and took care of each other. The thought of whoever sent that letter having any kind of harmful effect on him or Jonathan was more frightening than the thought of what they would want to do to her.

Ronan and Rob thought Jack was responsible for the letter but something in her gut was telling her he wasn't. It was a far more frightening thought. She could handle it better if it was Jack. At least she would know who she was dealing with but she didn't believe it. Emily didn't think Jack would do anything like this when there was the possibility he could be free soon. She expected Jack to make trouble for them but she wasn't sure he'd threaten her life knowing it could serve as a reason to deny his parole if he was caught.

But if it wasn't Jack, who else wanted her dead?

Ronan

Seated at a table in a small cement block room, Ronan folded his hands on the table and waited. He knew Emily was against him being there but he needed to see Jack face to face. He felt the only way he was going to know if Jack had written that note or not was to look him in the eyes. Anyone can deny an action but they usually had a tick or a give-away that would indicate they are lying. He was hoping that Jack would give himself away. If that happened they could form a plan to make sure Emily remained safe and Jack remained in jail.

He wasn't sure what he was going to say but there were things Emily made him promise he wouldn't say. He promised he wouldn't raise his voice, bring up the past, talk about June, make any threats, or directly accuse him of sending the note. Ronan knew he'd have to make some broad statements since he'd given his word to stay away from specifics.

The metal door opened as a guard escorted Jack into the room. Ronan thought he'd be handcuffed. He was surprised he wasn't. He was also surprised to see Jack dressed in a blue work shirt and pants. He had the old image of black and white stripes embedded in his mind. Ronan was almost disappointed Jack wasn't wearing them.

"So, what are you doing here, Ronan?" Jack asked as he took the seat across from him. The guard remained at the door. "I think you said the next time you saw my face you hoped it would be in a morgue. That was you, right?"

Ronan replied, "The last time I saw you was six years ago in court. I don't recall who might have said that to you." Ronan had, in fact, said it but he wasn't going to let Jack trap him into anything that might be construed as a threat.

"Why are you here?" Jack sat back in his seat.

"Your parole hearing is coming up."

"Are you here to tell me you're going to make sure I'm denied parole? Save your breath. I expect to see you and Emily at the hearing."

"No. I'm here to talk about what your plans are once you get out of here."

Jack sat up, looking surprised. "Wow. I guess you don't have a good case for the board since you're sure I'm getting out. That's good to know."

Ronan did not return the smile Jack gave him. He had to take a deep breath. It had only been a minute but he already wanted to give Jack a good right hook. "We'll see. I'm here to talk about your plans."

"Why?" Jack paused, then shook his head and let out a snort. "Are you afraid I'm gonna go after Michelle or Emily? Don't worry, I'm not. Do you want to know what I learned in here?" Jack leaned forward.

"What did you learn?" Ronan sat back, the further away from Jack the better.

"Neither one of them is worth it." He slapped his hand on the table and sat back. "No. Neither one. Oh, I could go after them. I could make their life hell in court for years, I suppose." Jack shrugged before continuing, "but why should I waste my time on them? You look like you don't believe me."

"Why should I?" Ronan asked. "You did nothing but lie to Michelle for years. You lied to everyone. You can see why it's hard for me to believe anything you say."

"If you think I'm only going to lie then why'd you bother to come in?" Jack lifted his chin and a smile crossed his face. "She told you to, didn't she? Jesus, Ronan, you're still so weak. Tell me, how high can you jump? I figure since you do it every time Emily tells you to, you must excel at it by now. So, how high?"

"Shut up, Jack. Emily didn't want me to come here. She was against it."

Jack raised his eyebrows. "She let you off the leash, did she? For how long? An hour or the whole day?" Ronan felt the anger stir as Jack sat back and laughed before he continued speaking. "You couldn't tie your own shoes without Michelle and now you have Emily telling you what to do. Were you born without balls or did you lose them somewhere?"

Ronan was gritting his teeth, his jaw tight. He had to wait a few seconds and take another deep breath before responding. If he hadn't, he knew he would have broken his promise to Emily. "Take all the shots you want, Jack. I'm not here to defend myself against your bullshit. I just want to make sure you will leave Michelle and Emily alone. That you will not harass them or harm them in any way. If you do, we'll see to it that you are put right back into your 6 x 8 foot cell block home."

Jack tapped the table. "Look, buddy, I hate Emily, got it? I wish she would have died that day in the street. But you're even dumber than I thought if you think I'd put my freedom in jeopardy. That bitch isn't even remotely worth it. She's trash as far as I'm concerned. As for your sister, I don't give a rat's ass about her. She was a pain in my ass. I never should have let her work for you. That's when it started with all that women's lib crap. Don't worry, Ronan. I couldn't care less if I ever see Michelle again. In fact, I have someone else waiting for me. Surprised? You shouldn't be. Even in prison I'm still one hell of a catch. She understands where a woman's place is. Yes, Ronan, I have plans and I have a life waiting for me when I get out of here. Those two can burn in Hell for all I care."

"And June?"

Jack shot him a look Ronan could only describe as menacing. "No one is going to keep me from my daughter."

"You know she doesn't want to see you."

"I'm sure her mother brainwashed her. The law will have a say in it. That's all I'm saying. I'm not going to discuss my daughter with you. We're done here."

Ronan stood up and pushed his chair in. "Yes, we are." He walked to the door and nodded at the guard, who opened the door.

Ronan couldn't help himself. He turned around and looked back at Jack. "Just so you know, June calls you Jack. She'll be happy to tell you it's because she will never acknowledge you as her father." With that, he walked out and let the door shut behind him.

As he got into his car, Ronan let out a deep breath. He was proud he hadn't lost his temper. He would have to tell Emily he'd brought up June but he felt he had to. He knew Jack was sitting in that prison somewhere stewing over what he'd told him and the thought made him happy. He thought about everything Jack had said to him. He realized that he was leaning toward believing Jack had been telling him the truth. They knew Jack was going to file for joint custody once released so his comment that no one was going to keep him from June wasn't surprising.

If Ronan was to believe Jack, then Emily and Michelle didn't have to worry if he got out. They would only need to focus on June. He wanted to believe that was true. He wanted to believe everything Jack said about a woman waiting for him. Ronan hadn't bothered asking if he was already harassing Emily since Jack had stated he wasn't going to risk his freedom. He realized he was no longer sure it was Jack who had the note sent.

As a thought slowly entered his mind, he rubbed his face in frustration. If it wasn't Jack, then who could it be?

Emily

"He has another woman waiting for him?" Emily was incredulous as Ronan relayed his visit with Jack.

"That's what he said. What kind of woman goes for a man like him?"

"A candidate for therapy," Emily replied as she finished putting Jonathan's stuffed animals back in the toy box. She walked over to the stereo and scanned the albums.

"You don't seem relieved that he won't be coming after you," she heard Ronan say as she picked out Simon & Garfunkel's Greatest Hits album.

"Oh, he's not going to leave me alone. Not entirely. It's that I was already sure he wasn't the one who sent the note." Emily put the album on the turntable and turned back to Ronan. "I didn't think it was him to begin with. I think he was telling you the truth when he said he wasn't going to risk going back to prison."

Emily watched as Ronan put the last of Jonathan's crayons and coloring books back on the shelf. She was proud of him for not losing his temper with Jack but she still wasn't happy that he'd gone. The less contact they had with Jack the better it would be for everyone. She remembered something Rob had said to her that afternoon and she knew Ronan went out of the need to protect her and Michelle. There was a time when she would have rejected any man if he began to feel the need to protect her. Since Ronan, she found comfort and a sense of security knowing that he would be there for her, that she didn't always have to be strong. It was a breakthrough for her to let those walls down and let him take care of her when she needed it. She knew that's what this visit had been about.

"I don't think so, either," Ronan said as he crossed the room to her. "Not anymore. I think he was telling the truth." She watched as

Ronan stepped behind her to the stereo, lifted the needle, and skipped over the first song.

Emily wrapped herself in his arms as 'Bridge Over Troubled Water', their unofficial song, filtered through the speakers. She melted into him and let him lead her. He'd skipped the first song on purpose and she loved him for it. She felt safe with Ronan, a feeling she hadn't known before him.

They swayed to the music, neither one talking, until it went into the next song. She felt Ronan move back a little, she lifted her face and kissed him. Without a word, he took her hand and led her to their bedroom. She wished she could freeze these moments. Jonathan fast asleep, dancing with her husband, the outside world blocked out. For six years, they'd built this family, this life and she had cherished every minute of it. As Ronan shut their bedroom door and took her in his arms she vowed nothing and no one would ever take this away from her.

Later, as they laid in bed, satisfied and tangled under the sheet, Emily couldn't stop the outside world from infiltrating her thoughts. She turned on her side and propped herself on her elbow.

"Ronan?"

"Mmm hmm?" came the soft acknowledgment.

"If it wasn't Jack, then who?" She knew it wasn't the opportune time to have this conversation but she also knew the question was the elephant in the room. She felt Ronan turn toward her.

"I don't know, honey. It could be someone else from your past or maybe a disgruntled patient."

"I thought about it being a former patient but I can't think of anyone I treated that would do something like this. I know therapy didn't help some patients but, again, none that I could imagine wanting to hurt me."

"I think if it was someone from back in your Corbyn days they would have made a move long before now. It's been fourteen years since you left there."

"So, we're back to the beginning." Emily laid back on her pillow. "Do you think someone saw my interview on TV and is being an asshole? That happens."

"Hmm, maybe it's someone who adores Reagan and heard you criticizing him for his policies. It's possible, I guess."

Emily sighed, "It's possible but I only criticized one thing and with valid reason. If I really wanted to make people angry I would have brought up how Reagan granting amnesty to the illegals is actually a good thing."

"That would have done it for sure."

"I know. People will never learn that politicians use them as pawns. Whenever something happens, like this recession, suddenly immigrants become the big boogey-man again. When is the country going to catch on that it's all a diversion, a political dog-and-pony show? 'Don't blame us for your hard times, blame them'. It's ridiculous."

"They will never catch on. I've been saying that for years. How long have they been using this trick? It's 1982. If they haven't caught on by now, they never will." Ronan let out a sigh, sat up and slid his legs over the side of the bed. Emily saw him run his hand through his hair. There was a moment of silence before he said, "Maybe you should consider taking Jonathan and going to Paris for a while, stay at the apartment, relax for a bit."

"You mean hide," Emily replied. "I'm not going to do that. I knew it was only a matter of time before you suggested that."

She met his gaze as he shifted sideways to look at her. "I don't mean hide. Maggie's over there now, isn't she? Staying at the apartment? Why not take some time and relax with your sister? You could take Jonathan to parks, teach him some French."

"Maggie's there on business. She's not relaxing. We already

planned to take Jonathan there after the holidays. I'm not going to let whoever sent it scare me into changing my schedule or hiding in Paris." Emily pushed the sheet away and got up from the bed. Pulling on her robe, she walked around the bed and sat down next to Ronan. "I know you're worried about me but Rob has someone watching. Who knows? Maybe it will turn out to be nothing, just someone who wanted to scare me but has no plans to do anything else."

Over the years she had treated quite a few patients who used psychological scare tactics to get someone to bend to their will. It was more common than most people would think. It was a form of mental abuse, not physical, usually associated with people who had a narcissistic personality disorder. She began to think of people she might know who would qualify as a narcissist. If she was dealing with one, the threat would be more psychological than physical.

She put her head on Ronan's shoulder as he put his arm around her. "Maybe," Ronan whispered into her hair. "I hope so." She felt him pull her tighter against him and then, without warning, pulled his head back and said teasingly, "Whoa, Em, do I see gray hair?"

Emily shoved him away and replied, "And each one has your name on it, buddy." She ruffled her hair. "Besides, there aren't too many, yet, maybe I'll just let them grow in and age gracefully." She batted her eyelashes at Ronan.

He leaned over and kissed her before getting up and heading toward the bathroom. "Redhead, brunette, gray, white, doesn't matter. You're beautiful and I love you."

Emily smiled. "I love you, too, Ro." She got up and turned on the small TV that sat on their dresser. She grabbed the cable box and pushed the slide to the letter for Home Box Office. It was the British movie *Breaking Glass* again. She should have known. It seemed they played the same movies over and over ad nauseam. She pushed the slide again until she landed on the cable news channel. She got into her pajamas and sat on the edge of the bed, waiting for Ronan to get out of the bathroom.

When Ronan returned to the bedroom, Emily was intently focused on the TV. "What are they talking about?" she heard him ask.

Without looking away from the TV, Emily replied, "What they're now calling Acquired Immune Deficiency Syndrome. The CDC identified four risk factors: male homosexuality, intravenous drug use, Haitian origin, and Hemophilia A. They shouldn't have published that. It's going to cause more hate crimes. They already said they strongly believe it's transmitted through sex and blood transfusions. They should be focusing on educating people on safe sex practices and making sure blood supplies are clean."

"At least they stopped calling it the gay plague."

"There are still reporters that laugh about it, Ro. They make jokes about being gay while people are dying. It's repulsive. People have been outwardly terrorizing the gay community and not a word from our esteemed president." Emily turned toward Ronan. "We have quite a few patients who have already been through so much trauma and the attacks keep coming. It's heartbreaking. This illness has moved beyond gay men but the media barely addresses that. It's an epidemic."

"Are they any closer to figuring out how it got here and how to cure it?"

"No. All they know is that it attacks the immune system." She got up and turned the TV off. "The Reagan Administration refuses to even acknowledge it. Their silence is deafening. Then this channel keeps repeating the same points and since they have to fill up 24 hours of news, they show gay men being harassed and physically attacked. That's not going to stop it, it's going to encourage more people to do it."

"Maybe a 24 hour news channel wasn't such a good idea."

"No, it wasn't. Not at all. Let's hope it goes off the air. This country doesn't need news channels bombarding them with crap like that all day, every day. News needs to be accurate and based on facts, not sensationalized."

Emily went into the bathroom as Ronan got back into bed. Her thoughts jumped from the threatening note to the men she had in therapy to how inadequately the White House was handling mental health and the epidemic. By the time she was finished, she'd come up with a new house rule.

Jumping back into bed, she turned to Ronan and said, "How's this for a new house rule? No TV news after sex or before going to sleep."

"Fine by me," came the reply and then, "What's on your agenda tomorrow? Maybe we can go out for lunch."

"Can't," Emily said as she turned out the light. "I'm in Brooklyn tomorrow until three and then Jonathan has his yearly checkup."

"Are you going to get back in time? I can take him."

"Are you sure? I wouldn't have to rush then."

"Absolutely. Nothing like a little father and son time bonding with the pediatrician."

Emily gave Ronan a kiss, "Thank you, honey." She burrowed under the covers as he put his arm around her. It wasn't long before they were both fast asleep.

Michelle

"I don't care if he has all of the Dallas Cowboy Cheerleaders waiting for him. I don't want June forced into seeing him." Michelle was sitting at her desk rehashing what Ronan had told her about his visit with Jack. He'd called her after their meeting the day before but she still needed to talk about it.

"That's if he's granted parole. If he's not, June won't have to worry about it. By the time he's up for it again she'll be over 18 and legally an adult. Neither Jack nor the court can make her see him."

Michelle nodded. Elbows on her desk, holding her coffee cup with both hands, she stared blankly into it. Her first priority was trying to keep Jack away from June. However, if she was being honest with herself, she'd admit that it stung when Ronan let her know Jack had someone waiting for him when he got out. It wasn't that she wanted him back. That was the last thing she wanted. What stung was the realization that the years she loved him and took care of him meant nothing to him. She knew it was foolish to feel that way. She didn't know what she'd been expecting. No, that wasn't true. She was hoping that he was sorry for the way he treated her. She had hoped Jack had given Ronan an apology to pass along to her. The fact that not only was there no apology but that he felt no remorse and still, on some level, blamed her for their failed marriage is what got to her.

Even though she'd talked to Emily many times the last few years, she still could not get past how she'd been raised. It had been instilled in her growing up that it was a woman's job to take care of her husband, to do what he said, he was the head of the household and her duties were to clean, cook and take care of the house. That part of her still struggled with the other side that knew women were more than that, women were just as smart and just as capable as men. It was an internal battle she thought she'd have for the rest of her life. It was this battle that sometimes caused her to wonder if she would have followed in her mother's footsteps, stayed home, made everything perfect, would things be different?

Michelle shook herself out of her thoughts. No, she knew they wouldn't be different. She would have been more miserable and it wouldn't have changed what kind of person Jack was. She hated when she fell back into that train of thought. She often wished she was more like Emily, who had never felt she had to be subservient.

Bringing herself back to the present, she looked up at Ronan and said, "Let's hope he's denied. Then the problem takes care of itself. In the meantime, have you heard anything else about the letter? If it wasn't Jack, and you seem to think it's not, then who do you think it is?"

She watched Ronan shrug and shake his head as he replied, "It could be anyone, Michelle. That's the thing. A former patient, someone else from Corbyn, someone who just hates women speaking out like she's been. Who knows? Emily even thinks it might be a one-time thing, someone who just wanted to scare her but won't do anything else."

"And you?"

"I think it's someone who definitely intends to hurt her. The fact that Rob has someone watching her is the only thing that keeps me a little calm about it."

"Has the private investigator found anything?"

Ronan shook his head. "Not yet. It's too early. I guess Rob told them to start with Jack and then branch out to other people, patients, co-workers, even relatives. They have cousins that they never speak to. I guess there was some feud between Emily's father and his brother and the families were estranged. It could even be one of them trying to settle an old family debt or something."

"I hope you find out soon. I can't imagine what it feels like to walk around with a target on your back."

"Emily's tough," Ronan replied. "Tougher than most people realize."

"Yes, she is," Michelle replied. "In the meantime, we still have a business to run here and it's picking up again. You have Mike and Bart out on Long Island today and Steve is over in the East Village. You don't have Kevin on today?"

"No need for Kevin today. Steve is on today and tomorrow."

"If it keeps picking up at this pace, you're going to have to consider hiring one or both of them full-time."

"We'll cross that bridge when we get there."

Michelle sighed, "We'll get there, Ronan. We were getting there two years ago before everything went to hell again."

"Haven't you heard? Reagan's going to fix it all and then I'll have to hire more than just Steve and Kevin," Ronan said with a sarcastic tone.

"Yeah, Reagan's going to fix it, sure he is. Just like he was *really* the one responsible for solving the Iran Hostage Crisis, right?"

"Don't get me started, Michelle. When they came back they went to visit Carter to thank *him,* not Reagan."

"I know, Ro. I love to wind you up, though. It's fun. Besides, Reagan *is* starting to get this economy turned around, so he's got to be doing something right. Carter's presidency wasn't exactly stellar, you know. Great man, but not a great president."

She noticed Ronan didn't reply at first. He got up and started to head back toward his office before turning back around. "I know Carter wasn't that good. Reagan, though? Yes, he's doing some things right, obviously. Of course he is. I won't deny that. Some other things, though? I think he's dead wrong. I think Emily was right. Did you notice after Lennon was shot they talked about Mark David Chapman's mental health? After Reagan himself was shot, they talked about John

Hinckley Jr.'s mental health. But did they do anything about mental health? No. They did the opposite. They repealed the act that was helping people who had issues. So, is that the trend now? Talk about mental health after something like a shooting happens but then never do anything about it? Not to mention this whole starting at the top thing. Does anyone really believe greedy corporate assholes are going to pass it along to their workers? I can tell you what it's going to end up like. It's going to be like dogs waiting for crumbs to fall from the table. Give me a break."

Michelle held up her hands. "Okay, then. Let's drop this before we get into another discussion where I literally have to pull a soapbox out from under you. How about we just get to work?" She scanned her calendar and then, "Aren't you going out anywhere today?"

"Not today," Ronan replied. "I have paperwork to clear up and later today I have to take Jonathan for his yearly checkup."

"That little boy is too precious."

"That he is," Ronan replied. "Also, giving amnesty to illegals is something I will give Reagan credit for. He did it even with members of his own party fighting him and, apparently, forgetting their ancestors were also immigrants. It's one of the things he got right. No soap box." With that, he turned and walked toward his office.

Michelle began going through the work on her desk. Her thoughts drifted toward her brother's family. She had to admit she was sometimes envious of how solid Ronan and Emily's marriage was. She hated to admit it to herself but she was envious of everything about them, even how they got over the revelation of who Emily really was. Then there was Ronan's over-the-top romantic proposal on the Pont Alexandre Bridge in Paris. They seemed to have a thing for bridges. She and June, along with Maggie and her family, had been with them on that trip and Michelle remembered it well. She had taken June to see the Eiffel tower lit up at night while Ronan took Emily to the bridge. When they met up again at the apartment, champagne was already flowing.

That was also the night everyone discovered what a beautiful singing voice Emily had. Michelle could still see it; Emily, feeling a little tipsy from the champagne, grabbing a candlestick to use as a microphone and singing Debbie Boone's 'You Light Up My Life". The look of pure love and happiness on Ronan's face was embedded in her memory. While she was truly happy for her brother, she couldn't help feeling jealous that night. No matter how much she wished it would, that feeling has never entirely gone away.

Emily

"How are you holding up?" Emily caught the worry in Jean's voice.

"I'm fine. There's no need to worry about me, Jean. I've been through worse."

"I know but still. Are you scared?"

Emily took a moment before responding. "For myself? No, not really. For my family? Yes. I'd be lying if I said I wasn't worried. If someone wants to come after me, fine, but no one better touch Jonathan or Ronan. That's what frightens me more. Rob has someone following me to, as he phrases it, keep me safe but I know how certain . . . entities, for lack of a better word . . . work. Families aren't always off-limits."

"Oh?" Emily heard the voice coming from behind her. She turned to see Theresa walking into the reception area.

"Hey, Theresa. I didn't realize you were in." Emily noticed Theresa looked tired and somewhat off again as she joined them at Jean's desk. Emily had been meaning to talk to her since the day after her interview, but then the letter arrived. She was worried about Theresa. Emily noticed she hadn't been herself since her minor surgery a few months ago. Though, a routine gallbladder removal would not account for the change in her demeanor.

"Yup, here I am," Theresa replied, setting her coffee cup on the desk and turning toward Emily. "Did I hear you correctly? Rob has someone keeping an eye on you?"

Emily nodded. "It keeps Ronan sane, if nothing else."

Theresa didn't respond. Instead, she flipped open the file she had in her hand and began to scan through it. Emily looked over at Jean, who only shrugged.

"Theresa, do you have a few minutes?" Emily asked. "I'd like to talk to you about something in my office."

"Sure." Theresa picked up her coffee and followed Emily into her office.

Closing the door and walking toward her desk, Emily noticed Theresa hadn't taken a seat. She'd walked to the window and was looking out over the parking lot. Emily sat down and watched Theresa for a few seconds. It wasn't like her to be standoffish. Normally, she would come in, take a seat and fire off a few smart ass comments before getting into whatever topic needed to be discussed. Lately, she'd been bordering on cold at the office and Emily hadn't heard from her outside of the office for almost a month. Emily had known for a while there was something going on with her. She began to wonder if something had, indeed, gone wrong with the minor surgery.

"I'm worried about you." Emily broke the silence.

Theresa continued to look out the window as she replied. "No need to be, Em. I'm fine. I just have a lot on my mind."

"You know you're not getting off that easy." Emily saw Theresa's shoulders drop slightly and heard her exhale. Whatever was happening, it was obviously something she hadn't wanted to discuss with her two closest friends. Emily grew more concerned.

"I said I'm fine." Theresa's reply came out clipped as she turned from the window and faced Emily. "You can unfurrow your brow, Emily. You don't need to worry."

Emily employed a practice she often used with her patients. She did not respond. She simply continued to look Theresa in the eye and waited. She did this with her patients when she could sense they weren't telling her the truth about something or were omitting something significant from the dialogue. It often led to them eventually revealing the entire truth. She felt a bit of relief as she saw it was working with Theresa. She watched as Theresa took a seat and inhaled deeply.

"It's only family stuff, Emily. There are some things going on with my mother and, naturally, my brother. It's getting very nasty. I really don't want to talk about it right now." Theresa paused and looked at the ceiling for a few seconds then closed her eyes, exhaled and looked back at Emily. "I've talked to you about my family but I never told you about our history. It's complicated and it's rearing its ugly head. It will be resolved soon but for right now, I just do not want to discuss it. I hope you understand that."

"Of course, I understand," Emily replied, softening. "I will be here whenever you want to talk. Until then, tell me how I can help you."

"You can't, but I appreciate the offer." Theresa stood up. "I have some things I have to take care of before my next patient." She headed for the door and then paused, turned around and said, "I appreciate your concern, but please don't worry. It will be taken care of soon." With that, she left Emily's office, closing the door behind her.

It was true that Theresa had talked about the dysfunctional dynamics in her family. Her brother seemed to be the source of most of the chaos when it erupted, but she usually talked to Emily about it. She knew Theresa's brother had anger issues for which he would not seek help. Theresa had tried a few times to get him into counseling but to no avail. She hoped that Theresa would be able to resolve it and wondered if picking up her patients for a few days while she took some time off might not be a bad idea.

Emily didn't have long to contemplate how she could help Theresa before she heard a knock on her door. Looking up, she saw Ian stick his head in her office.

"You got a minute?"

"Sure." She motioned to one of the seats opposite her desk.

Emily waited as Ian settled himself in the chair and fumbled with a sheet of paper. He stared at it for a moment and she noticed he hesitated slightly before he began speaking.

"Emily, there's no easy way for me to say this, so . . ." He put the paper on her desk and slid it over to her.

Picking up the paper without taking her eyes off Ian, she had a feeling she already knew what was on it. Thoughts of how to help Theresa were immediately replaced by thoughts of Ian possibly leaving the clinic and how she would have to find someone to fill the hole he would leave behind. She glanced down at the sheet.

"Your resignation," she said stoically.

"I know it's short notice but I've accepted a position with Columbia Presbyterian. I'll have Jean send out the letters to my patients."

"Ian -"

"I've made up my mind, Emily."

Somewhat taken aback by the finality in his tone, Emily took a moment to gather her thoughts. There had never been any indication from Ian that he wasn't happy working at the clinic. It came as a shock to her that he had been looking to practice elsewhere and she was feeling blindsided.

"Is there -"

"No."

"Can we talk about this?"

"There's nothing to talk about." Again, the finality struck her.

"When will you be leaving?" She began to think about sending out feelers and going back over the qualifications of the recent graduates.

"I'm already gone."

"What?!" It felt as if someone had thrown cold water on her face. Emily couldn't hide the shock.

Ian exhaled and held up his hands. "I know it's not professional. I know you're going to be upset with me but I need to take this job. It's a huge step. I already had Jean cancel my appointments for the rest of the week and I'll have her do the letters this afternoon."

Anger began to take over from the shock. "You're damned right it's not professional. What the hell, Ian? You could have given me a heads up before today. We're a team here. We've all been through a lot together to get this clinic where it is, not to mention the Tribeca clinic. You'll excuse me if I'm having a hard time understanding this. I thought you were happy here. Your patients have nothing but praise for you. I'm not even sure what to say. It's appalling to me that you have so little respect for the rest of us that you couldn't afford us the decency of some notice."

Ian lowered his eyes and remained silent for a few moments. He shifted in his chair, ran a hand through his hair and looked back at Emily. "I'm sorry, Emily. I really am. It's something I can't turn down. Yes, I've been happy here. I think the work being done here is tremendous but I feel I can also make a difference up there. I know I can. We all know mental health still isn't being taken seriously enough. Between here and Tribeca, you guys have this covered. I want to focus on in-patient care now. I think it's important. You know people are being released who aren't ready to cope yet. You know more people are either going to end up at Columbia Presbyterian or on the street once the effects of the repeal start being felt." He fell silent again. Emily did not respond. Ian fidgeted with his tie for a second before concluding. "I think I'm needed more there than I am here."

Emily mulled over everything Ian had said. She continued to look him in the eyes. She knew everything Ian said was true, but something felt off about it. She couldn't place her finger on it yet she couldn't argue with his reasoning. "What you've said is true," she said carefully. "I'm not 100% sold as to it being the entire reason you're leaving us, though. Is there anything you would like to add?"

She noticed Ian avert his eyes for a second before looking back and responding, "No, that's it. You can see it's a great opportunity."

Emily nodded. "I guess there is nothing left to discuss. That just leaves all the normal paperwork. I'll come by later this afternoon with the papers to sign. That includes all the privacy notices as well as non-compete, etc."

Ian stood up. "Thank you, Emily. I'll always be grateful to you for picking me up right after graduation. I hope you know that."

"I do," Emily acknowledged, though she felt something was not genuine in his tone.

After Ian exited her office, she literally dropped her head on her desk. She felt the beginnings of another headache starting to form. Her next patient wasn't due for another 40 minutes; a man whose father had been verbally abusive and who had fallen into depression when he realized he had turned out just like him. They'd been making progress and she was optimistic he would be able to break the cycle and form healthier and more stable relationships. She was glad to have some time to take some aspirin and recover from the inconvenient news Ian dropped on her before he arrived.

She heard a soft whispering noise and lifted her head to see Marcus sitting in the chair Ian had vacated. All thoughts of Theresa, Ian, and her patient fled her mind as she stared at the impeccably dressed man she had expected to see days ago. She had thought he would appear the night the letter came but he hadn't. As the days went on, she began to wonder if he had abandoned her, if he felt her soul was no longer "worth saving", as he had put it all those years ago.

"Rough day?" Marcus asked.

"Where have you been?" Emily didn't bother with formalities. "I expected you to show up right after the letter came. I need to know who sent it."

Marcus raised an eyebrow. "My, it has been a rough one. Darling, you know I can't tell you that."

"Won't," Emily corrected.

"Both. I can't and I won't." Marcus sat forward in the chair. "Emily, you need to be careful. More so than you have been. There's been a . . . ," Marcus paused for a moment as if he was searching for the right word, "development. Not everything is as it may appear to you. You need to look deeper than you have in the past."

"Deeper where, Marcus? What isn't as it appears? My God, that's such an old trope." Emily rolled her eyes and mimicked Marcus' speech pattern, "Nothing is as it seems." She went back to her usual voice. "What am I supposed to do with that?"

"I understand your frustration, Emily. I understand your mood. I'm afraid I have used the wrong words. Let me rephrase this. Everything is as it appears . . . on the surface. It's what's underneath that is not what you may think it is. You need to look deeper, under the surface."

"Again, deeper where? Give me a place to start, Marcus."

"That is all I can say."

"Are you telling me someone I know wrote the letter?" Emily's question was met with silence. "Family? Patient? Corbyn?" She prodded but was met with more silence. "You have to give me something. I know a lot of people, Marcus. I've worked with so many people over the years. First at Corbyn and now with patients, colleagues, professional groups, not to mention all the groups I've been an activist with."

"I do not have to tell you that humans are a complicated species. One may appear to be happy and adjusted one day only to attempt suicide the next. Every day, in everyone's mind, there are thousands of unspoken thoughts, unexpressed emotions. Among those thoughts and emotions are the details that make up that person. While everything is as it appears on the surface, it's the thoughts not spoken, it's the *knowledge* not revealed, that always holds the answers to puzzles such as this."

Emily sat back. She considered what Marcus had just said. There was an absolute truth in it. "I need to start with what I don't know." She saw Marcus give a slight nod. "The problem is that old saying – I don't know what I don't know."

"You have always been a thorough person, Emily. Although, there is an area you weren't thorough enough. I must be on my way, but before I go there are two things: first," Marcus paused for dramatic effect, "that was an awful impersonation of me." The corners of his mouth rose into a slight smile before becoming serious again. "The second is . . . you know who to ask for help in discovering things you do not know about people."

He was gone before Emily could say anything else. Rubbing her hands over her face she thought about the ending of the conversation. *Start with what you don't know. You know who to ask,* she thought. It clicked almost immediately. She grabbed the phone and dialed.

"Rob? It's Emily. You may need to hire another investigator. We need to go much deeper."

Ronan

Ronan heard the familiar chaos in the front office as Mike and Bart returned from Long Island. He glanced at the clock. It was only a few minutes past noon. He was sure that job would have taken the rest of the day. He walked out to find the guys around Michelle's desk, teasing her as they usually did.

"Hey, I didn't think I'd see you two until tomorrow. What's up?"

Mike turned around, saw Ronan and then side-glanced Bart. "We ran into a little problem. Seems there are electrical wires that need to be rerouted before we can continue. We weren't prepared for that. The guy is fine with it. We scheduled to come back Friday and finish up." He tilted his head to Michelle. "I just told her to add it to the calendar."

Ronan took a second before replying. "Bart, I thought you looked everything over before we did the quote."

Bart was still turned toward Michelle, appearing to wait for some kind of retort to something he said. When he heard Ronan address him, he turned his head and said over his shoulder, "Yeah, I did. He didn't tell me about the wires. It's cool. We'll go back Friday." He turned his attention back to Michelle.

"It's not cool. We won't be charging for the extra time. We also have other jobs scheduled for Friday. How are you going to be in Long Island and the West Village at the same time?"

Bart gave Michelle a sheepish look as if to say 'oops, I'm in trouble with the boss'. Turning around he said, "It's fine, Ronan. That job will be two, two and a half hours at most, to finish up. The place in the West Village is fixing some of the vents. We're not talking an all day job there. Don't worry."

"Question for you," Ronan folded his arms. "When you looked

the place over, did you happen to ask if there were any wires going through that wall? That's a pretty standard question when it comes to something like, I don't know, cutting a hole in the wall for a pass-through. And if you're at the point where you found wires, that means you didn't get the frame in and it's going to be longer than two and a half hours to finish it."

"Look, Ronan," Mike started but Ronan held up his hand.

"Bart?"

"I asked. He said he didn't think so."

"He didn't think so," Ronan shook his head then addressed Michelle. "Call Kevin. Have him go with Mike on Friday to the West Village. I'll be going with Bart to Long Island. Make a note of it."

"Got it," Michelle said as she began to write on the work calendar.

"What?" Bart looked irritated. "You don't trust me?"

"I want to make sure the job gets finished Friday to the client's satisfaction."

Bart stared at him for a few seconds before asking, "Is there a problem?"

The truth was this wasn't the first time Bart had missed something important while looking over a place. He also tended to talk bigger than he could deliver. Bart had been highly recommended to Ronan when he was looking for another full-time employee and he'd been pleasant and professional in his interview. Over time, he seemed to slip into a different personality. Mike had complained about him on several occasions and Ronan had reprimanded him more than once.

"We'll see on Friday if there's a problem." Ronan began to turn back to his office.

"What are you saying? Are my days here numbered?"

Ronan spun on his heel. "What?"

The sudden move from Ronan seemed to take Bart by surprise.

"Whoa, I'm just sayin' it seems like you're looking for a reason to let me go."

Ronan looked toward Michelle, who seemed to have the same reaction he did, although Mike looked as surprised as Bart did. Ronan inhaled and paused. He reminded himself it was a common enough saying. He couldn't suspect everyone who used it to be the person who wrote the note. He looked at Bart and said, "I'm not saying anything. Let's just get the job finished and go from there. In the meantime, take the van and pick up the order at Garber. I was going to pick it up in the morning but it seems you got some time now. Mike, can I see you for a minute?"

Mike followed Ronan into his office where they discussed Bart's recent attitude and unprofessionalism. Mike relayed Bart had foreseen Ronan being upset with him but didn't seem to care. They discussed several options but in his gut Ronan was leaning toward letting Bart go. He'd taken notes and Bart had signed the reprimands when they happened, so his paperwork was in order should Bart try to sue or take any other legal measure against him. He wasn't sure it was the answer but he was covered if it was.

After sending Mike out on an errand to the lumber yard, he walked back to Michelle's desk. She was concentrating on typing when she noticed Ronan walking toward her. Ronan saw her stop typing and swing her chair toward him.

"Bart's a pain in the ass, Ronan." She said it flatly as a statement of fact.

"Yeah, I know. Gotta say, when he asked if his days are numbered it threw me."

"It threw me, too, but it's a phrase a lot of people use."

"I know." Ronan glanced at the clock. "I gotta run and take Jonathan to his appointment. Anything for tomorrow the guys can get done today?"

Michelle shook her head. "Only one they could do quickly but the guy's not home. I left a message on his answering machine but I doubt he'll call before the end of the day."

Ronan nodded. "Okay. When they get back, tell them they can call it a day. I'll see you tomorrow."

Leaving the office, Ronan headed to the elevator. In the beginning, he thought Bart had been a good fit. He was pleasant enough and his work was good. When his attitude began to change, so did his work ethic. It was disappointing and Ronan hated it, but all signs pointed toward letting him go. His mind ran through what other options there were, including a suspension or a probation period. When he reached the loft, he still wasn't sure which way was the best.

"Jonathan's all ready," Ellen announced when he entered the loft.

The patter of little sneakered feet running toward him told Ronan his son was more than ready to leave the loft. He scooped Jonathan up and gave him a hug.

"Ronan, are you having work done on your bathroom?"

He looked at Ellen curiously. "No, why?"

"You didn't call a plumber?" Ellen asked.

Ronan put Jonathan down and turned to the babysitter. "Did something happen, Ellen?"

Ellen hesitated a moment and wrung her hands. "It might be nothing, but a little less than an hour ago a man rang the bell. You know how you get those feelings sometimes that something might be wrong?" She looked at Ronan expectantly and he nodded. "Well, I had a feeling something wasn't right. You guys told me not to unlock the door and to never let anyone in unless you told me in advance they are coming. So, I just asked who it was and he said he was the plumber I called. Well, he didn't say me in particular. I mean, I didn't call a plumber, he said 'I'm the plumber you called' like I live here, you know?" She paused and

Ronan nodded again. "I told him we weren't expecting anyone and maybe he should come back when you were home."

"Let me make sure I got this straight. A man came and said he was a plumber that was called to come by today but he didn't use my name or Emily's?"

"No, he didn't use either of your names. You hadn't said anything to me about it and neither did Emily. So, I didn't open the door. I kept it locked and told him to come back."

"We didn't call a plumber, Ellen. You did the right thing. Thank you."

"I don't mean to sound like a scaremonger but do you think it might have been the person who wrote that note?"

Ronan sighed. "I don't know. Maybe." Seeing the frightened look on Ellen's face, Ronan switched course. "Maybe not. Probably not. He could actually be a plumber that got the wrong apartment number. It wouldn't be the first time something like that happened."

"That's true," Ellen said. "It's just the feeling I got. That feeling of danger, you know?"

"Daddy, daddy, daddy. Let's go!" Jonathan began tugging at Ronan's jeans.

"I know," Ronan said to Ellen, then bent down and picked up Jonathan once again. "You did the right thing, Ellen. You have a whole new set of rules for this job, now. Just stick to them and let us know when something happens, like today. I don't think you have to worry about this, though. People mix up apartment numbers all the time."

"You're right about that. I once got a pizza I didn't order," Ellen said and appeared to relax.

Once outside and in a cab on the way to the pediatrician, Ronan tried to focus on Jonathan but his mind kept going back to the plumber. He calmed Ellen's fear but he hadn't calmed his own. It was true the guy could have gotten the wrong apartment. He wasn't lying when he said those things happen. It had even happened to him a time or two. That could very easily be what happened. But, then again, maybe not.

Michelle

"I said no, June," Michelle was exasperated. "I don't care who else is going. Your curfew is 11 o'clock. End of story, young lady."

"Young lady? Gag me with a spoon," June's voice sounded tinny through the receiver. "You're so old-fashioned. And over-protective. And uptight. Amy's mother is letting her go and you know Amy's mom. You know she wouldn't let Amy go unless it was safe."

"Safe? June, we're talking about a concert in Midtown. Safe is not the word I would use."

"A cab up and a cab back. That's pretty safe. It's not like we'll be taking the subway or walking around Times Square all night. Come on, Mom!"

"You have my answer," Michelle replied as she heard the office door open and saw Bart walk in. "I have to go now. I will see you when I get home."

After hanging up, she steeled herself for more of Bart's comments. There were times he was genuinely funny but mostly he was crass and offensive. She often wondered how his wife managed to put up with him. But who was she to judge anyone when she'd been married to an embezzling cheater. Bart was many things but at least she knew he wasn't stealing from the business.

"Kid trouble?" Bart asked.

"What else is new?" Michelle answered. "I'll never get used to the expressions kids use today. Like gag me with a spoon. And what the hell does 'grody' mean?"

Bart laughed and replied, "I think grody means something is nasty. I think. I could be wrong. But we all had our own expressions, like it was all groovy, you know, daddio?"

Michelle put her head in her hands and laughed. She looked up and gave Bart the peace sign with her fingers. "Peace, brother."

"Don't tell me you were a flower child!"

"Oh Lord, no. I was too busy being the perfect little housewife." Michelle rolled her eyes. "But I could have been. I should have been. Maybe they'll come back around."

"Maybe." Bart shrugged.

"Anyway," Michelle sat up straight. "Ronan said you can call it a day. You leave the order in the van?"

Bart nodded. "Locked up tight." He paused and then, "Everything okay with your brother? He seems uptight lately."

Michelle eyed him for a second before replying. "He's fine. Busy schedule with Jonathan and the business, that's all."

"Where's his wife? Shouldn't she be helping with the kid and stuff?"

Michelle noticed the shift in his voice. The light-heartedness vanished and was replaced with a slightly hard undertone. "You know his wife's name and you know what she does. You also know she does a lot with Jonathan." She squinted at him. "Why the attitude? You don't like her?"

Bart shrugged again and made a face. "Don't really know her. She seems like kind of a big shot or she thinks she is, anyway. Kind of snooty, don't you think? Especially for someone who tried to hide her past."

"Like you said, you don't know her. She's not snooty at all. She didn't try to hide her past, Bart. She overcame it. Big difference." Michelle's irritation showed in her voice.

"If you say so. A leopard can't change its spots, though. Isn't that what they say?"

"I don't know what you're getting at, Bart, but I'll say it again. You don't know her. Shouldn't you be concentrating on yourself and getting that pass-through done on Friday. I'll be honest, I don't think Ronan bought you asked about the wall. I think you should do yourself a favor and focus on your work."

"Look, *I'm* gonna be honest here. I'm a good worker and if your brother is thinking about getting rid of me I'm going to have a problem with that. He's going out with me Friday because he doesn't trust me. I already have a couple reprimands because of Mike, that fucking suck up. I do quality work. I'm goddamned good at what I do."

Bart paused for a moment, rubbed his hands on his face and then continued in a calmer tone. "I can't afford to lose this job."

"No one said you're going to," Michelle answered.

"I see the writing on the wall." Bart's tone and demeanor changed again. "Ronan's got a nice cushy life going with that woman up there. A woman you say overcame her past, I say a woman who thinks she's better than everyone else. I saw her interview on TV. She wouldn't even admit the poor guy she fired got the raw end of the deal. Ronan's got someone like that chirping in his ear and he talks to her about this business; before you know it, I'm out on the street. While they're up there living the high life, what do you think me and my wife will do? She better not convince him to fire me. That's all I'm saying."

Michelle was startled. "Bart, you are so wrong. Emily doesn't say anything to Ronan about this business. He's his own man. Ronan and I run this business. We're the ones you should be concerned about, not her. Right now, you're not making a good case for yourself. This is completely inappropriate. Emily has always stayed out of this. She has no say whatsoever in what goes on around here and I don't understand why you would think she does."

"It's absolutely appropriate when my boss is married to someone like her. I'm not concerned about you and Ronan. My work will speak for itself. He'll see that on Friday."

"Look, I don't know what your problem is but this isn't helping you."

Michelle saw Bart narrow his eyes. It seemed as if he wanted to say something and then changed his mind. Even though she knew he was right to be concerned about his job, she was dumbstruck with his attitude toward Emily. Michelle wasn't even sure they had ever met. To her, his apparent anger seemed irrational.

"You may not think Emily Corbyn has a say in this business but I guarantee you she does." Bart's tone was calmer but no less hard. "Someone like her always calls the shots."

The fact that Bart called her Emily Corbyn instead of Emily Byrne was not lost on Michelle. "Jesus Christ, you really have a bug up your ass and you don't know her at all."

"I don't have to know her, Michelle. I read the book."

Michelle sat in shocked silence as Bart left the office.

Emily

Emily sat in silence as Michelle relayed her conversation with Bart. Assembled at the table in the loft, she, Rob, his two investigators and Ronan listened as Michelle wrapped up her story by letting them know it appeared Bart's problem with Emily came solely from reading Lyle Kettering's book. Emily had initially asked for this meeting in order for her to explain why she wanted the investigation to go deeper than originally thought. She had no idea Bart, who she had only seen in passing a few times, had harbored animosity toward her.

"So, if he feels like that," Michelle was saying, "there might be others out there that feel the same way after reading the book. I don't know how you would even go about finding out how many or where they are."

"We don't." Emily's voice was calm but firm. "I don't believe it's a random person who read the book and developed a hatred of me. I believe it's someone I know." She sighed heavily. "I know that covers a lot of people between Corbyn, college, my work, my advocacy, but it's someone I've had contact with on some level."

"You've had contact with Bart," Ronan broke in, more than just a little angry. "Tomorrow that son of a bitch gets his walking papers. I'll make sure he doesn't come anywhere near you."

Emily was about to speak when she noticed Rob lean over and speak quietly with the investigator he introduced as Troy. Troy reminded her of Telly Savalas from *Kojak*. She had to remind herself that wasn't his name. She was also fighting the urge to ask him where his lollipop was. More than that, she wanted to speak to why she asked them all to meet.

"Rob, would you like to share?" she asked.

"It's nothing important, Em," Rob answered. "I was just reiterating we won't waste our time on random people who may have read the book. However, I think we should look into the cross section of who you know that might have read it."

Emily wanted to tell him not to waste time on that, either, but she was getting tired and her headache from earlier was returning. She also had no desire to explain that between her gut feeling and her conversation with Marcus, she was certain the book had nothing to do with it. It was troubling enough that she would have to sit down and have a conversation with Ronan about Marcus. Marcus was the one thing she never fully explained to Ronan. She referenced him in a vague sense of being a guardian angel but she was sure Ronan accepted the concept of a guardian angel as most people do - not one that actually appears and has full conversations.

"Okay, that's fine, but I'd like to get to why I wanted to talk with everyone," Emily began, "before Michelle let us in on Bart which, to be honest, I wasn't expecting and I must say he is showing definite signs of paranoia and someone might want to suggest he see someone."

"His wife can worry about that. After tomorrow, he's no longer our problem," Ronan interjected.

"He's our problem if I'm the focus of his paranoia," Emily responded. "Regardless, I believe we need to dig deeper into the lives of the people in our circles. All relatives, friends, co-workers, the people in my advocacy groups." She turned toward Troy and his partner, whose name was escaping her. "I will give you a list of those groups before you leave."

"How deep are you talking, Emily?" The question came from Rob.

"I'm talking everything. Go back as far as you can. Not just what they're doing now but what they've done in the past, what schools they went to, what groups they might have been a part of, where they lived, what their parents did, who their friends were in high school, college, who their friends are now and if those friends are in any specific groups. Look for anything I might be tied to either now or in the past at any point. I need to know what I don't know about the people in my life."

Troy let out a breath and sat back. "That's a lot of work. It'll take some time given the number of people you know." He turned to Rob. "We'll need more people if you want it done sooner rather than later."

"As many as you need. We need to figure this out soon. Between Bart's sudden rant about Emily and the plumber that came to the door this afternoon, I don't want to take any more chances." He paused. Emily noticed he glanced at Ronan before he continued speaking again. "Emily, I want you to go to Paris."

"No."

"Honey," Ronan started, "I think-"

"No."

Emily heard Rob sigh. She watched as her brother got up from the table and headed to the refrigerator, asking if anyone wanted a beer or anything else. She stood up and grabbed the wine bottle off the counter. She filled her glass and then Ronan's. She knew Ronan wasn't happy. He'd asked her before to go to Paris. She took note of the locked jaw and tense muscles in his neck. Once seated again, she waited until Rob came back with his own beer and one for Troy's partner.

"I'm not going anywhere. I understand why you want me to go, but I'm not leaving my family. I'm not going to run away." She picked up her glass and took a sip. "You already have someone watching me. I'm fine with that. I won't take any unnecessary chances. I'll go to work and I'll come home. I'll limit my movement but I'm not leaving my family." She reached over and grabbed Ronan's hand. She felt him squeeze it and knew he understood.

"I agree with her," Michelle chimed in. "Emily has never been one to back down. I don't expect her to start now."

"Well, you're right about that. Okay, then, I'm not about to argue with both of you," Rob said. "We started with Jack and his associates." He turned to address the investigators. "Dig deeper into them. You have a list of everyone employed at Safe Haven and at Byrne Improvements. Get those done first and then go into our cousins. You have their names. They're not exactly fans of ours. Find out what they've been up to lately. Fan out from there, Emily's college years, even the professors, the advocacy groups, etc."

"You got it," Troy responded.

"Troy," Emily interjected, "I meant what I said before. I need to know everything. I strongly believe the answer is in something that I don't know that I should know. I almost feel like it's just one little piece of information that I either overlooked or was just not aware of. I would like updates daily, twice daily if you can. As soon as you learn something new, I want to know about it."

"Yes, ma'am. We'll be very thorough," Troy responded.

"I'm sorry," Emily said to his partner, "I'm not sure I caught your name earlier."

"Marc, ma'am," the quieter one replied.

Emily suppressed a smile as she asked, "Marc with a c or with a k?" Though she was fairly sure she already knew the answer.

"C, ma'am."

"Thank you for taking this on, Marc. I appreciate what you and Troy are doing. Very much so, but please call me Emily. I don't feel old enough to be called ma'am. Not yet, anyway. Is Marc short for something? Maybe Marcus?"

"You can just call me Marc," he replied. "There's one other thing, though. Don't talk about this with anyone. Not even your closest friends or other family members. Don't let anyone in on the fact you have hired investigators. I know there are people both of you would be eager to cross off the list but, trust me, you never know what goes on in people's minds. I've been doing this long enough to know that no matter how well you think you know a person, you end up finding out how little you actually knew."

"I had a similar conversation earlier today, Marc. A thousand unspoken thoughts."

"Exactly, Emily."

After Emily gave them the list of groups she had once advocated for and with, and they were once again alone in the loft with Jonathan fast asleep, she sunk into the sofa and closed her eyes. She heard Ronan cleaning up and making sure everything was locked up. She felt the sofa shift as he sat down beside her.

"What made you change your mind?"

Emily opened her eyes and looked at her husband. "What do you mean?"

"Yesterday you were thinking it might be someone who just wanted to scare you but wouldn't do anything else. Today, you want to dig deeper and speed up finding out who it is."

Emily sat up and turned toward him. She knew she would have to tell him the complete story of Marcus and not the vague version she'd given him in the past. They had already been through so much together but she wasn't sure how Ronan would take to knowing she had an actual guardian angel - if that's what he even was - that had appeared to her, spoken to her and even guided her.

"Okay, there's something I need to tell you. There's . . ." she paused, trying to find the right words.

"There's what? A thousand unspoken thoughts?"

Emily raised her eyebrows. "There are. That's not what I was going to say but, yes, there are. It's an interesting point."

"You told Marc you had a similar conversation about it today. It seemed like both of you were on the same page about that. Do you know him from somewhere?"

"No, I didn't meet him until tonight. But I have a feeling I know who or what is guiding him."

Ronan

Two days after Emily revealed the truth about Marcus to him, Ronan found himself sitting in his office once again thinking about it. It sounded so outlandish, so unbelievable, something that a science fiction show is made from. Yet, he knew it was true. As Emily had laid it all out for him, he understood more clearly her reactions to certain things. Her nervousness at the beginning of their first date and the way she left before things had gotten too personal for her. What cemented it for him was remembering how she had run out of Michelle's house that day. She was adamant they leave immediately. He now knew it was because she had to tell him she had been Emily Corbyn before Jack could. If Jack had gotten to it first, he wouldn't have remembered what happened that night on the bridge when she had stopped him from jumping.

Ronan understood the concept of a guardian angel but it didn't seem Marcus was within that realm. Emily told him she had asked several times but never received a straight answer so the easiest explanation was to describe him in that way. He recalled during the time they had been working things out Emily had often explained certain things to him and would use the phrase 'my guardian angel must have guided me'. On one hand, he knew she had been telling him the truth . . . or as much of the truth as she thought was appropriate without sounding insane. On the other hand, he couldn't shake the feeling of disappointment that she hadn't told him all of this upfront or at least at some point over the last few years.

It's not that he didn't understand, he did. He knew he would have thought it was crazy. He knew he would have thought she was fabricating it, especially if she would have told him while they were working on things in addition to dealing with the fallout of Jack's arrest and trials. It would have been too much for him to handle or believe at that point. Still, he couldn't shake the feeling and it bothered him.

"He called again." Michelle's voice shook him from his thoughts. Ronan looked up to see her standing in the doorway. He knew she was talking about Bart, who he had let go the day after their meeting with the investigators.

"What did he say this time?" He asked the question in a way that let Michelle know he really didn't care and didn't want to deal with it.

"Same thing," she replied. "He's not going to let this go. He's saying exactly what we expected him to say, that you discussed him with Emily and she convinced you to let him go. That train of thought makes no sense to me but he wouldn't listen to reason. He's threatening to sue."

Ronan sat back in his chair and didn't reply right away. He didn't care if Bart sued. He had all the paperwork in order as well as witnesses. The only thing he wanted was for Bart to go away. He was sure if he saw him in person again he would let him have it for talking about his wife to Michelle the way he had. Bart had no reason to have any resentment toward Emily, regardless of the fact he read the book. She had been nothing but nice to him the few times she'd come in contact with him.

Taking Mike out to Long Island early this morning, they finished the pass-through and had gotten back in enough time for Mike to head to the West Village to help Kevin with the vents. At least Bart hadn't cost him any clients so he found at least one silver lining. That was it, though. If he never saw Bart again it would be too soon.

"Let him sue," he finally replied. "It won't get far."

Michelle walked in and sat in the chair opposite Ronan's desk. Ronan could feel her steady stare. He could also feel the concern almost jump off her. He knew he'd been unusually quiet the last few days. He should have known Michelle would eventually want to know why. He was tired and there was no way he was going to let Michelle in on

Marcus. He picked up the pen on his desk and began to play with it.

"Talk." Michelle broke the silence.

"I'm not really in the mood, Michelle."

"Is it bad? Did the investigators find something?"

He knew Michelle had been on edge since the meeting. She had told him she was hoping he was wrong and it was Jack behind it. She had gone through all the reasons it made sense that it was Jack. Ronan knew she was right about everything she had said, however, he didn't believe it was. Now, after the meeting and his talk with Emily, he felt anything was possible. He no longer racked his brain trying to figure it out because he now felt it could be anyone. He looked at everyone with suspicion from the mailman to Mike.

As promised, the investigators had updated Emily on their progress. They had dug up a lot of information but, so far, nothing that Emily either hadn't already known or she felt it was of no consequence. She also began doing what she had promised. The last two days she had gone to her office on the bottom floor and came right back up to the loft. Next week would be different as she had her days in the Brooklyn office. She had reluctantly agreed to let Carl, the man assigned to watching her, escort her.

"Ronan? Did they find something?" Michelle asked again.

"Nothing important."

"Is that what's weighing on you?"

Ronan decided to take the easy way out. "Sure is."

"Ro, maybe I'm wrong. Maybe it isn't Jack. Maybe it's exactly what Emily said days ago, that it's someone that just wanted to scare her and won't do anything else. It could be, you know. Nothing has happened since the letter."

He knew Michelle was trying to ease his mind but it wasn't working. "You forgot about the plumber and, of course, Bart's delusional rant."

"Well, Bart *is* delusional. I doubt it was him. And you, yourself, said it was very possible it was actually a plumber who got the wrong apartment. You know, that's easy enough to check on. Just ask your neighbors in the building."

"Already asked most of them, none of them called one. I still have a few more to ask, though. Yeah, I know it's possible but it just seems like too much of a coincidence. Look, Michelle, it's been a long day. I really just want to wrap things up here, go upstairs and see my boy."

Michelle nodded and got up. "I understand. I have a moody teenager I have to get home to. She's still upset that I won't let her see Peter Gabriel but at least I learned how to program the VCR so she won't miss this big video premiere."

"Cut her some slack, Misha, she's a good kid."

"Ro?"

Ronan looked up to see Michelle staring at him with more concern on her face than she had when she walked in. "What?"

"There are only certain times you call me that."

"What? Your name?"

"Ro, you called me Misha." Michelle sat back down. "You're not okay. What is it? I'm here to listen whether it's about finding who threatened Emily or whether it's Bart or whatever. Talk to me."

Ronan sat silent for a moment. He didn't realize he'd called her Misha. She was right that he only used it at certain times. Ever since that night he almost jumped he only used it when his depression reared up and he was going into one of his rough patches.

"I'm just overwhelmed," he started, trying to reassure her. "It's a lot to deal with. Plus, Jack's parole hearing is not far off. It's more exhaustion than anything. I haven't been sleeping well. Too much going through my mind. No need to worry."

Michelle regarded him for a moment and then rose from the

chair again. "Okay, but you know I'm here. Call me if you need something."

He gave her a nod and Michelle walked out. Leaning back, he shook his head. In the past, he had always been able to feel when the storm was coming. Until Michelle alerted him that he used her nickname, he hadn't realized the storm had already arrived.

Michelle

Walking into the apartment, Michelle immediately knew something was wrong. She found June sitting on the living room sofa, hugging her legs, chin on her knees. The TV was on but she didn't seem to be watching it. Michelle set down her purse and keys and slowly walked over to her. She could see June's eyes were red from crying. Instead of asking her any questions, Michelle sat down next to her and wrapped her arm around her. When June leaned in and rested her head on Michelle's shoulder, Michelle knew it was something more than not being able to attend a concert.

After a few minutes, June broke the silence. "Jack called."

That was something Michelle was not expecting. It took a moment to gather her thoughts before she answered. "Well, his hearing is soon. I'm sure he just wanted to talk to you."

June sat up and wiped her forearm across her nose. She shook her head and looked at Michelle through teary eyes. "It was more than that. I mean, in the beginning he did say he was looking forward to seeing me but he kind of got angry when I wasn't responding. Mom, I didn't want to talk to him."

Michelle reached out and took her hand. "I know, sweetheart. I'm so sorry I wasn't home to intercept the call."

Guilt crept through Michelle. She should have been there. If she hadn't taken the time to talk to Ronan maybe she would have been. June comes first. That was always her rule, but lately it seemed the letter and the issue with Bart had taken over. She checked in with June daily, by phone during the day and at night before they went to bed, she kept on top of her schoolwork and where she went with her friends on weekends. Michelle thought she'd been sticking to her rule, but she realized now she'd been distracted with everything else. She was doing what she had always done but her mind had been somewhere else.

"He was angry," June continued. "He insisted that you had brainwashed me against him. I told him you didn't, that I remembered what he did that day and that showed me all I needed to know about him."

"How did he react to that?"

"Well, he said I was too young at the time and I couldn't possibly remember what happened exactly as it did. He said that I must have listened to you and Uncle Ronan and my mind turned it into something worse than what it was. He said I wasn't being fair." June paused, her eyebrows furrowed. "Am I remembering it wrong?"

Michelle had spent enough time with Emily to understand exactly what Jack was doing. He had done it to her more times than she could count. In retrospect, it seemed it was the entire basis of their marriage.

"June, I know I'm going to sound like Aunt Emily when I say this but you need to understand this. Your father-"

"Don't call him that!" June's voice was shrill and Michelle felt June's nails dig into her hand.

"I'm sorry, honey. Jack. You need to understand what Jack is doing." She felt June's hand relax. "He's doing what people in Aunt Emily's profession call gaslighting."

"I don't know what that means." June sniffed and wiped her eyes.

"It means when someone tries to make you question your reality. In this case, Jack was trying to get you to believe you didn't remember things correctly. He wants you to believe you've been wrong about it and because of that, you've been unfair to him. When you admitted to me that you remember that day, and you described it, I'm here to tell you that you absolutely remember it correctly. Do not let Jack make you question your memories, your feelings, or anything else."

Michelle watched as June absorbed what she had just said. She remained silent as June nodded and processed the information. Michelle could see her putting the pieces together as the look of worry on her face was replaced with something that looked like resolve.

"I hate him, Mom. I really do. For what he did to you, to Emily. For pretending to love us when I know he doesn't." June's voice was soft but serious.

Michelle reached out to hug her daughter but June leaned back and held up her hand. In that moment, she knew there was more to the conversation than Jack trying to get June to doubt herself. She wasn't sure she was ready to hear it.

"There's more, Mom," June said. She removed her hand from Michelle's and wiped both her eyes. When she looked up again, Michelle could see worry and anxiety had returned to her eyes. "Like I said, he was angry. He kept saying the three of you brainwashed me. He said Uncle Ro didn't have a mind of his own so he blames you and Aunt Emily. He said both of you were going to regret it, especially Aunt Emily."

Hearing this reinforced Michelle's thought that Jack was behind the letter. She wasn't surprised Jack thought it, he'd said as much to Ronan, but she was surprised he had verbalized it to June. As she looked at June, she realized that for as much as her daughter tried to act mature and able to handle anything thrown at her, Michelle found herself looking at a scared child who needed reassurance and needed to feel the strong family bond that had been created between them, Ronan and Emily.

"Honey, the only person who is going to feel regret is Jack. He's making empty threats from jail, that's all." She noticed June give her head a slight shake. "I'm going to make a phone call. Stay right here. There are things you need to hear from someone who could say them better than I can." Michelle got up and went to the phone, dialed it and talked softly. She then stretched the cord over to the sofa and handed the receiver to June. "Uncle Ro wants to talk to you."

As June took the receiver, Michelle walked into the kitchen and poured herself a glass of wine. She knew Ronan would find the right words to remind June of the love she was surrounded. For as much as she wanted to be the one with the right words, she also knew that children didn't always take their parents' words seriously. She knew that more often than not, children seemed to feel parents were only saying things because they had to but didn't really mean them. She knew hearing it from Ronan would get through to her more than if she would have tried. Michelle also knew that the same held true for Emily and, once again, she felt that small pang of jealousy. She tried to squash it. She knew it was ridiculous but she couldn't help when it surfaced.

Listening to June's end of the conversation, she knew Ronan was reaching her. She relaxed a little and took a sip of her wine. Her thoughts went to Jack's words. She would call Emily later and tell her to have Troy and Marc look further into who visited Jack and who he called from prison. She wanted nothing more than to find something concrete to keep him in prison longer. From there, her thoughts went to Ronan and how he had used her nickname earlier. She felt another pang of guilt that she had laid this on Ronan when he was probably going into one of his bleak phases. Realizing she really didn't have anyone else besides Emily to call who would make a difference to June eased the feeling. June came first. She wouldn't be distracted again.

Setting down her glass, she walked back into the living room and sat next to June. Michelle could see June was feeling better, engaging in the usual silly banter with her uncle. She wrapped an arm around her and felt June lean in, again. Inside, Michelle made herself a promise that Jack would never see her daughter, no matter what she had to do.

Emily

Gathered in the loft living room, watching The Wonderful World of Disney's *Blackbeard's Ghost* on TV with Jonathan, Ronan, Michelle and June, Emily began to feel normal for the first time since the letter came. Seated on the floor in front of the sofa with Jonathan between her legs, Emily wanted this moment to last. This is what she had dreamed about, a family that did things together, completely unlike the one she had grown up in. It didn't matter if they were watching a movie, going out to dinner, taking a vacation at the apartment overseas, or walking in the park, all that mattered to her was the togetherness and the feeling of love that always permeated these moments.

Emily felt grateful every day for this family, including her brother and sister, who had become just as integral as Michelle and June had. There were moments she wondered if things like the book, Jack, and this letter were a way to punish her for the mistakes she had made. If it was the universe's way of letting her know in some way it would always come back to remind her and disrupt the life she had built with this family. Monday morning wasn't far away and she would have to deal with everything again. Tonight, she only wanted to be present in the moment and soak up the atmosphere and feeling of normalcy.

"Come on, guys," Emily heard June's whine. "Jonathan is almost asleep over there. Can't we turn on *Silver Spoons*?"

"Why? Do you have a crush on that blonde kid?" Ronan teased.

June rolled her eyes. "Gag me, Uncle Ro. No way."

"You don't have a poster of him in your bedroom?"

Making a face, June replied, "I'd rather have Pat Benatar. The show's funny, though. Jonathan's falling asleep. Can we change the channel?"

Looking down at her son, Emily saw June was right. She looked up at Ronan and smiled. "I'm going to put him to bed. Put on *Silver*

Spoons if you want to."

"I'll come with you," Ronan replied.

Settling Jonathan into his bed, Emily gave him a kiss on the forehead and pulled the covers over him. She stood looking over him with that feeling of love only a mother can experience. She looked over at Ronan, who was making sure Jonathan's favorite stuffed bunny was beside him under the covers. Her heart was ready to burst with the love she felt for both of them.

She had been worried about Ronan the last few days but she noticed that his low periods were farther apart and he wasn't sinking as deep into his depression as he had been in the past. The combination of his current medication and continued therapy was working the way it was intended to. He still called these periods 'the storm' but that term no longer seemed appropriate. He would deal with depression the rest of his life but his commitment to not letting it control him or his life was one of the reasons she loved him.

The news of Marcus being more than a concept had thrown him, as it would have thrown anyone. But he didn't question that it was the truth. That he didn't ridicule it or dismiss it meant he trusted her completely and knew she wouldn't fabricate something that sounded so outrageous. As Emily watched Ronan, it reinforced once again that she would never do anything that would break his trust in her.

As they walked out of Jonathan's room, Emily reached for Ronan's hand and stopped him. She turned him toward her, ran her hands through his hair and stopped, leaving her hands on either side of his face. "I love you, Ronan Byrne. I know life with me hasn't exactly been smooth sailing, and yet we've built this incredible life together. You've built a successful business. You create the most exquisite furniture. You're smart, you're creative, you're so grounded and solid and caring. You've done an incredible job being there for June, for me, for Jonathan. I know these last few days haven't been easy for you, but you were still there for all of us. I don't tell you often enough how much I appreciate you, how much you've influenced me and how much I love you."

As Ronan gently touched her cheeks, Emily felt that strong connection. It reassured her that no one and nothing could ever break them apart. She closed her eyes and breathed in. If only they could pause time and remain in this moment with their family.

"I love you more than you can possibly fathom, you incredibly brilliant, incredibly complicated, and incredibly wonderful woman. I wouldn't have a life if it wasn't for you. You inspire me every single day. What you have given me, what you have done for me goes beyond words. I wouldn't be half the man I am today without you." Ronan bent into a kiss and for a few moments, Emily felt loved, complete, and at peace.

As they moved apart, Emily smiled at her husband, though it was a smile that conveyed the moment of peace had passed and there was a reality that had to be contended with. She slid her hands down his arms and grabbed his hands. "We've gotten through everything else. We'll get through this, too."

She felt Ronan squeeze her hands as he said, "You know it. And as soon as this is all over, as soon as the parole hearing is over, we're getting out of here. We'll take everyone to Paris and spend a week eating rich French desserts and listening to June complain you can't see the Eiffel Tower from the apartment."

"Sounds perfect!" Emily laughed as she turned and led him back into the living room.

"I heard my name. What'd I do now?" June asked as soon as they entered.

"I guess we'll be listing eavesdropping as a skill on your college application," Ronan teased his niece.

"I wasn't eavesdropping! You guys were talking too low,

anyway. But I did clearly hear my name." June had her legs draped over the side of the chair with a bowl of popcorn balanced on her stomach. "So, what about me?"

Emily stopped as Ronan walked over to June, took a handful of popcorn, and said, "Just that you're a giant complainer who's lucky to have such a cool uncle."

"Who said you were cool? They lied." June threw a few pieces of popcorn at Ronan.

"Your mom." Ronan threw one back at her.

Michelle laughed, threw a piece of popcorn from her hand at her brother and said, "I never said you were cool, you big dork!"

Ronan threw a piece back at her and it only took a second before the three of them were throwing popcorn at each other. It ended when June stood up and emptied the bowl into the back of Ronan's shirt.

Emily stood back, watching and laughing at them. She shook her head as she walked over and took the bowl from June. "I'm not cleaning that up." She turned to Ronan. "This is another reason we should get a dog."

"To clean up popcorn?" Ronan began shaking the rest of the popcorn out of his shirt as Emily walked to the kitchen with the bowl.

"It would be cleaned up by now," Emily said as she turned and began walking backward, lifting her shoulders and spreading her arms out. "That's all I'm saying." She turned again and put the bowl in the sink.

She heard June ask if they were really getting a dog as she turned the water on and filled a glass. She'd been talking about getting a dog but Ronan was resistant, given their schedules and the work it would require considering they lived on the fifth floor of a building in a busy city. Emily felt a dog would not only be good for Jonathan but, now, she also felt a dog would be good for alerting them to things like an intruder in the middle of the night. She knew the loft was safe but after Marcus' visit she found she slept very lightly and heard every noise from the creaks in the building to the noise from the street.

Finishing the water, she returned to the living room. She walked into the conversation as June was trying to decide what kind of dog they should get.

"I think," Emily interjected, "we should get a tiny female Chihuahua. A white one. I could put bows on its ears and make your uncle carry it around in a little duffel bag. Her head would be sticking out and she'd have her bows and rhinestone collar, maybe even a pink sweater."

"Nooo," Ronan dragged the word out. "I think we'll get a big Saint Bernard and watch your aunt try to take it for a walk as it drools all over her."

"I'm voting for Uncle Ro carrying the girly dog around," June laughed.

"Thank you, June," Emily turned to her niece, "We'll make sure the carrier is also pink and studded with rhinestones."

"And sequins!" June added as she got off the chair and began picking up the popcorn.

Ronan bent down to help June and whispered to her, "Traitor."

Emily sat on the sofa next to Michelle as Ronan and June continued to clean up the popcorn and trade barbs. She was happy they had formed the bond they had. She knew Ronan served as a father figure for June and she was thrilled June had taken to it, even thrived under it.

Her thoughts turned to Jack and her smile faded. He would not have been half the father to June that Ronan had become. Michelle had let her and Ronan know about Jack's phone call. Ronan had June write down everything Jack had said. She knew Ronan was thinking it could be used against him at the hearing but she wasn't sure it would work. It would show anger and resentment but he had made no specific threat. Unfortunately, even though it was easy to interpret what he said as a threat, it contained no mention of direct harm and the law wasn't about what you thought or believed but what you could prove. It would be hard to prove he meant them any physical harm. She knew his lawyer would argue it that way.

"Hey," she felt Michelle nudge her. "Are you okay?"

"Yes," Emily replied. "Some unpleasant thoughts crept in, that's all. I'm not looking forward to having an escort to work nor am I looking forward to the hearing. I wish we could stay here, like this, without any worries."

"I know what you mean," Michelle said. "I wish Jack would stay in prison for the rest of his life and June would never have to think about him again."

"Hopefully, he'll be there for a few more years," Emily responded.

Michelle nodded and then, "Did you hear from Troy or Marc today?"

"This morning. Nothing relevant yet, but they've got a lot of people to go through. I think we were able to cross a few people off the list. Neither of us believes it's anyone we work with, but Marc was right. You have to look at everyone. You never know what's in a person's mind. A thousand unspoken thoughts."

"What are *your* thoughts?"

Emily sighed. "I'm not sure anymore. It could be Bart or it could be Jack but I doubt it. Then again, it could be Jean. There could be a few people who could be holding a grudge or hanging onto resentment."

"Jean?" Michelle snorted. "You could have crossed her off the list from the beginning. There's no way she would ever want to hurt you. What about the people from your office downstairs?"

"Claire is only 20, barely out of high school. I highly doubt it. She's a good receptionist, though. Patrick and Theresa see patients downstairs like I do. They were both already on the Brooklyn list. The only other one is Jared and I gave Troy his name. But, again, I doubt it's any of them."

"I ran into Jared a few times. Kind of nerdy but seems sweet."

"He is. Patients are very comfortable with him. But, yes, he is a bit nerdy, as you say. He saw Star Wars ten times in the theater. I couldn't get through it once." Emily let out a chuckle.

"In my opinion, I think you could cross Jean, Claire, and Jared right off the list. I can't imagine any of them having it in them." Michelle held up her hands. "But what do I know?"

Emily smiled. She wished she could share Michelle's sentiment but she didn't. It was another side-effect of Marcus' visit. She now viewed everyone in her life with suspicion. She'd gone over every conversation and interaction she'd had with those closest to her. Although she couldn't come up with any reason to doubt any of them, she also couldn't rule any of them out. Not until she knew the thing she didn't know.

She hoped whatever it was would be uncovered soon. Emily looked around the room. It had to be soon, she thought. There was no way anyone was going to take this away from her. Her parents had robbed her of having a real family by refusing to be one. No one would rob her of a family again. Especially this family.

Ronan

Hanging up the phone after hearing Emily was at the Brooklyn office safely, Ronan put his head in his hands and closed his eyes. He was exhausted and it wasn't only from the events of the last weeks. His motivation was still low and he was facing having to pick up the void left by letting Bart go. Emily was right when she noted his low phases were farther apart and not as bad as they'd been in the past, but they still happened. June called them "blue moods" and Ronan agreed that was more fitting to the recent pattern than "storms".

He felt like he'd been going through the last few days robotically. He did what he needed to do and tried to be present, but instead felt separated. There were moments the other night he felt more than present and, like Emily, had wanted to stay encapsulated in those moments. He thought he was coming out of this phase more quickly than before, only to wake up the next morning wanting to stay in bed and sleep the day away.

Now here he was, Monday morning with a full work schedule ahead of him and no desire to get started. Ronan got up from his desk and got himself another cup of coffee. He decided he'd caffeinate himself through the day.

"You gotta get going if you plan on getting that molding done this morning. The couple on 53rd is expecting you at noon to start the kitchen remodel. Mike said he'd meet you there when he's done with the bathroom on 41st." Ronan could always count on Michelle to light the fire under his ass on days like this.

Grabbing his coat with his free hand, he gulped his coffee and headed out. Focusing on the jobs in front of him and concentrating on each step with the precision he was known for got him through the workday. By the time he got back to his office, he was a different kind of exhausted.

Michelle looked up as he walked in. "Good day?"

"Cathartic," Ronan replied.

"Good to hear! Kevin got done early, so I told him he could call it a day. You're going to have to bring either him or Steve on full-time soon."

"Things keep going the way they are, I might bring them both. Did our favorite ex-employee call today?" Ronan braced to hear Michelle give a run down of another nonsensical call from Bart.

"Nope," Michelle replied. "Not today. I think what Emily said was right. He could have some kind of disorder. He definitely is paranoid. I didn't see it when he was going on last week but looking back on it, yeah, he definitely sounded paranoid."

"I hope he gets the help he needs. I really do, but that's his wife's problem. Let's hope she sees it and gets him some help. In the meantime, I'm going to finish up here, go home and take a much needed shower. Why don't you get out of here?"

"No need to tell me twice," Michelle smiled.

Locking up the office after Michelle left, Ronan walked to the mailboxes to pick up the mail. Flipping through it, he sorted out the junk mail and threw it in the garbage can by the door. He never heard the office phone ringing on Michelle's desk.

The elevator seemed to be taking forever. Ronan hit the up button again, knowing it wasn't going to get it there any faster. When the doors finally opened, he got in and leaned against the back wall. He was feeling better than he had that morning. He thought maybe tonight he'd get a solid night's sleep. He heard the familiar ding and the doors slid open to his floor.

As he walked closer to the loft, he heard the phone ringing inside. By the time he reached the door, he was irritated that Ellen hadn't answered it yet. Opening the door, he was about to call for Ellen when he saw her making a mad dash for it. She picked it up but was too late. She looked sheepishly at Ronan.

"They hung up."

"If it's important, they'll call back," he replied as he closed the door. "That's what my mother always said, anyway." He threw his keys on the table and walked further into the loft. "Can you stay for a little longer while I jump in the shower?"

"Sure, we were in the middle of building a castle fit for a king, anyway."

Just as she said the words, Ronan heard Jonathan running toward him. "Daadddy!!" He scooped him up and swung him in a circle. He let Jonathan give him a rundown on his day, which included coloring, Sesame Street, lunch, and building a castle. Not necessarily in that order. After sending him off with Ellen to finish the castle, Ronan headed for the bathroom.

Stepping into the shower, he let the hot water run over him. He bent down and rubbed his right knee. He hated to admit Emily was right and he needed to get it looked at. He stood up and closed his eyes, reveling in the warmth of the water. He stayed like that for a few minutes before starting to soap up. He stopped as he heard thumping coming from the living room area. He listened for a moment but it seemed to stop. Ellen and Jonathan must be playing a game, he thought. Just as he continued washing he heard it again. He turned off the water and listened. He heard shuffling and another thump but no talking or laughter that usually comes when Ellen is playing with his son.

He quickly got out of the shower and threw on his pants. Rushing into the living room, he found Ellen lying on the floor unconscious. He screamed Jonathan's name but was met with silence. A chill went through him as a feeling of terror he had never known before took over. He ran through the kitchen area and saw the loft door hanging open. He ran into the hall and down the hallway. The elevator doors were shut. He looked up and saw it was heading down. He opened the door to the stairs and ran, taking the steps as fast as he could. Flying through the door on the bottom floor, he ran to the elevator. The doors were shut and it was on its way back up. He ran out to the street, looked both ways, but saw nothing, only the usual everyday scene. He couldn't see Jonathan anywhere. Running up the street, he turned into the alleyway and around to the back of the building. No sign of Jonathan.

His heart beating out of his chest, Ronan ran back inside and into the offices of Safe Haven. He didn't have time to explain to Claire. He grabbed the phone and called the police. After hanging up, he told Claire to call Emily to come home but not to tell her anything, he'd do it when she got here. Back in the hall, he pushed the elevator buttons but couldn't wait. He took the stairs back up two at a time.

Back in the apartment, he went to Ellen. She was breathing steadily. He checked her over for any signs of blood. He didn't see any. He felt around her head but found no lumps to indicate she'd been hit with anything. He tried to wake her up but she only murmured and wouldn't open her eyes.

The phone rang. He jumped up and grabbed it to hear Claire tell him no one was answering in the Brooklyn office so she was sure Emily was on her way home. He hung up and dialed Rob's number. His secretary told him Rob was unavailable but she'd make sure he got back to Ronan as soon as possible. He told her it was an emergency, she needed to go find him and have him call back immediately. He called Michelle's apartment. When June answered, he told her that both of them needed to come to the loft as soon as Michelle got home.

He sat down next to Ellen and tried to wake her up again. She murmured and her eyes fluttered slightly but she wasn't coming to. He heard the police in the hallway just as the phone rang again. He went to the phone and picked it up.

"Ronan!" Rob nearly screamed through the phone. "Marc has been trying to get in touch with you and Emily." Ronan remembered the phone ringing earlier and Ellen getting to it just a second too late. He listened as Rob explained what Marc had found.

Ronan looked at the officers as they entered the loft. Receiver still in hand, he shouted to them, "You have to get to my wife! Call the police in Williamsburg! You have to get to my wife at the clinic!" He hung up on Rob and dialed Emily's direct number.

Emily

Emily rubbed her eyes. It had been a long day, but she was thankful there had been back to back patients. Focusing on them for a few hours relieved her of the anxiety she had been feeling that morning. Now that the last one was gone, she sat at her desk finishing her notes. It was the last thing she had to do before she could leave for the day. She decided she'd do the billing at home.

She checked her calendar and saw she had two interviews lined up for the next day. Ian's patients had been given the option to stay with the clinic and see either herself, Patrick, or Theresa, or waiting until another doctor was added. Emily wanted to get someone on board as soon as possible to avoid any gap in treatment for those patients who might choose to wait for a new doctor. She was grateful tomorrow would be another busy day.

Realizing she was out of the forms she'd have to take home with her, she got up and headed toward the reception area. Finding it empty, she walked to Jean's desk and saw her purse and keys were gone. It was unlike Jean to leave without telling her. The feeling of suspicion crept through her again. She hated it. She shook her head. Michelle was right, Emily told herself, Jean did not have it in her to harm her. Knowing where the forms were kept, she opened the desk drawer, grabbed some and walked back to her office.

Seated at her desk again, she felt a feeling of unease and then she realized why. The office was quiet. It was too quiet. Jean was gone and it sounded as if the others were as well. The unease grew. She knew Carl was in the parking lot waiting for her. She shoved the forms and a few files into her briefcase and was about to stand up when she felt a whoosh of air and the picture of Jonathan toppled from her desk. She looked up, expecting to see Marcus sitting in one of the chairs. He wasn't. . .the chairs were empty. At that moment, she knew she'd just been sent a sign. She was certain Marcus had just let her know that something had happened to or was about to happen to Jonathan. The unease gave way to panic.

The phone rang. It startled her and she let out a sharp cry. Emily realized it was the first time her phone had rung in hours. Between that and the deserted office, she knew, beyond a shadow of a doubt, that whatever was going to happen as a result of that letter was happening now. She picked up the phone.

"Emily, are you okay?" Ronan's voice was urgent and worried. She listened to Ronan and as she realized he was giving her the piece of information she'd been looking for, the one she didn't know, the one she needed to know, to understand who was behind the letter and why, she saw her office door open.

"I understand, Phil," Emily adlibbed, hoping Ronan would understand why. "We can talk about it during your next session. In the meantime, use the breathing exercises we discussed and I will see you Thursday." She hung up the phone.

"Why don't you come with me, Emily? I have something to show you. Or rather, some*one*."

"This is a surprise," Emily hoped she sounded calm. "I hope whoever it is brought some wine."

Emily walked around her desk and followed, putting the puzzle pieces together in her mind. Remaining calm, she followed down the hall and past the reception area. She knew that Ronan had called the police and that Rob, Marc, and Troy were either with him or on their way to the clinic. Hopefully, her cover of pretending to be talking to a client had been believable. The last thing Emily wanted was there to be any indication authorities were alerted. Her mind whirred as she hoped against hope that Jonathan was okay. The only thing she was certain of is that she, herself, would end up in jail if any harm had come to her son. Emily prepared herself to engage in combat. She went through the door on the other side of the reception area and down the steps. Not a word was said. At the bottom of the steps, she turned right and walked down toward another door and into a small room. Emily knew who she'd find in there and her heart raced as she entered.

"Jonathan!" Emily cried when she saw her son sitting at a small table, coloring, with a juice box sitting beside a coloring book and a cookie in his free hand. She ran over and picked him up. She looked him over and made sure he was okay.

"He's fine. He's been a good boy."

"I want to finish, Mommy," Jonathan squirmed.

Emily sat down in the chair with Jonathan on her lap and let him begin coloring again. She brushed his hair with her hand, squeezed him tightly, and kissed the top of his head. She took those few moments to figure out how she was going to start this.

"Let's talk about this, Theresa."

Ronan

"I'm going with you!" Ronan was ready to run to Brooklyn if he had to but he couldn't get past the officers in his loft.

"No, Ronan," one replied. "We already have guys headed there. We know who we're looking for. Let us do our job. We'll bring your wife and your boy home."

"She might have taken Jonathan somewhere else. We don't know who came here." Ronan was pacing. Limping around is more accurate. His knee was screaming from the toll of running down and back up the stairs but he couldn't sit down and he couldn't stand still. He was angry at himself. If he would have taken off work, if he would have gotten out of the shower the first time he heard something, if they would have gotten someone to watch the loft. With both of them having offices a few floors down, they hadn't thought it was needed. A hundred things he could have done differently went through his mind. The anger traded places with the fear that the police wouldn't get to Theresa in time.

"Let us in!" Ronan heard Michelle's voice in the hallway.

"That's my sister and my niece. I called her. Let them in."

"Do not touch anything, ladies," an officer informed them. "You can go to the kitchen area but do not go in the living room area and, again, do not touch anything."

Michelle almost ran to Ronan and threw her arms around him. "What happened?" She took in the scene, officers doing what she assumed was looking for fingerprints, Ellen on a stretcher near the kitchen with a paramedic hovering over her.

Ronan tried to explain what had happened but he kept jumping between what happened while he was in the shower, Rob's call, and his brief call with Emily. He kept looking over at the officers to see if anything else had developed. He heard their radios crackle but couldn't make out what was being said. He stopped talking to Michelle when he saw the officer in charge, Peters, walking toward him.

"Mr. Byrne, the Williamsburg unit apprehended a man outside the clinic. Dante Morelli. Apparently, the brother of Theresa Morelli. Are you familiar with him?"

"I've heard the name."

"Have you had any contact with him recently? Know anything that might be relevant?"

"No," Ronan replied and then remembered. "Wait, Emily told me that she was worried about Theresa. I guess Theresa told her she was having family problems and her brother had something to do with it. From what I understand, her brother isn't very stable. That's all I know."

Ronan watched as Peters spoke into his radio and began to walk away. "Possibly unstable. Carpenter and I are leaving now. We'll be there in 15." The radio crackled again. Ronan was only able to hear a few words, 'looks empty', 'two PI's", "go in". The officer replied, "Hold. We're bringing in McGuire. He'll be there before us."

"I'm going," Ronan approached Peters. "You can't stop me."

As the officer was about to reply, they heard Ellen murmur from the stretcher. Ronan went over to her as a paramedic began speaking to her in soft tones. Ellen's eyes fluttered open and she looked momentarily confused. Then, as if a switch flipped, she looked at Ronan, her eyes wide.

"I'm so sorry," Ellen's voice was raspy and strained.

Ronan wanted to hear Ellen explain what happened but the officers took over. One was to wait until Ellen was coherent and comprehended what was happening around her and then get her statement. The others, who were combing the loft, were to finish and report anything they found. Peters was leaving for Brooklyn with his partner. Ronan had no intention of staying behind.

In the back of the cruiser, Ronan's question as to how they were going to make it to the clinic in ten to 15 minutes was answered. With lights and siren blaring, they bypassed cars and were speeding across the Williamsburg Bridge. He'd already gotten the lecture of remaining in the car once they reached the clinic, to stay out of the way and not to get involved. Ronan tried to reassure himself that Theresa wouldn't hurt his family. He was positive she wouldn't hurt Jonathan, that she was only using him as a pawn. He wasn't as certain that Theresa wouldn't harm Emily.

Regardless of how fast they were already traveling, Ronan felt like time was standing still. Memories of Emily were flooding back to him; when they first met and the feeling they shared, her confession of who she was on the Brooklyn Bridge, working together to put Jack away, the silly times they had while they were figuring out their relationship, the look on her face when he proposed to her on the Pont Alexandre Bridge, her beautiful rendition of "You Light Up My Life", giving birth to Jonathan, watching her develop into the mother she never had but wanted to be for their son, her smile during their late night pillow talks, her funny comebacks to his stupid jokes.

Ronan felt his eyes begin to water and he blinked back the tears. He reminded himself that his wife was more than a brilliant psychologist. She was strong and she was resourceful. She had gotten through a lot of things in her life. Emily would find a way to protect herself and their son. He would have his wife and son back soon.

He hoped.

Emily

"There's nothing to talk about." Theresa leaned against the wall, looking at Emily with calculating eyes. She gave a short snort and continued. "You think you're so brilliant. Clearly, you're not as thorough as you think you are. Do you know who I am?"

Emily did, thanks to Ronan's call, but she wasn't going to let Theresa know that. "Why don't you tell me?"

Theresa's eyes narrowed as she considered Emily. It took a moment before she spoke. "I was born into a unique family. Yes, I've talked to you a few times about them. There's been a lot of trauma and dysfunction in my family for the last decade. I've shared some of it, but I didn't share it all." Theresa took a deep breath and folded her arms. "When I was born, my mother decided I would not carry my father's name. Instead, my brother and I have her maiden name, Morelli. You'll understand shortly why she did that. There were certain elements she didn't want us connected to." She leaned forward slightly. "When you did your background check on me everything came up Morelli, correct? All my college records, high school records, all Morelli. You would think, though, that someone like you would have been a little more thorough."

"Meaning?" Emily wanted Theresa to spell it out for her. She wanted to take up as much time as possible to give the police time to get to the clinic.

"Someone who crossed as many people as you did should have been a little more thorough, but the only way to know what I mean would have been to look into my parents. You didn't, though, did you?" Theresa didn't wait for an answer. "Of course you didn't. No one looks into someone's parents during the hiring process. You only saw the important things; grades, papers, skills, clinical practice, and, of course, background check. You found me to be a squeaky clean graduate with fantastic grades ready to join forces with you to help the world." She paused and gave Emily a level stare. "You really should have looked at my father, though. His name was Rocco Bernardi. Does his name ring any bells for you?"

Emily didn't respond. Of course she knew who he was. She knew where this story was heading and the horrible ending it had.

Theresa threw her hands in the air and shook her head. "It doesn't, does it? Of course, it doesn't ring any bells. Why would you care about him?" Theresa pulled out the chair opposite Emily and sat down. She considered Jonathan for a minute before she looked back at Emily. "Do you want to know the one thing that always bothered me when you did those interviews and answered questions when Lyle's book came out? The one thing that drove me crazy? The fact that no one - not one reporter - ever asked you about your ties to the families."

"Family," Emily corrected her. In her time at Corbyn she had only dealt with one of the several organized crime families in the area.

Theresa ignored the correction. "Everyone knew your father had those ties and you picked them right up when you took over for him. It's how you managed to take control of the company when you were only, what? 26? 27?"

Again, Emily did not respond. Instead, she looked at Jonathan's drawing and talked to him about what kind of animal it was and what he should add to it. Eventually, she looked back at Theresa but still did not respond.

"Why didn't anyone ask you about those connections?" Theresa didn't wait for an answer. "Did you tell them ahead of time it was off limits? It doesn't matter. I know what you did. I know how you severed the tie. Do you remember the deal? Do you? Do you remember it backfired?"

"I remember the deal." Emily's voice was even. She remembered everything clearly. Before she turned over the company to her brother and sister, she had to find a way to break the connection between Corbyn and the Acardi family, whom she had made deals with. It should have been a simple deal. The Acardi family wanted in on the gun deals the Lombardi family had control of. She met with the Lombardi family, got them to hand over one of the contracts to the Acardi family and, in return, Emily created a shell company for the Lombardi family. The shell company then controlled three properties in the Lombardi territory that Corbyn owned but signed over to the shell company. The result was that the Acardi family got something they had been trying to get a stake in for years and the Lombardi family would benefit more from the properties than the one contract they forfeited. Corbyn would be free and clear from any future involvement with either family.

In the end, it worked. However, not without bloodshed. No one knows exactly what happened the night the two families met. There was only speculation and rumor. Gunfire erupted and two men were killed. Rocco Bernardi was one of them. The story in the press was that it appeared to be a drug deal between the two men that had gone terribly wrong. It was clear it had been set up to appear that way as there was no trace of either family at the crime scene and various drugs had been found. There was never any mention of the families or the deal Emily brokered.

"If you remember the deal then you remember what happened." Theresa's eyes narrowed and her next words dripped with acid. "You are the reason my father was killed."

"No, I'm not, Theresa." Emily kept her voice calm. "I brokered the deal, yes, but I wasn't there that night. What happened is between the two families. You should be angry with the Lombardis not with me. But, as word on the street had it, the Acardi family pushed for more than was agreed upon. Words were exchanged, shots were fired. If that's what went down, then Don Acardi overstepped and got a little too greedy. Greed killed your father, Theresa."

"Well, you would know all about greed, wouldn't you? How much did you make when you ran Corbyn? Never mind, I already know. Does Ronan know that you use the money, what you would now call blood money, from that part of your life to fund these clinics?"

While Emily was surprised Theresa knew how the clinics were funded, she hoped she didn't let it show. She kept her face neutral and in response only raised an eyebrow.

"I always wondered how these clinics were able to function, even become as successful as they are, based on the low rates you insist on charging. You always said there was an investor. So, I dug into it. You put away a very large amount of money. A very hefty sum, actually. The rent and operating expenses for the clinics are paid for from the interest off that money."

Emily tilted her head. "You're correct. The money from that time is serving a useful and good purpose. Do you have a point?"

Theresa tapped her fingers on the table. "I guess I need to spell it out for the brilliant Dr. Byrne," she said sarcastically. "At the end of the day, you have that original sum intact, you have income from the stake you still have in Corbyn, plus what you make at Safe Haven. Not to mention the apartment in Paris. If we add in what Ronan makes from his cute little business, well, don't you have the best little set up, there? You wouldn't have to work another day in your life and still die a very rich woman while my father has been six feet under for the last 12 years. He's there because of the deal you set up. You may not have pulled the trigger but you might as well have."

"Why now, Theresa? You found out who I was in '75. If this is all about your father, why didn't you confront me then?" Emily paused for just a moment before continuing. "This is about more than your father."

"Don't you dare analyze me, Emily. My father is dead because of you. End of story. Why now? That's easy." A smile crept across Theresa's face. "I wanted to wait until you were happy. I waited until you built your perfect little life with your perfect little family. A time when you thought you would never have to face the things you did again, a time when you were settled, at peace and happy."

Emily nodded and tightened her hold on Jonathan. "What are you planning?"

"You'll see. Tonight is the night my father will get justice."

Michelle

Left at the loft with one officer, Michelle and June began to clean up as much as they could. Both were on edge and tried to keep busy. Michelle had watched as the officers had finished combing through the living room. She had held Ellen's hand and reassured her everything would be alright before they transported her to the hospital. Now, after the flurry of activity, the sound of crackling radios and the chatter between officers, the silence was too much for her. She had already washed and put away every dish and utensil she found in the kitchen, cleaned up Jonathan's toys that had been scattered near the dining table and was about to scrub the bathroom. They had been told to leave the living room area alone. Michelle suspected that was one of the reasons the sole officer was left behind, in addition to the reasons they were told; to make sure they remained safe and to watch the loft in case anyone else tried to enter.

"Mom, stop." June's voice broke the silence. "Sit with me."

Michelle hesitated for just a moment before she followed June to the table and took a seat. She rubbed her face and clasped her hands under her chin. She had always been a devout person, but she had never prayed as hard or as long as she did the last hours. She prayed for Jonathan, she prayed for Emily, but also prayed for Theresa. She prayed Theresa would find her conscience, find her faith, and let Emily and Jonathan go.

The account Ellen gave the police identified Theresa as Jonathan's kidnapper. It had been easy for Theresa to convince Ellen to allow her in the loft. Since she was both a colleague and a friend of Emily's, using the excuse of dropping off files was all that was needed. Ellen didn't remember much, except that a man had been with Theresa and pushed his way into the loft as soon as Ellen had opened the door, nearly knocking Ellen over. Theresa had gone straight to Jonathan and picked him up, instructing the man with her to make it quick as they hadn't expected Ronan to be home. Ellen asked what was going on, but the man put something over her face and everything went black.

Michelle was shocked to learn that Theresa's father had been involved with one of the city's crime families. Ronan had given her all the information he had, but it didn't make sense to Michelle. From her point of view, too much time had passed since she'd learned Emily was Emily Corbyn. Theresa had worked alongside Emily for a long time, pretending to be one of her closest friends. Michelle couldn't figure out how she could spend all those years with Emily and be plotting against her the entire time.

"They'll be okay, Mom." June broke into Michelle's thoughts.

She tried to give her daughter a reassuring smile. "I hope so, honey. It's just so hard to believe this is happening."

"You don't think Theresa will hurt Jonathan, do you?" June's voice was quiet.

"No," Michelle didn't hesitate. "Theresa's problem is with Emily. I'm sure she used Jonathan to scare her and get Emily to go along with whatever she has planned."

June fell back into silence as Michelle's thoughts went to Jonathan. It was another thing that didn't make sense. What was Theresa planning on doing with Jonathan once she was done with Emily? Michelle shuddered as she thought about what Theresa and her brother might be planning to do with Emily.

"I know you told me some things about Aunt Emily," June started again, "but what did she do that made Theresa do this?"

Michelle sighed, "She . . . I don't know a whole lot about it, but she was involved with some horrible people when she ran Corbyn. Theresa's father was involved with those people and he was killed. I guess she blames Emily."

"But Aunt Emily didn't kill him, right?"

"Of course not! Like I said, I don't know much about it. I'm not sure Ronan knows the whole story, either."

"I know Aunt Emily did some horrible stuff that made people hate her. I mean, I know her whole story with Jack. It's just that I can't imagine her being like that. She helps so many people, she goes out and talks about women's rights, and she joined that group that helps women whose husbands beat them up. I can't see her being mean or hurting anyone."

"You can't imagine it because she's not that person anymore. She no longer has it in her to be mean."

"What made her change?"

Michelle gave her daughter a genuine smile this time. "Your Uncle Ronan."

"Really?" June smiled back.

"There's more to it than that, but yes, actually. Ro had a whole lot to do with Emily leaving that person behind and discovering her passion to help people. Emily did a lot of work on herself and she's worked extremely hard to be the person she is and to put her clinics together."

June nodded. Michelle wasn't ready for the next question. "You don't always like her though, do you?"

Michelle's eyes widened. "Of course I do! Why would you say that? I love Emily."

June looked down and twisted her fingers before looking back at Michelle. "Well, I see the way you look at her sometimes." June shrugged. "It's like you get mad at her even though you don't have a reason."

Michelle closed her eyes. While she had been cleaning up, she had been feeling guilty for all the times she had been jealous of Emily. As she was scrubbing, she admitted to herself that those feelings had come from the discontent she had with herself. The things she was envious of were the things she found lacking within her. She had made a deal with God that if he returned Jonathan and Emily safely, she would never be envious or jealous again. She would, instead, learn from Emily. She would work on herself to become stronger and less insecure.

"Oh, honey, it's not that." Michelle met June's eyes. "I adore Emily. The truth is that there have been times I've been a little jealous of her. Sometimes I feel inferior to her and I know that's my problem, not Emily's. I need to fix myself, not be jealous of someone who has already managed to do that."

Michelle realized by June's confused look that she didn't understand. She almost regretted telling her. She hadn't liked admitting it to herself, let alone someone else. Shifting in her chair, she began to feel uncomfortable. The last thing Michelle wanted was June to view her mother as weak. She wanted June to grow into an independent woman and tried her best to set that example for her.

"Mom?"

Deciding to be honest with her, Michelle began, "Ever since Jack went to prison I've struggled. I've tried to keep it together, I've tried to be strong and create a good, stable environment for you, but I've been second-guessing myself every step of the way. I know I'm not great at getting you to understand things or sometimes I think that you won't believe me, so that's why I usually have Ronan or Emily do it. That bothers me. I feel like I'm failing you in that way." She paused for a second and looked down before continuing, "I would never have imagined my life would have turned out like this. I thought once I got married, that was it. I'd spend my life being a good wife and a good mother and I wouldn't have to worry about anything because I would have my husband to take care of me." She let out a snort and shook her head.

"Like Grandma?"

Michelle looked at June and nodded, "Yes, like Grandma.

That's how I was raised. That's how most girls my age were raised. Learn to type in high school, find a clerical job somewhere, find a husband then quit your job and be the perfect housewife and raise a family. There's absolutely nothing wrong with that, if that's what you want to do, if that's what you want to be. Some women do, and that's great, but it should have been one of many options. It shouldn't have been presented to an entire generation of girls as the only option."

"What did you want to be, Mom?"

The question surprised her. No one, outside of Ronan, had ever asked her that. She took a moment before replying. "I wanted to be a novelist." She saw June raise her eyebrows and give a slight smile, so she went on. "I read a book by Agatha Christie when I was young and I loved it so much that I went to the library every week and checked out one of her books until I read every one the library had. I wanted to be the next great murder mystery writer. Then life sort of happened. Dean was killed in the early days of Vietnam and then I met and married Jack and that was it."

"But why?" June asked. "Why couldn't you write after you got married?"

Michelle lifted her shoulders and said, "Because that's not what I was supposed to do. I was supposed to keep a neat house, cater to my husband and raise a family. According to my mother, anyway. Well, according to most people at that time, including Jack."

"That's not right."

Looking June in the eyes, Michelle continued. "You see, that's why I would be jealous of Emily. She didn't let all of those societal norms influence her the way I did. She was strong, she went after what she wanted and it didn't matter that she was a woman. She found ways to move forward regardless. Yes, she took a wrong and illegal road when she ran Corbyn, that's true, but she made the company a lot of money. I'm not excusing what she did. It was wrong on many levels.

I'm only using it as an example of how she was strong. Then when she came out of her coma, she worked hard to build the clinic in Brooklyn and get her doctorate at the same time. She did all that while she was also trying to heal her relationship with her brother and sister and also while trying to make it up to the people she hurt.

"She was also working on healing the parts of herself that were hurt when she was younger, most of which you know. Even when she met Ronan, she didn't stop. She was still out there advocating for women, putting together another clinic, plus helping me get through all the crap with Jack. Whenever she set her sights on something, she would find a way to make it happen. So, yes, there were many times I looked at her and I was jealous. Jealous that I wasn't like that. Jealous that she was independent and could accomplish these things without having to rely on a man. She doesn't depend on Ronan to survive and Ronan doesn't depend on her. They are partners who support and encourage each other. I was jealous of that, too. I envied her strength and her determination. But, I think mostly I envied that she was able to accomplish her dreams."

Michelle went silent. It was only at that moment that she realized the real reason she had been jealous. It was Emily's strength and determination, sure, but it was more the fact that Emily had gone after and accomplished what she wanted where Michelle had given up on her dreams. Once again, Michelle had to admit to herself that it was her own fault she gave up on them. She could have bucked the norms as Emily had. Instead, she gave into them.

"I have a couple things to say about all this, Mom." June interrupted Michelle's thoughts. "I love Aunt Emily but you're forgetting something, I think. She had money. I think it's a little easier to get things done when you have money."

"No," Michelle cut her off. "I mean, yes, she did have money but that doesn't make anyone a good person. It's not about the money,

June. She could have very easily woken up from that coma being the same person or even turned into someone much more ruthless and conniving. She didn't. Besides, I didn't need a bunch of money to write. All I needed was paper."

June held up her hands. "Okay, I get that but, Mom, who said you weren't strong? Who said you haven't done some of the things that Emily's done? Mom, we live in the East Village in an apartment you pay the rent on because you helped Uncle Ronan build his business. It wouldn't be as successful as it is without you. Uncle Ro probably wouldn't have started a business without you. I know Uncle Ro and Aunt Emily helped us out a lot but, you keep it going. You didn't give up. You pushed through, just like Emily did."

Michelle ran her hands through her hair and sighed. "I appreciate that, June, but I don't really want to talk about this right now. I don't want to talk about me. I know I need to work on things. Right now, I just want Ronan to bring Jonathan and Emily back safely. All of my jealousy has been stupid. I know that now. I even bargained with God."

"You did?" Michelle caught the surprise in June's voice.

"I did. I promised him if Emily and Jonathan come home I would never be jealous again and I'd fix the things that make me feel that way."

June nodded. "Maybe all you need is some paper."

"Maybe we should pray for all of them. Ronan has done his own work over the years to get where he is. He loves Emily so much and that little boy is his whole world. I have never seen him happier and more at peace than these last few years. Not even when he was with Carrieann. He helps so many people, too. You don't know this, no one but Emily and I know, but Ro does work for free quite often."

"He does? Why? I mean, okay, I don't know anything about running a business but I don't think that's how you make money."

"Well, he never forgot what it was like to be unemployed and hungry with no money. He feels that if he could help someone in that situation then he should. He believes in community. A community helps each other out, they don't hoard everything for themselves while letting their neighbors struggle. At least once a week, if not more, he fixes things for people who can't afford to call someone. Last week, he practically re-did an entire kitchen for a single mom in the Bronx. He balances that loss out by selling his furniture, and since that part of his business has picked up from word of mouth, he doesn't worry about doing the free work. He says he likes it more, to be honest. He says they are the ones that are easier to work with and he can feel their gratitude where some of the rich people look at him as far beneath them."

"Wow," June replied. "I didn't know that. I've seen Uncle Ro give spare change to people on the street. I know they drop off blankets and clothes to the shelters. Uncle Ro has always drilled into me about helping people who don't have much." June paused for a moment and then went on. "Actually, I remember something he said not too long ago. He said it was something Emily had told him. He said countries don't find peace; people find peace. I remember he said that once he understood that, he understood that to make the country a better place we first had to find peace ourselves then we can help others find it. He said if giving someone a coat gives them some warmth and some peace in the cold, that's a start. I really didn't think about it too much because, well, sometimes Uncle Ro goes on and on and on about things, but I get it now. In his way, he helps people. Like, I don't know how to say it . . . like by fixing stuff he's giving them some peace because it's something they won't have to worry about. And Aunt Emily helps people find peace by helping them mentally. I get what he was talking about now."

"This is what I mean!" Michelle's eyes filled with tears and her voice began to shake. "He's such a good man, he's been the best brother. He doesn't deserve any of this. And Emily. She's worked so hard to overcome everything. All they both want to do is help people." The tears began to slide down her cheeks. "And that poor boy. I just can't . . ." She trailed off.

"We have to believe they will all be okay." June reached out and took her mother's hands. "If there is a God, if there is a higher power at work, I can't imagine they would let anything happen to them."

Michelle heard the crackle of the officer's radio. She had almost forgotten he was still there. She turned to listen but could only catch a few words. After the officer replied that he'd received the transmission, he turned to Michelle and said, "They've arrived at the clinic. Ms. Morelli and the hostages are still inside. Don't worry, ma'am. They'll make sure your family is safe."

"Hostages," Michelle repeated the word. A chill went through her spine. She bent her head and began to pray.

Emily

"What are you planning on doing with my son?" Emily tried to keep her voice calm and light so it didn't upset Jonathan.

Theresa looked up from checking her watch and smiled. "You don't need to worry about him. No one is going to hurt him. He'll be just fine."

"Then why did you bring him here?" Emily knew the answer but, again, she wanted to keep Theresa talking. She was hoping Theresa would give her an opening where she could reach the logical, intelligent side of her.

Emily was met with silence. She watched as Theresa seemed to mull over how she would respond. Emily knew this was about more than her father's death. If that was the only reason, Theresa could have made a move at any time over the last seven years. No, there was something else and Emily was fairly sure she knew what it was. She went back over the last year of interactions, dinners, and conversations with Theresa. She pinpointed the change in her demeanor to almost four months ago, shortly after she'd had minor surgery.

"Why did you bring him?" Emily repeated.

Theresa sighed, checked her watch again and stood up. "There are many answers to that, Emily, but as I told you before, you don't need to worry about him. No harm will come to him."

Emily noticed that Theresa was also keeping her voice calm and friendly. She believed Theresa wouldn't harm Jonathan but she also knew Theresa had no intention of returning him to Ronan. She had to figure out a way to make that happen. If she couldn't get herself out of this, she was going to make sure Jonathan wasn't separated from his father.

"Do what you want with me," Emily said, "but don't take Jonathan from Ronan."

"I fully intend to do what I want with you, Emily. You will pay for my father and for everything else you've done. The only reason you're in this little predicament is because of your own actions. It's time you were finally held accountable."

"No." The single word came out quietly but with a strength that made Theresa freeze for a moment.

"No?" Theresa said after recovering. "No? Do you think you have a choice? You don't. You're not going to skate through the rest of your life and not face some consequences for what happened."

"No," Emily repeated. She looked up to meet Theresa's eyes. "No. I'm done. I spent years dealing with the guilt over things that happened back then. I spent years making it up to people that I wronged. I went through my own therapy for a long time to come to terms with it. I can't go back and change any of it. What I can do is exactly what I did. I reached out to people I hurt and I atoned for the horrible decisions I made. I made peace with as many people as I could. It's true a few refused to speak with me, but I understood why and I even tried to help them. It took me close to a decade to finally forgive myself and move on from it. You are not going to drag me back down into it, Theresa. I made a fair deal to extract any family ties from Corbyn. It was a good deal. It should have gone through without anything going wrong. It is not my fault things took a turn. It is not my fault your father died."

"Is that what you tell yourself so you can sleep at night? Why was my father there that night, Emily? He was there because of the deal *you* put together. He was there because *you* wanted it to happen so *your* life could be better. Yes, it most certainly is your fault."

"Maybe if your father would have chosen a different line of work he'd still be alive. Are you going to blame me for your father choosing a life of crime?"

"Shut up!" Theresa yelled.

Jonathan jumped and dropped his crayon. He turned in Emily's lap with wide eyes. Emily calmly talked to him, making up a story about why Theresa was upset but it was all okay, it had nothing to do with him.

"Are we going home soon?" Jonathan asked.

"Soon, honey. Soon." Emily stroked his hair then gave him his crayon back and told him he'd better finish his drawing because his dad was waiting at home for it.

"Oh, look at you," Theresa's voice was calm again but dripped with sarcasm. "Saint Emily with the perfect life, the perfect husband, and the perfect son. It all came so easily for you. I've been watching you since you first hired me. I was so foolish. I admired you so much. I thought you were so brilliant and caring. I bought into the whole idea of making a change in the world, keeping the rates low, caring more about the people than the money. I believed in you." Theresa stopped and shook her head. She glanced at her watch again and then at the door.

Emily watched and waited. She knew Theresa wasn't finished. She knew there was more Theresa wanted to say so she prompted. "It didn't come easily, Theresa. You know that. You know some of the things I went through."

"Oh, yes," Theresa replied. "I know. You were assaulted. I used to feel empathy for that. I don't anymore. You got away with what? Some cuts and bruises and a bloody lip." She paused. "Now, I don't mean to downplay assault by any means. I'm a psychologist, after all. But your case was much less traumatic than many, *many* of the patients we see. See what I mean, my dear? Even in the worst of circumstances, you manage to get away with minimal harm."

"Do not pretend to know everything I've gone through, Theresa. You don't. Do not pretend to know the extent of the trauma I've worked through. You don't."

"Ah, yes, I forgot about your parents," Theresa giggled. "Your dear, *rich* parents didn't care about you. Boo hoo. You know, it's hard to feel sorry for someone when their parents left behind a ton of money. That kind of softens the blow of their death, don't you think?"

Emily didn't respond. She murmured encouragement to Jonathan and pointed out a few things he could add to his drawing. She wasn't going to take the bait and let Theresa unravel the years of hard work she'd done to come to terms with all of it. This was a game, Emily reminded herself and she knew Theresa wasn't done with her move, yet.

"Here's some interesting information I bet you didn't know. Did you think what happened with your parents was really an accident?" Theresa smiled and then let out a little laugh. "It wasn't, dear Emily. It was the Lombardis." She laughed again. "Your father was stupid. He should have heard Don Lombardi through, but he didn't. Did he really think only dealing with the Acardis was going to work? They got rid of him and then made sure you were installed so you'd be the useful idiot for both families."

Emily had known from the beginning the car accident that killed her parents hadn't really been an accident. The news did not surprise or shock her. The only thing she hadn't known was which family had orchestrated it.

"You're wrong," Emily replied. Looking Theresa directly in the eyes, she continued. "Neither family helped me take over the company. I learned more from my father than he ever realized. I knew exactly what rules, laws and company policies I could use, along with blackmailing our lawyer, the Vice President and the board chairman. I did that on my own. It wasn't until that was finished that the Acardis approached me. They reminded me of the setup they had with my father. I could have found a way to cut the ties then if I had wanted to. I didn't, though. It was useful for me to keep them in my pocket. You see, Theresa, they were *my* useful idiots. But it worked. The Lombardis wanted to horn in but the Acardis stopped them. It was a dangerous game I played. Very dangerous.

"I made that company a lot of money and guys like your father were just pawns. Your father was a pawn to me and he was a pawn to the Acardis. He never rose above a soldato. You could have been so much more than your father ever was. You are an intelligent woman, Theresa. You handle your patients with amazing care and skill. You are one of the best psychologists I know. I've always been so proud to call you my colleague and equal. Help me understand what's really happening here. If this was about your father, you could have killed me at any time. If this was about money, you could have left the clinics years ago and made more money somewhere else. What's this about, Theresa? What is this really about?"

Emily saw in Theresa's eyes that she was faltering. Theresa had wanted to minimize and ridicule Emily's past traumas so that Emily would react emotionally. Theresa wanted to undermine the years of work Emily put in to heal. The idea of the families installing her was to shake her confidence and question herself. Theresa was counting on emotion. Emily hadn't given it to her. Instead, she praised her. Emily could see it was beginning to have an effect.

"Theresa, talk to me. Tell me what's going on with you. Whatever it is, we can work it out. We've been able to work through anything, we can work through this."

"I don't know if that's possible." Theresa sighed and looked at the ceiling.

"Of course it's possible. Whatever is going on, we can get through it. Together." Emily paused and then she took a gamble. "The surgery you had recently wasn't your gallbladder, was it? Theresa, did you have a hysterectomy?"

It was the wrong move. Theresa's head snapped back down and she leveled an icy stare at Emily. The final puzzle piece fell into place. Emily knew why Theresa was doing this and what her final plans were.

"Cancer, Emily. I had cancer." Theresa spat then took a breath and continued more calmly as she glanced at Jonathan. "Nothing puts life into perspective more than having cancer. Oh, wait. There is one thing. It's that the universe likes to play cruel jokes on you. The tumor is in your uterus, the cancer hasn't spread, you'll survive with surgery and radiation, but guess what? You will never have the one and only thing you've always wanted."

"Why didn't you tell me? Theresa, you know–"

"Know what, Emily? That you'd help me? How? You can't give me my uterus back and no amount of talking and healing will ever change that. Nothing will ever change that. No, I wasn't going to tell you. You are the last person I wanted to know. You. You, who should be the poster child for changing and healing, who has this husband who is so goddamn perfect it's like he fell out of the sky for you, who has this beautiful little boy . . . and who deserved none of it!" Theresa fought back tears as she went on. "Not only did you get my father killed but you have everything I have ever wanted and you don't deserve to. I deserve to." Theresa began poking herself in the chest. "I deserve to! I deserve to have a wonderful husband; I deserve to have an apartment in Paris. I'm the one who did everything right my entire life, even with the weight of what my father did hanging around my neck. I deserve to go to conferences and have my name recognized and celebrated in magazines. I deserve to go on television. I worked just as hard as you, I'm just as good as you. I'm the one who did everything right, who stayed away from things like blackmail and the families. That was me, not you." Theresa took a choked breath and wiped tears from her cheek. "I did everything I was supposed to do and I was good at it." She took another ragged breath. "I deserve a child."

"Theresa–"

Theresa held up her hand. "Don't. Just don't." She ran the back of her hand across her eye.

Emily remained quiet and let Theresa calm herself. Once again her thoughts ran through the last year of their interactions. She felt her eyes well with the realization of how much pain Theresa was in. Emily realized there was so much she didn't know about Theresa. The family problems Theresa talked about took on a different light now that she knew who Theresa's mother had been married to. Emily's mind went in several different directions. Her brother's unstable nature, the signs that should have been evident but weren't, the pressure Theresa must have been under to overcome and move beyond who her father had been.

"Mommy, is Auntie T okay?" Jonathan's voice brought her back to the room and the situation she was in.

"Yes, honey. She will be. She's a little sad right now."

"Does she need a hug?"

Emily looked over at Theresa. Fresh tears began to fall from Theresa's eyes.

"Not right now. Let Auntie T calm down a little bit. Okay?"

Jonathan nodded and turned to look at Theresa. "You'll be okay, Auntie T."

Theresa nodded at Jonathan and he went back to his drawing. Emily was unsure of what to do next. She had no idea if she could reach the rational side of Theresa or if saying anything would set her off. Theresa spoke first.

"Isn't this what you like to call a broken bridge?"

"There's no bridge that can't be fixed."

"Oh, I disagree, Emily. I don't think this bridge will be. In fact, by the end of the night this bridge is going to be burned to the ground." Theresa straightened up, sniffed and ran her hand through her hair.

Emily realized appealing to Theresa's rational side was not an option. She opted for logic and reality. "Theresa, let us go. You know this isn't going to end well for anyone. You'll be caught. There's no way out of this."

As the last words came out of Emily's mouth, the door began to open slowly. A man in black pants, a black shirt and ski mask entered the room.

Theresa smiled at Emily. "Yes, there is." She turned to the man. "It's about time. We have to get out of here."

The man nodded and began to walk toward Emily and Jonathan. Emily was frightened that he was going to take Jonathan away from her and hand him over to Theresa. She tightened her grip on Jonathan as she watched the man approach. Then she noticed he was walking with a slight limp that was very familiar to her.

Ronan

When they arrived at the clinic, Ronan immediately jumped from the car and went to the officers already on site. They filled him in on what they knew. Carl, who had escorted Emily to work and was tasked with looking after her, was found unconscious inside his vehicle and was being taken to the nearest hospital. Dante Morelli had, indeed, turned out to be an unstable person. He alternated between a tough guy persona and being fearful of what might happen to him. Dante was clearly afraid of his mother's reaction, but to what, the officers still could not discern. Going to jail or failing to do what was planned?

Upon hearing that Dante was expected to meet Theresa in the basement backroom, but that Theresa was armed, it was decided an officer would go down in Dante's place. Ronan realized no one was as tall as Dante except himself. It took persuading but it was agreed upon that Ronan was the only who could pass as Dante in black clothes and a ski mask. Sergeant McGuire, who was trained and specialized in hostage negotiations, was against the idea. He insisted negotiating with her would be the best plan, especially if she knew her brother was already in custody. However, Dante would not tell them what type of firearm Theresa had with her. He implied she would take out Emily before ever surrendering. McGuire conceded.

The captain stationed officers around the perimeter, at every possible exit and two were going down with Ronan, with instructions to wait outside the room, inconspicuous, until Theresa exited and was able to be apprehended. Both Troy and Marc wanted to go into the building with Ronan but were told to stay out of it. Marc went off to the side, seemingly fading into the background.

Ronan could hear his heart beat grow louder and louder as he entered the back door and took the stairs to the basement. Once at the bottom, the officers stationed themselves where Theresa would not immediately notice them upon exiting the room. Both had their guns drawn. Ronan paused for a brief moment, inhaled deeply to calm his nerves and opened the door.

"Yes, there is." He heard Theresa say but he was flooded with relief when he saw Emily and Jonathan sitting at a table, unharmed. He didn't catch what Theresa had said next. He began to walk over to his wife and son.

"Is it ready?" Ronan realized Theresa was asking him a question. He looked over at her and nodded.

"Good. Get them up and let's go. We can't be here any longer." Theresa began walking toward the door.

Ronan looked at Emily and saw she purposefully looked at his knee, up to his eyes, back to his knee again and then turned to Jonathan and gently tapped his pinky finger. Emily knew it was him. She had often held up Jonathan's pinky finger and would tell Ronan that his son had him wrapped around it. Still, he had a part to play. He grabbed Emily's arm and tugged it upward.

"Okay, honey, it's time to go." Emily gathered Jonathan in her arms and grabbed his drawing from the table.

"Are we going home now? I'm hungry." Jonathan began to whine.

"Yes, we are," Emily answered. "Don't you worry."

"Let's go!" Theresa had her hand on the door knob.

Ronan held on to Emily's arm as they walked toward the door. His mind was working furiously. If he could get Emily and Jonathan out first, the officers on the other side would have an easy job grabbing Theresa on her way out.

"You get the tickets?" Theresa asked, ready to open the door.

Ronan nodded again.

"Great. What time is the car meeting us?"

Ronan realized he couldn't verbally respond or the game was

up. He waved his hand at the door in an impatient gesture he hoped would indicate "Dante" wasn't interested in conversation and wanted to get out of there. His heart sank as Theresa paused and stared at him.

"Why are you still wearing that stupid mask?"

Ronan shrugged and pointed at the door knob. With one hand Theresa knocked his hand away as she reached in her waistband for her gun with the other hand.

"Take it off." Theresa leveled the gun at Ronan.

Ronan couldn't explain it then nor could he explain it later, but he instinctively knew what was about to happen and what he needed to do. Emily and Jonathan were slightly ahead of him to his right. He quickly pulled them back and against the wall, simultaneously stepping in front of them and away from the door.

The door flew open hard from a strong kick, knocking Theresa forward. Marc rushed in and grabbed Theresa around the waist with one arm and jammed a gun into her side with the other.

"Drop it!" Marc shouted. With that, the two officers that had come down with Ronan ran into the room.

Ronan didn't hesitate. He grabbed Emily and pushed them from the room, up the steps and out the back door.

Emily

"She jammed the phone lines and sent everyone home with a fake story," Michelle said. "That's why no one could get through. But, wait. Ronan got through. How?"

Although Emily knew the real answer was Marcus, she replied, "That's a bit of a mystery. The connection to my direct line was somehow restored."

Seated at the dining table in the loft, in the wee hours of the morning, Emily was doing her best to explain Theresa's motives. The police had taken Theresa and her brother into custody. They would have their due process according to the law. Emily would advocate for Theresa to have psychological assistance before having any type of jail sentence. Ronan wanted them both to pay severely for what they'd done and although Emily understood why he felt that way, she also understood Theresa's breakdown.

She hesitated to call it a psychotic break as Theresa was fully aware of what she was doing. What Emily had not known, and could only guess at, was when Emily had revealed who she really was, both Theresa's mother and brother began to apply pressure on her to avenge her father's death. Theresa hadn't blamed Emily for her father's death. She had tried repeatedly to make them see her father had chosen that life and knew the risks that came with it, but to no avail. For several years, when her family raised the issue, she had been able to dissuade and distract them, but it continued to be raised and the conversations became more volatile.

Emily tried to explain that in addition to the pressure her family must have been putting on her, Theresa also possessed a narcissistic side that had not been evident before. As Emily became more renowned for her work with the clinics, the more conferences, lectures, and appearances she was invited to, the more Theresa felt she was the one who deserved it more. It started as a slow burn that eventually turned into a deep resentment and a skewed view that Emily was taking the spotlight away from her.

The final straw for Theresa was the hysterectomy and the realization that she would never be able to have children, something she had always wanted. Not only had Emily stolen the accolades Theresa felt she deserved, Emily also had everything else Theresa had wanted but didn't, and couldn't, have. The deep resentment turned into irrational rage and a belief that Emily was the source of all Theresa's problems, which now had included her father's death.

Theresa's plan was to get rid of Emily and make it look like an accident. Her mother would provide an alibi for both her and Dante if they were ever questioned. She planned to move away from New York City and pass Jonathan off as her own. Though there were many holes and missteps in their plan, if Marcus had not been in Emily's life they may have gotten away with it, though Emily did not voice that part to the people sitting around her table.

"Sending that note was a stupid move," Rob said. "Why alert you? You would think Theresa was smarter than that."

"She is," Emily replied. "Dante sent it. He wanted to scare me. He wanted me to walk around constantly looking over my shoulder."

Ronan interjected, "Why did Marc come down? How'd he know Theresa would be standing right in front of the door when he kicked it in? I know he said he just knew but there were already two guys down there. They said he literally flew down the stairs and immediately kicked the door in, not saying anything to them. How did he know?"

Once again, Emily knew that answer but she let Rob reply. "Pure instinct, Ronan. He apologized to the officers and told them he was sure all of you would have gotten out safely even if he wouldn't have gone in, but he says he had the instinct that he should move, so he did."

Emily smiled and looked at Ronan. "It's exactly how you knew to pull us back and against the wall, away from the door. You said the same thing; you couldn't explain it, you just knew."

She watched as Ronan considered it for a moment, saw the realization dawn on him and nod. He smiled back at Emily and took her hand.

Turning her attention to Rob, she asked, "What are the chances of keeping all this out of the press? I've had enough of that in my lifetime and with Jack's parole hearing coming up, there'll be more of it."

"Troy and Marc are already on it. It should be minimal. If Theresa and Dante both plead guilty, and don't push for a trial, we can keep it down. I hope. I can do many things, Em, but I'm not a miracle worker. I can't stop nosy journalists."

"Let's hope something catches their interest and this is relegated to the back pages. Too bad the World's Fair still isn't going on in Knoxville. Maybe there will be a new break in the Tylenol case or they'll still be talking about that thing that came out last month," Emily turned to Ronan, "What was that?"

"A CD player," Ronan replied.

"Right," Emily replied. "Although their time would be better spent learning more about Acquired Immune Deficiency Syndrome so their coverage isn't so homophobic and disgusting. If the media only knew how many people they hurt with their careless words and inept research, not to mention the blatant bias. Maybe I should write a paper. Between Vietnam veterans and the gay community, the statistics of how media coverage affected them is astounding. The paper would literally write itself. They never should have created that 24 hour news channel, either. It's only going to get worse. Seriously, report the facts and leave the personal commentary out of it."

"Emily!" Michelle nearly shouted, "you were held hostage with a plan to kill you and you're talking about how the media should be more responsible?" Michelle's eyes were still wet with the tears she had cried when the group had finally returned home. "We could have lost you and Jonathan tonight and you're thinking about how other people are hurt. I . . ." Michelle trailed off as fresh tears began.

Emily got up from her seat, knelt next to Michelle and put her arm around her. "But you didn't lose us, Michelle," Emily's voice was soft and reassuring. "We're here and we're safe." She drew Michelle into a tight hug and whispered, "You're not going to lose us. We're family." She pulled away and smiled. "You're not getting rid of me just yet."

Michelle wiped at her eyes and tried to smile back. After a moment she put her hands on Emily's arms and looked in her eyes. "Don't ever do that to us again. We love you. June and I . . . we don't know what we'd do without you." She paused for a moment before continuing, "You are the best thing that has ever happened to my brother. He loves you so much. I just can't imagine what we would have done if . . ." She trailed off as the tears started once again.

"You don't have to imagine, Mom." Emily heard June say as the girl got up from her seat and joined Emily. "It's okay. No one is leaving you."

Emily was both surprised and impressed that June had recognized not only Michelle's anguish but also her mother's core fear of abandonment. Between losing her first love to war and Jack's betrayal, the signs were clear. She tried to help her overcome it, but knew it still lingered. What she didn't know was that June had noticed and correctly identified it. Maybe there was another budding psychologist in the family.

Without hearing him approach, Emily felt Ronan's arm encircle her as he grabbed Michelle's hand with the other. "We're strong, sis.

You know that. There's nothing any of us can't get through together."

Emily watched as Rob also walked over to join the circle. "If Maggie were here she'd say we're stronger than steel."

At that moment, Emily couldn't help but smile. She took a moment to look at each person. Michelle, June, Rob and finally, Ronan. The man who had a huge hand in her journey to become the person she was and her continuing journey to be the person she wanted to be.

Everyone in the room was a work in progress. Everyone had their own journey. Together they helped each other along the way and would continue to do so. There truly was nothing they couldn't handle together and they were, indeed, stronger than steel. But they were also so much more than that.

Emily smiled, closed her eyes and tried to draw them into the tightest hug she could muster.

"We're family."

Ronan

Strolling down the Av. du Marechal Gallieni, Ronan felt a sense of peace he hadn't felt for months. He'd stayed true to his word. Once the dust settled with Theresa's failed plan and Jack's parole hearing had concluded, Ronan wasted no time getting his family together for a much-needed getaway.

It had taken no convincing at all. Theresa and Dante pleaded guilty to the charges and, based on Emily's advocacy, Theresa was being treated at an inpatient facility. After that, her prison term would be determined. The board denied Jack's parole based on the evidence from his former law firm and, surprisingly, testimony from June regarding his phone call. Even more surprising was a call from Bart's wife letting Ronan know that Bart was diagnosed with paranoid schizophrenia and was getting the help he needed for it. He had wished them both well and asked her to keep him updated on his progress. A week after the hearing, the entire family boarded a plane to meet Maggie at the apartment in Paris.

Now, walking toward the bridge where he'd proposed to Emily, holding her hand and chatting easily about the beautiful architecture and history of the city, Ronan knew in his heart the worst was behind them. He also knew that whatever life had in store for them, as long as he was holding Emily's hand, everything would be okay. He intentionally asked June to make a fuss over keeping Jonathan at the apartment with her so that he could have this time alone with his wife.

After crossing the street, Ronan dropped Emily's hand and put his arm around her shoulders as they walked onto the bridge. He could not have asked for a better evening than this. It was chilly, definitely, but the sky was clear and the lights from the city were dazzling. He thought they might take a walk down toward the Eiffel Tower to see it lit up. He chuckled to himself. After all, he thought, isn't that what they do in all romance movies? It wouldn't be a romantic night in Paris without seeing the Eiffel Tower.

"What's that smile for?" He felt Emily nudge him.

"Nothing in particular," he replied. "I'm just a happy guy right now."

"And I'm a happy gal who's glad her man is happy."

"Well aren't we two rays of sunshine," Ronan began.

"In the middle of winter," they finished in unison and laughed.

"Only it's true this time," Ronan said as he slowed his walk and pulled her to the side. "It's been a rough year."

"That's an understatement," Emily retorted.

"True, but we made it through and here we are." Ronan bent his head and kissed her. He felt the same passion and love for her that he felt the day he proposed to her in almost the same spot.

He was reluctant to let go when he felt Emily slowly pull away and smile up at him. He watched as she turned, leaned over the rail and looked out over the Seine River. Her resilience never ceased to amaze him. She sought her own counseling after the kidnapping while simultaneously going back to work and caring for Jonathan. She'd told him there were people out there that needed her help and she wasn't going to let them down. She promised to continue seeing her counselor after this trip. Ronan may not be as well-versed in mental health as his wife but he knew the toll it took on her. He would make sure she kept her promise, but more than that, he'd keep the promise he made to himself: to keep her safe and happy.

"Hey, did you notice June didn't complain once so far?" Ronan asked.

Emily nodded. "She's growing up. She's surprised me a few times over the last few weeks. That girl understands more than we give her credit for. She's not a little girl anymore. Graduation and college aren't too far away."

"I'm sure boys are somewhere in there, too."

Emily fell silent. He was sure she would come back with some joke about boys or the birds and the bees, teen idols, or football players, but she didn't.

"You don't think she'll be interested in anyone?" he asked.

"Ro, for how much time you spend with her, I'm surprised that you have not noticed yet." She looked up at him. "Your niece is gay."

The statement took Ronan by surprise. He opened his mouth to say something but closed it again as different conversations with June went through his mind. He realized it was right in front of him and he hadn't noticed. The comments about girls, the posters on her wall, her never-ending chatter about one of the VJ's on the music channel.

"Wow, you're right. I didn't notice and I should have. It makes sense now."

"It's fine, Ro. We're conditioned to default to the boy-girl relationship. It's expected."

"I know, but still. Now that I think about it, I see it. Does Michelle know?"

"No," Emily replied. "No one does. June hasn't said anything to me in case you're wondering. It's something that I suspected, but over the last year, it's become evident. June is still navigating the feelings. I'm not even sure she's completely come to terms with it herself. I've talked to her about sexuality in a very general way, and I've let her know the door is open whenever she wants to talk. But, Ronan, this is her path. When she's ready, she'll talk. It is not for anyone else to push her along or force her to admit it. She will when she's ready and not a minute sooner. She may come out to us tomorrow over dinner or she may never come out. It's her choice when or if she wants to tell anyone. Understand?"

Ronan nodded. "I understand. I mean, I want to talk to her about it, and let her know that it's all okay, but I understand what you're saying."

"Good. If and when she does tell us, she's going to have a rough time. The U.S. still isn't accepting of the gay community, especially now. She'll need all of us for support."

"And she'll have all of us. There's no question there. Nothing's going to change my love for that girl."

"I know. I was never worried about that." Emily smiled at Ronan and turned back to the river.

As Ronan reflected on his recent conversations with June, he found himself lost in thought. He couldn't help but wonder if he had unintentionally offended her whenever he brought up the topic of boys. Pondering this more, he realized that June was more than likely uncomfortable than offended, feeling uncertain of how to express herself.

Ronan made a conscious decision to approach it from a different angle moving forward. He would actively listen to June's comments and expand on them, rather than change the subject to boys. Ronan became determined to create a safe environment where June could feel free to be herself without the fear of rejection.

"Ronan?" Emily's voice shook him from his thoughts.

He could tell by the tone of her voice that she'd turned serious. "Yes?"

"I've been pondering this question since the night I sat in that room with Theresa." Emily paused for a moment. Ronan thought she seemed to be deciding whether or not she wanted to ask the question. He knew something was weighing on her. He was about to tell her whatever it was, it was okay to ask when she continued. "Do you think the universe ever forgives you?"

Ronan wasn't quite sure what she meant by that and gave her a quizzical look.

Emily turned back to the water. "Do you think the universe will ever forgive me for the things I did when I was younger or do you think that something else will come up again?"

Ronan turned and looked out over the river as well. "I think," he began, "that the universe has already forgiven you. If it hadn't, I don't think we'd be standing here right now." His eyes traveled down to the water below him and a thought hit him. He turned toward her and took her hand, making sure she was looking at him. "Emily, for whatever reason, the universe sent you Marcus. In turn, it put you on the bridge the night I was ready to take a leap. It brought us together that night. A night we were supposed to forget, but a part of us remembered, and then the universe made sure our paths crossed again. And along the way you opened two successful clinics, helped countless people, and gave us the most precious little boy on the planet. Theresa is getting the help she needs, Lyle Kettering is long forgotten, and Jack is exactly where he should be. We're here on this bridge because the universe *has* forgiven you."

He saw her eyes begin to water and a slight smile begin to form. "I hope you're right."

"I'm always right." A big smile crossed his face. "Besides, I'm sure Marcus will definitely confirm it for you."

Emily took a deep breath. "Well, I only see Marcus when there's trouble. I would love to see him again and have a normal conversation without there being some kind of problem, but I don't think that's how it works. I've never known how it works, exactly, and he's never told me."

Ronan gave a slight nod and then, "I know you think he broke some rules the night Theresa had you."

"Oh, I'm pretty sure he did," Emily replied. "He always said everyone has free will and they weren't allowed to intervene with that, but he got through to Marc and to you. Not to mention that I'm positive he's the reason my direct line was reconnected. Maybe whoever is in charge, his superiors or whatever they're called, allowed him to do that, I don't know. Maybe I'll never know."

"Maybe you won't, and that's okay," Ronan answered. "I'm sure he's still watching over you and that's okay by me." He took her hands. "We're in one of the most beautiful cities standing on one of our bridges–"

Emily's laughter made him pause. "Michelle always said we had a thing for bridges."

"We do," Ronan agreed. "Although, in all honesty, while both bridges are architecturally gorgeous in their own way, I prefer the Brooklyn Bridge."

"Why's that?"

"Because it's where my life with you started." He saw that smile, the one that not only brightened her face but reached her eyes and made them sparkle.

"I will always, always be grateful to the universe for sending me Marcus so that I could be on that bridge with you that night and on this bridge with you today."

"Me, too. And, no offense to him, but I hope you never see him again."

"That makes two of us."

Ronan wrapped both arms around her and felt her snuggle into him. They both turned their heads slightly to look out over the river, and as they did so, a light snow began to fall.

Epilogue

Christmas 2022

They sat in their overstuffed chairs, their hands entwined resting on the table between them. They loved this part of the day, sitting together, gazing out the window and watching the sunset on the city. It was a habit they had gotten into in recent years. Every night after dinner they would retreat to their study and settle in their chairs with a glass of wine or a cup of tea. This day had been busy as the entire family had gathered for the Christmas holiday, but they still held to their routine.

After retiring over a decade ago, they moved to Weehawken, New Jersey, into a building along the Hudson river. They made sure their apartment faced the water so they could have a view of the river and see the bright lights of the city at night. For them, it was the perfect place; out of the hustle of the city they loved but only a ferry ride away to visit it.

Children's laughter filtered in to them, along with the sounds of their son and his cousins cleaning up the dinner dishes and putting things away. They were grateful the family was able to come together this year, though there were holes in the gathering. They had lost Michelle to cancer in 2014. June joined Save Haven after receiving her doctorate from Columbia and was now running both clinics with thoughts of opening a third in Queens.

Rob had passed away after a sudden heart attack two years after they lost Michelle. They didn't often see two of his children as they had moved away after having lost their mother within a year of losing their father. Rob's oldest son had followed in his father's footsteps and was the current President and CEO of Corbyn.

Maggie, divorced and never remarried, stayed in New York along with her two children - neither of whom wanted any part of Corbyn. One was appearing in plays on and off-Broadway and the other was a senior editor at a publishing firm. Having their niece and nephew in these positions was quite convenient. Not only did this help them decide which play to see on their date nights, but they were also given advance notice of which books were must-reads and which ones weren't.

Jonathan knocked softly before entering the room. "Mom? Dad? Do you guys need anything?"

Emily turned slightly to look at her son. "No, honey, we're fine. Come take a seat."

Jonathan and Ronan began talking business, as they often did after Jonathan took over Byrne Improvements. It seemed Jonathan had inherited all of Ronan's creativity and love of crafting wood and none of Emily's passion for psychology. What he did inherit from Emily was a quick mind and sharp intellect. That, combined with the compassion and a desire to help those who struggled, which he'd inherited from both parents, had taken the business to levels neither Ronan nor Michelle could have imagined. Jonathan had transformed it from strictly home improvements to include interior design as well. His furniture pieces and designs were often featured in magazines and newspapers. Jonathan had established himself as one of the most sought-after designers in the northeast, while still providing the free-of-charge services his father had established to those who needed the help.

"No, no," Emily interrupted the men, "no shop talk. It's Christmas. Where's Sophie?"

"She's in the living room having a slight disagreement with little Em," Jonathan replied.

Ronan chuckled. "Your wife and daughter are having a disagreement. Wise move to stay away, my son."

"You alright, Mom?" Jonathan asked. "Do you need anything?"

Emily gave her son a look. "I'm fine. I wish everyone would stop making such a fuss."

"You had COVID, Mom. Of course, we're going to worry. You must have been a nurse's worst nightmare in the hospital."

Ronan laughed and Emily shook her head. She'd battled a nasty strain of the virus and had been hospitalized for well over two months. Once she tested negative, she was released from the hospital but still had a cough and, occasionally, was short of breath.

"I was the perfect patient," Emily told her son.

"Yes, you were," Ronan added, "when you were sleeping."

Emily slapped her husband's hand and then smiled at him. Ronan squeezed her hand and brought it up to his lips for a quick kiss.

"You two still act like teenagers," their son observed.

"Ain't that the truth!" June exclaimed as she walked in.

Ronan turned, "There you are! Why couldn't Hannah be here today?"

"She couldn't get anyone to cover her shift at the hospital. She tried. Trust me, Uncle Ro, any chance she has to spend time with you, she takes it. She adores you."

"The woman has good taste," Ronan smiled as June patted his shoulder.

Bending down next to Emily, June asked, "How are you doing, Aunt Em?"

Emily patted June's hand. "I'm fine. I wish everyone would stop asking. It's only the little cough that won't go away. That's all it is now. Don't you worry about me. I'm more worried about you and Hannah."

"Don't be," June sighed.

"Oh, honey, I've been around long enough to see the signs. Once they managed to overturn Roe vs. Wade, I saw the writing on the wall. You and Hannah take care of each other. You belong together and don't let anyone tell you differently. They'll come for same-sex marriage, mark my words."

"Don't worry, we're ready. I know how to advocate, Aunt Em, remember? I learned from the best." June smiled warmly at her aunt.

"Hey, hey," Ronan spoke up, "no shop talk. It's Christmas."

"It's not shop talk, dear," Emily replied. "It's . . . well, I don't know what it is, but at least it's not business."

"That reminds me, Mom. Little Em's been asking a lot of questions lately," Jonathan said. "Especially after they overturned Roe. I told her you were probably the most qualified to answer them."

"Well, get her in here, then," Emily replied. As Jonathan got up and began to walk from the room, Emily grunted. "And stop calling her little Em. She's 17, for God's sake. I'm fairly certain she hates it." Jonathan shook his head and left the room.

"I'm going to check on Aunt Maggie," June told them. "She fell asleep in the guest room right after dinner. I also need to make sure those grandkids of hers and Uncle Rob's aren't wrecking the kitchen." They knew the kids' parents were in there, but Emily and Ronan also knew June wanted to give them some time with their granddaughter alone.

Ronan reached for Emily's hand again. He smiled at her and gave her hand another squeeze. "We're lucky people, Emily. All those kids and grandkids? They're good people. Michelle did good, Rob and Maggie did good. We did good."

"Yes, we did," Emily smiled. "Jonathan is so much like you. He has your heart, your patience and your spirit. I'm so glad."

"You were a wonderful mother, Emily. He wouldn't be the man he is without you. Jonathan may be more like me but his daughter takes after you. "

"Talking about me?" Ronan's granddaughter put her arms around his shoulders from behind and gave him a squeeze.

"There's my girl," Emily said as her namesake came over and kissed her on the cheek. "Your father said you've had a lot of questions lately. Anything you want to talk about?"

Little Em, as she had been called since birth, sighed. "I do. I wasn't planning on talking about anything today, though. It can wait.

We don't have to discuss all this on Christmas."

"Pfft," was Ronan's response. "It's as good a day as any. What's on your mind?"

"Well," she started, "I mean, I don't understand so much of what's happening lately. I mean, yeah, I do understand, but I really don't. I don't know if that makes much sense."

"In these times, it makes perfect sense," Ronan answered.

"In a lot of ways these times are no different than any other decade. In other ways, they are very different," Emily said. "Women are fighting for their rights, black people are protesting to be heard, there's inflation, higher gas prices and immigration is a big issue."

"I know," Little Em replied.

"Oh, you think I'm talking about right now? No, I'm not. I'm talking about the 1960s, the 1970s and even the 1980s."

"What?"

Emily laughed. "Nothing's changed, my girl. Nothing has changed. You know, I started out at a time when women couldn't have their own bank account or credit card. Sometimes they couldn't even have a medical procedure without their husband's consent."

"You have got to be kidding me," her granddaughter replied, incredulous.

"No, I'm not. Women have clearly come a long way, but now we're going backwards to where we have to fight for rights again. This country has been arguing over the same issues for decades and the parties in power have no desire to fix any of it."

"That's what I mean. It's like all they do is argue with each other and blame the other party. They're supposed to work for us, aren't they? But I don't see that happening."

"There's a reason for that," Ronan replied. "If you think they care about the American people, you're wrong. Oh, I'm sure some of them do. I'm sure there are a handful in the parties that do work for us, but the majority? No. They care more about getting and retaining power than they do about us. They are getting rich from lobbyists and special interests at our expense. They make up their own rules to meet their own agenda."

"The sad thing is the media doesn't help the situation," Emily chimed in. "You never hear them say anything was a win for the American people. It's always one side or the other. Politicians and the media have successfully divided this country so much that when one side does something, even if it's harmful, people will cheer like it's a football game and their team just scored a touchdown. It's become ridiculous."

"Become? It's been." Ronan snorted.

Emily nodded. "Em, we've lived through so many things and for as much as things changed, some things have stayed exactly the same." Looking down, she noted little Em had her phone in her hand. It seemed everyone was attached to them these days. "Technology sure has changed. You know, when I first used a telephone it had a cord that hooked to the wall and it came with a party line. Now, you have that little thing in your hand that you carry everywhere."

Little Em looked down at her iPhone and then asked, "What's a party line?"

"When two separate households shared the same number," Ronan answered. "You could pick up the phone and you'd hear the other people having a conversation. You couldn't use your phone until they hung up."

Emily laughed at her granddaughter's shocked expression. "It's true." Then she sighed and continued. "Your grandfather and I lived through so much; the assassination of John F. Kennedy, the Vietnam War, the Civil Rights Movement, 9/11, so much more right up to this pandemic. We have long memories, but the country? The country has a short memory."

"I don't think that's true. It's all in our history books," Little Em replied.

"Not accurately," Ronan corrected. "Do you know what the Tulsa Massacre is?"

Little Em thought for a moment and then, "No."

"Exactly," Emily said. "You need to read about that and then you need to find out why it isn't taught in your history classes."

"There are many things that aren't being taught in that white-washed history you're being fed," Ronan continued. "But what your grandmother means by a short memory is that there are certain issues that have spanned decades; issues that we're still fighting about today, issues that the parties don't want fixed because they are used during every election cycle to get votes."

"Let me guess," Little Em said, "immigration is one of them."

"I knew you were a smart cookie," Ronan chuckled. "For decades politicians have ranted and raved about immigration. It could have been fixed 50 years ago, but it still isn't. First, politicians will convince you immigrants are the reason for all your problems. They're the scapegoats. Focus on them before you realize it's actually the policies of those in power that are the reason for your problems. Think about it. Were immigrants responsible for the crash in '07? No. Are immigrants the reason we're experiencing this inflation? No. Are they responsible for the Columbine shooting? Parkland? Las Vegas? No. Then there's fear-mongering. They tell you immigrants are the reason for crime, even though more people have been murdered by our own citizens in mass shootings in one year than all murders committed by immigrants combined. Immigration comes up every election cycle and then it goes away right after. Well, until it's time to campaign again."

"You forgot one," Emily interjected, "The one that cracks me up is that politicians keep saying immigrants come to take the jobs away from U.S. citizens. Immigrants can't *take* a job from anyone. Employers are *giving* them jobs. There's a difference, but politicians don't talk about those employers, they only talk about the immigrants. If they wanted to rid the country of illegal immigrants, they would have deported all those meat plant workers that wouldn't get tested for COVID, but they didn't. Why didn't they? That's not hard to figure out, is it?"

"No, it isn't," Little Em replied. "Cheap labor means higher profits so politicians overlook it. That's what you're saying, isn't it? You're saying immigrants have been used as pawns for over 50 years and I see your point."

"Google it," Emily replied. "You'll see more. While you're at it, Google gas prices and who is really in control of that, Google women's rights and see how long we've been fighting for those, Google the Civil Rights Act and then Google how black people are paid versus white people. Google the history of universal healthcare in this country. There's a book out there that will tell you exactly why we are the only industrialized, first-world country that doesn't have it."

"That's another question I had. I don't understand why we don't have it."

"Racism is the short answer. The idea of universal healthcare was floated as far back as the 1920s but those in power didn't want black people to have access to healthcare, thinking it was a way to get rid of them. So they twisted and turned a basic human right into something that needed to be earned through employment. They were very successful in convincing a large swath of people that you needed an employer to hire you to earn the right to be healthy. Since the majority of black people at that time were not properly employed – instead, they were living off tips for services, they were denied healthcare. Like I said, there's a book on the topic."

"So, here we are today," Little Em said, "where some people are forced to sell their houses in order to pay for medical bills for major illnesses and it's all because . . . I can't even finish that sentence."

"It was racism for decades and now it's coupled with corporate greed. My dear, there's so much more we can tell you, but, instead, I think it's best that you go read about the true history of this country. I mean *read*, darling, from long-standing, credible sources. Do not rely on cable news. The 24 hour news cycle was the worst thing to happen. Too much misinformation and bias goes out over those so-called news shows. Some exist solely to get their viewers to hate the other side."

"In short," Ronan said, "turn off your television, YouTube, that TikTok thing and whatever else you watch and go *read*. And don't expect any politician from either party to save this country. Both parties have their own agenda that has very little to do with helping the American people."

Ronan gave his granddaughter a big smile and a pat on the hand. "What was that for?" Em asked.

"It warms my heart to see your generation so engaged in what's going on around you. I'm telling you," he patted her hand again, "it's your generation that's going to set things right."

"Yeah, because the generations before us screwed it all up." Little Em laughed.

"You're not kidding," Emily said. "It's the same battles over and over - inflation, recession, unemployment, racial and gender inequality, division among ourselves, violence against the LGBTQ community; none of that is new. We're fighting the same issues for decades. Like I said, short memory."

"Grams, has there been any violence against June and Hannah?"

"Thankfully, no physical violence, but they've had their fair share of discrimination and harassment. I know some politicians like to act like it's new but gay people have been around since the dawn of time. As for trans people, we heard about sex change operations back in the 60's. It's not new, it's not an agenda from a political side. They have always been there. The only thing that has changed is they want to live their lives openly without torment. That's not a big ask when you think about it and take out all the rest of the noise. They *should* be able to live freely without being terrorized."

"They *shouldn't* be terrorized. What is wrong with people?" Little Em shook her head.

"You want the short or the long answer," Ronan laughed. "The media and politicians are our biggest problems. You see it every day. They tell people what to get upset about and people will follow without finding out what's true and what isn't. They'll turn on their own family if their network of choice told them to."

"I can't believe we are arguing over things that history has already shown us to be horrible." Emily shook her head.

"Grams," Little Em said quietly, "I *have* done some reading based on something that's been happening and it scares me. It's one of the things I wanted to talk about."

Emily took her granddaughter's hand. "I'm sorry, sweetie. Your grandfather and I do tend to go off on tangents sometimes, don't we? Now tell me, what have you read about?"

"Book bans, the calls for change in public education, stuff like that. I remember reading about that in history class when we were studying World War II, so I read more about it when the book bans started."

Emily nodded. "So, you see that it's all been done before and it didn't end well."

"That's what I don't understand. Why can't people see that?"

"Because they don't want to," Ronan replied. "They are afraid of losing their superiority, their privilege, so rather than have equality and harmony among all the diverse people in this country, they'll fight tooth and nail to maintain the status quo. The system has always been rigged toward white people."

"A little clarity, sweetheart," Emily interrupted. "You really meant to say the system has always been rigged toward white *men*."

"I won't deny that," Ronan answered.

"What you're really talking about is white supremacy," Little Em replied. "But not all white people are racist. None of my friends are."

"No, you're right," Ronan said. "A lot of white people aren't, especially in your generation. However, a lot of white people still *are* and that's why they will support and praise whatever politician demonizes those *other* groups of people."

"I can't wrap my mind around it. I really can't. I mean, I want to shout at people that the Holocaust didn't start with Hitler rounding up the Jewish people, it started . . ." Little Em sighed.

Emily continued. "It started with him changing the educational curriculum and banning books. It started with him forbidding any history be taught that was in direct contrast to his policies and did not show the country in a very positive light. It started with him convincing people not to trust experts, scientists, teachers. It started with him convincing people that his was the only way and anyone who didn't show allegiance was a traitor."

"That sounds like Florida and that's what I'm talking about. It's happening here almost in the exact same way and people think it's okay. It scares me. I don't understand why people can't see that different ideas, different cultures, different art, different anything can co-exist and, in fact, make a country much more beautiful."

"The Netherlands understands that," Emily said. "In fact, if you think the United States is the freest country, go visit Amsterdam. After two days there, you'll see that the United States is free-*ish*. We are definitely not the most free, by any stretch. France is even freer than we are."

"Is that why you love going to France?"

"I love their sense of community. I love that their culture is one of taking care of each other and their community. It's not every man for himself."

"Don't get us wrong, Little Em," Ronan said, "we love this country. There has been a whole lot of good that has come from this country. What we're saying is our government is broken."

"We do love this country," Emily agreed. "It's why we tried to make a difference in our own way. I would not want to live anywhere else. This country is worth fighting for. I used to say that countries don't find peace, people find peace, and that still holds true."

"That seems contradictory," Little Em replied.

"It's not. Think on it for a bit, and you'll get it."

Little Em stood up and stretched. "I know there's a lot about the government that no one knows . . ."

"And shouldn't know," Ronan interrupted.

". . . but I don't see either side doing anything to make our lives any better. I see what you're saying about still arguing over the same things decade after decade, and certain issues being used as tools for elections, but I don't know. I don't see how one person finding peace helps the country."

"You'll figure it out," came Emily's reply.

Little Em wandered to the far wall, where pictures of various scenic views hung. She paused and considered the large picture of the familiar bridge in Paris. "Not to change the subject, but I think Aunt Michelle was right. You guys really do have a thing for bridges."

"Maybe that's because bridges represent a lot of things," Ronan answered.

"The alchemy of bridges is certainly something you should ponder, honey," Emily chimed in. "It might help you find the answer to your previous concern about finding peace."

Little Em considered her grandparents for a moment and then

replied, "A bridge brings opposite ends together, whether in physical or metaphorical form."

"You're getting it," Emily smiled at her. "Wherever there is conflict - in the world, in a country, in a city, in a family, between friends, and even in one's own mind - there is always a bridge that can fix it if one can figure out what foundation to use and if they possess the will and courage to build it."

"I get it." Little Em smiled broadly at Emily.

"Now, skedaddle, young lady, I think your grandmother needs to rest." Ronan had begun to hear the strain in Emily's voice.

"I'm fine," Emily chided her husband.

"I think Grandpa's right, Grams. I should let you rest." Little Em made sure to give both her grandparents a kiss before leaving the room.

"I really am fine, darling," Emily's cracking voice betrayed her.

Ronan reached over the table and took his wife's hand again. "Just close your eyes and rest, my dear. It's been a long day." He pulled her hand closer. "I love you. I've loved you from the moment I laid eyes on you."

"I love you, too," Emily smiled again. "We did good, Ro. We did good with our family and we did some good in this world. But you, my dear Ronan, you by far have been the best part of my life. Every day with you has been a blessing."

"Shhhh. Get some rest," Ronan replied. "There's plenty of time to stroke my ego later."

Emily let out a little chuckle before relenting and closing her eyes. It wasn't long before she fell fast asleep.

~~~~

Emily stirred slightly and opened her eyes. She blinked a few
~~~~

times and took in the room. She wasn't in the library anymore. Ronan wasn't in a chair beside her. This room was sparse. She could only make out different shades of beige. She closed her eyes and shook her head. Opening them again, she was still in the unfamiliar room.

"Greetings, my dear Emily!"

The voice was one she hadn't heard in 40 years but she recognized it instantly. Emily sat up and looked around the room. In the corner sat Marcus in an ornate, over-stuffed chair.

"Marcus!" she exclaimed. "What's happening? What's wrong?"

"Nothing, my dear, nothing. It's my duty and, I might add, my honor, to welcome you."

"Welcome me?" Emily was confused. She shifted positions and then realized that none of the pain she'd been experiencing in recent months was present. She looked down and gasped. Her hands were no longer wrinkled. She lifted them up, even with her eyes, and turned them back and forth several times.

Dropping her hands, she looked over at Marcus, who only continued to smile at her. In her peripheral vision, she caught a mirror hanging on the wall beside her. She slowly stood up and walked over to it. The image she saw staring back at her was not the same one she'd seen in her bedroom mirror that morning. She turned to Marcus and then back to the mirror. She should be frightened, but she wasn't. She should be worried, but she wasn't. Emily felt nothing but a calm, peaceful feeling as she stared at the reflection. Staring back at her was her 27-year old self, looking exactly as she had the night she first saw Ronan on the Brooklyn Bridge.

"Well," she started after a long moment, "I suppose I've passed on." She turned to look at Marcus.

"Yes."

Emily walked back to what appeared to be a chaise lounge, sat down and nodded. "My family?" she asked.

"That is why it is my honor to welcome you." Marcus stood up and walked over to her. "But before we get to that, you need to come with me." He extended his hand.

Hesitantly, Emily took his hand, stood up and followed him out of the room. She began to feel as if it was a dream, it was bright but hazy, clear but the edges were blurred. She looked around her but couldn't make anything out. She almost ran into Marcus when he came to a complete stop.

"Look around, Emily, and tell me what you sce."

"I have been. It's almost looks like a fog, but also, it looks like images that won't come into focus."

"Give it a minute."

Emily stood still and looked forward, focusing on one area, hoping she'd be able to see something, anything, that would let her know where she was and what Marcus was trying to show her. Without warning, the images became clearer, but came and went so quickly, it was hard for Emily to catch them all. One after the other, image after image flew by; families, construction workers, small towns, large cities, a man on a hill, teenagers fighting, children by a waterfall, someone with a gun, a boat on the ocean, couples talking, friends laughing, crowds protesting, they kept coming in what she thought looked like a fast moving slide show. She backed up and looked away.

"What was that?"

Marcus smiled. "It takes getting used to. Try again but will them to slow down."

Emily eyed him warily, took a moment, and then looked back. Once again, the images had a speed she found hard to keep up with. She focused in and concentrated. Eventually, she could see each image for a full second or two before it flashed into the next. She watched in amazement until the realization dawned on her. She let her eyes drift away until the images were gone.

"That's how you knew," she said without looking at Marcus.

"Yes," he replied, "and no. That's one part of it."

"And the other part?"

"We'll get to that," Marcus smiled. "But first." He gestured in front him, toward movement coming forward.

Emily could see it was the shape of a person but she couldn't make how who it was. Her mother? Michelle? Rob? For more than just the obvious reason, she hoped it was Rob. She had missed him more than she had been willing to admit to anyone.

"Oh, the others will come, Emily," Marcus said. "Don't worry. You will see who you wish to, but this one has had something she's wanted to say to you for quite some time."

"Are you reading my mind?" Emily asked. Marcus did not reply. He nodded toward the approaching figure.

Emily watched as the figure became clearer. She had seen the face before, but only in pictures. Her mouth opened slightly and her breath left her as the woman came closer. Emily thought she was more beautiful than any of the pictures she had seen and she felt a warmth and kindness emanating from her that filled Emily's heart.

"Carrieann." It came out in a whisper.

The woman smiled. "Emily."

Emily closed the gap between them and enveloped her into a hug. "Oh, Carrieann, he loved you so much," Emily whispered as she drew her in tighter.

Carrieann squeezed Emily fiercely for a few seconds before relaxing, taking a step back, and grasping her hands.

"I know, but it was my time. I had to leave."

"You never left his heart."

Carrieann nodded. "You gave him the room he needed. You showed him there was enough space for everyone; for Michelle, for June, for you and Jonathan . . . and for me." She paused for a moment, her smile fading. "I saw his depression starting. I didn't know what it was, though. I saw the change in him and didn't know what to do. After I was gone, I could see him . . . on occasion . . . when I focused and tried hard enough . . . I could see him losing himself and I couldn't do anything about it."

"Don't—"

Carrieann held up her hand and Emily stopped. Carrieann continued. "Then I saw you. I saw you that night on the bridge and I knew he would be okay. What I have wanted to say to you for quite some time now is . . . thank you. Thank you for being there, thank you for taking care of him, thank you for supporting him. But mostly, thank you for loving him. He wouldn't have found a new life – a life he loved – without you."

"He cherished his life with you as well," Emily replied.

Carrieann smiled, "Yes, he did. But, as you'll see, the universe does work in interesting ways. I must leave now. I was only given moments here. Thank you, Emily. You gave Ronan the life he deserved to have."

Giving Emily's hands a final squeeze, Carrieann turned and walked swiftly back the way she had entered, fading slowly until Emily could no longer make out her form.

"Why was she only given moments?"

Marcus inhaled. "Carrieann is a beautiful, kind soul. Unfortunately, she is not one of us and, therefore, cannot stay in this realm for too long."

"In this realm?" Emily sighed. "Even in the afterlife I can't get straight answers from you."

Marcus smiled again. "You'll understand it all. Come." He took her hand again and began walking until they came upon a bench much like the one they sat on the night she stopped Ronan from jumping. "Sit."

Emily sat down and looked around. Once again, it felt odd. White, cream, beige, seemed to swirl into each other. Emily felt as if she could see things, but not clearly, hear things, but not distinctly. She tried to focus but it shook her. It sounded like thousands of voices at once, but silent at the same time.

"Emily, you've been chosen to be one of us. You asked me several times what I am. This is what I am. It will be clear in just a moment, but I would like to explain something to you first. You see, many, many years ago we were given the name of someone who would make a huge impact on the world. A positive impact at a time of impending darkness. An impact that would invoke change. That name was Emily Byrne."

"What?" Emily was dumbfounded.

"When you were born, I did not know that you would cross paths with Ronan," Marcus continued. "I saw the goodness in you, and as I've told you before, I always believed your soul was worth saving."

"I remember."

Marcus nodded. "It wasn't until that night on the bridge that it occurred to me you might possibly become the Emily Byrne in question. However, I had to do what was required and wipe the memories, with the hope that someday you would cross paths again. We still do not understand how the two of you managed to bury part of it somewhere in yourselves, but you did."

"There is a scientific name for it, Marcus," Emily laughed. "You know that. Although, I doubt science means much here, wherever we are."

Marcus went on. "Regardless, you did, indeed, cross paths again and you became Emily Byrne."

"Wait," a thought crossed Emily's mind. "Carrieann. She said the universe works in interesting ways. If she had lived, he wouldn't have been walking the streets. I wouldn't have followed him. There would have been no night on the bridge. There would be no Emily Byrne."

"Carrieann was not collateral damage, if that's what you're worried about. We do not give someone a sudden heart attack or a brain aneurysm. No, that was exactly as she described it. That was the universe making way, as harsh as that sounds."

"It is harsh. How can I believe you, though? You admitted you saved my life more than once. How do I know you or whoever you work with decided Carrieann wasn't worth saving?"

Marcus inhaled deeply. "I told you; you will understand soon enough. Carrieann, while being an exceptionally kind and wonderful person, wasn't on our radar, so to speak."

"But I was?"

"Yes."

"Well, then, who is the joke on? Her? Or you?" Emily shook her head. While she was beginning to understand the concept, there was something glaringly obvious to her. "Clearly, I did not make a huge impact that invoked change at a time of darkness."

Marcus did not reply, instead he slowly moved his hand in front of them. Slowly, a scene came into focus. Emily recognized the setting. It was the loft in Tribeca that Jonathan and his family now occupied. It looked like a party. No, not a party. Everyone looked somber and dressed in grays and blacks. It was a memorial.

"Is that *my* memorial?" Emily's eyes widened.

"The luncheon after the memorial."

"How can it be so soon? I just died."

"Time is somewhat fluid here. Please watch."

Emily fell silent as she watched and listened. She saw many of her past colleagues, along with June, Maggie and her children and grandchildren, Rob's children and grandchildren, and Jonathan. Sophie and Little Em were standing by his side. She was more than surprised at the number of former patients that attended. Her heart broke when she saw Ronan sitting alone at the table, his head bent. He looked tired and older than his years. She wanted to reach out and let him know she was okay. It was all okay.

"You can."

"Stop that!"

Marcus laughed. "It's one of the perks here. You'll enjoy it once you get the hang of it."

"So how do I let him know?"

"Think of something only the two of you know. Then think of how you can get that across to him. Focus. Concentrate."

It only took Emily a second to think of something. She focused on the scene in front of her. She moved her gaze to the window. It was gray and it was snowing. She concentrated as hard as she could manage until she saw two rays of sunshine come through the window and fall across the table in front of Ronan. She held it for only a few more seconds until she felt herself become weak. She exhaled and the rays were gone.

She had seen Ronan look puzzled, then look up at the window. She saw the slow recognition cross his face and the small smile appear. He knew it was her. It was all she needed.

"Message received," Marcus said. "That, too, will get easier as time goes on. You won't get as weak. Now, continue watching."

Emily returned to the memorial. She saw people speak to Jonathan, who would only nod and smile. She watched as people filtered out and the group became smaller. Her eyes began to water as she listened to some of her patients describe how she had helped them through some of their toughest times. Tears slid down as one of them credited her for saving his life. She laughed when June told the story of a time they went to the Catskill Mountains and got lost on a hike in the forest. Then she saw Little Em get up to speak.

"My grandmother was many things," Emily heard her granddaughter start. "She started out in the business world, but it wasn't her calling. Her true calling was to help people. She did that by opening up two clinics and providing outstanding, professional mental healthcare that she made sure was affordable to working families. She was adamant the cost remained low while the services provided were of the highest quality. It wasn't an easy feat but she did it. She championed mental health for decades. She was an advocate for everything from women's rights to voting rights to same-sex marriage. She did all that while also having a family that she loved more than anything. My Grams and my Grandpa were, if I'm being honest, sometimes sickening to be around."

Emily heard the laughter from the group and glanced at Marcus. He raised an eyebrow at her. She smiled, shrugged and went back to listening.

"They loved each other, no doubt about that. I hope I find a love like that one day. But, I think, there are a few other things I will take with me from my Grams. She said that countries don't find peace, people do. But she also said that this country, with all its problems, is worth fighting for. At first, I thought those two things were contradictory statements, but then she said to ponder the alchemy of bridges and once you do that, answers will come.

"Those are some wise and powerful words. I don't think my Grams, for as brilliant as she could be, really knew how powerful they are. We fight for our country not by fighting the government or by fighting each other. We fight for our country by building bridges with our neighbors. We find what connects us and we build on that. We find the commonalities between races and we build the bridge so that one can learn from the other because bridges go both ways and there is much to learn from different races. We understand intersectional feminism and we build that bridge to learn from each other, to understand each other. We drop the hate based on politics and find the foundation of what we all care about, build that bridge and let the ideas for a better country flow both ways instead of being stuck on one side.

"It's not a particularly new idea, it's been said in different ways in the past. Except what is new is leaving the government, the politicians, the media, out of it. We can make a better country for ourselves and for future generations if we stop listening to them and start listening to each other. If we start listening to each other, embracing each other, learning from each other, we'll also learn how to meet each other half-way, to compromise, to build and to grow.

"I'm taking that from my Grams. I'm taking her passion to help people, her courage to use her voice and her enthusiasm for bridges of all kinds. She was a one-in-a-million person and I'm glad she was my Grams."

Little Em's voice began to fade away. Emily continued to watch as people approached her, hugged her, spoke with her. She saw the occasional laughter. Finally, the only people left in the loft were Jonathan, Sophie, Ronan, and Little Em. Emily held her hand over her mouth as she watched Ronan hold his granddaughter and cry. He always did think Little Em took after her. She held back tears as she saw Little Em motion for her parents and they stood in a tight circle, letting their grief out if only for a few moments.

Eventually, Sophie broke from the circle and moved toward the bathroom, leaving the three of them. Emily stared at the love of her life, her beautiful son and her exceptional granddaughter. She let the tears slide down her cheeks. She knew they would be okay.

After several moments, she wiped the tears, composed herself and looked at Marcus.

"It's not me."

Marcus smiled. "You started it. You laid the groundwork. You led by example. You laid the foundation for her but, no, it's not you. It's *that* Emily Byrne that will have the huge impact."

"How long have you known that?"

"As I've told you before, I thought it quite possibly was you, but we don't interfere with free will. Things could have turned out differently. You could have chosen a different location for your second clinic and never saw Ronan again. He could have chosen to stop seeing you once he discovered who you really were. There are a thousand variables with everything. When you married Ronan, I thought it was definitely you. That is, until your granddaughter was born, then it became clearer as the years went on."

"You could have chosen *not* to interfere the night Theresa kidnapped Jonathan."

Marcus took a sharp intake of breath. "Shhhhhh. We don't discuss that anymore."

Emily nodded. "Okay. I understand." She paused and then asked, "Will you be there for Little Em the way you were for me?"

"In the same way, yes."

"Okay, I think it's time you show me how this all works."

Marcus moved his hand and the loft slowly vanished. The bland colors and vague scenes returned, along with the silence – or thousands of voices - Emily still couldn't decide.

"They're voices." Marcus smirked.

Emily shook her head. "I can't wait until I can do that. So, what do I do now?"

"You look forward, you silence yourself, you focus, and you listen. That's it."

Emily did as she was instructed. At first, she heard too many voices to distinguish just one, so she closed her eyes, shook her head and refocused. The second time, it took a bit before one voice came through among the others. She opened her eyes and she could see the man whose voice she was hearing, she could also see a slight red-gold glow around him. As soon as it all came together, she knew. Her mind was filled with information.

"And that is where it gets tricky," Marcus' voice brought her out of it.

Emily sharply turned from the image, the voice exited her head. "What do I do with that? It's too much information about him at one time."

Marcus nodded. "That's where it's like walking a tightrope. What you received was the different scenarios based on what decision he makes. You may clearly see the best decision that would lead to the best outcome but you cannot interfere with his decision-making. He must make his own decision."

"And if he chooses the wrong one?"

"Then you know what the outcome will be and whether or not he is still someone to watch or someone who is delegated back to a regular."

"A regular?"

"A regular person - someone who will not have much of an effect on his community or the world one way or the other."

Emily nodded. "So, am I in training? Are you my trainer?"

"Okay, Emily, I give up. You can finally put a label on me. I am your trainer."

"Finally!" Emily clasped her hands together. "So, I'm being trained for . . . . . . not a guardian angel . . . . more like a monitor of people. What would the title for that be?"

Marcus stood up. "Let's go, Emily. There's much to show you, much you need to learn. The world didn't end because you passed on. There's work to be done."

"I'm ready," Emily said as she stood up. "Now tell me what the title is. After you finish training me and we go in the field, so to speak, what's your title then?"

"Is it really relevant to have a title? We've been in contact for over 50 years, Emily."

"I know, and now you can finally tell me."

Marcus turned and began to walk away.

"What are you, Marcus?" Emily asked as she hurried behind him. "What are *we*?"

"I'm in control and I can see you're going to be a pain in the ass, as usual."

"Yes, but I'm your favorite pain in the ass."

"Don't push your luck."

It continued that way through Emily's training. In fact, it will always continue that way as Emily is, indeed, Marcus' favorite pain in the ass.

Acknowledgements

This book was truly a labor of love. There were many nights I would go to bed thinking about Emily and Ronan and how this world needs people like them; those who selflessly help others in order to make their community a better place; those who lend a helping hand and expect nothing in return and those who want to unite and build those bridges instead of being constantly divided.

With that said, there are some people I want to thank who fit that description. First and foremost, I would like to thank Linda Howard, whose assistance with this book was invaluable – from pointing out every missed comma to the insightful questions that made me step back and rethink things. Linda, I cannot thank you enough for everything. I would also like to thank Ericka Csencsits for letting me bounce off ideas to see how they would land, for providing insight and helping me fill in words and phrases when I was drawing a blank – and for reminding me of the Great Potato Famine! Then there is Adam Steppke, whose willingness to help meant so much. His honest and in-depth critique was appreciated beyond words.

Thank you to Kel for being patient while I spent hours writing. And a big thank you to my family and friends who kept encouraging me to write and who believed in me. You know who you are.

Charlene Williams is an author and part-time photographer. She is a graduate of Kutztown University of Pennsylvania with a degree in Education, minor in Psychology. When she's not writing or taking pictures she can be found gardening, hiking, reading and going to as many local theater productions as she can. Her debut work, a collection of short stories, *Unexpected Places*, can be found on Amazon. Charlene currently lives in Pennsylvania with her husband and daughter, her dog Sasha, and her cat Melanie.

Visit her website at:
www.charlenewilliamsofficial.com

9 798988 441557